AUTOGRAPHS

I0534931

TIME TO LOVE-RELOADED-TIME WILL REVEAL 3

"Reloaded version 2013"

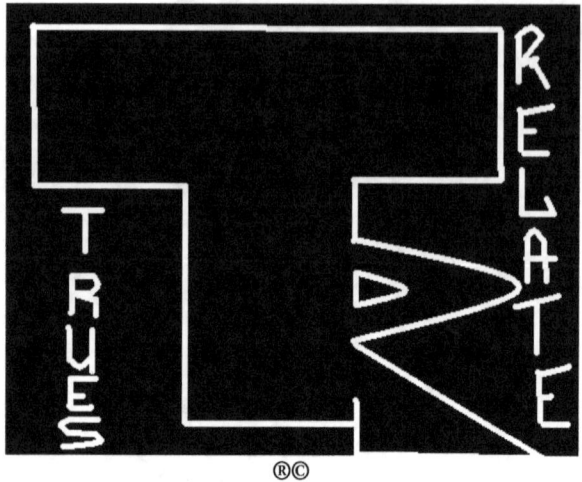

®©

TIME TO LOVE-RELOADED
TIME WILL REVEAL PART 3 ®©
BY
BLACK COFFEE ®©

TIME TO LOVE-RELOADED-TIME WILL REVEAL 3

Published by: True's Relate Publishing
Time To Love-RELOADED (Time will reveal: Part 3) ®©
Library of Congress Control Number: Txu-1-726-696
Copyright ©2003, 2008, 2010, 2013 True's Relate Publishing/LTBROWN
All rights reserved

®REGISTERED TRADEMARK-MARCA REGISTRADA
ISBN: 978-0-9844701-3-6 & 978-0-9892092-1-2
Printed in the United States of America
Set by: True's Relate Publishing
Cover design: Gregory Spencer of Misvision Graphics info@misvisiongraphics.com
Logo design by: JayRocOne [age 15] JayRocOne Designs
Requests for information on ordering, scheduling the author for signings and
appearances should be addressed to:
Black Coffee's websites
http://www.blackdollone.com
http://www.truesrelatepublishing.com
http://twitter.com/LTBROWN

www.facebook.com/BlackCoffee

Facebook Group: Black Coffee's Crew Nation-The Movement
Facebook: **True's Relate publishing and Black Coffee's Books**

Manuscript Preparation: Black Coffee
blackdollone@att.net
True's Relate publishing company
P.O. Box 2911
Gulfport, Ms. 39505

PUBLISHER'S NOTES

III

TIME TO LOVE-RELOADED-TIME WILL REVEAL 3

[Favorite Quotes and Reviews(no spaces)]

Love will find away to happen, if it's meant to be. There's no set formula, no blueprint, no guidelines to follow. It simply takes perseverance. Despite all opposition and discouragement. If it's true love, it'll prevail. If your heart, soul and mind are all in it. Love takes time to happen. When it does, it is it's own reward.-Black Coffee [From Time To Grow-Time Will Reveal pt. 2]

1. "When I read the original copies of the book, I instantly fell in love with the story and didn't think that anything could top them, until you rewrote the story line and added new facts which made me instantly fall back in love with these books. Because no matter how many times I read the books, I still laugh, cry and get mad at the same parts, as if its my first time reading the book. Lol. I am proud to be part of your book (cover girl part 1). All I can say is keep up the GREAT work and I can't wait for part 3."- Shanny Smith-Gulfport, MS. [Cover model for Time To Learn-part 1]

2. "I read the first book because my mom said she knew you. I really liked it and couldn't wait until the new one came out. When i finally got Time To Grow- Part 2 I was so happy. I didn't put it down until i got done. I really enjoyed the book. I hope you come out with a movie or play for the it. I have now read it 8 times that's how good it is. Can't wait for the next book."-- Shell Smith-Gulfport, MS [Black Coffee's Book club Admin]

3. "Time to Learn was captivating to read. This book kept my attention for a full day, I finished it that quickly. For me to do this, I had to really enjoy what I was reading and I must say that I thoroughly enjoyed this book. It gives you a true outlook on family, friends, love, and life overall. I believe it is a great read for any man, woman, boy or girl, as it speaks on how life truly is for some people and there's no sugar coating anything. I almost felt as if I was there starring in a role because it was so intriguing. Overall, Black Coffee, has really impressed me and I can't wait to read part 2. Keep up the great work!"- S. Stewart- Virginia Beach, Va. [Emerge Tradeshow & FunkeyFlashBack Gear].

4. "About 3 days ago I got to meet a great woman. She talked me into buying a book called Time to Learn. I bought it and we began to talk. Thank you, Black Coffee! The other day I met you at the mall when I had 3 of my 5 children and the lil one that I baby sit. You ask me to buy the 2nd book because most people finish the book in a day. I didn't think I needed too but I bought it anyway. When I got home 3 nights ago, I laid all the kids down and began to read. The following night, I read some more after the kids were in bed and then yesterday morning, I finished the book [part 1]. I

IV

am now halfway through the second book....You were right! Lol.............
Part 2 had me so stuck it only took me a day and half and I am done! I am
absolutely mad because I want to read the next four so I know the life story!
I couldn't help but read every bit of the book before bed last night. I love
the books and I can not wait for more to come!"- Mrs. Shantae Warren
Baltimore, MD
5. "I just finished reading the first two books in the "Time Will Reveal"
series. Sister, you have phenomenal literary skills, and I look forward to
reading more of your work. I could not put those books down until I
completed them. I cannot wait until part three comes out. Your cousin,
Tina, turned me on to your books, and I am happy she did. I wish you
continued growth and success. Thank you for sharing your God-given
talent with the world. Much love."-Shanette "Shaye" Beard-Houston, TX
"Okay, miss lady. There's only 1 word to sum up these books. [REAL] I
don't like to read but once I got into it, oh, it was on. I got wrapped up in it
cause this shit happens for real and I'm pretty sure everybody can relate to,
at least, one character. This shit is as real as it gets, for me. [Lol] I was
ready to get done [with part 1] and get to part two[2]. Now that I'm done
with part 2, I'm ready for part 3. You know I will support you, 100%. Keep
doing what you do and you will go beyond your expectations. Stay making a
name for yourself and pretty soon, it will be a worldwide, household name.
I LOVE YOU, COUSIN and I'm so very proud of you!!!!" Bettina Carter-
Poet from Houston, TX [by way of Gulfport, MS] [Subtitle description
assistant & Black Coffee's Book club Admin]
6. "In order to understand how awesome this book was, you had to read
"Time to Learn." Time to learn revealed the growth of these young people.
I cried most of the book, but to understand the love between Anthony and
Ebony, as Anthony just wants to protect Ebony. Girl you have done it again
with the blessing of the Lord. I can't wait to enjoy the next part. I know it
will be even better. God Bless you, Love you."- Clara Randolph-Brown-
Gulfport, MS [Family]
7. "Now you know I read the original version of Time Will Reveal, and I
loved it. I thought I read it too many times but since I have received Part 1
and Part 2 I would say I did not read it enough. I love all of which you have
written and I know I will love the ones to come!!! You are an incredible
writer, so keep doing what you are doing and continue to keep GOD
first....and the rest will fall in place. Now Hurry Up with Parts 3,4,5,6 and
the other books you have in the making. I cannot get enough of your work
(you are amazing)!! You catch the attention of different genders, ages, and

V

race. Continue to be a blessing to others."-Venitia Crawford-Aisola-Smryna, GA [by way of Gulfport, Ms] [Black Coffee's Book club Admin]

"If you love to read about characters with whom you can get deeply involved, you will love these books. The writer has done a great job with bringing out the meaning of love and friendship with the characters. I can't wait to own the whole series. Love your work and keep it up."-Julie Hamilton Vonreed-Hattiesburg, Ms [Rural Relief Carrier, USPS]

"Hi Black Coffee,

8. This is Ronnisha. You met my mother at Security Square mall and she told you that I'd authored a book in the 3rd grade. She gave you her business card from my school (Kipp Ujima Village Academy). Well I finished your book and I thought that it was FANTABULOUS!!!!!!!!!!!!!!!!!! I cant wait to get the following books that come afterwards. The relationship with Ebony and Anthony, remind me, of me and my boyfriend (also named Anthony) and how we go through life. Keep on writing."-Ronnisha Sye-Baltimore, MD [Student, future author]

9. "When I purchased Time To Learn-Part1, I thought it would be quite boring. Little did I know, after I started reading it, I found it to be very interesting. So interesting that I couldn't wait for Time To Grow-Part 2 to be released. When I went to purchase, Part 2, I was a little shy but I survived. Talking to you actually inspired me and made me realize that I can conquer all fears and I can do anything that I set my mind to do. Thank you." -Saalihah TooCute Jackson-Pascagoula, MS.

10. "Ms. Black Coffee, Keep doing what u do, girl ! I like what I've read thus far but, the suspense is killin' me. I love Ajay and Ebony. These 2 have what it takes to make a relationship work, with sooo many ups and downs, trials and tribulations. *"Time Will Reveal"* is truly #1 in my book !!! "Gimmie more! Gimmie more!"- Gwen Cooper- East Orange, NJ

11. "ADDICTED! Can you say ADDICTED? Everywhere I look I see Ajay and Ebony. (haven't seen them yet) Every storyline, every song. WTF is going on? I'm about to go read both of them again... LOL :-) These are wonderful books. It took me a little longer to start Part 1, because of all the build up of the characters. But when it got down to it, there was no putting it down. Part 2 was even better. Talk about an emotional rollercoaster... LOL I laughed, cried, got angry on more than a few occasions. I just felt like this was my family and I was going through it with them. Thanks for the entertainment. It was wonderful. "-Tenischa Jones- Delisle, Ms

12. "I absolutely love the Time Will Reveal series. Once I started reading, I couldn't put the books down. I can't wait for part 3. I'm hooked and I ain't

VI

ashamed to admit it Lol."-Nickeia Sylve [Hair Stylist]- New Orleans, La

13. "TimeToGrowPart2Review: Black Coffee has done it again! Another Wonderful Read. This book took me on an Emotional Roller Coaster, from the beginning to the end. The Crew really went through some tough ordeals. But they pulled together like family and *"Handled it."* I can go on and on but I can't give any details away. I Love the Book, Coffee!!!!!!!!! Ready for Part 3~ Better yet just mail me the complete series!!! LOL S/N: I'm proud of how the Crew handled things with Alana & Angel so far!!!!!!!!!!!! But I know its not over....... And I also love the dates 6/28-my birthday & 9/15 my anniversary."-Trina Hall-Willis- Great Lakes, IL.-[by-way-of-Gulfport,-Ms]-[School-Teacher]

14. "OMG" This book is REALLY GOOD. I Could not get enough of "AJAY". He TURNS ME ON. I CAN'T WAIT UNTIL PART 3, comes out. I NEED MY AJAY "FIX"! This book was great! I can't wait to see what the crew are up too. Good Luck with part 3. GOD BLESS YOU and the crew!"- Tanya Casteal- Gulfport, Ms. [Campaign manager to city Constable, district 4]

15. "So far, I love part 2, just as much as I do, part 1. I feel like I know these people. I can feel their emotions. Oh My God!"- Shante' Walker- Glen Burnie, MD

16. "Again, this Author has captivate us with these characters. You become more involved in their lives, feeling their joy and pain. Another page turner! I am going to have such a hard time waiting to read part three!!! Congrats Coffee, you have done it again! A great read!!"-Linda Scarborough-Sanders-Biloxi, Ms.

17. "Dear Black Coffee, You go girl!! Another book. Well count me in. I think you are wonderful. I love the series. Can you sign part 3, like you did with parts 1 & 2? They're special to me, as was meeting you at Emerge."-Diane White- Venice, Fl [Side-Cap designer]

TIME TO LOVE-RELOADED-TIME WILL REVEAL 3

Also by Black Coffee:
Be sure to pick up the sequels to this Time Will Reveal Series
Time To Learn-RELOADED-Time Will Reveal part 1
Time To Grow-RELOADED-Time Will Reveal part 2

[AVAILABLE]
(Time Will Reveal, short stories)
#1 MORE THAN 4 ADMIRERS-RELOADED
#2 MR. WRONG AND THE RATS-RELOADED
#3 THE CREW'S PRIORITY[TBA]

And more of the Time Will Reveal series!
Time To Know-RELOADED-Time Will Reveal part 4
Time To Feel-RELOADED-Time Will Reveal part 5]
The Making of AJAY-Every Man-RELOADED [Print only]
TIME TO SHOW-RELOADED-part 6 [TBA]
AJAY AND EBONY 1- Time Will Reveal 7-Time To Give [TBA]
AJAY AND EBONY 2- Time Will Reveal 8-Time To Live [TBA]

(<u>Dedication</u>)
TIME TO LOVE-RELOADED-Time Will Reveal part 3 ®©
To all the readers who love this
series and wanted more, right away……..,
ENJOY!
#CREW4LIFE ®©

VIII

Time To Love-*RELOADED*-Time Will Reveal-part 3

Nina has been experiencing false labor since Friday. Today is Wednesday and still nothing has happened with the pregnancy. Tank is going crazy down in *Natty*. They are in constant contact with each other and Mr. Parkwood has agreed to fly Tank home when she goes into labor. This calms Tank down a bit. But not Nina. She's very impatient at this point and just ready to bring their little girl into this world.

The October celebration will be held 3 days from now, on Saturday night. Rob will turn 24 tomorrow. Rich turned 19 on the 1st and Greg Jr made 14, on the second. Rebbie's baby brother, Archie Jr turned nine years old yesterday. Stoney's day of birth, which is always included in the crew October celebrations, is the twentieth. He would be 25 years old, if he hadn't been brutally murdered nearly 4 years ago. Him and Bre's daughter CJ will be 3 years old on the eleventh. Nina has been helping mama Jackie with final preparations for CJ's birthday party at *Granny's House*. It's being held Saturday afternoon, prior the celebration at *The Chill Spot*.

Bre, Jb and Lynn fly home for the weekend. CJ has received a package, special delivery, at her grandma Debbie's home. Her grandpa Chester Lee sent her a baby doll and a card from prison. Both had been handmade by him. He is Stoney's father and he had kept his word to CJ and Bre that he would not lose touch with them. CJ loves her doll. She's very excited as she joins her crew for her birthday party. Both celebrations go off without a hitch.

Renee and Chill meet with the accountants today to go over the books for *Crew Enterprises*. Every business has been profitable. *The Chill Spot* is number 1 while *The Crew's House of Soul Food* is a close second. *Crew Cuts & Styles* is third but not far ahead of *Crew Details* and *Granny's House*. Rob's studio and record Store has shown enough profit to support itself. It's moving into it's own suite at *The CrewLand Mall*. The name they select for it is, *Jenkins Jams Company,* the name Rob has used, all along. Reaper has a single on the radio and he's nearly done with his CD. June's younger sister Brittany sings background vocals on 3 of his songs. He has 11 tracks recorded and mastered. Rob is shopping him to labels and trying to get him signed to a record deal. His father Archie Sr steps in as his manager, which frees Rob up to travel with the music.

But these days everyone in the crew are concerned about Nina. She's way past her due date. Not only is Tank going crazy and bringing everybody in Cincinnati along with him. But her parents, Al and Jo are just as anxious as her and Tank are. Meanwhile Tank's parents, Pearl and John are trying to keep everybody calm while trying to conceal their own eagerness. This is the 1st grand baby, for both sides of the family. So they are *all* anxious. Big John calls Pearl from the road, to check Nina's progress and to see how Ebony and Ajay are getting along since their arrest.

"Hey baby. How's everything at home?" he asks, while on 1 of his many calls to Cleveland.

"Nobody got hurt, locked up or suspended, so far," Pearl says sarcastically, "But it's still early."

Her and John share a laugh.

"Nina hasn't done anything yet, ha?" he asks.

"No baby," she says, "She's still wobbling around here. Poor thing. She seems *so* miserable."

It's the 18th day of October and Nina is 18 days past her due date.

"She's so tired of being pregnant, John," Pearl says as she laughs again. "Every time she comes over, I rub her shoulders and her back while she complains to me about how tired and miserable she is."

"What's Weston saying?"

"She's trying to wait for her labor to come naturally. But she gave her until Monday. If she hasn't done anything by then, we're going to induce her."

"She's got about five days to get it jumped off?" he asks.

"Yes and Tank is about to worry me, her and Jo to death, about it," she says, "He's so afraid he's gonna miss it."

"Well baby, the man wants to be there to see his first child born and that's a very good thing," he says, "And I expect that from him. But the baby's not coming until it's ready to come."

"I know but Jo and I want her to have it naturally, if she can," she says, "Instead of a cesarean section."

"Uh huh. Okay," he says. Then he changes the subject to something

10

else that's been on his mind. He asks, "They still got Angel locked up?"

"Oh yes and she'd better not get out either," she says.

"Ajay will kill her, if they do let her out. Ajay don't play that type o' shit and I like that. He ain't gone tolerate nobody hurting baby girl."

"Like *you*," Pearl says as she smiles.

"Like me? You *think*?" he asks as he laughs.

"John, Ajay acts more and more like you as the years pass. I can see it clearly now," she says.

"Then can you see why our baby girl loves him?" John asks.

"Yes. I've *been* able to see it," she says, "I just wasn't ready to accept it, back then. But she loves a man who's just like her daddy."

"She can't help herself then," he gloats, "Her father is way to irresistible."

Pearl agrees with John and they laugh as they discuss they're feelings about Ajay and Ebony's relationship.

"They're doing good, Pearl," he says, "I visited with all of them when I went through Cincinnati, last Tuesday," he says, "That's a nice mansion they got them in."

"Oh, I know," she says, "Me and Jo love the house. But we still don't want Nina to take the baby down there to stay though."

"Y'all know it's their decision. We'll have to accept it if they want to take her to Cincinnati," he says.

Pearl says she understands but she doesn't have to like it.

"They come home every chance they get," he says, "They're gonna want to go to the club. You and Jo will have her the whole time."

"I know. They run the streets the entire weekend when they *do* come home," she adds with a laugh.

"Nina's ready to have that baby," he offers, "So she can get back down there with them."

"Oh yes. She's been working at the salon. But she's missing baby girl, T-baby and Rebbie, like *crazy*. Not to mention Jeremy," she says with a slight chuckle. Then she says, "Just like I'm missing you."

"I should be there around three or four. No later then five, tomorrow morning," he says, "You're gonna keep it hot, right?"

"You know it," she answers with a smile.

He's traveling from Iowa, this time. Pearl says she'll be off from work tomorrow and she'll be home when he arrives. She's going back to the graveyard shift for the fall, so she can help out at the mall in the mornings. They exchange hugs, kisses and "*I love you*," Then they hang up.

11

TIME TO LOVE-RELOADED-TIME WILL REVEAL 3

Wednesday morning starts out normal for Nina. Just like every other day of her pregnancy. She has backaches, uncontrollable bathroom urges and swollen feet. She drags herself out of bed, gets dressed and goes to work. Only to get there and be told she could've taken the day off.

"Nina you know you could've stayed in bed, if you wanted too," Tonya says as Nina wobbles through the door.

"I know. But I get too depressed and bored just laying around the house," Nina says, "I can't wait until Friday, when my baby gets home."

She's missing Tank, terribly. They're closer now, then ever. And they have been discussing marriage a lot. Jo and Pearl asked them to promise they would allow them to give them a wedding. Nina doesn't want to get married while she's pregnant anyway. They're waiting until after their baby girl arrives. Then they'll get engaged and set a date.

"Since I'm here, I may as well take a few heads," she say as she sets up her station. "Hopefully the moving around will bring her on down."

Her and Tonya usually have a light schedule on Wednesday mornings. By the late afternoon, business picks up and it stays busy clean through until the close of the day on Saturday. Which is at 6pm. On Sunday and Monday the salon and barbershop are closed. Nina has already hired and trained a replacement for when she'll be out on maternity leave. Her name is Justine Carr. She's Jackie's niece by marriage. She's actually the niece of Jackie's husband Jason. The crew met and saw her a few times, over the years. Justine has just recently come to live with Jackie and Jason since they moved back to Cleveland. She attends night school at CSU, where Tonya is in grad school. Justine already has experience in Cosmetology. She's worked in a few shops in Columbus but she's been slow to choose a real career. She's 23 like Tonya and Jr. But she had dropped out of high school and didn't do anything for awhile. Her uncle Jason took custody of her before she turned 18 and made her get her G.E.D. Finally she's on the right path and trying to get her life straight. The crew gave her an opportunity and so far, she's working out great. Chill and Renee had introduced her to Kilo. His government name is Kejuan Thomas. They've been seeing a lot of each other, lately. Things seem promising. Justine has stepped up her responsibilities. She's already at work when Nina comes in.

"You're ready to drop that load. Ha, Nina?" Justine asks.

"Yes. It's time out for this," she says, drawing in a deep breath.

"Or you alright, cousin?" Tonya asks as Nina *is* her first cousin by marriage.

"I don't know. My butt and everything is hurting," she answers.

12

"You're in labor, I'll bet," Justine says and they all laugh because they've said that *every morning* for the past 3 weeks.

Tank calls just as Nina is putting her 1st client under the dryer. He's on his usual morning call to check on her.

"How are you, baby?" he asks.

"Pregnant," she answers sarcastically.

"I know you're tired, baby. But it won't be long now," he says.

He's said that *every morning* for the past 3 weeks too. They hang up after a brief conversation and he heads to class.

About an hour or so later, as Nina is finishing up her 5th client, she finally gets some *real* action.

"Tonya, y'all I can't stop peeing," Nina says.

"What?" Tonya asks.

"I've been to the bathroom seven times, already. It's just eleven forty five," she says, "I can't even cut if off, really."

Before Tonya can respond, Nina sits down in her station chair and all of a sudden, her water breaks and spews across the floor in front of her station.

"Call Tank back!" Justine yells, "We're having a baby, today!"

She runs to get towels and a mop while Tonya helps Nina. Justine throws towels on the floor to catch the amniotic fluids. Then she calls mama Jo before she starts to mop. Nina is finally in active labor. Tonya and Justine scramble to contact Tank and the rest of the crew, in Cincinnati. They need to be on their way, if they want to be here in time for the birth.

Tank and Parkwood are going to fly. He's telling Nina and running through the Cincinnati airport, at the same time.

He says, "I'm flying out in twenty minutes."

It's only been a half hour since her water broke. During that time, Nina goes from the salon to lying in the prone position in the labor and delivery unit of East General. Dr. Weston is there and so are Jo and Pearl. Nina's on the phone with Tank, who's flight is ready to take off in minutes.

"You'd better hurry, baby. My water broke and I'm dilated to four centimeters, already," she says, just as she gets her 4th huge contraction and screams out.

Pearl takes the phone while Jo helps Nina with her breathing.

"Come on and get here, son," she orders, "This baby ain't gonna wait for you."

Mr. Parkwood's jet is ready to go. Him and Tank take off for Cleveland.

Ebony and the rest are driving up. They left Cincinnati over 30 minutes ago. They're driving and having very stimulating conversation.

13

June brings up the subject of sexual positions. Ebony is too embarrassed to talk in front of the guys. Her girls say very little too. Rich adds his 2 cents. But Ajay teaches the class. He not only names more positions than anyone else. He also explains how to do them. Ebony is so embarrassed, she turns a lighter shade. Ajay thinks it's funny. So funny in fact, he teases her along the drive home.

"We're gonna try all of them tonight, baby," he jokes.

"The sutra one too?" Rebbie asks as they all laugh.

The foursome doesn't even know what that means yet.

"No not until we're married," he says.

"When will that be?" T-baby digs.

"I don't know but we're going too," he says.

"All y'all wanting to get married at the same time?" Rich asks.

"Yes," Rebbie and T-baby say, simultaneously.

Ebony doesn't offer an answer. She just looks at Ajay.

"That's *too* many damn people," Ajay says as they all laugh again. They continue driving with plenty of conversation about weddings, babies, sex and all. Ajay senses that Ebony is uneasy about the whole wedding talk. He doesn't know why, right now. But they'll talk about it in private as soon as she's ready too.

Nina has been in active labor for 12 hours. She's finally dilated to 10 centimeters. Tank's here. The crew, John, Al and papa are all here too. The crew are all hoping she can hold out for another 20 minutes or so. Then their baby girl can be born on Stoney's birthday.

It's 11:50pm. Her and Tank are in the delivery room. Ebony, T-baby and Rebbie are in there with them and so are Jo and Pearl. Nina is doing great and it's finally time to deliver.

Another half an hour later, she gives a final big push and Dr. Weston yells, "It's a girl!"

"Oh God!" Tank yells, "I'm a daddy! I got a little girl!"

"Yep. Now it's payback time," Al says as he chuckles.

NAME: Jerica Eloise Brown
BORN: October 20, 1994
TIME: 12:37AM
WEIGHT: 8lbs, 2 ounces
LENTGH: 20 Inches

14

TIME TO LOVE-RELOADED-TIME WILL REVEAL 3

Ebony, Rebbie and T-baby are crying as they watch Tank cut the umbilical cord. He's shaking so badly. Everyone is doubtful he'll be able to sever it. He eventually cuts the cord and the nurse takes Jerica to get her vitals done. She's healthy and has a great set of lungs.

"That's a beautiful baby," Jo says to Nina and Tank.

Tank holds her first. Jerica opens her eyes and smiles at her daddy. She remembers that voice that's been whispering to her for 9 months. He's in tears. He's so happy and proud. John puts a hand on his shoulder and says, "There's no better feeling in this world than this one, son."

"Look at daddy's baby girl," is all Tank can say at the moment.

He holds her for 10 minutes. It seems like a lot longer to the others who are waiting to hold her too. He eventually lays her in Nina's arms.

"It's about time you got here," Nina says to her new daughter.

She's been crying every since the announcement of Jerica's arrival.

"She's gonna be slow to move, just like Tank," Pearl says as they all stand around the bed.

"And Nina too," Jo agrees as they all laugh.

No one can take their eyes off of this beautiful baby girl. Dr. Weston goes out and announces Jerica's arrival to the rest of the crew. She tells them they can go back and see her. Soon there are over 30 people in the delivery room.

"New crew!" Chill yells as he comes through the door.

They're all so excited.

Later, Tank and the guys go down to the gift shop and buy *It's a girl* cigars, lots of gifts, flowers and toys for Nina and Jerica. She's being spoiled already.

Even later, in Nina's private room, Ebony, Rebbie and T-baby hog all of the lap time with Jerica. Ajay watches Ebony as she holds his and her niece. He's thinking of the baby they would be receiving in a few more weeks had it not been for Angel's evil. He removes the thought of Angel from his mind. She's still incarcerated and no doubt, having as rough of a time as Tameka. He isn't going to let thoughts of her ruin such a precious and wonderful day in his families life. He finally gets to hold his niece.

"Hey, Jerica," he says as he looks down into her little eyes, "I'm your uncle Ajay. I'm gonna look out on you. Anything you want, that your mama and pops won't get for you. Call me for it. I got you, okay?"

Everyone laughs. Even Jerica smiles.

Welcome to the world, Jerica Eloise Brown!

15

TIME TO LOVE-RELOADED-TIME WILL REVEAL 3

{Three weeks later{

Jerica is already 3 weeks old. Nina is home from the hospital and settling into motherhood. Tank is back at school but he'll be home this weekend. He's been home every weekend and some weeknights, since Jerica arrived.

It's November 11 and all is well with the crew. Their November Celebration of Thanksgiving and crew birthdays has been scheduled for Saturday the 26th. All of the crew will be home for Thanksgiving.

Ebony and T-baby's opening college game is scheduled for November 29 in Cincinnati and Nina is planning to attend.

Renee will turn 25 on the 21st. The James twins celebrated their 8th birthday last Saturday at *Granny's House*.

The Cincinnati crew are home this weekend also. Ebony, T-baby and Rebbie are at Jo's house with Nina and Jerica, as everyone expected. While Tank goes to help with the Friday night opening at their club. The foursome are still mesmerized by their new little princess.

"I love my little niece, so much," Ebony says as she feeds Jerica her bottle, "She has big mama's name and my middle name. She's the fourth generation *Eloise*." Then talking to Jerica she says, "Your great great-grandmother Eloise gave big mama the name and she gave it to us, as our middle names. Your mama gave you my middle name because I'm her best friend. Your nana Pearline has your late great-grandmother Pearline's name because she was our big mama's best friend. You look like *me* though. I'm your auntie Ebony. I'm your dad's only sister. I'm gonna marry your mom's only brother. Your uncle Anthony," she giggles as Jerica smiles, "When we have a daughter, y'all will be best friends too."

"She looks just like you and Tank," Nina says.

"I think so too," Ebony says proudly.

"We would have three babies to care for if everything had gone right," Rebbie says.

"Our baby would be due a week from today, on November eighteenth," Ebony adds.

"We all have one now," Nina says as she picks out an outfit to dress Jerica in, "This is the outfit for her, today."

"Yes. I like that one," Rebbie says.

"Yes. That's because you bought it. Right, kid?" Nina asks.

"Exactly," Rebbie says as she giggles.

Nina had received many gifts at her surprise baby shower. It had been held at the salon, the weekend of the August celebration. She had more than

16

enough clothing, furniture, bottles and diapers for Jerica.

"On Thanksgiving weekend, mama and mama P are gonna keep her," Nina says, "So I can go out with y'all to the celebration. I missed partying with my crew."

"It's gonna be *on and poppin*," T-baby says, "We have so much party time to make up for. We missed you too."

"The foursome are in full effect again," Ebony says and they all laugh as they help Nina bathe and dress Jerica.

"It's like having our own little living baby doll," Rebbie says.

"I want a baby, more now. After seeing Jerica," Ebony says kissing Jerica on the cheek.

"Me too, kid," T-baby adds, "And we haven't given up."

"She ain't like a baby doll, though," Nina says as she smiles, "This doll eats, pee pee's and poo-poo's too. And it all has a smell. A *bad* smell. Plus her favorite play time is when I'm the sleepiest."

Then turning to Jerica, she says, "Ain't that right, mama's baby? But I wouldn't trade you for the whole world."

They all crack up laughing as Jerica is now dressed and bundled up. They head out to Tank's jeep and strap her into her car seat first. They all get into the tracker and head to Ajay's apartment.

They meet their guys there. Their guys had just finished helping Chill open the club. The guys have the kitchen and patio for their drinking and smoking, so the foursome stay in the living room with Jerica.

Previously, Nina and Ajay had discussed her moving into the apartment with the baby. Tank was against it, then. He's still against it now. Their parents are as well. Her girls don't want her to do it either.

"If you stay at mama Jo's, you'll have her help and mama's too," Ebony says, "You're coming to school in January anyway. It doesn't make sense to move out here for two months."

"Yes. I am coming to school soon," Nina agrees, "I know and I'm ready. I'm not gonna move. I decided that already. Because I love having their help and Jeremy ain't wit it anyway. Mama has been in my ear this whole fall season. But her and mama P wanna keep Jerica *here*. *No way*. She's coming to Natty *with me and her daddy*. Point blank. And y'all, I am so ready to get back to regular classes. I don't like home study."

They're listening to Nina's *Aaliyah* CD. *Age Ain't Nothin But A Number. At Your Best* is Nina's favorite song.

"This song makes me think about Jeremy," she says, "I've been playing it to death and missing him, so much, this whole fall season."

17

"You know what song makes me think about Rich?" T-baby asks.

"Which one?" Rebbie asks.

"*Weak*," T-baby says, "By *SWV*. *Sisters with voices,* kid."

"Oh yes. I love them too," Ebony adds, "*It's About Time* is my favorite."

"And, *Right Here* ," Rebbie offers.

"Uh uh. *Downtown*," Nina adds as they start to sing it.

"*That's the way to my love,………, Downtown.*" They all laugh.

"All me and Ajay been listening to lately is *Tupac*," Ebony says, "He's the truth. That *Thug Life* he just put out, is the bomb."

Ebony tries to change the subject but her girls want to keep talking about oral sex. T-baby has a question for Nina.

"Are you still getting it like that, kid?" she asks.

"Hell yea. And girl it's so *good*," Nina says, "Jeremy is the master."

"Hell no he's not," T-baby says, "Rich is the man. He can make me cum in less than six minutes. *Six minutes, Dougie fresh you're on.*"

Ebony and Rebbie frown at the 2 of them. The girls are in the living room while the guys are still in the kitchen, playing domino's quietly. While listening and now peeping in on their girls. The foursome continue their discussion on oral sex, oblivious to the fact that their guys can hear them.

"Oh don't knock it until you've tried it," Nina says.

"Ajay ain't gonna do that," Ebony says, "Not anytime soon."

"June either," Rebbie says.

"I bet they love when y'all do them. Don't they?" T-baby asks.

"Well actually, I don't do him," Ebony says, "He don't want me to do him. We haven't gotten to that yet."

"Me and Brian are not there either," Rebbie says, "We'll never get there, if it's up to me."

"Just don't say they never will," Nina says, "Because I didn't think Jeremy would either. But he started when I was pregnant and it's so good."

"Rich started right after we got back together," T-baby adds, "I think it was because of Craig doing it to me. But Rich is the best. *Oh God.*"

"Well Ajay haven't done it and he don't want me to do it to him either," Ebony says again, "He always say *that's* why he kisses me. Because I don't do oral sex on him."

"A*nd you don't call me Ajay either*," he says from the kitchen and the guys all laugh.

Ebony is embarrassed that he overheard her. Then the guys turn the music back up loud on the kitchen and patio speakers, giving the girls the false

18

impression that they can't hear their conversation anymore. The ladies continue their discussion.

"He'll start licking it, one day," T-baby says as she giggles, "Watch what I tell you, cousin. Because the rest of the crew are. Except for him and June. Renee, Lynn and Tonya told me that, last year. Rob do it and Stoney use to do it too. All of their guys do it."

"Jb!?" Ebony asks stunned.

"Hell yes," Nina says, "Lynn told me they been doing that since before they went to Tech. Since high school. And the younger crew are doing it too."

"Kim *told* me her and Bruce do it," T-baby says.

"It don't matter to me if June do it or not," Rebbie says, "Because if he starts, he's gonna want me too. And I don't know *how* too."

"He'll show you what he likes" Nina says, "And you're gonna have to show him too. Because he don't know how too either."

They spend the whole evening talking sex, oral sex and the new sexual positions they've tried since the trip home for Jerica's birth. The foursome are young women now. They're all 18 and in secure relationships with their guys. Sex talk is a natural progression for them. Their mothers have these talks and always have. They use to find good hiding places so they could eavesdrop on them when they were little. Now they're having them.

"I know Jeremy and I are gonna stay together," Nina says, "He says he wants us to get married soon."

"Alright now!" T- baby says, "Y'all get it started. You know we're gonna follow."

"Let's each do our own," Ebony says, "With our favorite colors."

The guys stay in the kitchen playing bones and pretending they aren't listening. But they are and they do plenty of snickering too.

Two weeks later, at the celebration, Reaper performs with Brittany. The foursome sing songs by *TLC, SWV, Xscape, Mary J. Blige* and *Aaliyah.* Everybody has a wonderful time. Ebony and T-baby remind them to come to Cincinnati on Tuesday for their first college game.

"You already know we're coming," Renee says.

On Sunday, all of the college students return to school. The December celebration has been scheduled for December 23, the day after Nina turns nineteen. The celebration is on Friday, this month. Because Saturday will be *Christmas eve* and more of Chill's crew have to play *Santa*

19

TIME TO LOVE-RELOADED-TIME WILL REVEAL 3

Claus, these days. Nina and Tank are looking forward to their 1st year.

December also means basketball seasons are in full swing at UC and Tech. Jb and his team have an undefeated record in their first 4 games. Bre's team has lost only 1 game of their first five. Ebony and T-baby's team are 5-0. Ajay and the men's team are undefeated in 4 games.

June and Rich's UC football team had finished well enough to be invited to a bowl game. They'll play in New Orleans on New Year's Eve.

}December 23{

The CrewLand Mall is decorated beautifully for the *Christmas* season. Each shop coordinates with the other. Nina turned 19, yesterday. Ebony will be turning 19 on Christmas day and lil Kenny will be eleven. He had his birthday party last Saturday at *Granny's House.* Rich's only sister Ruthie or Roo, turned 13 on the eighth. Tonight at the celebration, they initiate her to the crew. The crew call her Roo which is short for Ruthie. This year is her official coming out and Jesse is very excited that she's finally turning thirteen. He had asked her to be his girlfriend, a year ago. She said yes. They've talked on the phone nearly every night since. They stick close to each other at the celebration. Jesse asks Tank if he'll drive them to Chill's house so they can be together. Tank does. This is the 1st time for both of them. Tank, Jb and big John have been talking to Jesse about sex a lot, over the last 5 years. More specifically, about his 1st time and his girl's too. He feels well prepared for it but he's still nervous about how Ruthie will feel. Being that it's going to be painful for her.

"This is kind of an on-the-job training thing. The first time is painful for the girl, bro," Tank says, "You can't fix that. But you'll never know how you can make her feel until after the first time."

Roo has talked with her mother Anna and all of her crew girls. They have schooled her on the do's and don'ts. Anna put her on birth control pills at 12 years old, as soon as she started menstruating. Tank and Nina drop them off, give them a few more words of encouragement, then return to the club.

In the months that had led up to the celebration, there had been much talk about the guys plans to propose marriage to the foursome, this Christmas. Tank had gone to Al and asks for Nina's hand and he had given his approval with no questions and no hesitation. Ebony knew Ajay wasn't going to propose. They had discussed it since losing their baby and he had said, "When I propose. I'm doing it by myself and make it all about you. When we get married. We'll be the only couple up there, *getting married.* That day has to be all yours, baby. It'll be your day and you're not gonna

20

share it. You just tell me where to be and what time to show up."

She's fine with that. She has always imagined a fairy tale wedding with just her and her Prince Charming, standing in front of the altar, alone. Tank has always said him and Nina would have a single wedding too. But T-baby and Rebbie are hell bent on a quadruple wedding. Rich nor June have ask big Greg or big Archie for their hands. A quad wedding seems very highly unlikely, at this point. Nevertheless, they're all having a great time at the celebration. After all of the music and dance performances, the crew have 1 more event for the crowd to witness.

Tank, Ajay, June, Rich and Jb take the stage. They start off rapping 1 of the songs they use to do back in their early days. Then they start singing *Forever My Lady* by *Jodeci*. Afterwards, big Al sings *You Are My Lady* by *Freddie Jackson*. Tank had asks him to sing it as his dedication to Nina. Him and Nina dance solo, for this song. Then John takes the stage to sing *Just Be My Lady* by *Larry Graham,* as Tank continues to dance with Nina. T-baby and Rebbie are disappointed now. It's obvious to them at this point, they aren't going to be proposed too. After John finishes singing, he gives the microphone to Tank, who stands in the center of the floor with Nina. All of the attendees surround them. He takes to 1 knee and you can hear a sigh in the crowd, then silence.

"Nina, you have always been my love, my lady, my crew and my friend. My *best* friend. We have a beautiful baby girl together, who has changed my life. I love you, very much. In front of God, the crew and all these folks. I would like to know, will you marry me?"

"Yeah, Jeremy! Yes! Yes! Yes!" she answers with tears streaming down her cheeks, "Yes! I'll marry you, baby," she says again.

They kiss as everyone applauds. They dance together to *At your Best* by *Aaliyah*. The crew couples join them on the dance floor. After the crew, the rest of the partygoers come back to the dance floor too. T-baby and Rebbie are visibly upset with Rich and June for not proposing to them. They want to talk about it in the back office.

The 4 of them go to the back to have their discussion. After confirming that June and Rich aren't going to propose to them, T-baby and Rebbie go congratulate Nina and Tank, then leave. They go outside, get in Sandy's car and leave without saying another word to Rich or June.

"What's wrong with them now, man?" Rich asks June.

"Just being a bitch about it," June answers as they leave in pursuit of their ladies.

Ebony and Ajay stay at the celebration until it ends. Then they go

21

to the U. Tank and Nina are staying downtown, at the hotel, tonight. Jerica is at Jo's. Her and Pearl are going to keep her throughout the weekend, while Tank and Nina celebrate their engagement.

At Ajay's apartment, him and Ebony go straight to bed. He's horny, as usual. She's in the mood as well. But before he can fuck her, he has to know that she's mentally okay with tonight's events.

"How are you, baby girl?" he asks.

"I'm okay."

"Are you *sure*, baby?" he asks, "Did you want me to propose to you tonight, when Tank proposed to Nina?"

"No, Anthony," she says, "You always told me we would do our thing, solo. And that it would be *my* big day. Where the attention was on me *only*. We both stressed that even more after our baby was killed and we couldn't get married, earlier this year. I wanna do it the way we talked about since then. Your way. And before we make another baby. I know it'll be off the hook. You go all out for me, so I'll wait for it."

"You're damn right, I will," he says, "I don't want the attention to be on nobody else but my baby, when we get engaged *and* married. I'm so glad you understand that and didn't go off like your girls did."

"Tee and Ree Ree are just use to our *all for one* vow, baby," she says, "They'll be okay after they think it through. Nee and Tank wanted to get married, first and alone. They did everything else first." She giggles, then continues, "They was the first couple out of the foursome. Nina had sex first and they had a baby first. T-baby has always wanted to be the first one *of us* to do everything. But Nina always gets that spot. She just hasn't gotten over that yet. But her and Rich had oral sex first, so she does have that *one* first time, in her vault."

"How do you feel about them getting oral sex and you're not?"

"I don't feel anything about it. We talked about that too."

"And you remember what we said about that, then?" he asks.

"Yes. We said we're gonna wait until we get married," she says.

"And are you still alright with that," he asks.

"Yes."

"Are you sure," he asks, "Cause I can start licking this clit tonight, if you need me too. I'm all about pleasing you, Ebony. At all cost."

She looks at him as he rubs her already throbbing clitoris. She smiles at him and says, "I'm sure, baby. You said we're gonna save something so that something can be new to us when we get married. I want that to be our

22

something new. That's the way we planned it, after we lost our little girl. And that's the way I've been looking for it to be."

"So is the sex still satisfying to you without the extra?" he asks.

"Yes. Very," she says with a shy smile.

"I love to fuck you, Ebony," he says as he starts rubbing her breast. "You got the best pussy in the world. Your pussy is *so* tight. Oh *Jesus!*" He yells as he chuckles and pulls her to him.

"My pussy is tight or your dick is big?" she asks, shocking him.

"Your pussy is tight *and* my dick is big," he clarifies, "But I've been in enough pussy to know when one is *extra* tight. Yours is as tight as the day you gave me yo cherry. Uh huh. And I love the way you say dick too. But nah. I'm not in a hurry for you to suck it. Keep this virgin mouth." He starts to kiss her with fervor while rubbing her breast at a fevered pace. He's ready to fuck. He's feigning for her, like he hasn't had her in months. Even though they share a huge bed together down in Cincinnati. In a room nearly the size of 1 whole floor of this apartment.

"Give me these clothes, baby girl," he says as he strips her, "You know not to wear clothes in my bed."

"Oh. Uh huh. That's my bad, baby," she giggles.

He's already playing with her clitoris, causing her nipples to stand at attention, before she can even shed her t-shirt and panties. He waste very little time serving them with his cool tongue. While tugging at her t-shirt until he finally gets it to release her elbow. She's completely nude now. He's free to browse her playground with his hands, fingers and tongue. Which he certainly does. He lets his tongue roam her upper body from her ears to her navel and back up again. She can tell he's toying with the idea of eating her pussy. She doesn't want him to take away their something new, Which they've been saving for their honeymoon. She pulls upward on his shoulders and he slides back up her body and on top of her. He stares her right in the face, momentarily. He smiles slyly, then he's back to her breast. She's ready to fuck.

"Oh *sweet* baby," she moans, "We don't need extras, Anthony. You make me feel so good with the things you do *already*."

He agrees with a series of grunts while sucking on her nipples like a starved man at a smorgasbord. She pulls up on him again. This time, he knows she isn't going to be denied. She wants her dick and she wants it now. He gives it to her, as they both release pleasant moans.

"You better make sure you let me know you're enjoying that foreplay, baby girl," he says, "Cause that something new won't be *so* new, if

23

I *ever* get the feeling *daddy* ain't pleasing this body *or* this pussy. You understand me?"

"Yes, baby. I understand."

With that said and understood, they spend the better part of the next 2 hours enjoying the fuck out of their something old and familiar. Which just happens to stay fresh and new, thanks to her lover man's determination.

Ebony's 19th birthday is extra special, this year. For her Christmas and birthday presents, she gets another car. John, poppa, papa and Ajay put the money together and get her a brand new 1995 Toyota Camry. It's dark blue with almond colored leather seats, dark blue trim and carpet. Ajay put big money into the details. She has a 6-disc CD changer with top-of-the-line stereo equipment and speakers, a security system, built in cellular phone rack and power, *everything*. Navigation, Dayton rims in white gold, tinted windows and chrome trim, inside and out. Natty alumni had pitched in with Ajay.

"I love my car!" she exclaims, "This is *tight!*"

Ajay hands her a 2nd gift while they're all admiring the car. She opens it. It's another *Ajay's Girl* tag for the front of her new car. She attaches it immediately, smiles and says, "Now it's complete."

Her and Ajay go for the first ride. She rides her girls next. They strap in the baby seat and Jerica comes along too. They listen to *R. Kelly's 12-Play* CD while they ride. It's 1 of Nina's gifts from Tank.

"I like *Seems like you're ready*" Ebony says as they head back to Shaker Heights.

"Yes and you're ready to get to Ajay when you hear that song. Ha, Ebony?" Rebbie asks as she grins.

"Yes. Uh huh," she responds with a smile.

"Nina, they play this shit *out*, at school," T-baby adds.

"Oh yea? Well Ajay is gonna give her some of that twelve play, one of these days," Nina offers as she laughs.

Ebony smiles at the thought. But dismisses it almost as soon as Nina says it.

"Big mama said we shouldn't be listening to R. Kelly, though," Ebony says.

"Grandma Sally won't let us listen to it. My mom and dad won't either," T-baby says.

"Mine either. Because they say he was going with Aaliyah," Rebbie adds.

"My mama *been* said that," Nina says, "When she first saw her

24

Video, she said it," Nina says, "She said, 'W*hy the hell is his old ass in a video with that little girl*,' when she first saw *Back and Forth.*"

"That's why we only listen to it in Natty," Ebony offers, "Misses Pearl don't *wanna* hear it either."

Later, they meet up with the crew at Chill's house, after their Christmas dinner. They're going over final preparations for the trip to New Orleans, for June and Rich's football bowl game next Friday. All of the crew are going. June and Rich's families are too. Jackie and Jason's family including Justine, are going. Kilo, Arthur, Wayne, Michelle and Courtney Freeman, Wayne's friend girl, are going to New Orleans too. Ron, Carolyn, April and Charles, David, Yolanda and their Houston crew will meet them there. Little Miss Jerica is staying home with Pearl and Jo for New Year's while her parents go to the game. This will be Nina's 1st time being away from her new baby overnight.

They leave on a flight for New Orleans, 2 days before New Year's. Nina misses Jerica from the moment they leave for the airport. Once they get to New Orleans, the crew will show her a great time. She's missed hanging out with her crew and they've missed her too.

New Orleans is wonderful. The food, the drinks, the atmosphere, *The French Quarter, the beignets* and the party people are all perfect for a group like the crew. A group who knows how to have a good time. Kilo is at home in New Orleans. Him and his family show the crew a great time in the *Big Easy*. Cincinnati's football team wins the game which was the best part.

Another week later, the winter semester finds all of the college crew back in school and Nina goes to Cincinnati.

"Finally got my roommate back," Tank laughs as they get her things settled in their room.

With 7 bedrooms and 9 bathrooms, each couple has their own room and bath with 2 bedrooms and 4 baths to spare. Jan has a suite for her and Rob. He's in Cincinnati as often as he can be. One of the remaining rooms is decorated as a guest room. The last one is a nursery for Jerica.

"She needs to be here in her own little room," Nina says to the others as she views the nursery for the 1st time.

Her crew and the alumni women had decorated the room as a surprise for her while she was in Cleveland waiting to give birth.

"It's so beautiful, y'all," she says, "I love the wallpaper, the drapes and the matching patterns are fit for a princess," she says and adds her own finishing touches and makes it absolutely perfect for Jerica's arrival.

25

They spend the next couple of weeks getting into their new schedules plus basketball and cheering practices. T-baby is having a hard time in practice. She's tiring more easily than usual. Coach Sanders suggests she go to the clinic and get checked out.

Friday afternoon, after basketball pre-game shoot around is over, Ebony, Nina and Rebbie go with T-baby to the clinic. She has some familiar symptoms. At her check up she finds out she has brought a little something extra back from her trip to the crescent city. She's pregnant again.

"T-baby, I knew you wasn't taking your pills, girl," Rebbie says.
She confesses to them that her and Rich had planned to get pregnant. They both want this baby. They had planned to try again until they succeeded.

"We was heartbroken when we lost the first baby," she offers, "Especially with the way we was at each others throats, during that time. We figured maybe God was punishing us for fighting and treating each other the way that we was."
Ebony listens intensely. She fully understands where T-baby is coming from. Her heart still aches at the lose of her own baby. If her baby's death had been punishment for the sins of her and Ajay. Then *oh God*, what more will they have to endure. The bible states *an eye for an eye*. She has been personally responsible for lose of life. She knows Ajay has been also. She has no idea just how much or how many for him. But she knows her and Ajay account for more contribution to the crew's sin tally than just Raymond White. She dismisses the thought, for now. She's definitely going to support T-baby with this pregnancy. She even goes with her to tell coach Sanders the results of her test.

Coach is disappointed but admits she isn't surprised. She suspects Ebony has similar plans. Ebony admits she wants a baby but Ajay isn't in agreement.
Coach Sanders says, "I have to make it a point to personally thank Ajay for suggesting that you all wait until after college is done."

Sandy and Greg aren't surprised either. T-baby had expressed to her mother that she wasn't going to give up trying to have a baby. Even though Sandy and Greg had suggested she wait, she was determined. Her and Rich have to tell the rest of the Crew. They'll do that when they come down for the ladies game in Cincinnati, tonight. T-baby doesn't dress out for the game. But it's after they get the entire crew and their parents and Jerica back at the Natty house, that everyone is told. They're all loving and supportive as usual. T-baby isn't going to loose her scholarship either.

26

TIME TO LOVE-RELOADED-TIME WILL REVEAL 3

She'll come back next preseason. Her due date is September eighteenth.

In February, Rob has good news to share. He has been offered a job in Los Angeles with an up-and-coming record label. The label is interested in signing Shannon *Reaper* Wilson also. They offered Rob the opportunity to produce his 1st project with their label.

"They also offered me a salary to continue managing him," Archie Sr adds, "And I mean, I'm his daddy and he's only fourteen. I'm not about to send any child of mine to Hollywood alone. I got an actress and a rapper, so far," he gloats.

"We got stars in this family," Jo says, "And they're getting brighter every year."

Ajay has been invited to the Olympic trials this coming spring, along with Jb and Lynn. Ebony and T-baby have invites as well. But T-baby will forfeit her invitation because of her pregnancy. She's deep into her morning sickness stage. Ebony doesn't even want to go. Lynn has an invitation for track and the whole crew agree, she has the best shot at making the Olympic team and getting a gold medal. Ajay doesn't try out.

By March, the basketball season's come to a close. Tech's men and women plus UC men and women go to the tournament but neither advance past the Elite 8. Ajay's team got eliminated by 3 points spoiling their chance at a final four bid.

But the most notable event in March is when the crew mourn the lose of their favorite rapper/producer *Eric Eazy-E Wright,* on the 26th, to AIDS. His death shined a light on the Aids disease within the Hip-Hop and rap communities. No other AIDS case had drawn as much concern from Black people since Earvin *Magic* Johnson announced that he had been infected with the HIV virus, several years back.

Angelise Taylor's murder trial is big news for the month of April. The crew have looked forward to it and are definitely present the 1st day. But they're all sorely disappointed during the opening day of the trial. Angel's court appointed attorney ask for and is granted a continuance. The new trial is set for November. Ajay is upset and still he has to comfort Ebony because she's angry and let down. She wants justice for their unborn child. Wheeler assures them he'll stay on the prosecutor's back. He will make certain Angel is put away and Alana is dealt with, as well.

27

TIME TO LOVE-RELOADED-TIME WILL REVEAL 3

The rest of April is spent planning the next crew wedding. Nina and Tank have set a date to get married but it won't be until March 16 1996. However, there's a triple wedding planned for this June. Jb is marrying Lynn. Ced is getting married to Bre and the 3rd couple will be Rob and Jan. They'll be joined in a large triple wedding ceremony, on the 24th.

It's May and as the crew anticipate this month's celebration, they note that this is the first time in 5 years they don't have anyone graduating from high school. However, Jb and Lynn are graduating from Georgia Tech. Lynn is enrolled in Officers Training School and will begin serving active duty at *Dobbins AFB* after their honeymoon. She has also qualified to compete in the *1996 Olympic games*. It will be hosted by the city of Atlanta GA, a city her and Jb have grown to love. They plan to make it their permanent home.

CJ is still living between her 2 sets of grandparents Debbie and Bradley Wilson Sr and Jackie and Jason Carr. Bre has 2 more years to go before completing Georgia Tech. She wants a military career also. She's following in her father's footsteps. She'll attend Officers Training School in Sacramento at *McClellan AFB*.

At the Celebration on the 27th, Kim celebrates sweet 16. Pam turns 13 and is officially recognized as crew. Jan's only brother Sam Logan Jr is her boyfriend. With the nickname Cupid, which is what the crew call him, it wasn't a surprise that he brought flowers to present to Pam on their first official date. After the celebration is done, the crew devote their attention to the triple wedding taking place next month. Starring the crew ladies known as, *Three the Hard Way*.

REST IN PEACE TO:
ERIC "EAZY-E" WRIGHT
MARCH 26, 1995

We pray for your family in this time of grief.
The whole Hip Hop nation grieves with you.
We loved Eazy like family.
He will live on with this crew eternally and
he will never be duplicated!

28

CHAPTER   24

EXPANDING AND BUILDING

YOU ARE CORDIALLY INVITED

TO ATTEND THE TRIPLE WEDDING CEREMONY

OF

LYNORA SHONTAY JACKSON

TO

JOHN BROWN, JR

———

JANICE MARIE LOGAN

TO

ROBERT LEON JENKINS

———

BREANNA SHONTIA WILSON

TO

CEDRIC LEROY HAMILTON

———

SATURDAY JUNE 24, 1995
AT
4:00P.M.

THE FIRST BAPTIST CHURCH OF CLEVELAND, OHIO

WHAT GOD HAS JOINED TOGETHER, LET NO ONE PUT ASUNDER!

TIME TO LOVE-RELOADED-TIME WILL REVEAL 3

Prelude...Soft Music
Lighting of the candles...Host and hostesses
Entrance of the Grooms ....John Brown, Jr.
....Robert Leon Jenkins
....Cedric Leroy Hamilton
Honorary Best man...........................Mr. Cheston W. Coleman [deceased]
Best Men...Jeremy Marcus Brown
....Kenny Ramon Payne, Sr.
.... Bradley Lee Wilson, Jr.

Processional...Wedding Party

The Wedding party
Bridesmaids.........Escorted by..............Groomsmen

Ebony Eloise Brown..Anthony Devante' Jackson
Latrisha Nicole Brown.............................Richard Trevon Williams, Jr.
Rebbie Shantell Wilson.......................................Brian James, Jr.
Alicia Mallory Wilson..Bruce Dalvin Wilson
Brittany Neon James...Shannon Tyreek Wilson
Erica Maureen Jackson.......................................Gregory Brown, Jr.
Ruthie Nakia Williams......................................Jesse Lee Brown
Pamela Darius Jackson.......................................Samuel Logan, Jr.

Matrons of Honor...Renee Stewart Payne
....Latonya Walker Wilson
....Jacquel Coleman Carr

Maids of Honor..Nina Shalon Jackson
....Kimberly Celina Logan
....Chaundra Laurnea Coleman

Entrance of Junior Groom..........................Kenneth Ramon Payne, Jr.
Entrance of Junior Best Man.............................Steven Davon Brown

Junior Bridesmaids...Escorted by....Junior Groomsmen

Charlotte Elaine Coleman.............................Archie Joseph Wilson, Jr.
Brina Shawnice James....................................Brandon Shawn James
30

TIME TO LOVE-RELOADED-TIME WILL REVEAL 3

Junior maid of Honor................................Destiny Jalene' Shante' Payne
Honorary Flower Girl................................Jerica Eloise Brown
Flower Girls
Valene Amiya Hamilton............AAliyah Janeese Hamilton

Ring Bearer
..............................Bradley Lee Wilson, III ....

Entrance of Junior Bride...............................Chastity Jacquel Coleman

.........................ALL STAND PLEASE ....

ENTRANCE OF BRIDES
....Lynora Shontay Jackson
Given by her Father.....................................Allen Devante' Jackson, Jr.

....Janice Marie Logan
Given by her Father..................................Samuel Logan, Sr.

....Breanna Shontia Wilson
Given by her Father.............................Bradley Lee Wilson, Sr.

PLEASE BE SEATED

Devotion...Pastor Larry Tucker
Prayer..Mrs. Sally Greene-Logan
Duet.........*Always*....................Mr. and Mrs. Allen & Joanna Jackson
Poem...Mrs. Eloise Wilkes *Big Mama* Jones
Scriptures..........................Mrs. Annabelle Elizabeth Johnson Wilson

PLEGING OF THE VOW.

EXCHANGING OF THE RINGS

Lighting of the Unity Candles .... Soft Music
Song..................... *Here and Now*................Mr. Gregory Brown, Sr.
Song ....*All This Love*...............Debbie Jalene Williams Wilson

....................SALUTE THE BRIDES AND GROOMS..............................
31

TIME TO LOVE-RELOADED-TIME WILL REVEAL 3

Prayer...Mr. Charles Leon Wilson

Moment of silence in Remembrance of:
Cheston Wayne *Stoney* **Coleman**
And
Mrs. Pearline Anderson *Granny* **Brown**

Poem To the Couples.............*Percy* **Poppa** Jones and Jackson *Papa* Brown

Song...........*We're Going All The Way*....................Mr. John Brown, Sr.

Blessing of the Couples.....................................Mr. Joshua Logan, Jr.

ALL STAND PLEASE

....Recessional..................................

Coordinators...

Mother of the Groom..................................Mrs. Pearline Jones Brown
Mother of the Bride...............................Mrs. Joanna Williams Jackson
Aunt of the Groom...Mrs. Brenda Jones James
Mother of the Groom...................................Ms. Roberta Elise Jenkins
Mother of the Groom..................................Mrs. Sedina Faye Hamilton

Seamtresses..
Mother of the Bride....................................Mrs. Belinda Carter Logan
....Mrs. Sandra Logan Brown
....Mrs. Rena Baker Wilson

Hostesses...

Mother of the Bride ....Mrs. Debbie Williams Wilson
....Mrs. Anna Wilson Williams

Host...

Father of the Bride.......................................Bradley Wilson, Sr.
Father of the Groom...........................Mr. George Leroy Hamilton
32

TIME TO LOVE-RELOADED-TIME WILL REVEAL 3

Father of the Bride...............................Mr. Allen Devante' Jackson, Jr.
Father of the Groom............................Mr. John Brown, Sr.
Father of the Bride............................Mr. Samuel Logan, Sr.
....Mr. Richard Trevon Williams, Sr.
....Mr. Gregory Brown, Sr.
....Mr. Brian James, Sr.
....Mr. Archie Joseph Wilson, Sr.
Ushers...
The ladies and gentlemen of Delta Sigma Theta Sorority and Omega Psi Phi
Fraternity

Decorations and floral:.........................The Mothers of the Crew

Catering and Wedding cakes:..................The Crews House of Soul Food

Photography: ....Que Psi Phi Pictures, Co. Arthur Lee Owens, CEO

Reception follows at: The Chill Spot, Sounds by Jenkins Jams Company

Thanks to God for his blessing of these unions. With him all things are
possible. Thanks to our parents who have weathered the
storms known as our lives. Thank you for your unconditional love and
support.
Thank you to our crew, friends and families for sharing
in our special celebration. We love you all, dearly.

Thanks to each other for the patience, endurance, consideration and
support. Thanks for caring, sharing, loving and being my best friend.

PRESENTING:
Mr. and Mrs. John & Lynora Brown, Jr.

Mr. and Mrs. Robert & Janice Jenkins

Mr. and Mrs. Cedric & Breanna Hamilton

Saturday June 24, 1994
Forever

33

TIME TO LOVE-RELOADED-TIME WILL REVEAL 3

The crew execute another breath taking wedding. The reception is so full, they have to turn people away. The 3 couples are going on the same honeymoon excursion that Chill, Jr and their wives had taken. They're leaving on Monday morning. But for the rest of the weekend, they're staying in a lavish hotel in downtown Cleveland. They won't see the crew and their families until they return from their cruise.

The June celebration is included with the reception and starts after the newlyweds leave for the hotel. Big June will be 20 in 2 days and for his birthday, he gets a fully loaded 1995 Acura Legend. It's registered in him and his parents names. It's rumored that the car is a present from the UC alumni. A token of appreciation for his contributions to the UC football bowl game win, in January. There are also rumors of a possible NCAA investigation into the practices of UC athletics because of the crew's lifestyle. But their businesses are profiting enough to account for the monies it would take to make any of the purchases the crew claim to have made. Rich will receive a fully loaded 1996 Caprice Classic for his birthday, once the investigation news dies down. His will be registered to his parents and him as well.

Chill turned 26 years-old on the 14th of June. He received a diamond and platinum watch from the crew as an appreciation gift. He had worn it as best man to Rob, at the wedding.

Ally turns 12 on the 3rd and she's still begging Rena and Archie Sr to let her go to the crew parties. They haven't given in. She has to wait until next year for her coming out party. She has her last party at *Granny's House* but she doesn't like having it there. In defiance, she hangs with the active crew at the reception and celebration. Rena and Archie Sr decide to take her home with them when they leave. She isn't happy but she felt a little better when she saw that Steven had to leave too. They like each other. Rebbie and T-baby are excited that their little sister and brother want to date.

Chill, Renee, Jr and Tonya celebrate 4 years of marriage this month.

Ebony replaced her car, last Christmas. June and Rich are car owners now. Which leaves the crew with a nice list of cars.

Chill and Renee own a 89 and a 92 Blazer. Bre and Cedric own a 90 Jeep Cherokee and the 88 Chevy van, from Stoney. Jr and Tonya have an 81 Cutlass, fully kitted and restored, a 92 Bonneville and a 94 Toyota Camry. Rob and Jan own a 85 Cadillac Seville and a 91 Toyota Corolla. Jb
34

and Lynn have a 88 Regal and 94 Sentra. Ajay owns a 64 Chevy Impala convertible while Ebony *had* a 91 Accord. She now owns a 95 Toyota Camry. Tank owns a 93 Tracker while Nina has a 95 Camry just like Ebony's. Only Nina's is white. June has a 95 Acura Legend. Bruce owns a 92 soft top Cutlass while Kim has the 87 Sentra which was given to her by Bruce, by way of Tonya and Jr. These cars are regulars at their detail shop for cleaning and maintenance, on a strict schedule. They will upgrade plenty, during the coming years and trade some too. And in some cases, they'll pass them down to younger siblings or crew.

The crew have planned the July celebration for July 1st. Ajay's assault trial is July 17th. The crew hope he'll beat this one too. They'll have to wait for the outcome because they know anything can happen with the *injustice system*. None of them are over confident about him having an easy time. Still, the entire month of July is filled with celebrations.

The females throw T-baby an awesome baby shower at the salon, on the last day of June. Jb's 22nd birthday is the 4th of July and Ajay turn's 21 on the 11th. The 2 of them do it real big with their party being sponsored by their Alumni. T-baby's 19th birthday is the 24th and most of her gifts are for the baby, as she had requested. She receives money gifts for her birthday. Her and Rich start a trust fund for their unborn son with most of the money. Little Destiny Payne turns 2 and has her party at *Granny's House*.

The celebration is wonderful but the crew have another surprise for their guest. June and Rich are proposing to Rebbie and T-baby and the girls are totally surprised. The guys do their rap song first. Then sing R&B oldies, just as they had done for Nina and Tank's engagement. T-baby and Rebbie are elated as they finally get to show off their engagement rings. They plan to get married next June in a double ceremony.

"Ebony, you know we can make it a triple wedding if you and Ajay come on in," T-baby says.

"We're not ready, kid," Ebony says, as she's truly happy for her girls.

Again, Ajay thinks she's sad. But to his surprise, she isn't. She has come to accept and love his plan that they're going to stand alone when they take their vows. However, he already knows *when* he's going to propose to her, where and *even how*. But he's keeping it a secret. For now, he's going to make sure she doesn't feel left out. He's giving her gifts of jewelry, accessories for her car, clothes, shoes and accessories for her. And anything

35

else he thinks she may like, at every turn. Still he learns that all she *really* wants from him is private and quality time. His dominance in basketball takes him away from school a lot, to participate in other leagues and All-star events. Time alone with him would be enough for her. They're a very happy couple these days and noticeably more private and secluded. More so than they was before college. Even Pearl and Jo mentioned that they've noticed it more, each time they visit from college. They spend most of their time alone, at Ajay's apartment. Or sometimes, they don't even come home with the rest of the Natty bunch. They go to another town or just stay in Cincinnati when the others come home.

"They're growing up and becoming independent," their mothers had said and they like seeing them more independent.

They always knew Ajay would become more selfish when it came to even sharing Ebony with the family and crew. He's already adopted both of their fathers mentalities, when protecting her is the issue. But he's become more like her father in his young adult life, when it comes to spoiling her. He doesn't want her to miss out on anything. If it's new and popular amongst females, he's going to make sure she has it. Still, all she *demands* is his time.

T-baby and Rich go to Dr. Weston. every 2 weeks now. But they'll start going weekly, in August. T-baby is forgoing the beginning of the 1st semester until after their son comes. She'll start off the fall on home study, same as Nina had done last year. Nina had reclaimed her scholarship after Jerica was 6 weeks old. T-baby and Rich had an ultrasound last month. They know they're having a boy. Rich is already beside himself with excitement. He wants him to be named after him and his father. T-baby agrees with him on the name. That doesn't matter as much to her, as him being born healthy. She misses being able to train with Ebony during the summer months. She'll also miss a lot of the preseason workouts. But she knows she'll get her rhythm back, in no time. She loves playing basketball more than Ebony does. Ebony is just more of a natural talent. But Ebony would rather support Ajay's game, then to play herself, these days. Ajay still pushes Ebony to play to her full potential and she does.

}July 17{
Ajay's trial starts today and the crew attend. Ebony has paid all her court fees and fines. She has also completed her community service for her misdemeanor assault charge against Angel. Hardin had her fine down to less the $75. She's all clear. Now her focus is on her man and his trial.
36

TIME TO LOVE-RELOADED-TIME WILL REVEAL 3

The trial only last for 2 days. By Wednesday, Ajay has received a sentence of 5 years. Which is suspended immediately with the expressed understanding that if he has another felony within 24 months, he will have to serve out his 5 years, day-for-day. The judge said he was spared, only because Angel has a trial pending for murder and attempted murder. His jury had no sympathy for her as a plaintiff. Not after they learned of the violent charges against her. Furthermore, the acts she had committed was against Ebony Brown, who is considered 1 of Cleveland's most prominent citizens, nowadays. Same as Ajay. The jurors were sympathetic to Ajay's actions. They saw it as him trying to protect his girl and he's a prominent citizen as well. He receives 2 years probation and he isn't happy about it at all. Until Ebony reminds him that a year ago, this time, they were grieving the lost of their 1st born and he was dreaming about murder. This could've been a whole lot worse. She isn't happy with probation either. But she's happy he doesn't receive any jail time at all. With the trial being over, the crew can now turn their attention back to August and the celebration at hand.

But first, they lease Arthur a suite at *The CrewLand Mall* for his video and photography studio. Aptly titled *Que Psi Phi Photography and Video studio*. He leases the 7th suite in the first tier of *The CrewLand Mall*. Now their original strip mall is nearly filled to capacity. All businesses are already very profitable and with Rob leaving for Los Angeles this fall, Jr will be 1st in charge of *Jenkins Jams Company* with Archie Sr as manager of operations.

Next, the crew break ground for an additional strip mall adjacent to the original one. They have more businesses to open, in the future. Mr. Parkwood's real estate and investment savvy, has afforded them some very high stake purchases. Ebony does some student work at his firm in Natty. She's majoring in Real Estate and Investment banking. She can see the crew's dream and she knows with her major, she'll play a very intricate roll in guaranteeing their investments, land purchases and leases. As well as their pensions and retirements.

Before returning to Cincinnati for the new semester, the crew have their August Celebration at The Spot. Jr is 24 by the 14th and Jan will turn 21 on the last day of the month. Ajay feel like he needs another classic car. He buys the 1978 Cadillac Seville from papa Brown, as a celebration gift to himself for not going to jail. His love of antique cars comes from his fathers side of the family. This fall will be his senior year in college. So Al and Jo actually pay papa for the car and Ajay puts the money into the detailing

37

and extras. Papa loves what he has done with it, so far. And he tells him so.

"Next year we're gonna have our first annual car show at Crew Details," Ajay announces at the celebration which doubles as a birthday party for Rebbie, who turns 19 the same day.

****

This fall, it's T-baby and Rich's turn to play phone tag. The Labor day festivities have come and gone. Rich is into his junior football season and Mr. Parkwood is called upon again for his assistance in getting him home for the arrival of his son. And once again, Mr. Parkwood is willing to help the crew. The September celebration will be the last day of the month. Which gives the college crew a chance to work out their schedules.

Jb and Lynn have built a home in Smyrna, a subsidiary of Atlanta. She's training heavily for the 96 Olympic games and is now an active duty 2nd lieutenant in the U.S. Air Force. She is stationed at *Dobbins Air Force Base*.

Bre and Cedric are living with them right now and they all share the expenses. Bre starts her junior year at Tech. While her husband Cedric Hamilton, who had graduated from CSU in 91, works for a major credit bureau in Atlanta. All 4 of them will fly home on September 30, the day of the celebration.

}September 30{

T-baby and Rich are 12 days overdue. The crew are in town for the big party tonight. But this morning, the foursome treat T-baby to breakfast at their restaurant; *The Crews House of Soul Food*. She isn't able to keep anything down. She's having a very bad day, so far. She suggest to the crew that she go home and lay down. Rich is there with Ajay, Tank and June. They all decide to go to Ajay's apartment and relax before tonight's festivities.

Tonya turns 24 today. Bre had celebrated her 21st birthday on the 9th with Jb, Lynn and Cedric, down in Atlanta. Reaper made 16 on the 24th and he's doing very well in football. But even better with his music. He has a 2nd single on the radio and Brittany is featured on it. He has been to Los Angeles with Rob, twice. Rob is due to leave next month for an extended stay in LA. Reaper expects to join him during the Thanksgiving and Christmas holidays. Archie Sr will go to the west coast with him. Rob will be returning to Cincinnati with the UC crew, on Monday. He will
38

TIME TO LOVE-RELOADED-TIME WILL REVEAL 3

remain there until shortly before he has to leave for his trip to Los Angeles, to start his new job.

Brad III had his birthday party at *Granny's House* on the 2nd. He turned 4 years old this year and started preschool.

At the U, T-baby isn't fairing much better than she was at the restaurant, so Ebony calls aunt Sandy at the salon.

"T-baby isn't doing good," she tells her aunt, "She's complaining that everything hurts and she's throwing up. What should we do?"

Sandy says she'll call Dr. Weston, then call her back. When Sandy does call back, she's calling from her cell phone.

"Doc wants her to come on to the hospital," she says, "I'm going to get her bags and I'll meet y'all there."

Ebony relays the news to the rest, then they all leave taking T-baby to the hospital. Nina and Tank will meet them there, after taking 11-month old Jerica to Jo's house.

The others arrive at the hospital within minutes. When T-baby has her 1st exam in labor and delivery, Weston is pleasantly surprised to announce that she's already dilated to 6 centimeters.

"Looks like we're having a little boy, today," Weston smiles.

Ebony and Rebbie do phone duty. By the time Nina and Tank arrive, T-baby is at 8 centimeters as Nina says, "Kid, you're moving fast."

Sandy and Greg are in the delivery room along with T-baby, Rich, Ebony, Nina and Rebbie. Anna and Rich Sr are in the waiting room with papa. For papa and grandpa Joshua, this is their great-grandson. The 1st great for Joshua. But for papa, Jerica was the 1st. Other crew are filing in, hoping she'll deliver early enough so they can announce the birth at the celebration, later tonight. They get their wish. She delivers in record time for a 1st baby. Technically, her first *delivery*. She doesn't experience very many hard contractions before she's allowed to push. She's fully dilated within 4 hours of arriving at the hospital. The birth goes prefect and their baby boy is born.

NAME: Richard Trevon Williams, III
BORN: September 30, 1995
TIME: 5:35pm
WEIGHT: 7lbs, 10 ounces
HEIGHT:22 inches

39

TIME TO LOVE-RELOADED-TIME WILL REVEAL 3

Rich cuts the cord, then after Rich III vitals are checked and normal, he's allowed to hold his son. He's very emotional.

Chill yells, "New crew in the house," his classic line for the labor and delivery room.

They all share a laugh but T-baby is worn out. Her girls are in tears as she takes her new son into her arms. She holds lil Rich for a short time. Then ask if she can get some sleep. She hasn't slept in 4 days. The crew leave her side, so she can rest.

Rich takes his son to the nursery for his 1st attempt at feeding. Ebony is staying at the hospital with T-baby and aunt Sandy. Ajay has gone with Rich, his parents and big Greg to the nursery. The rest of the crew go to the celebration to share the news with partygoers.

Welcome to the world...*Richard Trevon Williams, III.*

Jb had gotten an invitation to the Atlanta Hawks open tryouts, earlier in the summer. He didn't make the team. However, he did meet a lot of great contacts. Those contacts will help him with his new career as a sports representative and sports agent. He already represents 2 NBA athletes and 4 in the NFL. He has negotiated 6 figure deals for 5 of his 7 clients. 1 of his NFL clients has a multi-million dollar contract with major endorsements and Jb is just getting started. His plans are to represent for everybody from his crew, who gets drafted. He feels that's going to be a lot of them, starting with Ajay.

T-baby is home from the hospital with Richard III and both are doing great. She's helping the staff of *Granny's House* with the final preparations for the October kids party. She also helps to plan *The Chill Spot's* October celebration. It will include Rob's going away to Los Angeles celebration, as well. The parties are going to be held on the 28th with a Halloween theme. The kids honored will be Archie Wilson Jr who turns 10 on the 4th and he's already good at basketball. Ajay is whom he credits as being his teacher and role model. CJ turns 4 this year and receives another gift from her grandpa Chester. Jerica will celebrate her 1st birthday on the 20th.

The adult Celebration will follow at *The Chill Spot*. Halloween is the theme for it, as well. All guest are required to wear costumes. Belinda, Sandy and Rena are the main seamstresses in the family. They have designed costumes for everyone in the family. They will have their own
40

TIME TO LOVE-RELOADED-TIME WILL REVEAL 3

Store, soon. It will be the 1st business in their newly completed strip mall.

Saturday, Rich is in Cleveland with his little family, as his son turns 2 weeks old. He received his birthday gift last weekend. A 1996 Caprice Classic and proudly drives it home this week. Tank and Nina make the trip with him. They're picking up Nina's car from Jo's house and taking Jerica shopping for her birthday gifts. The grandparents have already spoiled her with many things. Nina comments to her mother about the many gifts she has for Jerica.

"Ma, you didn't leave anything for us to get her," she says.

"I'm not waiting on anybody when it comes to my first *grand* baby," Jo says, "Besides, half of this stuff came from Pearl and John."

"Jerica *is* the first grandbaby on both sides," Tank says proudly, "She's suppose to be spoiled."

"Just like Jb, Jr and Jan was," Jo says.

"Lynn is the oldest grandchild on big Al's side, right?" Tank asks.

"No. Allen's sister Jessica has a son named Terrell. He's two years older than Lynora," Jo says.

"I thought Lynn was older then Terrell," Tank says.

Al's older sister, Jessica Jackson-Layton, lives in Boston. She had married Jonathan Layton, her sweetheart from *Kent state*. He's white and according to Jessica, a step up from being a 2nd class citizen. That's not-at-all how Al sees it and neither did their parents. Jessica looks down on Jo because she came from *"poor roots"* as she had put it and didn't want her only sibling *marrying down*. Their has been friction in the family, for years. At the time their father passed away, the friction hadn't been mended. Al believes that's why Jessica hadn't been *considered* in their fathers Will. Their parents hadn't approved of the way Jonathan looked down his nose at them. Or of the changes in their only daughter. Their son Terrell Layton is an only child. Jessica and Al aren't close anymore. They talk, about once a year. Jo stays on him about reaching out to his only sister. She wants them to stay in touch, being that they're all the family each other has left. Al has always told Jo that he tries to get Jessica to come for visits but she won't. She flat out refuses. Jo knows the reason Jessica doesn't speak to Al now, is partly due to his marriage to her. And because Al was named sole executor and beneficiary of their parents *Last Will and Testament.*

"So Rell should be about twenty four or twenty five, by now ha?" Nina asks.

"He's twenty five," Jo answers.

41

TIME TO LOVE-RELOADED-TIME WILL REVEAL 3

Nina and Tank look through the new things their daughter had acquired since last weekend.

"We're still taking her shopping," Nina says, "She needs some more stuff for her room at school."

Jo suggest she take the things Jerica will need, from her room here or at Pearl's. But Nina wants to leave the rooms just as they are and buy new things for the Cincinnati nursery.

"We've got to get some more stuff for lil Richie's room at school too," she says and once again Jo suggest she first check with his grandmothers, Anna and Sandy.

"They have just as much stuff between their two houses, as me and Pearl have at ours. He's their first grandbaby too," Jo reminds them.

Nina says they'll check with T-baby and Rich before buying anything. Her and Tank buckle Jerica in her car seat and head out to *The CrewLand Mall*.

10 minutes later, they arrive, park and head inside *Crew Cuts*. Tonya and Justine have a full shop of clients and they still have their usual sense of humor.

"We need to start selling clothes up here," Nina says to Tonya as she enters the salon.

"Girl, we already do," Tonya says as she laughs.

She's referring to Justine and Kilo, who have been bringing garments in to sale to the customers, every weekend for the past 2 months.

"They be serving the whole strip, kid?" Nina asks as her and Tonya continue to laugh.

"We got all these businesses covered," Justine adds as she laughs.

"Child please. People be placing orders for specifics like she's a catalog," Tonya says with more laughter.

"We're laughing but that's an idea for the other business," Nina suggests, "Y'all know aunt Belinda, Sandy and Rena can sew their butts off."

"We'll check into it," Tonya says as she looks at Justine.

"Just let me know what's happening," Justine says.

Tank and Nina pick out several outfits for Jerica and Rich III.

"Ebony and Rebbie didn't come with y'all, this time?" Justine asks.

"No. We all got practice tonight," she answers.

"We have to get back before seven, ourselves," Tank adds, "We just came to take daddy's little girl shopping for her birthday."

He's playing peep-a-boo with Jerica as she sits in her walker.

"We're fixing to go see T-baby, Rich and lil Rich. Then we're

42

going to the stores to shop for awhile," Nina says as they prepare to leave.

"I thought you was gonna take some heads, when I saw you walk in," Justine says with a sly grin.

"I wouldn't mind taking some customers, if I had more time to be here," Nina says.

She does a few shampoos to help her partners get ahead. Then her, Tank and Jerica head to Sandy and Greg's house to visit Rich, T-baby and their new baby boy.

The salon was full of customers. Sandy is going in to help with the rush since Rich is at the house with T-baby and their son. She leaves Nina, Tank and Jerica at her house visiting and heads to the salon.

"She's trying to get to him, isn't she?" T-baby asks Nina.

She's referring to Jerica, who's nearly falling out of Tank's lap trying to get to Rich III.

"That's your cousin, girl," Nina says as she laughs.

"They're *second* cousin's. On both sides," Rich adds.

"They're definitely gonna have to date outside the crew," T-baby says as she laughs.

"Jerica is not dating until she's twenty one," Tank offers.

They all laugh as they discuss the fact that all their children will be born, blood related.

"It's sad none of our kids can date each other," Nina says, "Like we all did."

"Twenty years from now, crew will be all new blood," Tank says.

"Yes indeed, man. There's no telling how many different families will be connected by then," Rich adds.

They dress the kids in matching fall outfits and all 6 of them go shopping.

After shopping, T-baby and Rich III go back to Sandy's. T-baby is keeping Nina's car, this week. Rich drives to Pearl's house to drop off Jerica. Then him, Tank and Nina head back to Cincinnati.

The October Celebration starts promptly at 9pm. This year Rob turns 25 on the sixth. He's leaving for Los Angeles, Monday. Rich made 20 on the 1st. Greg Jr is 15. The crew also celebrate his achievements in football, this season. He has been selected to the national junior all-American AAU football team as a high school freshman.

The Georgia crew fly in the Friday night before the party. Rob and the Natty crew arrived early this morning. Everyone go and get their costumes from Sandy at the salon.

43

"Aunt Sandy, y'all did your thing!" Tank says after viewing his costume.

They all love them.

The celebration goes very well until someone picks up the phone in Chill's office upstairs. It was a call from Angel, from jail. Someone had hooked her up on the 3-way so she could call. Kilo was the person who answered. He hung up on her. He relays the info to Chill, who tells him to forget about it for tonight. They'll look into it later. He knows that most likely it's Alana, up to her old ass tricks again.

Jan and Rob leave early and go to his apartment at The U, for the last time. He gave up the lease and shipped his furniture to Los Angeles, last week. Tonight, him and Jan share an air mattress in the middle of an other wise, empty living room.

"I'm gonna miss you, baby," she says.

"I'll miss you too," he says, "But you're coming out for the holidays. Thanksgiving and Christmas."

"And you're gonna try to come back for my season opener in March, right?" she asks.

"You know I am," he says as they kiss.

"We're gonna have a long distance relationship, Rob," she says after the kiss.

"A longer distance relationship," he corrects her, "We've had that for the past three years. Remember that," he offers and they agree.

"We can handle it," she says, "We always do."

They make love in the empty apartment. Several times throughout the night and a few more times before Church, the next morning. Then they get dressed and head off to church. They have an important commitment to fulfill today.

Everyone is at Church, this Sunday. Jan and Rob are Christening Richard Trevon Williams III. Then after Church, all of the families gather for dinner at *The Crews House of Soul Food,* before the Georgia crew's flight has to leave. The Cincinnati crew leave around 7pm.

Jan stays in Cleveland to bring Rob to the airport. She's very emotional about saying goodbye to her husband. Chill, Renee, Tonya and Jr go with them. Jan and Rob share a long kiss goodbye.

"A part of me wishes you was pregnant, right now," Rob says, "Then a piece of me could be with you. Until I get back."

"I got your heart, baby," Jan says, "I'll hold onto that and send mine with you."

44

TIME TO LOVE-RELOADED-TIME WILL REVEAL 3

They share another kiss. Then he boards his flight to Los Angeles and it departs. Jan takes a flight to Cincinnati, shortly afterwards.

Chill contacts Ajay during the next week and makes him aware of Angel's call to the club, during the celebration.

"That bitch wants me to kill her, bro," Ajay says, "She must be out of her *fuckin* mind to be calling for me. She killed my baby and tried to kill my heart. I could kill that bitch, a hundred different ways. She don't get it."

"I'm just glad her ass is still locked up," Chill says, "She plays a stupid ass game. *Like* what muthafuckah *don't know* that you nor this *fuckin* crew, don't have no love for her?"

"That's why I say she's doing it just to fuck with me and baby girl, bro," Ajay says, "I'm not going for this stupid shit, Chill. I'm on paper and this bitch *playin* dangerous."

"I'm gonna have to alert Wheeler on this, Ajay," he says, "I can't even risk you blowing your cool, lil brother. You got millions of dollars on the table. You are *too fuckin* close to the league for me to allow some dumb ass, fatal attraction to fuck it up."

"Call Wheeler then, man," Ajay says, "Because I've got things to do and a life to live out here, with my love. I don't even feel like being upset about her dumb ass."

"I got you, man," Chill says, "I got it handled. She's nervous about her trial coming up, probably."

"And I don't give a fuck," Ajay says, "That bitch needs to go to the chamber."

45

CHAPTER   25

JUSTICE FOR EBONY?

The highlight of November is the Angelise Taylor's murder trial, on the 6th.

T-baby is back at UC and back into the groove on the court. Their season opener was the 16th of November. She dressed out but her play was limited. She had only been back in school a week. She returned to practice on the 4th and has held her own since. Her and Ebony are captains this season and they still love to push each other.

"Cousin, you didn't loose anything while you were pregnant," Ebony had said during the 1st week shoot around drills.

She knew it wouldn't be long before T-baby was back on the starting team and helping her demolish their opponents. They won their first 3 games then packed up and headed home for their holiday break.

Ebony is still shaken from Angel's trial. The entire family are, for that matter. That is evident during Thanksgiving week. The crew's holiday celebration is almost overshadowed by speculation of what Angel's prison sentence will be. The celebration is Saturday the 30th of November.

Angel's trial had been held on November 6, just 24 days ago. She had been officially charged with Vehicular Homicide, Attempted Murder and Fleeing Interstate Jurisdiction. All 3 are class A felonies. Alana's trial had been held before Angel's or Ajay's.

Alana had been tried in January and received 5 years, just as Ajay had. Just like Ajay, Alana's sentence had been suspended too. She was given 3 years probation. 1 more than Ajay. After 2 failed attempts to be promoted to 12th grade, she'd dropped out of MLK and moved back to Pittsburgh. Darlene didn't want her around her place anymore, after learning that she had been an intricate part of Angel and Ajay's encounter ever coming to be. That information had come out during her trial and that's when Darlene told her she could no longer live at her apartment. The terms of Alana's probation was that she had to finish school or get her G.E.D. Since leaving Darlene's apartment and Cleveland, she has taken classes in Pittsburgh and gotten her G.E.D., ahead of schedule. She's now attending a community college and has custody of her daughter Olivia. The Pittsburgh authorities were quoted, saying, "S*he only straightened up her act to avoid jail."*

Michelle tells Arthur that *most likely,* after Alana saw how hard

TIME TO LOVE-RELOADED-TIME WILL REVEAL 3

Tameka was having it in jail, it convinced her to try to get right. Michelle had severed her ties with all of the above. But she's considering reaching out to Tameka upon Arthur's approval. Alana had claimed she had severed all ties with Angel and Tameka as well. Michelle says it's not true. They'll find out later that it was just 1 of the many lies Alana had told.

"Time will tell, Arthur," Michelle says as they talk, while sitting in VIP at the November celebration, "Those bitches could lie for a living. They're just that good at it. Angel and Alana, that is. Tameka wasn't a bad person. She thought she had to be because of them. They was her only *so called* friends. Before me. You'll see the real her, if she ever gets out. She wasn't like them, at all."

"I just know Angel better not get no fucking probation," Arthur says, "Cause I'm gonna do her yamp ass myself, if she ever see the sun."

During her trial, back on November 6, Angel had hoped for some leniency from the judge too. Since 1st Alana and then Ajay had been spared. But Wheeler pressured the prosecution to get a sound conviction with maximum jail time. Angel's court appointed attorney was out of his league. He wanted to deal her out of the charges but the prosecutor sought the maximum and she wouldn't dare bend on what Wheeler demanded.

Michelle, who had been the star witness in Alana's trial, was called in Angel's trial also. The foursome was witnesses to the telephone threats Angel had made to Ebony, prior to the incident. Ebony was angry and very emotional on the stand. Which had only infuriated Ajay, farther. He was already upset after he had to testify about his involvement with Angel. Alana was called as a witness for the prosecution. Angel's stepfather, Tony Mangrove, testified and officer Jacobson gave testimony as well. Angel had planned to take the stand in her own defense. But the defense opted against it, after hearing testimony from a young man named Mario Scott.

Mario gave vivid testimony about his relationship with Angel. Which had taken place prior to Ajay. He said their relationship was only a sexual one. When he broke it off to date his present girlfriend, Angel had threatened his new girl and she'd tried to stab her with a butchers knife on 3 separate occasions. Mario also testified that Angel claimed to be a virgin before him. But he found out she had dated 2 other guys from Smith High, where he attended school. She'd had violent cases with their girlfriends also and didn't even admit to those relationships until after she met Ajay. Ajay was calmer during Mario's testimony. He even offered his opinion to Chill, who sat next to him and Ebony during the trial.

47

TIME TO LOVE-RELOADED-TIME WILL REVEAL 3

"I already knew that bitch wasn't no virgin," he had whispered to Chill, "Word's been out. She was wide open. You know the streets talk." Mario's testimony had almost mirrored Ajay's. Angel's 2 former lover's, Mario and Ajay, painted a clear picture to the jury about her obsessive behavior with guys she had been involved with. After their testimony on Wednesday, the prosecution rested. The guilt was clear.

The defense's case or lack there of, was presented on Thursday. Angel's mother was their only witness. Before the defense rested, all previous witnesses were recalled and cross examined. Closing arguments were done by 4pm on Friday. Then the jury was allowed to deliberate. They reached a verdict in just under 2 hours and court was called to order again at 6pm. The Jury foreman stood and read the verdict. Ajay put his arm around Ebony and braced for it. The verdict was read as such;

"On the charge, count one of the indictment, Fleeing Interstate Jurisdiction. We find the defendant, Angelise Taylor, guilty."
The courtroom had erupted in applause and cheers and the judge had called them to order. The verdict on the next charge was then read.

"On the charge, count two of the indictment, Vehicular homicide. We find the defendant, Angelise Taylor, guilty."
The courtroom erupted a 2nd time and was called to order again. This time with a warning. Mama Jo had motioned to the crew to be calm. Ajay and Ebony was holding each other, at that point. They wanted guilty on all 3 counts. The Foreman read on.

"On the charge, count three of the indictment, Attempted Murder. We find the defendant, Angelise Taylor, guilty as charged."
The courtroom erupted a 3rd time. Which resulted in the judge calling a sidebar. It was then that he told the prosecutor and defense attorney they would convene in 3 weeks, for sentencing. He decided to make the sentencing phase private, due to all of the outburst after the reading of the verdict.

Yesterday, November 29th was Angel's sentencing day and it had stayed closed to the public. Ajay, Ebony, their parents nor any of their crew was allowed to attend. Only Wheeler could go. And still today, November 30th, Ajay and Ebony remain very emotional about the guilty verdicts from 3 weeks ago. They're anxious to know Angel's sentence. They're even more agitated about not being allowed to give statements, at her sentencing, for killing their first child. But even worse than that, the sentencing phase has gone into it's second day. Still, only Wheeler can attend and he's going to contact them with the outcome, as soon as he knows it.

48

TIME TO LOVE-RELOADED-TIME WILL REVEAL 3

They're still emotional tonight. Wheeler hasn't called yet. He's still in court. Ajay still wants what he demanded to have from the start. *Justice For Ebony* and their unborn child. *But why is sentencing such a problem?*

Tonight, the crew are celebrating the verdicts at their event. They feel confident that Angel will receive the maximum sentence. Ajay and Ebony stay at the U. They don't feel a celebration is in order. Not until they get that call from Wheeler. Hopefully with news of a lengthy sentence.

It's 6pm and still no word. Ebony doesn't want to celebrate. Not until she knows when Angel is being sent to a *real* prison. Like the Ohio State Penitentiary and for how long. Ajay agrees with her.

"I just want her out of our lives, baby," she says.

"She *is* and has been, for a long time," he offers.

"Not long enough," she says.

"I apologize for Angel and everything she did," he starts, "If I could go back to the first time I met her and change history, I would. I can't do that, baby. But what I can do is promise you I'll never put you through nothing like this again."

"I know, baby," she says, "I'm sorry too."

They talk for hours about Angel. He tells her the whole story of how he had met her at Jeremy's 16th birthday party. The night she had her career high game at Smiley high school in Houston.

"That party was really a turning point for all of us," she says.

"Yes. But I didn't hook up with her *that* night," he says, "You called from H-town and I was busy talking to you, on the phone. So she left with her girls."

"When did you hook up with her?" she asks.

Ajay thinks for a minute. He remembers when he had his 1st sexual experience with Angel. But he didn't have intercourse with her.

"The first time, she gave me head. That's all," he says reluctantly.

"Whatever," she says, "But when was that?"

He hates telling her that the night he had first been intimate with Angel, was the same night Raymond had attacked her. But he does tell her.

"What?" she asks in disbelief.

"I hated her guts after I realized that," he says, "I never messed with her again. Not solo. Not since you came back and got back to being yourself. It was always something creepy and dishonest about her. I can remember asking her questions, all the time. Because she just didn't seem genuine. I told her shit, point blank. And I treated her like shit too."

49

"She's phony," she says, "She wasn't no virgin like I told her."

"I knew she wasn't a virgin. I knew *my love* was the only virgin I'd ever had," he says and smiles. She smiles back. He continues, "I just figured if I would've been somewhere calling you. Or had you at big mama's early, to wait for my call, the shit with Raymond wouldn't have happened."

She's quiet briefly. Then she says, "You can't blame yourself for either one of those monsters," she starts, "God's got a plan for us. All we have to do is stick to it."

"And stick to each other too," he says as they share a laugh.

Ring! Ring! Ring!

The phone rings. It's Wheeler. He has called with the news on Angel's sentence. After finding out the sentence, they call their parents and tell them. Then they asks them to share the news with the crew at the celebration, for them.

"You two aren't coming?" Jo asks.

"No. We're gonna stay in," Ajay answers.

"Are you okay?" Pearl asks.

"Yes," Ebony answers, "Just let our crew know, we just wanna be by ourselves tonight."

They hang up the 3-way call. Then they make love, twice before falling asleep. Each of them sleep rather peacefully tonight.

The kids party at *Granny's House,* which had been held on the 25th, honored the James twins. June's youngest siblings had made 9 years old, on the fourth. Stoney's baby sister Charlotte, turned 11 on the third.

Renee had turned 26 on the twenty first. She's the only active crew member with a birthday in November. Ebony and Ajay sent the sentencing announcement by their parents and turned in for the night.

Chill and Renee get the word on Angel's sentence. The party goes into overdrive. They tell the crew it's good but don't say exactly what it is. They want to announce it. The crew want to know what Angel's sentence is now. Before they put holes in the walls and maybe a few people too. Instead of prolonging the suspense, Chill call Renee on stage to let it be known.

"At this month's celebration, we're gonna switch things up, once again for y'all," Renee says as she takes the microphone from Chill, who'd just announced the celebration's official start. Though the crew has been partying for over 3 hours already. Renee gives this months announcements.

50

TIME TO LOVE-RELOADED-TIME WILL REVEAL 3

"This month, we'll honor wedding anniversaries in our extended crew. As y'all know, the crew is four generations strong now! This month celebrating their twenty third year of marriage, we honor mister and misses John and Pearline Brown Sr. They was married November sixteenth, nineteen seventy two. Also celebrating twenty years of marriage yesterday, we have mister and misses Archie and Rena Wilson Sr. They was married November twenty ninth, nineteen seventy five. Give it up to them!"

The club applauds as Pearl and John, Rena and Archie, take the dance floor for a slow dance.

"That's gonna be us, one day, baby," June says to Rebbie as they watch her parents and his aunt and uncle slow dance.

"I know that's right," Rebbie responds.

After the dance, big John and Pearl take the microphone and announce the outcome of Angelise Taylor's sentencing.

"She has been officially sentenced," Pearl says as the cheers start and grow louder, "It was a closed proceeding. She received a sentence of 25 years to life. With eligibility for parole in two thousand and seven."

"In other words," John reiterates, "She has to serve those 12 years before she has any chance of meeting with the parole board. Her attorney is appealing the verdict. But ours is going to appeal *his* appeal."

The crowd laughs and continues to cheer. Pearl and John are joined by Jo and Al. The 4 of them have a slow dance in honor of the justice which their daughter and son has been granted. For now, Ebony and Ajay are free to celebrate, as their crew do the *public* honors for them. Next, Renee dances with John while Chill dances with Pearl.

"Hey! She got some moves, baby," Chill says to Renee referring to Pearl.

"Where do you think her motivation comes from?" John ask Chill. He's referring to the gyrating Pearl is doing.

Meanwhile, Ajay and Ebony had stayed at his apartment and celebrated alone, until they feel asleep. Ajay wakes up to his house phone ringing. He has to stretch but he doesn't want to disturb his sleeping princess. He hears yelling on the other end, as he answers.

"Hello," Ajay says, waking from a light slumber.

"Hell yea, family!" June yells into the club office speakerphone. Him, Rich, Tank, Nina, T-baby and Rebbie had to call them after hearing the sentence. Ajay switches to speaker and nudges Ebony to wake her.

"I guess y'all heard, ha?" he asks.

"Yes! That shit is the bomb!" T-baby screams.

51

"She should've gotten death!" Nina yells into the speaker and Rebbie cosigns her.

"In two thousand seven, I'll be there to object to her ass getting out," Ajay says, "If I can't be, y'all better be."

They scream concurrence. All the noise wakes Ebony, as she listens to her crew celebrate her justice.

"I might have somebody to knock her ass on off while she's in there," Tank adds as they all share a laugh before hanging up.

The party continues for the crew. Ajay and Ebony lay in each other's arms and talk more.

"Angel is out of our lives, baby," Ajay whispers.

"For good," she responds.

"If she ever comes back around us, she's *gonna* be gone for good," Ajay says, "I put that on my first born son. *She's going to the chamber.*"

}December 1995{

John is home and will be, through December 3rd. He attends Ebony and T-baby's 4th game on December 2nd at Ohio State. He doesn't have to return to the road until the 4th. Ajay sits next to him and they talk.

"I got tickets to the last Browns game. I was hoping you would be in town to go with me and pops," Ajay says to John on the night of the 2nd.

"When's the game?" John asks.

"The seventeenth."

"I'll make it a point to be there," John says.

"Word," Ajay says with a chuckle.

Ajay is pleased with John's answer. It's important to him that he ask John for Ebony's hand in marriage. Al had suggested it to Ajay and was pleased to know that was the way Ajay had planned to do it, all along.

"She deserves a traditional everything," Ajay had said to his father, "Because she's a traditional lady."

In the days leading up to the *Cleveland Browns* game, the crew do a lot of protesting with other fans. They don't want to loose their *NFL* team. There are many protestors on hand at the dome. Not only are the crew there. But Tim's clique is there also. Ajay sits on his '64, signing autographs for a group of teens, when he hears, "Hey stranger. What's up?"

He turns around to see Raquel Perez or Roc, smiling at him.

"What's going on?" he asks, returning the smile.

"Not much. Just out here with Timmy and them. You know.

52

Protesting," she says, "He don't even cheer for the Browns. He cheers for the Bengals. He's just *frontin,* like usual."

"We all out here too," Ajay says as he searches the crowd but doesn't see Tim. He finishes the autographs and the teens leave. Then he asks, "Where's he at?"

"Oh he's way over on the other side," Roc starts, "I saw you when we first got here. So I told them to meet me on the other side. I didn't want any trouble when I came to *holla* at you."

"Well as long as he minds his fucking manners, it won't be," he says convincingly.

Roc agrees as she asks, "Where's Ebony?"

"She just left with her girls to go check on the babies," he says.

"I was sorry to hear about what happened to yours," she says. He thanks her and she says, "I hear that girl Angel, got life."

"Yea she did."

"So do you really make the women that insane, when they can't have you?" she asks, smiling.

"That bitch is just crazy. That shit didn't have nothing to do with me," he says, "She knew Ebony was my woman. I tell every girl that."

"That's true," she says, "I know you told me."

She confesses to Ajay that she is and always was attracted to him. But she hadn't pushed it any further, after the fight with Tim and his shooting.

She says, "Because I figured you was mad at me too. And two, because I knew you wasn't gonna leave Ebony."

He agrees with her on the 2nd point. But he tells her his fight with Tim, even though it led to him being shot, was nothing against her.

"You didn't have anything to do with that," he says.

"Well I still would like to…," Roc says as her eyes survey his body.

"Like to what?" he ask as he smiles.

"You look like you can really put it down, Ajay," she smiles as she plays with the pen he has in his hand.

"I can," he says confidently, as he slides his hand from hers and smiles, then looks at her.

"You think you could meet me later, somewhere?" she asks.

He thinks about it for a few seconds.

"You must wanna see me kill that bitch ass nigga of yours, for real?" he asks.

"He ain't my man, no more, Ajay" she says quickly.

"Let me get back to you on that," he says as Chill approaches.

53

"What up, Roc?" Chill asks, "Where's your clique?"

"That's not *my* clique," she says quickly, "But they're around on the other side."

"Well you'd better get back to em, then," Chill suggests, "Because if they come around here with that bullshit, they won't make it home alive, today."

Roc takes that under advisement and prepares to leave. Before she walks away, she tells Ajay she'll try to see him later, at the club.

"It'll just be me and the girls, if I do come," she says.

He says, "Alright."

She walks off. But continues to look over her shoulder and smile at Ajay. Chill peeps it and he has to mention it.

"Is she still trying to pull your dick, bro?" he asks.

"Nah. She wanna fuck me now," he says, "The whole time I been in Natty, nothing ever jumped off. Ebony's there and *now* she wanna fuck."

"That's how it be, man," Chill says as they both laugh.

"She can suck it. But I don't wanna fuck now," he says.

****

The December celebration will be held on Christmas night. Instead of Jan going to Los Angeles as she had done for Thanksgiving. Rob is going to fly home. This event is billed to be *extra special*. Lil Kenny is the only crew kid with a birthday in December. He'll celebrate turning 12 with a party at *Granny's House* on the 23rd. Roo turns 14 on the eighth. Nina and Ebony will be 20 years old, this year. There are no active anniversaries for the crew. Ajay reminds Ebony that December 31, 1952 was his maternal grandparents anniversary. Mr. and Mrs. Allen Saul and Joanna Lynn Williams, Jo's parents, had been married on New Year's eve.

"They would be celebrating their forty third year, if they was still living," Ebony says to him, in amazement.

"They would be sixty and sixty one years old, now," he says, "We marry young in this crew and crew should do something with that date."

"Besides just celebrating *New Year's Eve,* ha," she says with a smile and he smiles too.

The crew are all home this weekend for the last *Cleveland Browns* football game. Today is Sunday December 17. All the males, including the grandfathers, fathers and sons are going to the game. Poppa is the only
54

grandfather not present. However, him and big mama will be present at the special celebration in 8 days. Ajay had called and invited them, personally. He has made big plans for Ebony's 20th birthday and wants everyone, who loves and cares for his girl, to be there. As for the Browns game, all of the other males in the family are going. They have 33 tickets. The only home male who isn't attending is Richard Williams III. He's only 11 weeks old. Rich wants him to come to this historical game. But it's much to cold for him to be out. Poppa will miss it because he's in Houston but Jb and Ced come in from Atlanta to attend. Rich, June, Tank and Ajay are home from Cincinnati. Rob is home from Los Angeles, for 2 weeks. Arthur, Kilo and Wayne are at the game. They all participate in the tail gate party prior to the game.

They finally head inside and take their seats. Ajay sits between Al and John, during the game. At halftime, he speaks with big John.

"I wanted you to come home for this game. Not only because it's the last one but because I wanted to ask you something," Ajay begins.

"Alright. I'm all ears, man," John replies with a smile.

"I plan to ask Ebony to marry me, on Christmas day. Her birthday," he says, "And I wanted your blessing."

John smiles. He knew this day was coming. The day when a young man would ask for his only daughters hand in marriage. He had realized, over the last few years, that Ajay was going to be *that* young man. He accepted their relationship as solid. There isn't a doubt in his mind that Ajay loves Ebony and wants to be her man. He's about to give him his official approval.

"I give you my permission to marry my baby girl," he starts with a smile, "And I will definitely give you her hand. But I want you to promise me *two* things."

"Okay. What's that?" Ajay ask as he pays close attention.

"When I give Ebony to you," he says, "It's for life, son. You will be making a life long commitment to love, honor and cherish her."

"Okay. That's on my life," he says, "She's not coming back home."

"She don't stay there *now*," John says as they smile.

"You're right," Ajay admits.

"One more thing," John adds, "Remember to make her a wife before you make her a mother, *again*."

"I understand," Ajay says as they shake hands.

Him, Al and John smile. He has John's blessing. He's free to propose to Ebony as planned. She had no idea he was going to ask her dad. She is
55

completely oblivious to his proposal plan. No one knows how he plans to propose. Papa, poppa, big mama, John and Al know they're suppose to be a big part of it. Jr, Chill and Rob only know he plans for the celebration to be Ebony's night, *only*. All of the males know he's going to propose at the celebration. They pretend to their wives or girlfriends that it's just an event for the December birthdays. All of the female crew will be surprised, along with Ebony, when the plan unfolds.

     Saturday night, December 23, is a late night at the club for the crew. The foursome celebrate Nina's birthday until after midnight. Then they leave to go pick up Jerica and lil Rich, then go to Ajay's apartment. For Ebony it feels strange not to have celebrated her birthday with Nina. She gets a hint from that, that the Christmas party will have a lot to do with her birthday. But she doesn't even know the half of it.

     Roc is at the club with her girls, tonight. The word on the streets is that Tim is no longer her man. But they're still in touch for the sake of their daughter. Tim and his crew had moved to the other side of town, after Ajay's shooting. But the streets still bring the crew info on their every move. Roc has hung around until after the foursome leave. She's hoping for a chance to talk to Ajay, again. She wants to know what his answer is to the proposal she made, earlier today. He's still there. She gets her opportunity.

"What's going on?" Roc asks.

"I'm bout fucked up," Ajay says, "What's up with you?"

"The same," she says, "So what are you about to get into?"

"Take it to the crib and chill," he says, "Why you wanna know?"

"I was kind of hoping we could leave together, if you know what I mean," she says as she smiles at him, flirtatiously.

"Nah. I don't know," he says, "What do you mean?"
He asks for clarity. But his body language says he's not interested.

"I wanna hook up with you," she says bluntly.
He thinks about the possibility of taking Roc to a hotel and banging her brains out. But for a change, he thinks about the consequences first. This could bring more trouble to his girl, if Roc turns out to be clingy. Or worse. If Tim finds out and confronts him, that confrontation wouldn't end well and for sure, not peacefully. He would take Tim's life, go to prison and ruin him and Ebony's dreams. He also considers what he promised John, at the game on Sunday.
Love! Honor! Cherish!
He thinks long and hard about what he's planning to do in 2 days. He
56

doesn't want to bring anymore drama to Ebony. Nor ruin the surprise he has for her. Roc has waited way to long to make her move.

"After all this time, *now* you wanna give me the pussy?" he asks. Then he says, "If it was another place and time, maybe we could. But I can't do that now. Ebony's waiting for me. I don't wanna fuck over her. She's been through enough shit because of me and these type of situations."

"I feel you," she says, "Ebony is a very lucky woman."

"Not really. I'm the lucky one," he says quickly, "They don't get any better than my baby."

And with that, he says goodnight to Roc and heads to his apartment to hook up with his future wife. He's proud of himself too.

His boys come and get their fiancée's and babies. They leave, leaving Ajay and Ebony alone. They love their alone time. They can really talk about anything when they're by themselves. He tells her what happened with Roc at the club. She's pleased that he'd stayed true to her.

"It's about time," she says, "After 8 years of dating, you finally kept *my* property in your pants," she giggles as he laughs.

"Say dick, baby," he says as he chuckles and hugs her tight, "You sound so sexy when you said dick, that night. Now I can't get you to say it again, for *nothing*."

She's not going to say dick. Especially not with him asking her too. But she's happy he'd taken the time to think about him and her. And what they've already suffered because of his *"girls on the side."*

"I told you, baby girl," he says, "I'm through with all of the bullshit. All them ho's and that drama. I don't wanna hurt you, anymore. I love you, baby."

She's pleased to hear that also. Very pleased, as she smiles big for him.

"Now that's the best birthday present I could ask for," she says as she continues to smile and they retire to the bedroom.

****

Rebbie's parents, grandparents and June have been planning to do something special since she got accepted into the school of Performing arts. They've decided to get her her own set of wheels, this Christmas.

"So which one do you like," grandpa Charles asks her.

It's Christmas Eve. Him, Archie Sr, June and Rebbie have just finished test driving new cars.

"I like the gold one," she says after test driving 12 cars, "The gold

57

one fits me. It fits my personality and it screams Rebbie Shantell Wilson." She makes sure they *all know* she wants the Gold Camry, as she cracks up laughing.

"I knew you was gonna follow your girls," June says with a smile, "Y'all always gotta match."

"Yes. Ebony got a blue one. Nina got a white one. I will have a gold one."

"This one is a ninety six, though," her dad says.

"Their's are ninety five's," Rebbie says aloud.

"Well, that's alright," grandpa Charles says, "They all look good and run great."

"Merry Christmas, baby," big Archie says, "You've worked hard to earn it and you deserve it."

Rebbie has done well in college and in her performing arts. She'll have the chance to participate in many plays and concerts, this coming spring and summer. She's on the Dean's list, as are all of the foursome. Her grandpa Charles is most proud of her because she hadn't gotten pregnant, thus far.

"We're gonna try to wait until we finish school," June adds.

"No. Y'all are *going* to wait until after y'all get married and finish school, hopefully," big Archie adds as they all laugh.

"I'll do my part," June says, "But you'll have to tell her to wait."

Rebbie explains to her father and grandfather how much she has wanted a baby since the births of Jerica and lil Rich.

"But I know we need to wait and we will," she adds.

Archie Sr and grandpa Charles do the paperwork and thank the salesman for coming in today.

"Oh that's fine," the salesman says, "We open every year, for Christmas eve. We do pretty good business too."

Archie had handled the financing, months ago. When Rebbie was accepted to Performing arts school last fall, he and Rena had discussed getting her a car.

"Now we both have a car," June says as him and Rebbie head to Chill's house to show it off.

"We all have our own car now," she says, "Except for T-baby and Jan."

"Ajay's got two cars," he says, "And so does Rob."

"T-baby has to get her own wheels, next," Rebbie says as she pulls into Chill's driveway.

She gets her girls, Jerica and lil Rich. They all leave for some last minute
58

TIME TO LOVE-RELOADED-TIME WILL REVEAL 3

Christmas shopping for the babies, their guys and the entire family.

Ajay helps to put the finishing touches on *The CrewLand Mall* decorations. He wants everything perfect, for tomorrow night. Then he heads to papa's house to go over his proposal plans with big mama, poppa and papa. Poppa and papa have booked *The OJays* and *Levert* for the celebration. Everything is in order.

⎰Monday December 25⎰
The celebration is packed as the crew had expected. Roc is here with her girls. Shantel and officer Jacobson are here. Coach Booker and coach Sanders have come, at Ajay's request. Mr. Parkwood is definitely here with his wife Barbara and other alumni. Dr. Weston, Dr. Stansfield and Dr. Mahoney are all in attendance. All of the crew's friends, parents, grandparents and the Houston crew are present. Of course, the Cleveland Crew, the Omegas and Deltas and their friends are here too. Mrs. Green, Pastor and Mrs. Tucker are doing babysitting duty at *Granny's House*. April and Yolanda hang tight with the foursome, as usual.

There's a definite buzz in the air which tells Ebony this will be a birthday and *Christmas* she'll remember forever. Her and her girls perform *What Do The Lonely Do* by *The Emotions*. Reaper performs a rendition of *Kurtis Blow's Christmas Rap*. Then he and Brittany J perform a song together. Brittany J does *Christmas Gift* by *Margie Joseph*. It's a magical night and everybody notices.

"I am having a ball," Yolanda says.

"This party is jumping, Ebony," April says, "Y'all always have the best parties."

"We get enough practice," she says as they all laugh, "But this one feels like they felt when I was a little girl. Everybody's here. Even our first generation. It's not like the club, tonight. It's like a family reunion. I have butterflies, for some reason. Like I think I'm gonna get something really special for Christmas and my birthday. I got a few gifts today. But my baby said he was gonna give me my big gift, here at my birthday party. Look at all of the people here. I think Anthony, my big mama and mama are up to something. I got a new Camry, last year."

"Maybe you're getting a Benz," April says as they laugh.

They're enjoying the performances. Papa, poppa and big mama do *The Christmas Song,* a classic which had been done by *The Whispers* as well as *Nat King Cole.* John sings a rendition of *This Christmas,* a song recorded by
59

the late great *Donnie Hathaway*. Ajay, Tank, June, Rich and Jb perform *Silent Night* by *The Temptations*. Then Al does *Please Come Home for Christmas* by *Charles Brown*, while Jo hangs on his every word. Nina and Lynn tease her after their father is done singing.

"Look at them," Lynn says as she laughs.

"They're trying to get frisky, like *The Cosby's*," Nina says and she laughs too as Jo and Al finish off the end of his solo with a dance.

Ebony has mistress of ceremony honors for this celebration and she finds it hard to hide her excitement, as she introduce *Levert* and *The OJays*.

First *Levert* performs. Then *The OJays* join them on stage. They do the *New Jack City* version of *For the Love of Money*. Which gets the party rocking, immediately. But before their last song, *Eddie Levert* calls Ajay to the stage. Ebony calls him over her microphone to make sure he had heard.

"Come on up here, baby," Ebony says, "He called you."

She's glowing with excitement. She just *knows* he's about to receive, either another key to the city, another award from the city of Cleveland or the state of Ohio. Or maybe he's about to dedicate another wall, a park, a plaque or something similar. He does that a lot, these days. While she speculates, he makes his way to the stage and grabs the microphone she's holding. He gives her a sweet kiss and she puts on her best smile. She's so proud of him, as she steps just down the stairs to give him the stage to himself. He begins to speak.

"Good evening, everybody," he says, "I'm really glad all of you could come out this Christmas night and celebrate with us. For all of you in here that know me, you know I've lived a pretty rough life, at *times*. I've had some run-ins with them folks and all, you know. There may have been times when y'all thought I would go all the way to the wrong side. But that didn't happen. One reason is because I have a strong family. The other reason is because I had real love and that made me *not* wanna lose at life."

Many in the audience applaud as he goes on.

"I've got my priorities straight now. I'm on the right track. I do have my family and crew to thank for a lot. But it was much more. I love basketball, no doubt. But it was still more than that. It was a stronger force that, for a long time, I wasn't familiar with."

The audience cheers again.

He continues, "Some of y'all may not know it but I learned something *very important* in the past seven years. And that is, life ain't worth living if you're not happy. So I wanna let all o' y'all know tonight, that I am happy. *Very* happy."

60

TIME TO LOVE-RELOADED-TIME WILL REVEAL 3

The audience applauds again as Ebony looks on and smiles. She has a major feeling that something very big is about to happen.
Is he about to announce he's going pro? Did he get a contract? He wouldn't announce it without telling me, first. No way! He's gonna be a lottery pick, for sure! Maybe he's just gonna tell all of his fans that he's got some big contract offers. He loves to make his fans apart of his world. You go baby!

She's still clueless as she smiles big.
He looks at her and continues.
"But the push behind that love and that force is also the biggest part of my happiness. That force of love, is a person. Her name is Ebony Eloise Brown."
He's gonna tell them I inspire him to play good. No! Of course he ....,

Her jaws drop when she sees the look in his eyes. Now there's no doubt in her mind that him being on that stage, has everything to do with her. But she still hasn't figured out what his real reason is yet.
Oh God! He's looking so damn good and he knows I'm turned on too. Look at how he's looking at me. He's thinking about fucking me while he's making his announcement about his career move. Is that his motivation when he's on the court? It must be. He just said it. Hmm. Well if he's ready to take it to the U, the answer is yes Anthony!

The others realize he's about to propose to her while she's thinking he's just giving her his bedroom eyes. That is until he calls her back to the stage. She knows it has to be about something else because they're definitely not going to relieve their sexual tensions there.
      "Ebony, can you please come back to center stage?" he asks.
She does as she's *asked*. She walks gingerly back up on stage, to cheers and applause. *Eddie Levert* holds the microphone for Ajay while he takes her hands in his.
      "Take your time, young player," Eddie Levert says with a chuckle, "You're gonna wanna get this one right, the first time."
She's still wondering what he's up to. But the next move he makes, leaves her with no doubts. He takes to 1 knee. She can feel tears welling up in her eyes. Big John and big Al, both stick their chest out and look proud. Jo and Pearl are near tears already. Everyone looks on in anticipation. Ajay looks up at Ebony and smiles that sexy smile that's sure to make her insides melt. He says, "Baby girl, you are so special to me. You helped me find my
61

patience when no one else thought I had any. I didn't even want any."
He chuckles as everyone laughs. She's smiling and crying.
He starts again.
"In nineteen eighty seven, my mama told me she saw a change in me and she wanted to find out what that change was, so she could preserve it and keep it around. Then when she found out it was you, she was scared because she didn't think I would act in a way that would say I deserved to have you. But big mama stepped in and told me, we was born to be together and to go for it. And don't let anyone stop me. First, our parents was saying we couldn't be together. Well, our mothers was. And our dads just had to go along wit it to keep the peace. That's something I'm sure I'll experience, one day."
Everyone laughs again as he holds up his hand for them to be quiet, so he can continue.
"But while you was gone to Houston, my mama admitted to me that she always wanted me to be with you. But she didn't think I was gonna do the right things *by* you. After she said that, it helped me to get up the courage I needed to go to your mom. I went to see mama Pearl and told her I would do whatever she wanted me to do, if she would agree to let me be your boyfriend. Because I had to past her test or it wouldn't be right. She told me to come by and talk to her, *anytime* I wanted too. And she would let me know when I was ready to be her son-in-law. So when you went back to Houston, mama Pearl and me, we looked out for each other, *every* day. She would come over to my house and talk to me, so we could just talk about you. I think that was her way of not missing you so much. I know it was mine. But it really didn't work for me. Not *too* well. I missed you like crazy, baby girl. Those were the longest days of my life and patience wasn't happening for anybody, without you around to keep me sane and relaxed. That's when I started leaving it all on the court."
The audience sighs. There is a lot more tissue being past around in the crowd, right now. Her girls are all tears and smiles. Renee is crying and leaning against Chill. He has tears streaming down his face too. This is big for their crew.
Anthony must've been really bad before I could come outside. Everybody was always trying to say he was mean and too street. But I never saw any of that.

Ajay says, "I know I don't always tell you. But tonight I want you to know, in front of God and all of these people, that I appreciate all of these years that you've put up with me. I love you, Ebony."
62

TIME TO LOVE-RELOADED-TIME WILL REVEAL 3

They smile at each other again. She can tell he's very comfortable with this. "*I love you too*," she says. The audience can hear her on the microphone and a chuckle moves through the crowd.
Ajay continues.
"I know it hasn't always been sunny. But you've always stayed loyal to me. That means more to me than I can ever express but I'm gonna try," he says as he notices big mama pulling her pink handkerchief from her purse to wipe her tears.
He pauses to make certain he doesn't become too emotional, himself.
Then he continues, saying, "I have always felt like I had to protect you. Every since way back when I was in second grade and you started Kindergarten."
Everyone laughs.
He says, "And everyday since September seventh, nineteenth eighty seven. When you gave me that job. I've given it everything I have. Whenever someone hurt you, I hurt them. Or I wanted too. Unless it was your parents. Because that was probably about me."
They all laugh again as he's goes on.
"But somewhere along the way, your pops and mine, along with papa and poppa, was able to show me how to be a man. The man that you deserved. And you added all of the approval I needed, the first time I heard you say you loved me. That changed my life, Ebony," he says as he smiles and continues.
"So now that I have a new outlook on life. And all of these reasons for living. I need an answer to just one question. Ebony, it would make my life complete, if I could have you in my life, *forever*. As my wife. That's the only way to bring this love that we have, full circle."
She starts to cry harder. He stands up to wipe away her tears. Then he leans her against his chest. He looks out over the crowd and gives her a few minutes to regain her composure. The audience is spellbound. His attention goes right back to Ebony as he lifts her chin, so he can look into her eyes again.
He continues, saying, "I wanna know if you'll continue to save my life and be my lady. Will you marry me, Ebony?"
She can't speak. All she can do is smile and cry. For more than a decade, she has thought about this moment and how she would react when he asked her to marry him. For more than 7 years, she has known she wanted that man to be, Anthony Devante' Jackson. Well that day is here. And now that
63

it is, she's overcome with joy. To the point where her words escape her. Chill takes the liberty as he yells out, "Hell yea dog!" and the audience applauds and cheers.

But that's not going to work for Ajay. He needs to hear his lady's answer. "Whoa. Wait a minute," he says to the crowd as he asks for quiet again. He says, "She didn't answer me yet!"

"Yes, Anthony! Yes! I'll marry you, baby! You know I will!" she finally screams, as tears stream down her face.

He pulls off the promise ring he had given her on her 1st trip to visit him down at Cincinnati, in 1993. He puts it on the ring finger of her right hand. They both smile big.

"You still have to wear this one too," he says as he kisses her on her forehead.

He pulls a black velvet box for his pants pocket and opens it. When he does, there is a sparkling glare which rainbows above his hand as the lights above their heads bounce off of the engagement ring. There's a sigh mixed with mumbles that wave through the audience. The Parkwood's smile proudly. They had insisted Ebony's rings had to be exquisite. They too, know how important she is to Ajay's *good days*. Ajay takes the ring from the box. Ebony's eyes become 2 sizes bigger as she does a double take. He puts the box in Eddie's hand. Then he places the huge engagement ring on the ring finger of her left hand.

"Oh my God, Anthony," she says, "Baby, this is *too* much. It's beautiful and it's *huge*."

"You're beautiful, baby girl," he says, "And it's not even close to what you're worth to me."

She hugs him tight and he returns the hug. Then they kiss, for at least a minute as the crowd hisses and cheers. Their kiss has obvious fever as the crowd starts to yell comments. Next, he leads her down the stairs and takes her to the dance floor. Parting the crowd as they head to the very center. Eddie Levert is still with them, holding the microphone. They want to get every word. Arthur and Michelle are videotaping it all.

"Merry Christmas and happy birthday, baby girl," Ajay says.

"You mean, *Anthony's* girl," she corrects him as she smiles.

Chill is 1 of the 1st people to congratulate them. He's almost as excited as they are.

"Didn't I tell you, a long time ago, baby girl. He was gonna get it together?" Chill asks as he hugs her.

"Yes. I'm *so happy*," she says as she continues to cry.

64

"Alright now. Y'all give us some room," Ajay orders as he looks toward the stage that *Eddie Levert* is making his way back too.

Once he's back on stage, *The OJays* begin to sing *Have Yourself A Merry Little Christmas*. Ebony and Ajay dance alone, on the dance floor. She gathers herself as she holds onto her fiancée. She's learned something else about him. He's loved her, for as long as she's loved him. Even longer.

"Anthony, I just figured out what your stare means," she says.

"What stare?" he asks, "You mean when I look at you?"

"Yes," she says, "The way you looked at me from the stage. The way you've looked at me, all of our lives. As far back as I can remember. I always thought it meant you was in the mood for sex. Now I know its the look of love, in your eyes. Not just that you wanna have sex with me."

"Nah. I wanna have sex too," he says as they both laugh. Then he says, "Well it's about time you get it. But I would never say anything, back then. Because I didn't know how to say it. Plus you was willing to give me mine, so I wasn't gonna talk you out of it. You was turned on tonight too. Wasn't you?"

"Yes, baby. I was and I still am," she says, "But you've had that look in your eyes for years. And I had it all wrong. You've loved me for years."

"Yea, baby girl. Longer than you've loved me," he says, "I've been trying to tell you that. I just had to learn how to express it. I learned that part from you."

They dance and hold each other as others stand around the floor. Their parents are proud. It's obvious as they make their way to the floor too.

"It's about time," Jo says to Pearl, as they hug each other.

"Lord, Jo. This make's three more weddings we have to do. And hopefully soon," Pearl says.

"I know that's right. Before anymore grandkids come," Jo adds with a laugh.

The 2 of them get with John and Al and join the happy couple on the dance floor. Ajay invites every couple to dance, as a tribute to his girl and him becoming engaged. This is truly a spectacular Christmas and birthday for Ebony.

Her Christmas gift to Ajay is a $5000.00 watch and gift certificates for 3 car monitors, from *Crew Details,* for his Seville. She knows he had plans of having them installed when he got it from papa. But lately, he'd been saying he didn't have the funds to do it, right then. Now she knows why. His main Christmas present to her is the engagement party and the

65

engagement ring. She doesn't even want anything else for Christmas or her birthday either. The ring will fill any void for the next 5 years and then some. The engagement ring he bought for her, cost him just shy of $100,000. It's a flawless 5 carat diamond solitaire with an entire carat platinum band. It has his name engraved in it. He tells her the wedding bands, for him and her, are already purchased. And the entire set had cost him $185,000.00.

"This ring alone, cost over ninety eight grand," he says.

"I must really be worth it," she says as she looks up into his eyes.

"It's not worth you, baby," he says as he smiles back, "And I'm gonna upgrade it every time the money gets bigger. I wanna make it a million, before I'm done."

He kisses and hugs on her as she holds onto him, all night. Which isn't hard to do because he's holding onto her too.

Roc comes over to congratulate them and she's all smiles. Ebony doesn't hesitate when it comes to making her aware that she knows about her propositioning her man.

"He told me what you asked him," Ebony says to her with a smile.

"Yes. But he let me know, right then and there, that it wasn't gonna happen. I'm okay with that," she says, "I am a hopeless romantic. I wish y'all luck. Your ring is gorgeous and Ebony, may I please get an invite? Because after witnessing how tonight went, I have to see how grand the wedding will be," she says before she leaves the celebration.

After Roc walks away, all of their crew make their way to them, 1 after the other. The Houston crew is right there too.

"I want to be in *this* wedding," April says.

"Me too," Yolanda adds.

Ebony assures them, they will be. The rest of the night is joyous, great and everybody has a wonderful time.

"When are y'all getting married?" Jesse asks.

"I don't know," Ebony says to her youngest brother, "We haven't set a date yet."

"We'll do that soon, though," Ajay says, "Because she said yes already. I have to get her married to me before she changes her mind."

"That's not gonna happen, baby," Ebony says.

She smiles as he kisses her again. Before long, they're ready to leave for their nice hotel suite downtown. She's been in the mood to fuck since before they got engaged. He's more than ready, willing and able to oblige her.

)New Year 1996!(

The new year comes in with a bang. Bruce is finally 18. He's also a

66

senior all-star and All-American, in football. He still plays on the basketball team and starts. But football is his *money* sport. He's Mr. Football at school and he has already signed a letter of intent with *Ohio State,* for the 1996-97 football season. The January celebration held on *Dr. Martin Luther King Jr holiday* weekend, includes a celebration of Bruce turning 18 on New Year's day. Also for Tank, who will be 21 and Jesse who made 15 on the 7th day of this month. Jesse is another standout on the freshman football team, at MLK. He's expected to do big things in his next 3 years. Tonight, him and Roo are going to the motel. Tank and Rich have gotten a room for them. Bruce and Kim are going to the same motel. The 4 of them ride together, in Bruce's Cutlass. The rest of the crew party until the early hours before going home.

By the February celebration, which is Saturday the 24th, the UC men's team are on fire. They boast a 29-4 win/loss record. In conference play, they're undefeated and they get an automatic bid for the *NCAA* tournament in March. Ajay led all major categories. His averages are 30pts, 12 rebounds, 8 assist, 3 steals and 2 block shots per game. He has enjoyed a great college basketball career. Everyone knows he's going 1st round, with a high seed lottery pick, in the *NBA* draft.

The main event for the February celebration is to honor Mr. and Mrs. Charles and Annabelle Wilson's anniversary. They are the oldest living couple in the crew's family. Their anniversary is February 21, 1952. This year marks 44 years of marriage. Birthdays this month are Sam Jr, who makes 15 and Erica turned 15, on the 18th. They're expected to do well in track, this spring. But Ajay's youngest sister Pam is now being compared to her oldest sister Lynn, who will be competing in the Olympic games in Atlanta, in 3 months. Lynn has made the Olympic team and will compete for gold in the 100 meter dash and the 4x100 meter relay. But there is another huge event that's going to take place prior to that one.

{Saturday March 9{

All new year long, the mother's of the crew have been preparing for Nina and Tank's wedding. While they have Rebbie and T-baby's in view and still wondering just *how soon* Ebony and Ajay's will be.

March 16th is the first one. Nina prefers an evening wedding. Her bridal shower, given by Lynn, her matron of honor and Ebony, her maid of honor, is tonight at the salon. They have invited male strippers for the shower. Tank got wind of it early in the week and tried to protest. But Ajay

67

warned him not to make trouble for Nina. As Tank's best men, Ajay and Jb have invited female exotic dancers to his bachelor party, on Friday night. Their reception will be the only celebration for the month of March. March birthday's and anniversaries, the crew will celebrate in April.

Nina's shower goes according to plan. Tank shows up but he isn't allowed to come in. Pearl and Jo see to that. June and Rich convince him to leave and come watch Ajay's game, at The Chill Spot.

Al, John, Chill and Jr, poppa, Ron and papa had flown to Florida for the 1st round of the NCAA tournament. UC wins their 1st and 2nd round games. They're going to the sweet 16 in Syracuse, early next week. Coach Booker informs Ajay that he'll allow him to go home on Friday afternoon, for the wedding ceremony. But he has to be at Sunday morning's practice and ready to go. The team is flying to Syracuse, Sunday afternoon. Ajay will be home for Friday's rehearsal, the rehearsal dinner, the bachelor party and the wedding on Saturday. He won't be able to stay for much of the reception.

Ebony is excited for him and his team. But she doesn't like that they haven't seen much of each other, this past month. He's been on the road with basketball, same as her. It seems like they barely have time to spend together since they got engaged. Her team was eliminated in their 2nd round game. They lost to Tennessee. Ebony and T-baby got a chance to talk with coach Pat *Head* Summit, after the game. Coach Summit expressed her sincere regrets about not being able to sign the 2 of them.

Tank is no longer playing basketball at UC. He's concentrating his energy on track. After Jerica arrived, he needed to free up his schedule so he could go home and visit her. But she'll be moving with him and Nina to Cincinnati, after their honeymoon. They'll honeymoon during spring break, in April.

The following week is filled with wedding party fittings and Nina's final fitting for her wedding gown. All of the flowers and decorations are here and the guest are starting to arrive.

"Everything is going according to plan," Jo says.

"Let's just hope they don't blow anything at this bachelor party tonight," Pearl adds as the mothers laugh while decorating the church.

TIME TO LOVE-RELOADED-TIME WILL REVEAL 3

The rehearsal dinner is over. It's time for the bachelor party. *The Crews House of Soul Food* catered the event. They'll cater the bachelor party and the reception too.

The guys go to the bachelor party in downtown Cleveland. Nina tries to find it, so they can crash it. They've tried to find every bachelor party since Chill and Jr's and haven't, thus far. Not tonight either.

Judging by the amount of action going on at the bachelor party, it's good she didn't find it. Nor any of her girls, for that matter. Or instead of new weddings, there would've been some relationships ending. Rumor has it, some of the girls from the crew's past, was present at the event.

None of the guys were willing to share their knowledge of the guest list. It's just another one of those infamous all male parties that will go down in crew history, as undiscovered by the female crew.

Ajay does come back to his apartment after he leaves the bachelor party. Ebony is in bed and she's already asleep when he glides into the room. But he wants her awake. He doesn't have a long time to be home and he wants to have and hold his fiancée, as much as he can before he has to report back to his team. He goes back into the living room. He wants to play that *Prince* song. The same song he'd heard for the 1st time, in Chill's Blazer, the night before Ebony moved to Houston the very first time. He bought the CD titled *"Prince"* as soon as it was available. The song *"With You"* is what he wants playing while he makes love to Ebony. He sets it on repeat, then goes back into the room. Ebony has rolled over. She's awake.

"I had to hear this song," Ajay says and smiles. Then he says, "Do you remember when I played it in Natty and told you when it became one of my favorites?"

"Yes," Ebony says, "When you was on the way to granny and papa's for dinner. I love it now too."

"Make love to me, Anthony's girl," he whispers as he lays down with her.

He has already removed his gear. She slides right up under him and gives him all of her tongue. After a long and heated kiss, he looks into her eyes and whispers, "As far as I'm concerned. You're already my wife."

"And you're my husband too. But we'll still watch Nina and Tank while they stand at the alter tomorrow."

They laugh before making sensuous love as *Prince* serenades them from the living room. In Mr. Ajay Jackson's heart, Ebony is already, Mrs. Jackson.

69

TIME TO LOVE-RELOADED-TIME WILL REVEAL 3

YOU ARE CORDIALLY INVITED

TO ATTEND THE WEDDING CEREMONY

OF

NINA SHALON JACKSON

TO

JEREMY MARCUS "TANK" BROWN

SATURDAY

MARCH 16, 1996

AT

6:00 P.M.

WHAT GOD HAS BROUGHT TOGETHER.
LET NO ONE PUT ASUNDER!

TIME TO LOVE-RELOADED-TIME WILL REVEAL 3

Prelude..Soft Music

Entrance of Mother's

Mother of the Groom..Pearline Jones Brown
Escorted by Father of the Groom............................John Brown, Sr.

Mother of the Bride...Joanna Williams Jackson
Escorted by Brother of the Bride..................Kenneth Ramon Payne, Sr.

Lighting of candles.............................,.............Host and Hostesses

Entrance of Groom...Jeremy Marcus *Tank* Brown

Honorary Best Man.........................Cheston Wayne Coleman [deceased]
Best Man 1..John Brown, Jr.
Best man 2...Anthony Devante' Jackson

The Wedding Party
Bridesmaids.........Escorted by.........Groomsmen

LaTonya Walker Wilson.................................Bradley Lee Wilson, Jr.
Breanna Wilson Hamilton...............................Cedric Leroy Hamilton
Janice Logan Jenkins...Robert Leon Jenkins
Latrisha Nicole Brown...........................Richard Trevon Williams, Jr.
Rebbie Shantell Wilson.................................Brian James, Jr.
Kimberly Celina Logan...................................Bruce Dalvin Wilson
Brittany Neon James.......................................Shannon Tyreek Wilson
Erica Maureen Jackson...Gregory Brown, Jr.
Ruthie Nakia Williams...Jesse Lee Brown
Pamela Darius Jackson......................................Samuel Logan, Jr.

Matrons of Honor
Lynora Jackson Brown...Renee Stewart Payne

Maid of Honor

..................Ebony Eloise Brown..................

71

TIME TO LOVE-RELOADED-TIME WILL REVEAL 3

Entrance of Junior Groom……………………...…...Bradley Lee Wilson, III

Entrance of Junior Best Man…………………...……KeJuan Thomas, Jr.

The Junior Wedding Party
Junior Bridesmaids….Escorted by….Junior Groomsmen

Alicia Mallory Wilson……………….…………………Steven Davon Brown
Chaundra Laurnea Coleman…………………...Kenneth Ramon Payne, Jr.
Brina Shawnice James……………..……………...Archie Joseph Wilson, Jr.
Charlotte Elaine Coleman………………………..Brandon Shawn James

Junior Maid of Honor….…………………...........Chastity Jacquel Coleman

Flower Girl………………………………......Destiny Jalene' Shante' Payne

Honorary Ring Bearer……………………….Richard Trevon Williams, III

Ring Bearer…………………………………....Demarcus Tremaine Owens

……………………….........ALL STAND PLEASE………………….................

Entrance of the Junior Bride and Daughter of the Bride and Groom

Little Miss Jerica Eloise Brown

Entrance of the Bride

……………………......Nina Shalon Jackson…………………………

Escorted by her Father…………..…….........Mr. Allen Devante' Jackson, Jr.

PLEASE BE SEATED

Devotion……………………………………….................Pastor Larry Tucker

Prayer……………...Eloise Wilkes *Big Mama* Jones
72

TIME TO LOVE-RELOADED-TIME WILL REVEAL 3

Song..............*Here and Now*.....................Mr. Gregory Brown, Sr.

Poem...Mrs. Sally Greene Logan

Scriptures...Mr. Percy Jones

.........................PLEGING OF VOWS...

Song.................*Always and Forever*...............John Brown, Sr.

Exchanging of the Rings...

Lighting of the Unity candle..Soft Music

Prayer..Mr. Jackson Brown

Duet- *If This World Were Mine*.......................Parents of the Bride

Poem-by the Bride and Groom.....................Read by Miss Justine Carr

Trio.......................*Tonight*............................Performed by
Ebony Eloise Brown.....Latrisha Nicole Brown..... Rebbie Shantell Wilson

Pronouncement of Marriage.......................Pastor Larry Tucker

++++++SALUTE TO THE BRIDE AND GROOM++++++

.................RECESSIONAL..................

Coordinators...
Mother of the Bride..........................Mrs. Joanna Williams Jackson
Mother of the Groom..............................Mrs. Pearline Jones Brown
Aunt of the Groom............................Mrs. Brenda Jones James

Seamtresses..
Crew mother..Mrs. Belinda Carter Logan
Aunt of the Groom...................................Mrs. Sandy Logan Brown
Just like an Aunt to the Bride....................Mrs. Rena Baker Wilson
73

Hostesses..

Aunt of the Bride.....................................Mrs. Debbie Williams Wilson

Aunt of the Bride.................................Mrs. Anna Wilson Williams

Crew mother...Mrs. Jacquel Coleman Carr

Host...

Father of the Bride.........................Mr. Allen Devante' Jackson, Jr.

Father of the Groom...Mr. John Brown, Sr.

Uncle of the Bride.....................................Mr. Bradley Lee Wilson, Sr.

Uncle of the Bride................................Mr. Richard Trevon Williams, Sr.

Just like an Uncle of the Bride...................Mr. Archie Joseph Wilson, Sr.

Uncle of the Groom...............................Mr. Gregory Brown, Sr.

Uncle of the Groom.................................Mr. Brian James, Sr.

Crew Father... Samuel Logan, Sr.

Crew Stepfather ....Mr. Jason Eric Carr

Ushers......The ladies of Delta Sigma Theta Sorority, Inc. & The gentlemen of Omega Psi Phi Fraternity, Inc.

Decorations and Floral.....................................The Mothers of the crew

Catering and Wedding Cakes...............The Crews House of Soul Food

Photography.............Que Psi Phi Pictures, Co.-Arthur Lee Owens, CEO

Reception to follow at The Chill Spot.................Sounds by Jenkins Jams Co

FROM THE BRIDE AND GROOM

We thank God for our love for each other and for his blessings. With God, all things are possible.

We would like to sincerely thank our parents: Joanna Lynn Williams Jackson and Allen Devante' Jackson Jr, Pearline Denise Jones Brown and John Brown Sr for your patience and guidance. We ask God that you'll continue to give us that unconditional love and support that you've shown us, all of our lives.

74

TIME TO LOVE-RELOADED-TIME WILL REVEAL 3

To our living grandparents: Jackson Brown Jr, Percy Jones and Eloise Wilkes Jones, we love and treasure your love and guidance very much. We love you.

To our grandparents who are deceased: Granny Pearline Anderson Brown, Mr. and Mrs. Allen & Joanna Williams, Mr. and Mrs. Allen & Bertha Jackson, Sr. We miss you so much and love you, even more. We know, in our hearts, you are here sharing this day with us.

To our Crew/Family: We love you, forever. Thanks for being there every minute of every day, with us. We are one.

To Cheston Wayne Stoney Coleman: We miss you, brother. We will always keep you in our hearts, minds and all of our future endeavors. Rest in peace until we meet at the *crossroads*.

To all our friends, teammates, in Houston, Atlanta, Boston, New York and Ohio family. We appreciate the support you show us. Thanks for sharing our special day.

To each other: We've been here and there, before today. Now together, we strive for tomorrow. And last but definitely not least;

To Jerica Eloise Brown. Our daughter:
Thank you for giving our love a true meaning. You will be the focus of our future and the reason for our success. We love you, baby girl.
Love, Mom and Dad.

PRESENTING:

MR. AND MRS. JEREMY [NINA] BROWN
AND
JERICA ELOISE BROWN

SATURDAY MARCH 16, 1996

ALWAYS AND FOREVER!

75

Nina is radiant. Tank can't keep his hands off of her, long enough to take the wedding photos. They are so happy. Jerica seems to know this is her day too. She's extra photogenic and plays with everybody. She's always a friendly baby. But today, she has no boundaries.

"Come here, Jerica," Al says to his granddaughter.

She comes to him and they take a photo together. John gets in the picture and she takes a photo with both of her grandfathers.

"One of these is for her," John says when they finish shooting.

"Put it in her baby book," Al says to Nina.

After the photos are done at the church, they all go to the reception. Ajay dances with Ebony, for a couple of songs. Then they say their goodbyes early and leave for his apartment. He isn't going back without private time.

"Y'all call me before you leave for Cincinnati," Chill says.

They say they will, then they leave.

Erica and Greg Jr have a disagreement at the reception. It's about a girl named Mya Dean, who attends school with them. Erica has been suspicious of Greg Jr. She feels like he's been messing around with Mya. Bruce gets wind of it and brings the 2 of them to the back office.

Chill smiles at Jr and says, "It's his generation, man. Let's let him try to handle it, first."

They go back to partying as Bruce handles the situation, for now. He sends Erica back to the reception and talks to Greg alone. He tells him what Chill and Jr had told him, a few years back.

"You have to be low key with *non crew* ladies," he says, "Don't show love to any other girl when you're around the crew, partner. If you do, you're gonna have a lot of crew to answer too."

Greg says he understands how he is to handle the Mya situation. He goes back to the reception and ask Erica to dance. While on the dance floor, he tells her he's sorry and she accepts. They dance through 4 songs, then 2 slow ones before Jo tells her to take a break.

"Girls, we've got six sets married off. Now we have to start all over again," Jo says to all the mothers.

The parents are all seated in 1 section. The mothers and fathers agree. The grandparents section thinks it's poetic justice. They're chuckling each time the parents complain about anything.

Later, during the reception, Ebony and Ajay come back to tell everyone they're leaving for Cincinnati. They hug Tank and Nina, then tell

76

everybody goodnight. They leave at 2:00 am. Ajay calls his teammate Jarvis Rhodes, to say he's on his way back. He has practice at 11:00am.

****

Erica has a fight with Mya Dean, at school today. She doesn't start the fight but she certainly finishes it. Mya leaves school for the emergency room. She has a broken jaw and has to have her mouth wired shut.
Pearl is on staff when Mya comes in. Her staff preps Mya for the procedure while the police officers take statements. Pearl discovers Erica is involved and presses the officer for details. She plans to call Jo and give her the information.
When Mya's mother shows up, she's visibly upset and in Pearl's opinion, she's way to dramatic. Ms Dean is flinging accusations and threats, wildly. Pearl steps in and suggest she calm down. Ms Dean has a few choice words for Pearl, who has a few in return. Pearl ask Joyce to take over for her so she can leave the area. Joyce does. Pearl takes her cell phone to the break area and calls Jo.
"Jo, this bitch is down here clowning because Erica beat her daughter's ass," she says, "And her daughter started it."
She tells Jo about the threats Ms Dean has made.
"She's not gonna touch Erica. That's all I have to say about that," Jo says and Pearl agrees with her.
They hang up and after she's calmer, Pearl returns to her duties. Mya has been released. But the feud between the 2 girls, isn't over by a long shot.

The very next day, they have a 2nd round at school. This time Erica has to call her mother.
"Ma, can you come pick us up?" Erica asks.
"Yes. Us *who*?" Jo asks.
"Me, Brit, Sam, Greg and Jesse," she answers.
"Erica, what *happened*?" her mother asks.
"We got into a fight and they suspended all of us," she says.
Erica tells her mother that Mya had shown up at school with her mother and 2 aunts. They had all come to fight her and the crew jumped in to help. The crew beat Mya again. Plus the 3 adults.
"I'm on my way," Jo says as she hangs up, then calls *her* crew.
Pearl, Brenda and Belinda, Sandy, Anna and Jo's sister Debbie are ready to ride when she fills them in. Jo is ready to fight, at this moment.
77

TIME TO LOVE-RELOADED-TIME WILL REVEAL 3

"There is no way a grown ass bitch is gonna put her hands on my kids and think I'm not gonna get back at them," Jo says.

Her, Brenda, Deb and Sandy are driving to the school. Pearl, Anna, Rena and Belinda are meeting them there. The faculty are holding all people involved, at school and waiting for the crew's parents to arrive.

When Jo and her crew get to MLK's freshman office, Ms Dean is still talking loud and making threats.

"That lil nigga ain't about nothing! If he was, he wouldn't be putting his hands on you!" she screams to Mya.

"I wasn't about to let y'all jump my crew and I wasn't getting in it," Greg Jr says, "You *must* be crazy."

"Just shut up, nigga," Ms Dean says, "I wasn't talking to you. I was talking to my child."

"*Then that's what you need to continue doing,*" Sandy says as she makes her way into the office with Jo and the rest of their crew. "Don't say another word to my son," she says, "I'm his mother and I'm grown like you. So you need to address me. *Not* him."

Ms Dean starts insulting Sandy and Belinda steps in.

"You don't want it with neither one of us," Belinda says, "I suggest you keep your cool."

Ms Dean continues to yell until the officers show up and threaten to arrest her for disorderly conduct. As it stands, she's already going to be charged with trespassing on school property and 5 counts of assault on a minor.

"If it's all the same to you, officer," Jo says calmly, "We can take her outside and settle this."

The officer smiles but objects to her suggestion.

"That's fine," Pearl says, "We'll probably have to deal with her sooner or later, anyway."

The officer arrests Ms Dean and her 2 sisters on the school's charges. Jo and her crew get their kids suspensions reduced to 1 day each. They all go home. The situation is cool, for now.

April is the beginning of Track season. Tank and Nina are going on their honeymoon. Ajay's team finished 5th in the NCAA tournament. Narrowly missing the Final 4. He's been on the road, so much, Ebony hasn't seen him in a week. She's looking forward to the event, this weekend. She has something special planned for him. He's flying into Cleveland on Saturday, from New York to meet her. It's the weekend before spring break. The March and the April celebrations are this Saturday night too.

78

TIME TO LOVE-RELOADED-TIME WILL REVEAL 3

From March, the crew have 2 birthdays. Brittany made 15 and Steven, who finally made 13, is being initiated into the crew. His parents Mr. and Mrs. Gregory and Sandra Brown Sr celebrate their 21st wedding anniversary. Big mama and poppa come from Houston. Carolyn, Ron and most of their crew, come too. Big mama and poppa or Mr. and Mrs. Percy and Eloise Jones, mark their 42nd year of marriage on the 3rd of April. Birthdays to celebrate are Lynn, who turned 23 and Chaundra turned 13. The crew are excited about her initiation. One of Stoney's sisters is officially crew.

Steven and Ally still like each other but she still has to wait until June before she can hang out with the crew. There are no kids in the crew family under 13, with a birthday in March or April. So there is no party set for *Granny's House,* this month. That's just fine with Belinda, Rena and Sandy. They have a double wedding to sew for. Rebbie and T-baby's double wedding ceremony is June 22nd. Rena and Sandy are very excited to finally be sewing for their own daughters wedding.

79

CHAPTER   26

ANOTHER STEP IN TIME

After the celebration, Ajay and Ebony take Tank and Nina to the airport to catch their flight to Miami. These newlyweds are taking the same cruise package as the honeymooners before them. Once they depart, Ajay and Ebony go to his apartment. He's been looking forward to this part. Alone time with his fiancée.

"Finally got you to myself," he says as he starts hugging and kissing on her, while he's removing her clothes.

"Wait," she says with a smile, "I have a surprise for you."

"What's up?" he asks, "Because even though I love your smile. You know I don't like surprises."

"You'll like this one," she says, "First, I want you to sit down in this chair."

She takes a chair from the kitchen table, places it in the middle of the living room floor and has him to sit down in it.

"You have to wear this," she says as she giggles and presents him with a blindfold.

"It's a surprise that I *can't* look at?" he asks, being facetious. "See *why* I don't like surprises?"

"Just wear it until I tell you to take it off," she says as he allows her to blindfold him.

"Hold this and when I tell you too," she says, fixing the remote control in his hand, "You can take off the blindfold and press play."

She had come to his apartment earlier, to set up this surprise. Now it's show time. She's still a little nervous about how he'll react. But she wants to do something special for him, to get him aroused. It's been more than a week since he's seen her and she knows he's ready for sex. She just wants to make it *as spicy,* as possible. This way when he leaves for next week's draft combine, he'll have a little something more on his mind. She gives him the remote and tells him to give her a few minutes to get ready. He waits but not quite, so patiently. All she needs is a few more minutes, then she'll tell him when to press play. She turns on his video camera and focuses it, so she can get a shot of the room and his reaction to her surprise. The camera is setup to capture both of them and his auto zoom lens will get his reaction.

"Everything in here is set," she says, "I'll be right back."

Before leaving out, she pours him a Hennessy on the rocks and puts the glass in his hand. She sits the bottle on the table next to his chair, then she goes into the bedroom to get ready. After a only 5 minutes, he's already impatient.

"What's taking you so *long*, baby?" he asks from the living room.

"I'm almost ready," she says, "Alright. You can remove the blindfold and start the music."

He removes the blindfold but doesn't see her. "Where are you?" he asks.

"Press play," she says.

He does and *It's About Time* by *SWV* starts to play. She sashays into the living room wearing a hot pink 3-piece lingerie set. Complete with the stockings, garter, heels and gloves. She starts her striptease. Her moves are very provocative. She makes her hips move like a belly dancer. From his immediate reaction, she doesn't know if he's enjoying it or not. He finishes his drink quickly and pours another. But he's barely taken his eyes off of her. He gets up to approach her. His eyes are very intense.

She tells him, "You're not allowed to touch the dancer."

"That's some bullshit," he says with a sly grin, as he reluctantly sits back down.

First, she removes the shoes. Bending over with her ass directly in his face. He touches her, anyway. She removes his hand.

"Tease," he snorts.

She can tell he's turned on now. And she can also tell that he isn't going to follow the rules. She removes the stockings and gloves, 1 by 1 and tosses them at him. He blushes. She places 2 of his fingers under her garter and allows him to slide it off of her leg. He does so, quickly. She continues performing. She's down to only the 3-piece. She removes the cover wrap quickly and tosses it to him. He catches it and lays it to the side.

"Come on wit it, baby," he says as his anticipation grows.

She teases him with the bra straps. Pulling 1 down and then, back up. She's smiling but he's not, as she does the same thing on the other side. She smiles seductively. He still doesn't smile. He can't take the teasing. He stands to approach her again. Again, she tells him to sit but he doesn't. He grabs her by her shoulders, seizes her mouth and kisses her, very aggressively. She doesn't resist. She know she's teased him, long enough. Quickly, he removes the bra and panty set. He caresses her breast while still kissing her.

"Umm, baby," he whispers, "I liked it. I liked it, a lot. But you know I'm not gonna keep my hands off you, girl. Never that."

He removes his clothes, then spins her around to face the counter. He leans
81

into her bottom, his weight forcing her against the island counter, as he plants kisses down her back. He sucks on the back of her neck as he enters her aggressively, from the back.

"Oh ssss," she moans, assuring him that she loves the sensation.
He's as hard as steel. Invasive even. But he slows down to give her juices a little time to kick in. They both moan.

"Oh, baby girl," he whispers, "You turned me on, baby. I really liked the dance. You feel what it did to me, ha? I missed you, baby."

"Umm, Anthony. I missed you, so much, baby," she whispers.
He strokes her hard, at first. She know he's *way to* anxious and this episode is going to be painful before it ends.

"I missed my pussy, baby. You smell so good," he whispers as he looks down to witness his work. He pulls her hair, bringing her head up with it. He kisses her. Then he smacks her ass and asks, "Do you like that?"

"Oh yes, baby," she whispers, "I've learned too."
He smiles. Minutes later, he pulls out and brings her with him. He sits back on the chair.

"Sit down," He orders, wanting her to face and straddle him, on the chair.
She does so. Instantly, she discovers that her man is still much to large for her to be trying this position.

"Oh no, baby," she tries but she can tell he's enjoying it.
He's sucking and licking her nipples which are as hard as rocks. He's moaning and pulling on them, as if he's starving and being fed from her. He isn't trying to stop, just yet and he lets her know it.

"Uh uh. You're telling me no, baby?" he asks. Then he says, "I'm gonna give you what you need. You know your man's gotta do that."
He takes 1 of her nipples into his mouth while caressing the other.
"Work me, baby," he instructs.
She does her best but he's too large for her, even when she's wet. He senses that she's afraid to push back and says, "Come on and lay down."
While she's still straddling him and he's still inside of her, he carries her to the couch and lays her down, gently. He's stays on top of her and positions his head so he can get his lips on her left earlobe. He sinks his dick back inside of her.
"Is Anthony doing you good, baby?" he ask as if he's in the 3rd person.
"Daddy missed you, baby. Shit yea, he did. Ooo this pussy is good, Ebony."
This sends a chill down her spine as he proves to be a man of his word. She is starting to spiral out of control as he continues to thrust his dick into her
82

very wet pussy, over and over. He's sweating. She shivers. He's breathing heavy while he's whispering in her ear. "I wanna feel you cum, baby. I wanna hear you screaming my name in that *sexy* ass voice of yours."

"Yes," she says, knowing he can take her to any height he wants.
He knows her body, almost as well as he knows his own, by now.
"Oh God, it feels so good!" she screams out and he loves that.

"Is your man doing you good, baby? Ha?" he asks.
"Oh baby, yes! God! I love you, baby," she manages.
"Come to me," he demands, "Come on, baby. Cum, baby."
He knows she's about to go to ecstasy and that's where he wants her to be.

"Oh Anthony! Oh baby! Yes! Yes! Yes! Anthony!" she screams as her emotions run wild and her juices run free.
"God! It feels so good, baby! Anthony! Oh do it, baby!"
He continues to talk into her ear as his wild kisses take over her neck, face and lips.

"I've been thinking about this, all week, baby," he whispers as he fucks her, thoroughly.
Then as he goes into the zone, she holds onto to him. She knows there's about to be some turbulence.
"Mmm. I love this shit, girl," he says almost yelling as he can feel his nut coming.

"Oh Anthony!" she screams back as his strokes go painfully deep.
He's buried his face into her shoulder. He says, "Uh huh. Let daddy work it out, baby," as he thrust harder and deeper.

"Oh God!" she manages, "Baby, please."

"That's what I do," he says as he continues to beat it up.
"Come on now! Let me wet it good!"
She just holds on and allows him to have his way with her. That's what he wants and needs.
"Take it, baby. Take it," he whispers as he reaches his sweet climax and lifts his head so she can see his face, in sweet agony.
"Oh shit! Ssss! Oh yes, baby! Ssss oh," he says as he *cums* hard, like he's been saving it up.
"Oh you feel so damn good, baby," he manages as he releases into her.
She holds back her tears, some what. The heavy ones, at least. He kisses her. They're out of breath as they lay on the large leather sofa, still intertwined and dripping with sweat. He holds her tight against his body. She can feel and hear his heartbeat. He's staring into her eyes. They trade breathing patterns for the next 5 minutes. Finally, he catches up to his breath.
83

TIME TO LOVE-RELOADED-TIME WILL REVEAL 3

"Damn! It was worth the wait, baby," he whispers and smiles.

"Yes it was," she whispers and smiles back.

After his breathing becomes normal again, she wipes the sweat from his face and they kiss again. With no energy left, they take a nap right there on the couch while still intertwined. They don't even bother to go the club. They're going to stay in tonight and tend to each other.

They wake up to another session, early Sunday morning. Then they realize they've overslept. He has to leave for New York with Jb, tonight. They have major press to do before leaving. Ajay has hired Jb as his agent. They'll visit his potential NBA teams, this week. The draft is in July. Ebony, Lynn, Jo and Al will fly to New York, on Tuesday. Ajay tells his crew he'll probably go to either Cleveland, Dallas or Miami. He doesn't care which team he gets selected too. He's more concerned with his contract. Jb has negotiated a great deal for him. He's negotiating at 55.5 million for 5 years. Plus *Reebok* apparel ads and 12 major magazine photo shoots per year. He has to do interviews on *The Tom Joyner Morning Show* and *ESPN*, this week after the draft combine is done. If he gets selected to Cleveland, then this summer he'll do *The Sports Report* for their local good morning TV talk show. If he goes to Miami or Dallas, he'll be the new anchorman on a local TV sports show. He and Ebony talk about the fact they'll have to be apart, a lot in the next 2 years. Until she finishes at UC.

"I think we should set a wedding date before I leave, baby," he suggest.

"Okay. When do you wanna do it?" she asks.

"Do what?" he asks.

"Get *married*," she says with a smile.

"Then why didn't you just ask it, like that?" he asks.

"Okay. When do you wanna get married?" she asks with a smile.

"That's up to you," he smiles, "But you have to remember. I'm gonna have a real hectic schedule, once I'm drafted. So keep that in mind."

"How about we get married on your grandparents anniversary?" she asks, "After all, we do need to do something *significant* with that date."

He loves the idea. Plus he wants them to be the only couple at the alter when they get married. And he wants their anniversary to be in a month where there's no one else from their crew. Just them. He wanted to do this date, all along. Which is evident by his next comment.

"I see you pay attention to me when I'm talking to you," he says with a chuckle, "Because that's the exact day I wanted to get married on.
84

So I can plan your birthday, Christmas and our anniversary, all at one time. Then do it big for a month and then again, after the season ends."

"Yes. I caught that, *'the crew needs to honor that date'* line at the Thanksgiving party and our engagement party too," she says with a smile.

"You're suppose to listen to your man," he says with a smile as he kisses her. He says, "That's right."

"I want you to take some time and get your feet wet in the NBA, first too," she starts, "So why don't we say, next New Year's eve?"

"December thirty first, nineteen ninety seven?" he asks for clarity.

"Yes."

"That's perfect. Because I get more time to play around," he says as he chuckles, then winks his eye, "I'll be there."

They laugh as they get up and take a shower together, before attending Church.

After the service is out, the entire family have Sunday dinner at their restaurant. They're hanging out until Ajay and Jb leave for the airport. Ajay and Ebony share their wedding date with everyone.

"That's still a year and a half away," Pearl says in disbelief, "Why so long?"

"I know. But we've got time," Ebony says as her and Ajay explain their reason for the delay.

Pearl and Jo understand it but they want them married, before another baby comes. They still don't realize that they've got a plan.

"You know what your daddy said," Jo reminds Ajay.

"I know. Big John said the same thing," he says with a chuckle.

They all share laughs for the next few hours. Then it's time to leave for the airport. Lynn and Ebony are taking them to meet their flight, then Lynn has to get back to track practice before flying to New York on Tuesday.

"I love you, baby," Ajay says to Ebony before boarding his flight.

"I love you too, Anthony," she says.

Lynn and Jb exchange hugs, kisses and love salutations too. Ajay and Jb head down the boarding ramp. Lynn and Ebony watch as they take flight.

"I miss him, already," Ebony says, "Lynn, I love your brother, so much. I can't remember when I didn't. I'm lost without him."

"I know, sis," Lynn says, "Get use to it. They're gonna be gone, a lot now."

Chill and Jr are at the club, on Monday, getting things ready for

85

the new week and going over the entertainment line up for the next month.

"I've been thinking," Chill says, "We need *Tupac* to perform."

"No shit, bro," Jr says, "He's the hottest artist out there, besides *Bone Thugs*. And *Biggie Smalls* making some noise too."

"I'm looking into it," Chill says, "I got a good contact for him. I'm gonna make it happen, if I can."

"That's the business, crew," Jr say as he smiles, "I can't *wait*."

On Tuesday, Ajay gets the best offer from Miami. They have the highest draft selection of the 3 teams he's visited. He seems most positive they'll draft him, 1st and at nearly 100% of what Jb took to the table.

"Well I guess I get to live in Florida, this year, ha?" Ebony asks.

"For *sho*. If that's where I end up," Ajay says with a smile.

They are in Harlem, eating at *Sylvia's,* along with Lynn, Jb and his parents.

"We have a lot in common with Sylvia and her husband Herbert," Ebony says, "They've been together since they was eleven and twelve."

"We've been together since the womb," Ajay says and they all laugh. Then always the hustler, he says, "We're gonna get Crew's house to this level, real soon. We got the clientele now and they're in the money."

"We should expand to other cities," Jo says, "Like Atlanta."

They discuss the possibility of opening more businesses in their new hometowns. Jb and Lynn have had discussions about opening a club or restaurant, in Atlanta, already.

"It's four of us there, so far," Lynn says, "Bre and Ced are gonna be moving to California, after she finish at Tech," Lynn says, "That's the only problem really, is having enough crew to run it."

"It'll be someone who can move down there before *that* time comes," Jb says, "If we decide to do it."

"You know we're opening a nail spa and a center for kids, from six to thirteen, later this year," Ebony reminds them.

"Yes but the reputation in Cleveland is already solid," Al says, "The new businesses already have a waiting list. They're gonna turn a profit, the first quarter."

"Yes they'll be profitable from the start," Jo says, "But she's talking about the new businesses because of the work force issue. We don't want to spread to thin. Nor do we wanna have to out source for our employees. Not more than five percent."

Ebony says, "Right. Because we started all of this, so that we could be self contained. Correct?"

86

TIME TO LOVE-RELOADED-TIME WILL REVEAL 3

"Yes indeed," Ajay and Jb say simultaneously.

Jo will be leaving Beachwood elementary school to manage and teach at *Big Mama's House*. A secondary childcare and intermediate aftercare facility scheduled to open in October. The crew plan to have *Big Mama's House* as strictly a home school option alternative and aftercare. Accepting ages 6 to 13 years old. They'll teach the kids self help skills, age appropriate trades and prepare them for taking care of themselves until their parents get home. *Granny's House* will continue to handle pre-mature to 5 year olds and offer after hours care for that age group, as well.

"We started these businesses to make and keep our money within our crew and our communities," Ebony says, "Auntie's Anna and Debbie will managed the new nail and health spa. They've already hired six nail techs. They have three masseuses and three dermatological experts, a dietician plus sponsorship from *Estee Lauder* and *Clinique* cosmetics. Our alumni got us that hook up."

"And that's the most *outside* employment we've done," Ajay says, "Other then, Crew's House."

"The restaurant and club are twenty percent out sourced," Al says, "It takes more people to run a club and a restaurant."

"And that's why I would be concerned about opening in Atlanta," Lynn says, "We'll need forty employees. It's going to be reservation only."

"Right. Which allows for prepping," Jb adds, "We can do it. We got crew coming from Houston too. They'll need new careers."

"Oh, that's right," Ajay says as he looks at Ebony, "Your girls and them, from Ron's crew."

April, Yolanda, David and Charles have already shown interest in joining the family business. Ebony loves the idea of having all of her family under the crew umbrella. Ron and his crew are family, *forever*.

There's more talk on the possibility of new businesses while they finish their dinner. They'll spend the rest of the week in New York, as Ajay participates in the draft combine, before flying back to Cleveland on Friday. Jb and Lynn will fly back to Atlanta, where Lynn will be on a strict training schedule for the next 3 months. She won't make the May celebration but she has been allowed time off for the weekend of Rebbie and T-baby's wedding, so she can participate.

Nina and Tank return to Cleveland, from their honeymoon, today. Tank had purchased the 1967 Chevy truck from big Al's shed, during the winter. He left it at Crew Details to be restored.

87

TIME TO LOVE-RELOADED-TIME WILL REVEAL 3

The antique truck is ready when he returns from his honeymoon. His parents paid the cost of restoring it. As a wedding present to him and Nina. They love it.

"I'm not taking it to Natty, though," Tank says, "We're gonna leave it in Cleveland for the car show, this summer."

"I wish y'all was leaving my baby here, too," Pearl says and Jo agrees with her.

"Ma, she's eighteen months now," Nina says, "We agreed we would take her to live with us, after she was walking and toilet trained."

"Well she's not done training," Jo tries.

"Then that'll have to be our job now, mothers," Nina says quickly as they laugh.

Jo and Pearl lets it go. They don't want Jerica to move to Cincinnati. But they don't have a choice, in the matter. Her mother and father wants her with them.

The UC crew leave early, Sunday morning. Ajay will have to report to his rookie NBA training camp in July, after the draft. Jb had gotten that pre-approved. It's for weigh-in and his training assignment, to help with his transition into the pros. He's looking forward to finishing up at UC but he knows he'll graduate late. Jan is going to graduate Cum Laude in May, with a degree in Pre-Med. Ajay will graduate in July with a degree in Sports Journalism and an emphasis in Radio, Television and film.

May 17 is the last day of classes at UC, CSU and Tech. Jan graduates on time with her pre-med degree, the next afternoon. She has already applied and been accepted to *UCLA* school of medicine. She plans to be a pediatrician. Rob is home for her graduation and the celebration, later at their club. The celebration includes birthdays for Kim, who turned 17 this year. Pam makes 14. May 21st will be 41 years of marriage for Mr. and Mrs. Joshua and Sally Logan Jr. They were married in 1955. Mr. and Mrs. Allen and Joanna Jackson Jr celebrated 24 years as husband and wife on the fifteenth. They were married in 1972.

The 1st Annual Crew Details Car Show is held Sunday, the 19th, at *The CrewLand Mall*. Tank wins the classic division with his 1967 Chevy truck. Ajay wins the Cadillac division with his 1978 Seville. Wayne Matthews, from the U, wins the overall competition with his 1996 Ford Expedition. He has everything you can want in a ride, in his Sport Utility Vehicle.

88

Bruce graduates on the 27th from MLK and will attend Ohio State in the fall, on a football scholarship.

JB is home for graduation to spend a few weeks in Cleveland. The first week in June, he buys a 1996 Lexus Coupe. He's going to ship it to Atlanta, after Crew Details finishes with it. Lynn is still in Atlanta training for the Olympics. The car is a surprise for her, to celebrate her making the Olympic team. But he's planning to drive it.

Chill heard back from Tupac's people. *Tupac* has agreed to perform at *The Chill Spot*, this fall. He'll be the entertainment for the crew's Thanksgiving Holiday celebration. They're all hyped about having him and *Bone Thugs* performing in their club, together.

"That *Thug Luv* is off the chain," Reaper says, "I get to open for Bone and Tupac."

"It don't get no better than that," Bruce says, "You got legends, who will be hearing you perform."

"Dude, I'm so honored to be in the same place with both of them," he says, "It's a dream come true."

"Now if we can just get a collaboration with you, Pac and Bone, together," Bruce says, "Then I want even have to try to make it to the NFL."

They laugh hard.

The June celebration has been postponed until July because of the crew's double wedding on the twenty second. Rebbie, June, T-baby and Rich are having their turn at the alter. Everyone is busy with preparations while Ajay finds out he will definitely graduate in July.

TIME TO LOVE-RELOADED-TIME WILL REVEAL 3

YOU ARE CORDIALLY INVITED

TO ATTEND THE DOUBLE WEDDING CEREMONY

OF

LATRISHA NICOLE BROWN

TO

RICHARD TREVON WILLIAMS, JR.

REBBIE SHANTELL WILSON

TO

BRIAN JAMES, JR.

SATURDAY JUNE 22, 1996

AT

4:00 P.M.

WHAT GOD HAS BROUGHT TOGETHER.
LET NO ONE PUT ASUNDER!

TIME TO LOVE-RELOADED-TIME WILL REVEAL 3

Prelude..Soft Music
Lighting of the candles...Ushers

..................Entrance of the Mothers..................

Mother of the Bride 1...Sandra Logan Brown
Escorted by Uncle of the Bride....................................Samuel Logan, Sr.

Mother of the Bride 2...Rena Baker Wilson
Escorted by Uncle of the Bride....................................Bradley Lee Wilson, Sr.

Mother of the Groom 2...Brenda Jones James
Escorted by father of the Groom....................................Brian James, Sr.

Mother of the Groom 1...Anna Wilson Williams
Escorted by Father of the Groom................Richard Trevon Williams, Sr.

ENTRANCE OF GROOMS
Groom 1..................................... Richard Trevon Williams, Jr.
Groom 2 ....Brian James, Jr.

Honorary Best Man........................Cheston Wayne Coleman-deceased
Best Men...........Anthony Devante' Jackson............Jeremy Marcus Brown

Processional..Wedding party
     Bridesmaids...........Escorted by..........Groomsmen

Renee Stewart Payne...............................Kenneth Ramon Payne, Sr.
LaTonya Walker Wilson...............................Bradley Lee Wilson, Jr.
Lynora Jackson Brown...............................John Brown, Jr.
Janice Logan Jenkins...............................Robert Leon Jenkins
Breanna Wilson Hamilton...............................Cedric Leroy Hamilton
Kimberly Celina Logan...............................Bruce Dalvin Wilson
Brittany Neon James...............................Shannon Tyreek Wilson
Erica Maureen Jackson...............................Gregory Brown, Jr.
Ruthie Nakia Williams...............................Jesse Lee Brown
Pamela Darius Jackson...............................Samuel Logan, Jr.

Matron of Honor...............................Mrs. Nina Jackson Brown
91

TIME TO LOVE-RELOADED-TIME WILL REVEAL 3

Maids of Honor...Ebony Eloise Brown
....Alicia Mallory Wilson

Entrance of Junior Groom

.............Bradley Lee Wilson III...............

Junior Best Man...Steven Davon Brown

Junior Bridesmaids-Escorted by- Junior Groomsmen

Chaundra Denise Coleman............................Kenneth Ramon Payne, Jr.
Charlotte Elaine Coleman.................................Brandon Shawn James
Brina Shawnice James.................................Archie Joseph Wilson, Jr.

Junior Maid of Honor...........................Chastity Jacquel Coleman

Flower Girls
Jerica Eloise Brown---Valene Amiya Hamilton---AAliyah Janeese Hamilton

Honorary Ring Bearer and son of Bride and Groom 1
Little Master Richard Trevon Williams III

Ring Bearer..Demarcus Tremaine Owens

Entrance of the Junior Bride
.............Little Miss Destiny Jalene' Shante' Payne...........

--------ALL STAND PLEASE FOR ENTRANCE OF THE BRIDES-------

Ms. Latrisha Nicole Brown

Escorted by her father...................................Mr. Gregory Brown, Sr.

Miss Rebbie Shantell Wilson

Escorted by her father......Mr. Archie Joseph Wilson, Sr.

------------------------------------PLEASE BE SEATED----------------------------
92

TIME TO LOVE-RELOADED-TIME WILL REVEAL 3

Devotion...................................Pastor Larry E. Tucker

Prayer: Grandmother of Bride-1......................Mrs. Sally Greene Logan

Duet.....*Very Special*..................Mr. and Mrs. Allen & Joanna Jackson

Poem: Grandmother of Groom-2.........Mrs. Eloise *Big Mama* Wilkes Jones

Scriptures: Grandmother of Bride-2 & Groom-1..Mrs. Annabelle J. Wilson

PLEDGING OF VOWS

EXCHANGING OF THE RINGS

Solo-*Somebody Loves you*:........mother of Bride-2-Mrs. Rena Baker Wilson

Lighting of the Unity candles....................Soft Music

Duet................*Am I Dreaming*...................Brides Best Friends
Miss Ebony Eloise Brown.....................Mrs. Nina Jackson Brown

Spoken Word Poetry to Brides and Grooms................Miss Justine Carr

}*Moment of Silence for the deceased family members*{
Mrs. Pearline Anderson Brown-Grandmother of Bride-1
Mr. and Mrs. Saul & Joanna Williams-Grandparents of Groom-1
Cheston Wayne Coleman- Crew Brother to both Couples

Prayer: Grandfather of Bride-1...........................Mr. Jackson Brown

PRONOUNCEMENT OF MARRIAGE

SALUTE TO THE BRIDES AND GROOMS

RECESSIONAL...

93

TIME TO LOVE-RELOADED-TIME WILL REVEAL 3

Coordinators..
Mother of Groom-2.....................................Mrs. Brenda Jones James
Aunt of Bride-2 and Groom-1..................Mrs. Joanna Williams Jackson
Aunt of Bride-1 and Groom-2.......................Mrs. Pearline Jones Brown

Seamtresses...
Mother of Bride-1...Mrs. Sandy Logan Brown
Mother of Bride-2 and Aunt of Groom-1.............Mrs. Rena Baker Wilson
Aunt of Bride-1...Mrs. Belinda Carter Logan

Hostesses...
Mother of Groom-1 and Aunt of Bride-2..........Mrs. Anna Wilson Williams
Aunt of Bride-2 and Groom-1....................Mrs. Debbie Williams Wilson
Mrs. Jacquel Coleman Carr
Miss Justine Carr
Host...
Father of Bride-1..Mr. Gregory Brown, Sr.
Father of Bride-2 and Uncle of Groom-1......Mr. Archie Joseph Wilson, Sr.
Father of Groom-1 and Uncle of Bride-2..Mr. Richard Trevon Williams, Sr.
Father of Groom-2..Mr. Brian James, Sr.
Uncle of Bride-2 and Groom-1..................Mr. Allen Devante' Jackson, Jr.
Uncle of Bride-1 and Groom-2..............................Mr. John Brown, Sr.
Uncle of Bride-2 and Groom-1.......................Mr. Bradley Lee Wilson, Sr.
Mr. Bradley Lee Wilson, Sr.
Uncle of Bride-1..Mr. Samuel Logan, Sr.
Crew father...Mr. Jason Carr

Ushers…..The ladies of Delta Sigma Theta Sorority, Inc. and the Gentlemen
of Omega Psi Phi Fraternity, Inc.

Decorations and Floral:…..........................All the Mothers of the Crew

Catering and Wedding cakes:...................The Crews House of Soul Food

Photography and Video….....Que Psi Phi Pictures-Arthur Lee Owens, CEO
Archie Joseph Wilson, Sr.-Mgr

Reception follows at The Chill Spot...............Sounds by Jenkins Jams Co.

94

TIME TO LOVE-RELOADED-TIME WILL REVEAL 3

Special performance:................Reaper F/ Brittany J. Siblings of Couple 2

FROM LATRISHA AND RICHARD, JR:
We thank God for all his blessings. We thank our parents for all the love and support. We thank all our families for the guidance and love. To our crew, we love you. Thanks for always being there. Our unborn child, we miss you being apart of our lives. To our Friends, always stay true. To our lost loved ones, please continue to watch over us. And last but not least; To our son, Master Richard Trevon Williams III. We love you so much. Thanks for being our reason for living on and staying together. You've brought so much happiness to our lives.

FROM: REBBIE AND BRIAN, JR.:
We thank God for his strength and blessings for through him, all things are possible. We thank our parents for showing us the way, with your guidance, love and undying support. To our crew, there are no words that can express how much you mean to us. You're our family. To all of our family, teammates, dance teams and friends, both living and deceased; Thank you for always being near. We love you all forever.

TO ALL OF OUR DISTINGUISHED GUEST WE PRESENT TO YOU:

MR. AND MRS. RICHARD [LATRISHA] WILLIAMS, JR.

AND

MR. AND MRS. BRIAN [REBBIE] JAMES, JR.

SATURDAY

JUNE 22, 1996

ETERNAL

The photo session ends, promptly at 8pm. Reaper opens the reception with his 1st single from radio. Brittany J joins him for the 2nd single. Rob takes over the wheels and keeps everybody rocking. The couples enjoy the reception, guests and food. T-baby and Rebbie both throw their bouquets to Ebony. Rich and June follow suit throwing the garters to Ajay.

"Real cute, y'all," Ebony says as the crew tease her and Ajay.

"Y'all planned this at the bachelor party," Ajay says to the grooms, "I knew y'all did."

"I told you, you're suppose to be up here, man," Rich tells Ajay.

"We got a year and a half to get it right," Ajay responds.

"Lil Rich can be our ring bearer," Ebony adds as they laugh.

Rebbie and T-baby look stunning in their wedding gowns. Their wedding colors are Navy, Blue and White, the original crew colors. Everything is perfectly coordinated. Ebony, Ajay, Nina and Tank got them 2 presidential suites at the Fillmore Hotel downtown. The couples will take a horse and carriage ride from the reception to the hotel. A limousine will be waiting for them, in the morning, to take them on to the airport for their flight to Miami. Their taking the 7-day cruise honeymoon.

Ajay and Ebony go to the U, after the couples leave. Tank and Nina bring Jerica and go to Jo's house. The rest of the crew take it in by 3am. They plan to have a professional athlete to celebrate with, for the next celebration.

}4 days later!}{

It's *Draft day* in New York city. Ajay and company are seated and waiting for the roll call to begin. He waits patiently on the platform with Jb, his parents, big John and Ebony.

"You look so handsome, baby," Ebony says.

"Thank you," Ajay says, "I like the suit too. It's fly."

"I could get use to this look," she says as they both smile and she adds, "You look so professional, in this suit, baby. I love it."

She had chosen the design, for him. After the selection meeting last February, she asked aunt Sandy, Belinda and Rena for help finding him a suit for draft day. They're the ladies of the crews next business venture, *Crew Gear and alterations.* She had asked them what would be a good start since they hadn't been able to sew it for him, because of the weddings. They had suggested she look into a present pro ball players line. They would've made a killer suit, especially for him. But with of the weddings they had to

96

sew for, it was impossible to devote the time it would've taken to do the perfect suit for this day. At least, that's how Ebony felt about it. Ajay had asked her to help him find a suit that she would like to see him in. So she had ask his parents for help in having *Hakeem Olajuwon's* company make him one and they did.

"I could get use to this look, you know," she says again as she straightens his tie and smiles at him.

He smiles back. She can see that he's nervous and who wouldn't be? He's about to embark upon the dream of every school and asphalt player in the world. He's at the *NBA draft* and he has played well enough to be a lottery pick. As *David Stern* approaches the podium, Ebony grabs Ajay's hand.

"I'm so proud of you," she says as she gives him a kiss on the cheek for luck and the selections begin.

}Ohio State Penitentiary{

The bullies on Angel's tier have commandeered the television for her benefit. They're assuring that she can watch Ajay in the draft. Only because she has to call his family, after he gets chosen, so they can talk to them too. Angel was already planning to call the club. She had called after the engagement and every other major event that's been about Ajay. Somehow she's still able to get information about whenever he's home. One reason is because of his high profile, nowadays. A simple trip home from college is newsworthy. Especially since he was usually hosting something for the neighborhood youth. Chill had stopped telling him about her calling. Being that her case was high profile, the word spread quickly amongst her fellow convicts, before she'd even gotten there. She's now *their* link to fame and fortune. She had been intimate with someone who's on their TV screen, weekly. So they demanded she give them that life line or else. They've also agreed to be her protection from those prisoners who are loyal to the crew. Angel is in maximum security. Nothing like the day camp, Tameka is nearly done serving her time in. Angel had to get protection, immediately. The female inmates she befriended, promised her protection. But for a price. The fact that she knows and can contact Ajay. Or at least his famous crew, gave her instant value. But to keep her protection, she has to call every time there is a chance he'll be near *The Chill Spot*. Basically, she's a bounty. She has to call, even if she hadn't planned too. Angel calls the club before lights out. Renee's receptionist answers and quickly makes waste of the 3-way call routed through Pittsburgh. She alerts Renee, immediately and they make a record of the number on the caller ID, for future reference.

97

TIME TO LOVE-RELOADED-TIME WILL REVEAL 3

}In Cleveland{

The Chill Spot is hosting the *Anthony Jackson NBA draft* party tonight and they have a packed house. *The Crews House of Soul Food* has catered the event. Tank and Nina aren't able to be there because Jerica has been running a temp since she left *Granny's House preschool* today. But they've already been made aware that Angel had called the club. They give their opinion about the call, then turn their attention back to caring for their daughter and watching the draft. Jerica has a fever from a mild ear infection. Instead of going to the club to watch the draft, on the large TV screens, Tank and Nina are watching the big screen at Jo's house. They're also discussing their future while waiting to see *how high* Ajay gets picked. They discuss him and Ebony's future, as well.

"It's time for us to start building our house," Tank says.

"Okay. Where do you wanna live?" Nina asks, "You still wanna move to Atlanta?"

"I've been thinking about it more and more," he says, "Especially with Jb and Lynn talking about opening a spot, down there."

"Wouldn't it be neat if all four couples could live down there?" she asks.

"You're always gonna include your girls, ha baby?" he asks as he smiles.

"I'm just so use to us being around each other," she says, "It would be weird not seeing them everyday. But if Ebony moves to Miami, then yes. I wanna move to Atlanta."

"Ajay and twin are *gonna* be in Miami," he offers, "They haven't picked yet. They're gonna pick Ajay, first. Watch."

She says, "They're getting more and more independent as the years go by. Aren't they?"

"They always have been," he offers, "As couples go. They act more like Jan and Rob. They're separated a lot too."

"That's why they're use to being on their own," she adds, "They make up for it too. Like we did when I had to stay here until Jerica came."

"Next month, they're gonna be apart again. When he reports for rookie camp," he says, "He's going first round. I just *know* it. Miami has the fifth pick. And we will always make up for lost time, Nina Boo."

"*Sho* you right, baby. But I'm so proud of him for sticking it out," she says, "Boy. At one time, I thought he was gonna go the other way."

"He got his shit together after twin's accident," he starts, "He damn near did a three sixty. He was always in love with twin. I knew that."

98

TIME TO LOVE-RELOADED-TIME WILL REVEAL 3

"He *has* changed a lot. But he's still stubborn as hell, though," she says, "Ebony is the only person who can get him to change his mind, once it's made up. Mama says that too. She says, *'him loving her is what got him to this draft,'* and I agree."

On the TV, they watch as Ajay is selected 1st round, 5th pick. To the *Miami Heat.*

"He got that Heat contract! A-T-L sound good to you?" Tank asks, "Cause I'll be graduating, this time next year. I want all of our stuff set up before then."

"A-T-L it is," she says and they both laugh and celebrate.
Ajay has made it to the NBA!

99

TIME TO LOVE-RELOADED-TIME WILL REVEAL 3

CHAPTER 27

THE MORE THINGS CHANGE............,

The July celebration is a 4-day event, which will last from the 4th through the 7th. This is their largest celebration, too date. It includes both the June and July anniversaries, accomplishments and the birthdays too.

In the month of June, Chill had turned 27, big June turned 21 and Ally had finally got crewed up, on the 3rd. Papa Brown is recognized for what would've been 43 years of marriage, for him and granny Pearline. June 30, 1953 was their wedding date. It's been 5 years since Chill and Renee plus and Jr and Tonya got married. Lynn and Jb, Jan and Rob, Bre and Cedric celebrated their 1st year of marriage, this year. Ajay was selected 1st round, 5th pick, to the *Miami Heat*, the last week of June.

In July, Jb turns 23, Ajay makes 22 and T-baby turns 20. Destiny Payne has her 3rd birthday party at *Granny's House*. Chill and Renee recall Destiny's birthday as the 3rd anniversary of their shooting, as well. And though it took them less than a year to get rid of the violators, it came at the cost of seeing Ajay get shot in the process. Something that could've taken his life or voided any real chance of him becoming the millionaire his is today.

Since the shootings, their focus unconsciously went toward putting the drama of the streets they'd gained a name in, behind them. They put their energy toward making their business dream a reality and enjoying some of the fruits of their legitimate labor. While making real strides, legitimately. But street life and the lessons that come with it, aren't so easy to shed. Out growing the drama is more of a façade, then a reality. Still they vow to keep it to a minimum while encouraging the next generation to do the same. Keeping a link to those streets that stayed loyal to them, proves profitable still.

Anniversaries in July, are Mr. and Mrs. Bradley and Debbie Wilson Sr. They celebrate 22 years of marriage. So does Mr. and Mrs. Richard and Anna Williams Jr. They were married on the 10th and was the 1st in the crew to have a multiple wedding ceremony.

Ajay will report to the Miami Heat rookie camp on July 29, for a walk through to get his locker and pick up his practice and preseason media schedule. Bruce will go to preseason camp at Ohio State, the same day.

TIME TO LOVE-RELOADED-TIME WILL REVEAL 3

However, the real highlight of July is Lynn competing for gold in the 100 meter dash and 4x100 meter relay, at the Summer Olympics in her new hometown of Atlanta. The families are going next weekend. Her events are Friday and Saturday. The crew can't wait to be her personal cheering section.

Her only brother Ajay, has a feat to conquer before he can cheer for her. As the newest rookie of the Miami heat, he meets media this week. Ebony and Jb travel with him while his parents fly to Atlanta for the pre-Olympic game ceremonies and events. Big John returns to the road and will meet them in Atlanta, on Friday. Ajay finishes his interviews and photo shoots by late Thursday. Then him, Ebony and Jb join the rest of the family in Atlanta.

On Friday morning, Lynn wins her quarterfinal heat in the 100 meter dash. She advances to the semifinal round. Her and the 4x100 meter relay team advance as well.

Later in the afternoon, she wins her semifinal heat in the 100 meter dash and a chance to compete in the finals, tomorrow night. The 4x100 meter team advance to tomorrow's finals as well.

"Lynn is doing her thing, baby," Ebony says to Ajay.

They're leaving Olympic Stadium after watching Lynn run her way into the finals. The 2 of them go back to their hotel room for naptime.

"She's gonna win a medal," he says, "I know she is."

"Two pro athlete's in the family, so far," she says.

"Speaking of. You know the women's league kicks off next week, right?" he says, speaking on the new *WNBA* pro league for females.

"I know," she says, not sounding interested.

"You don't wanna play after college?" he asks.

"No," she says with a smile, "I just wanna be your wife, the mother of your children, your best friend, co-homeowner, your homemaker, our kid's first teacher and counselor. Yours too, if you need me to be. A successful investment banker, real estate mogul and a businesswoman."

"That is a lot of hats, lady," he says, "But you're also a top ranked female basketball player. Top ranked in the country and the world. They billed us as the *Bonnie and Clyde* of *you see* [UC]. So you can be a pro basketball player too. The *WNBA* is writing to you. I've seen the letters."

"I wasn't hiding them. I'm just not interested."

"Just think about it," he says.

"I don't want a job that'll conflict with your schedule," she says,

101

"Also, I want a job with comparable wages and benefits to yours. That's why I'm getting this degree and going for my masters. Mister Parkwood said they already have projects waiting for me. Do you know how well an investment banker does?" she asks, "Better then a *WNBA player*. I have to compete with you financially too, Anthony."

"No you don't," he says quickly, "I'm gonna pay the bills and buy whatever you need. I'm paying for *everything*. I want you to get some fun out of life and not work. You've had enough grief, just growing up with me and trying to love me."

They both laugh, then he says, "But playing ball ain't like work to me. I really don't want you to work, just so you know."

"I will have fun doing all of those things I just named," she says, "Playing ball will take me out of the house, like you'll have to be. I can never remember my mama going halfway across the world and leaving me for days. Nor leaving my daddy's house without him."

"He does, though," he says, "He leaves every two weeks."

"That's my point," she says with a giggle, "He's the man of the house. He's suppose too. He does what it takes to support his household."

"I got me an old fashioned girl, for real."

"That's what you want," she says as she laughs more, "You had to hear some reassurance, right baby? You know who you're with, Anthony. The very girl you molded. But thanks for always being supportive."

"You're welcome and thank you too," he says as they giggle at each other.

He doesn't want her to feel like he's being overbearing. But at the same time, he doesn't want her to wake up 10 years down the road and wish she had played pro ball.

"I just don't want you to forget about your skills, just because I made it into the league," he says, "Do whatever you wanna do. But just know, I'll support you if you wanna play."

"I know you will, baby," she says, "I never doubted it. You're one of the reasons that I started playing and got *so* good."

"I know that's right," he says as they laugh again.

Eventually, they take their nap while listening to *Outkast's* new *ATLiens* CD on the radio, *first play*.

}Pittsburgh{

Alana has her own apartment through a section 8 program. She has her GED and she's taking classes at Allegheny College. That's all very

102

TIME TO LOVE-RELOADED-TIME WILL REVEAL 3

Good. But her trifling ways haven't subsided, in the least. She's on the phone with Angel, right now. They're going over the latest crew new she'd got from Angie and Nicole, her Cleveland reporters. What Alana can't find out from her aunt Darlene, she gets from them. Her obsession with having Jeremy "Tank" Brown hasn't and will not subside either. Just as Angel's fatal attraction to Ajay never escaped her. These 2 females are low key now. Only because they owe debts to society. But their evil ways, overbearing lust and their plans to forever taunt and haunt Tank and Ajay, are far from over. They was just getting started when they got arrested.

}Atlanta{
It's late night, when Ajay and Ebony wake up. He's looking over the room service menu. She's rubbing his shoulders while they talk.

"We're gonna take advantage of all the time we get to spend together, baby," he says, "Next weekend is my graduation. The week after that, I leave for Miami."

"See. That's why I don't want a job that puts me on the road a lot," she says and they agree on that point.

They decided to skip the evening events and spend more time alone. They kick back to watch some late night TV.

Suddenly, at 1am, a local breaking news broadcast reports that a bombing has taken place at Olympic centennial park. One person was killed and there was over 100 injured. Ajay and Ebony quickly confirm that none of their crew was harmed. No one has been arrested, so far. Ajay is worried for the safety of his sister and his entire family and crew. He isn't going to allow Ebony out of their room, that's for sure. Not until the final events, when the security is sure to be extra tight. He insist the rest of the family do the same. After the bombing, the crew stay close to each other but they're determined not to let it ruin their good time. They was out at an A-T-L nightclub, where Jb, Bre and Ced had taken them, when the bombing occurred. They stayed put. Lynn is with her team. Safe and focused on tomorrows finals. Everyone else is at the hotel or at Jb and Lynn's home.

Ajay and Ebony stay in all night and order a very late supper. Then they eat until they're content.

"Do you want some more of this food, baby?" he asks.

"Oh no. I'm full enough, as it is," she says with a frown.

He'd ordered Lobster, Steak and Shrimp dinners.

"I hope you got room for dessert," he says as he sits on the bed next to her.

103

"Is it you?" she asks with a giggle as he nods affirmative.

She smiles and says, "I've always got room for you."

They take a bath in their Jacuzzi styled bathtub. They bathe each other, then make love in the tub. After their session, she reminds him of how in demand he is of her time. And it would be impossible for her to be on a professional team *and* be available to him, at a moments notice.

"You're probably right," he says as he smiles slyly.

They towel off and return to the bed for another session.

He's rubbing her breast and clitoris. Kissing her wildly from the onset. Doing the things he *knows* will turn her on. But when he sticks his finger in her, she nearly jumps off the bed. He takes notice, immediately.

"What's wrong baby?" he asks.

"I don't like that and I never have," she says nervously, "You should know that by *now*."

"I'm sorry, Ebony," he says, "I was caught up in the moment."

She lays back down with him and tries to relax. "I'm sorry," he whispers again as he takes her into his arms, a second time.

"I should've remembered you didn't like that. I just got caught up in the moment. That's what happens when I'm close to you, baby girl. I *gotta* fix it now. Come here."

She allows herself to relax and they make passionate love. She falls asleep immediately after. But he's still awake, watching her sleep. He's watching her and wondering what it is about him putting his fingers inside of her, that makes her so uncomfortable. She'd rejected that action from day one. He knows it isn't about the Raymond assault. It's surely something which happened long before that. He knows there's a story behind it and he wants to know what it is. He *has* to know what it is.

What's going on?

From now on he'll make a conscience effort to *not* do it. But he still wants to know why that action has her so traumatized. He'll take the time and talk to big mama and Pearl, if he needs too. But he's going to find out. She's his girl, exclusively. His father had said something about her going though something in her life, awhile back. He figures his father knows what she'd gone through because he had made him aware of it.

He should know.

By Saturday, Al's sister Jessica Jackson-Layton and her son Terrell arrive in Atlanta. Her husband Jonathan didn't make the trip. He

104

isn't ready to mix with his black relatives. Olympic games or not. Al had invited her entire family to come to yet another event. This time she actually came, much to the credit of her son Terrell. Al reintroduces her to all of the crew and family. It's been 13 years since they've seen each other. The last time was 1983, when their father died. He had left everything to Al and his older sister wasn't happy, at all. He had even tried to offer her some of the estate but she was so stubborn about the Will, she'd refused it. He still put some away, for her and Terrell. He'll tell her about it later.

Meanwhile, Lynn competes in the 100 meter dash finals and places fourth, just missing a medal. But the 4x100 meter team finishes 1st and wins the gold.

Later the family, including Jessica and Terrell, talk and celebrate over a huge dinner in a popular soul food restaurant in the Atlanta area.

"The last time I saw you, you was about nine or ten," Jessica says to Lynn, at dinner.

"I was Nine. Terrell, you was eleven, right?" she asks Terrell.

"Yes. I had just turned eleven when grandpa died," he says.

"I was gonna be ten, the next month," Lynn says, "Ajay, you was eight. Nina was seven. Erica was two and Pam hadn't even made one yet."

"He passed two weeks before your tenth birthday," Al says to his oldest daughter.

"I know he's proud of you," Jessica says, "You're all doing so well and so is Terrell."

She tries to divert the attention to her son. Terrell is 25 now. He successfully produces music with a Boston production crew. They had a song nominated for an *AMA*, 2 years ago. He produces for Hip Hop and R&B artist. Him and Rob make plans to get together and discuss doing some tracks for *Reaper* and *Brittany J*. He had already expressed interest in working with Rob, after hearing about his company. He's also interested in hanging out with his only male cousin Ajay. And spending some time getting to know him again, now that they've had this chance to reconnect.

"Man, you went in the first round, cousin. Fifth pick!" Terrell says with excitement.

"Nothing but the best," Ajay says, "On and off the court."

"A torn right ACL put a stop to my hopes, in the tenth grade."
He's ignoring Ajay's *off the court* remark. "So I lost out on the NBA."
Ajay cracks up laughing and Terrell knows he's going to have to try to cover his tracks.

He says, "Okay. I wasn't going nowhere near the draft and we all know
105

that. Division one, maybe. But an NCAA finalist, I was not! But *you*. You got game, cousin. You always had game, man. Okay. On the court *and* off. I've been bragging on you since the eighties."

They all laugh, this time. Unaware of what Ajay and Terrell are *really* on.

"I remember you had a little cross over. But I also remember you had a *big* crush on Ebony too," Ajay says, making it apparent. "We all played basketball. Every time you came. *She* use to beat you. Lynn tried to play but I had to make her give it up. She's my sister and she was just, *alright*. I couldn't let the world get wind of that. I had to stop her."

"Shut up," Lynn orders and they all laugh. "Ebony's better than you. Now what?" she teases as now, Terrell is forced to recognize Ebony and make it apparent to the others that he's going to concede to Ajay. Ajay is a true Jackson man. Alpha male, through and through. Terrell has been watered down, some what.

"Your *girl*," he says, trying to hold on to the façade. "This is Ebony? Your neighbor, right? From next door?"

"Yea. You know who she is, man," Ajay says, not allowing him to leave any doubts with the others. He says, "She's my fiancée now. You, me *and* her, know you *never* had a chance. So you didn't lose out there either." They laugh hard, this time. Ebony leans on Ajay and smiles.

"That's what's up," Terrell says, not wanting a confrontation with Ajay. "You use to *say* she was gonna be your wife *too*. You was like seven, then. She's got game, though," he adds, "Is she checking out the pro's too?" He asks Ajay, knowing he's going to realize he's been keeping track of Ebony too. Terrell is a Jackson man. And though he's not as concentrated as Ajay, he knows the code. Never address a Jackson man's woman, without him first introducing her. Especially if there is history. He isn't going to address Ebony. Unless Ajay okays it. Ajay doesn't okay it.

"Not so far. She's the brainier side of our relationship," Ajay tells him with a chuckle. Knowing he's won this joust, he adds, "She's gonna be an investment banker."

"That's smart, baby," Jessica cuts in, trying to rinse whatever egg that may be left on her sons face. "She can make sure all of those millions you just got, are safe. While earning some of her own too."

"That's what I'm talking about," Ebony agrees, glad to see that Jessica recognizes her man is not only talented but wealthy too.
And with the intelligence to surround himself with intelligence, as well. She knows the history, just as her mother and her crew does. She knows part of the reason Ajay is so aggressive in his stance with Terrell, is because of the

106

TIME TO LOVE-RELOADED-TIME WILL REVEAL 3

heartache his mother Jessica has dealt to his father and his mother, over the years. But Terrell wants to shun all of that. He just wants his extended family back. Which is the reason he insisted on coming. He's grown and out of his parents home now. He was going to attend this crew event, rather his mother did or not.

"So cousin, you're graduating next week?" Terrell asks Ajay. He doesn't even dare look Ebony's way again.

"Yes indeed," Ajay answers, "We're leaving out at eleven, tonight. Going back to Natty. I have to get ready for finals. She's my tutor."

"Why don't y'all come for his graduation?" Ebony asks Jessica, as they laugh at Ajay's tutor comment.

"We will, baby," Jessica says, "I just told Al. We're gonna have to see more of each other. Whether Jonathan wants to come or not."

"Good for you," Pearl says, "I'm so happy to see that you two are reconnecting. Family is *everything*. That's what we teach our children."

Pearl is standing up for her best friend Jo, who didn't say anything to Jessica, as usual. Jessica does likewise. She's used Jo's family dynamic as her excuse for not having a real relationship with her own brother, since college. But Jo knows that's not even the biggest part of it. What it's about, is the fact that Jessica's husband, Dr. Jonathan Layton, would rather she not consort with or claim her brother. Nor his middle class family and friends. Jo also knows the only reason he'd allowed Jessica to come this time, is because Allen's daughter and son are now in the national news. They're big names in sports news. Which makes them money earners, outside of sports as well. Since they met, Jessica has always tried to be someone she isn't. She had labeled Jo as a fatherless girl, who wouldn't be morally fit for her brother. Jo saw her as far worse than anyone she could ever be. A girl who came up well off. But disowned her own, based on material *haves* or *have not's*. And considered herself marrying up because her husband was white. Still, Jo encouraged Al to reach out and try to maintain a relationship with his only sibling, for their late parents sake. For 13 years, Jessica rarely returned a call. And when she did, she lied about her reasons for not being able to come. She wanted Al to believe it was because of Jo. But Jo and her girls, all knew better. Jo and Jessica's friendship never bloomed. They haven't spoken in almost 20 years. That isn't going to change tonight.

{JULY 20, 1996{
Ajay graduates from The University of Cincinnati, in an afternoon
107

ceremony. Aunt Jessica and cousin Terrell attend, as promised. Afterwards, they follow the crew on into Cleveland.

Shortly after arriving, Ajay and Al discuss the *Ebony's sensitivity to fingers* issue. Ajay wants to know what his father knows about the problem.

"I know you said it's something that happened in her life," Ajay says, "Is that what this is from? I don't understand it, pops. We've been intimate for almost 10 years. I'm puzzled by this one."

"She just may not be comfortable with that sort of thing, son," Al tries, "People have different things they like and don't like about sex."

"I know. But it's more than that," he probes, "I know it's not about Raymond. She was freaking out about this, from day one. In eighty seven."

Al knows what the problem is. But he isn't willing to tell Ajay. Ebony will tell him, when and if she's ready too. That's what Al tells him.

"It may be deeply rooted, son," he says, "If she can and wants too. She'll tell you."

"She doesn't have to worry about Raymond, anymore. He's not coming back," he says, ready to confess what happened to Raymond White. He tells him the entire story. Al is quiet, for awhile, before he speaks again. When he does, he tells him he's been in similar situations with his crew.

"Why do you think we understand *every* aspect of your crew and what you're facing?" he asks, "We've been there, son. I've told you before, we did it all. John is willing to do this time, if they try to pin it on either of you. So am I. We all are. You'll see that before you move to Miami. I don't want you to worry about it. Either of you."

Al tells him he's going to handle the situation of Raymond's disappearance, for him and his crew.

"I don't want Ebony nor any of you, going down for it."

Ajay ask what he plans to do. Al doesn't tell him. But he assures him if anybody from their family gets hemmed up, it won't be him, Ebony or their crew. They finish their conversation. Then Ajay goes to meet Ebony at Chill's house. They go to the U to freshen up. He doesn't tell her anything about the conversation he had with his father.

Jessica goes back to Boston. But Terrell stays, so he can hang out for the remainder of the week. He's staying until Ajay leaves for Miami. Then he's flying to L.A. with Rob, Jan, Archie Sr, Reaper and Brittany J.

When John comes home, August 1st, Al tells him they need to talk. They get all of the fathers together. Al tells them what he knows about
108

Raymond's demise. John isn't the least bit sad to know that Raymond White is already dead. He had plans of doing it, himself.

"I sure was. If his ass would have ever surfaced," John admits, "My baby didn't deserve what he did to her. And those assholes questioned me, for *years*. Behind his bullshit ass. They know I wanted too. I'd cop to it, in a heartbeat, if it comes up again."

The fathers agree they'll take the rap before allowing any of their children to go to jail.

"It's our time, if anybody has to go," Brad Sr says, "We've lived free for over twenty years. And haven't served any *real* time."

"Yea," Rich Sr says, "I've done the only *real* time in our crew. But not for murder. Chester took the rap, way back. He's the only one."

"Many of us have some jail time in our past," Sam Sr says, "Much of it for being railroaded during segregation. Or what have you. But never as much as we would've gotten, if we had gotten caught on any of that murderous shit, we was doing."

"We need to get with Chill and handle this now," Brian Sr says.

They all meet with Chill. Al tells him what he knows about Raymond's murder. Chill tells them all the details about the situation. The fathers tell him, they're going to do a taped confession. A few sets of fathers will do separate videos, confessing to the murder. From the kidnapping to the burial site in Michigan. Chill tells them he has someone trustworthy to do the videos. He assures them that Arthur has been down with this crew since day one. And he was a big part of them getting Raymond to the chamber, in the first place. He tells them Arthur is the only 1 he trust to do these videos.

They go to Arthur, immediately. Not only does he do their video's, he does 1 of himself, on his honor. They bury them in Al and John's backyards.

"These tapes will only be dug up when one of us die. Or if our child gets nailed," Al says, "If it's my son or daughter, then I'll do the time" Al says, "And so on. Are we in agreement?"

All 10 men agree.

"We'll leave it up to the surviving heads," John says, "They'll explain this situation to the crew. After the tape or tapes, are presented," he adds, knowing their offspring will worry about their legacies, post mortem. Chill tries to do a video too. The fathers won't allow it.

"We're doing this for your crew," Sam Sr says, "Arthur did one on his honor. Which goes a long way with us. Chill you was *born* in."

"As a member of the crew that follows yours," Chill says, "I'm

109

honored. I know Arthur is too. We will not stop until we find a way to close this case. Without any lose to our family."

"You have our words on that," Arthur adds, "We'll find a case closer and it won't be anyone from *this* crew."

With that, the subject is closed. These men are the only ones who will know about this. They aren't to tell anyone else. Not even their wives or their crew. No one!

The August celebration is Saturday the 3rd. This month, all 3 generations attend. To celebrate Lynn's gold medal performance and Ajay going pro. He came home for tonight. But he has to return to Miami by Monday morning. Poppa, big mama and the Houston crew fly in too. Ebony tells April and Yolanda, she still has them in her wedding. She also tells them the date, her and Ajay have set. Ajay ask Terrell and Jarvis Rhodes to be the groomsmen for April and Yolanda. He wants his cousin and his wing man to be in his wedding. Ebony wants to go back to Miami with him but she has to start her junior year of preseason practice, this week. June and Rich are home from summer practice. They have to return Monday also. The foursome have practice on Monday. Tank and Jerica are returning with the 6 of them. Jb, Lynn, Bre and Ced are home from Atlanta. Jb is already working on deals for June, Rich and Tank, with the *NFL*. Tank tells him he prefers to be a businessman.

Jr turned 25, Jan made 22 and Rebbie turned 20, yesterday. Her and Lynn have some good news for the crew, as they all hang out at Chill's, before time to go open up their club. But first, they discuss this summer.

"They still got that bomber locked up?" Chill asks.

"Yea, so far," Ced says, "But probably not for long."

"Why not?" Tonya asks.

"Cause now they're saying he's not even the one who did it," Bre says, "They just grabbed somebody then, to shut the media up."

"Damn," Jr says, "So do they have somebody else in mind?"

"I heard somebody is copping to it," Lynn adds.

"We don't know the name," Jb says, "Give it a few more weeks."

"That was fucked up," Ajay says.

"Had us paranoid and shit," Rich adds.

"We wasn't leaving the hotel," Ebony says, "Y'all was partying."

"Yes, we was partying," T-baby says as they all laugh.

"We had a *good* time," Rebbie says, "Brian and me. We brought something back with us."

110

TIME TO LOVE-RELOADED-TIME WILL REVEAL 3

"Like what?" her brother Reaper asks.

"I'm gonna be a mother," Rebbie says suddenly.

"What?!" Nina shouts.

"Yes, kid," she says, "We found out yesterday. On my birthday. What a gift, right?"

"I finally sent one, man," June adds with laughter, as everyone congratulates them. "We're due on May first," he adds.

"Well, we're due on April, twenty fourth," Jb adds.

"Y'all pregnant *too*?" Ebony asks.

"Lynora is," Jb says sarcastically, as they all crack up laughing.

"We got 'em coming, two at a time," Renee says.

"That's all good!" Chill shouts and they are all excited.

"That's alright, baby," Ajay says, "We'll catch up."

Ebony smiles at him. She knows he wants kids, just as much as she does.

"We've got to wait until we get our stuff together, first," she offers.

"Y'all asses practice it more than anybody else in this room," Jb says, "Y'all should have twenty crumb snatchers, by now."

Everyone laughs as Ajay says, "We're just taking our time and getting it right." He's hugging Ebony who says, "We're gonna be alright, baby."

"At least y'all not some old married folks, already," Jesse adds.

"Not yet," Rob says, "But they got the date set."

"They're married," Jan says.

"May as well be," Bre adds, "Because they act like it."

"There's nothing wrong with it," Ced tells Jesse.

"We're gonna have to start acting like it too," Kim says.

"I don't know about all that," Bruce says, "You get everything I have, *now*."

"Except time," Erica adds, "Y'all be in the streets, so much. But don't want us to go *nowhere*."

"Tell him, girl," Brittany says.

"There ain't nothing to tell, bay," Reaper tries.

Greg Jr interrupts, "What do you mean, always in the streets?"

"Y'all are *always* gone! But let us try to go somewhere!" Erica yells.

The youngest crew members continue to disagree. Chill looks at Ajay.

He asks, "Who does that sound like?"

"Ebony and her girls," Ajay answers as the foursome disagree.

"The only reason we was *ever* fussing about y'all," Nina offers, "Is because y'all was *fucking around*, out in them streets."

"He is too!" Erica shouts, as she points to Greg Jr.

111

"Erica. Baby you don't know that!" Greg shouts back, "Damn! Stop believing everything them ho's be saying to you."

"I don't listen to no ho's, Gregory! I *know* you are!" Erica yells.

Greg Jr says, "You can't talk to me, no any kind of way!"

"Wait. Calm down," Ajay says to Greg, "She's still my *lil* sister." The younger crew members continue to argue as their voices grow louder and louder.

"Everybody chill the fuck out!" Chill shouts and the room goes completely silent. Then he says, "I still got it."

He laughs so hard, he nearly falls out of his chair.

"We didn't argue and yell like that," Ebony offers.

"Not you. Cause you knew I wasn't having it," Ajay says.

She blushes. She wants to object but he's right. She never got *out of pocket* with him, like the younger crew are now. She laughs with the rest of the crew as everyone else calms down. It's time to go get dressed and head to *The Chill Spot.*

Soon everyone is dressed and arrives at CrewLand early, so they can open up for the night. Once the club is set up, the doors are opened and the patrons come in, in droves.

****

The next week, at MLK, there is more tension for the crew. Erica and Mya are both football cheerleaders. Their beef is affecting the squad. Anywhere these girls see each other, there's friction.

"What the fuck are you watching me for, ho?!" Erica yells to Mya.

"You had to be looking at me to know I was looking at you, ho!" Mya yells back.

"If you see a ho, come get her foot out of your ass," Brittany adds.

"Ladies, you need to go to class!" Mrs. Tasha Gates yells.

Mrs. Gates is the student teacher who was hired to replace Debra Whitman. It's the 96-97 school year. Mya and Erica are football cheerleaders. Erica, Brittany, Jesse, Sam Jr and Greg Jr are all sophomores and better known as the *99 crew*. Reaper is a junior. Kim is a senior captain of the football cheerleaders. Roo and Pam are Freshman. They're very early into the fall semester. Erica and Mya have been to the office, 2 times already, for attempting to fight. Their cheerleading coach, Mrs. Pittman, warns them, "If you can't get along, there's no way you can be on a squad together."

Erica loves cheering and dance. She isn't willing to risk being thrown off

112

TIME TO LOVE-RELOADED-TIME WILL REVEAL 3

the squad, just for beating up Mya Dean again. She tells coach Pittman she won't fight, "Unless she hits me first."

After school, Erica tells her mother about the altercations. Jo calls and talks with coach Pittman. She tells her about the girls history, from last school year. And that Mya had started it then. She also tells her about Mya's mother and aunts coming to the school to fight the kids. Coach tells Jo, she's aware of the situation and she'll do her best to keep the girls in line. Jo extends herself to coach Pittman and tells her, "If you ever need me for my daughter. Just call me."

By September, preseason basketball practice at UC is in full swing. The women and men's teams have weight training together, again this year.

"I miss having Anthony here to spot me," Ebony says to T-baby.

T-baby says, "Even the house seems strange without him around."

"You want to be partners, captain?" Ebony asks her.

"Cool, captain," she says as they sign the log-in sheet.

From behind them, they hear, "Do you ladies need partners?"

It's Jarvis Rhodes. He's a senior basketball player at UC. He'd played 3 seasons with Ajay. He was 2nd to Ajay in all categories. Ajay calls him his wing man.

"No thanks," T-baby says, "We've got it covered."

"That's to bad," he says, "I wanted to be your partner, Ebony."

"I have a partner," she says and laughs, "He's in Miami."

"So how is Ajay handling it?" Jarvis asks.

"He's handling it *great*," she says, "He's gonna start. Didn't he tell you the other night?"

"I haven't talk to him," he says smiling, "Are y'all still together?"

"Of course we are, Jarvis," she says, continuing to laugh.

"And engaged to be married," T-baby adds, "As you know."

"Okay. Then I was gonna ask you out. But since you're still taken-"

"I'm still spoken for," Ebony interrupts, before grabbing 2 towels for her and T-baby and exiting the office. She says, "He just called you and asked you to be in our wedding, *wing man*. So you know we're still together. Stop trying to be low down, Jarvis. Oh *wait*. I wasn't suppose to know he called you, right? Right."

She laughs and goes on to work out. Jarvis smiles. He knew she would pass the test.

"Girl, he gotta come better than that," Ebony says as her and T-baby enter the weight room.

113

TIME TO LOVE-RELOADED-TIME WILL REVEAL 3

"You know Ajay keeping tabs on that shit," T-baby laughs.
They do their required workout, then hit the track to run their 5 miles. When their workouts are done, they go back to the crew's house. Tank is there with Jerica. He has a worried look on his face.

"Have y'all heard the news?" he asks as him and Jerica enjoy father and daughter time.
Nina, Rebbie, June and Rich are away, on a UC football trip to Texas.

"What news?" Ebony asks.

"Tupac got shot again," he says.

"Oh no! Is he alright?" T-baby asks.

"Yea. He's still living," he says, "You know Pac gets shot like this, all the time. He'll pull through."

"We got him performing for Thanksgiving," Ebony says, "Oh God, let him be alright. I'm looking forward to meeting him and chopping it up."

"For real, though," T-baby adds.

"You know he's a poet, like me," Ebony says with a smile.

"He *is* a poet," Tank says, "People put down on him because he claims thug. They just don't bother to see the meaning. Thugs mean: *True's Humbly United Gathering Souls.* Our Cleveland Thugs already cleared that shit up."

"Tupac is a soldier for the streets. A voice for the voiceless," Ebony says, "His mother was in jail while she carried him. And she's a panther, like our first generation."

"Black Panthers are his family too," he adds, "And I love *the Outlaws.* I know they must be ready to kill a muthafucka."

"I hope he pulls through," T-baby says, "Rich is gonna be sad to know he got shot again."
The ladies go on to take there baths, grab some food and then relax. Ebony talks to Ajay. They discuss *Tupac* getting shot. He's Ajay's favorite rapper, of all time. Same as Ebony. They're both praying for his full recovery and looking forward to meeting him this Thanksgiving.

Rich calls T-baby at 10pm to tell her they won their game and they're about to fly back to Natty.

"We'll meet you at the airport, baby," she says and they soon hang up, as she tells Ebony and Tank, "We're going home tomorrow to see our little man," she says heading into her room to get out her notes to study.

"I'm going to see my baby, Friday!" Ebony yells in the same tone.

The September Celebration is scheduled for the 14th. Ebony won't

114

attend because she's flying to Miami to see Ajay, for the weekend.

Tonya turns 25, Bre makes 22, this month and Reaper turns 17. Little Rich III is going to celebrate his 1st birthday with Brad III, who turned 5, this year. Their party is all set for *Granny's House*. Jan and Rob, lil Rich's godparents will be there. Ajay sends gifts for lil Brad and lil Rich to Jo's house.

<u>}August 13, 1996{</u>

Ebony arrives at the Miami International airport. Ajay and some team assistants are waiting as she comes into the terminal. Ajay is signing autographs but excuses himself when she comes off the gang walk.

"Hey baby!" she says as she runs and jumps into his outstretched arms. "I missed you, so much," she says as they kiss.

Right away, she notice he looks troubled.

"I missed you too," he says, "You haven't heard the bad news?"

"No baby. What happened?" she asks noticing he has a look of distress on his face.

"Pock died today," he says sadly.

"Oh baby no! When?" she asks as the tears flow immediately.

"A few hours ago," he says, "While you was flying here."

"I don't believe it," she says with tears streaming down her face, "No way. That can't be true, Anthony."

"I don't wanna believe it either," he says, "But it's all over radio and TV, baby."

As they drive along the highway, they notice other passengers looking dazed. They stop at a stoplight. The driver in the car next to them, ask if they'd heard the news about *Tupac*.

"Yea, man," Ajay says, "That's fucked up, right?"

"Yea. Real fucked up," the passenger says, "We lost a legend."

All along the streets of Miami, from the airport to Ajay's condo off of Lincoln Avenue and Ocean drive, people seem to be in a daze. Everybody is gathering in huddles at street corners, sports bars. Everywhere. They're discussing this great lose. As Ajay turns into his Condo complex garage, he spots 3 of his teammates.

"What's up, Ajay?" 1 of his teammates asks.

"Nothing much, man," he says, "Where y'all headed?"

"We're about to get together at my place and listen to some Pock, man," he says.

"That's what me and my girl about to do," he says as he introduces Ebony to his teammates.

115

"Nice to meet you," she says.

"He's good Ebony," another player says, "He's gonna be an impact player, for us."

She smiles proudly as she looks at Anthony and says, "I know he is. I'm so proud of him."

"She taught me everything I know," Ajay says and they all laugh.

Ajay grabs her bags and they go into his condo. The condos where he resides are owned by Miami Heat supporters and sponsors, which is how he found out about them. They're also popular for new professionals who move to the Miami area. Nearly all of his single teammates live here. This makes it a hot spot, frequented by many women who look to snag a rich celebrity. Or just to bed down with one. Ebony notices 3 women eyeing her fiancée as they're about to enter the secured property.

"I see you can use some better scenery, baby," she says and laughs as they pass the skimpy clad females.

The 3 of them turn completely around to get a longer look at Ajay. But he doesn't look their way.

"For damn sho," he says as the doorman lets them in, takes the luggage from him and calls the elevator. Ajay says, "Somebody will let them in, at some point. Then release them on the building when they're done with them," he says and laughs as he shakes his head. "They'll knock on doors until somebody else lets them in. Or gets security to come put 'em out."

"I wish somebody *would* come knocking at your door. I'll let her in *and* out," Ebony say as they continue laughing and the doorman laughs too.

"Don't open the door. Cause they'll know where I live," he says.

"Just let us know if they bother you," the doorman says, "We have plenty of security to escort them out. We try to keep up with who comes in, with whom. So we can make sure our residence are being responsible for the guest they bring in."

"She's the only one I'll be bringing here," Ajay says, "And I'm the only one she's gonna visit."

"Correct," Ebony says and they all laugh again, as Ajay opens the door to his condo.

The doorman brings her luggage in, gets his gratuity and leaves after his services are no longer needed.

"This is huge, baby," she says, "Why don't you think it's big enough?"

"It's big but not big enough for a family," he says with a smile.

"Are you expecting a family, anytime soon?" she asks sarcastically.

116

TIME TO LOVE-RELOADED-TIME WILL REVEAL 3

"Not right away," he says, "But that's why I'm telling you now."
"Telling *me*?" she asks.
"Yea. I'm telling you," he says, "So don't come down here and get caught up. Your man is lethal, right now. I've been holding on to this nut for six weeks," he says as he grabs hold of the bundle in his boxers, "In honor of pock, it's time to Christian this place."
She smiles. Then informs him of the encounter with Jarvis in the sports arena. He doesn't seem to be bothered by it. She'll find out later that he'd put him up to it. Just to see if she'd bite. They take a bath together. Then listen to *Tupac* records and indulge in each other for the majority of the evening.

During the late night, as they talk about the lost of *Tupac*, there are 2 separate knocks at his door that they don't bother to answer. His phone rings, once. He lets the caller know, in no uncertain terms, that he's not available. Ebony smiles. Ajay was always a lady killer. But what use to be *ho's* before the contract, are now *groupies* and still she's his priority. She lets it roll off of her back because he isn't frazzled at all. They reminisce on last March 26, w*hen Eazy-E* had passed away. Now, *Tupac* is gone. Both men are favorites of their family. They know when they call and talk to the crew, during the celebration tomorrow, there'll be much more reminiscing about *Tupac* and *Eazy-E*.

Jan replaces her Sentra with a 97 Rodeo, while she's home for the celebration. She leaves it at *Crew Details* to have it tricked out. Her, Rob, Terrell and Archie Sr will drive it to Los Angeles, in early October. They'll miss that Celebration, which will have a Halloween theme again this year. October 26 is the date for both, the big and little crew parties.
In October, they'll celebrate the grand opening of more businesses too. Mama Jo is managing *Big Mama's House*. The immediate and aftercare center. Pearl will help out when she isn't on duty at East General. Mrs. Green will help Jo, on a daily basis. Anna manages the *Crew Spa and Health center* with Debbie. They're already fully staffed. Sandy, Rena and Belinda open *Crew Gear and Alterations,* a clothing store, with mostly original garments made by the 3 of them. They already have a huge clientele and a reputation for being able to make anything their customers describe to them. With a new building and plenty of room for their machines, equipment and merchandise, they're sure to do even better. They have given Justine and Kilo a half wall and window, to add their clothing. All 3 of the new businesses are in the new strip mall which is adjacent to the
117

TIME TO LOVE-RELOADED-TIME WILL REVEAL 3

original one. It's directly across the street from the original strip of CrewLand Mall. It will carry the same name. The crew are having an over-the-street crosswalk put in to connect the 2 strips. The newest strip has 8 spaces, in various sizes, just like the original one. Their having a 3rd strip built in the very near future. That will give them 24 total suites, in various sizes. Plus *Crew Details* which sits independently, at the entrance of the property.

Just over the cliff ridge, on the back side of this new strip mall, you see the area where Ebony's accident occurred. You can also see Cleveland State University and the University apartments or the U. Reaper has taken over Ajay's old apartment since Bruce left for Ohio State. Rena spends so much time trying to watch out for the *goings on, down there* that sometimes it seems she can barely focus on her sewing projects.

"It's only a matter of time before some shit hit's the fan, down that hill," she says to Sandy and Belinda as they sew and hem garments in their new store.

"We're all going through the same thing," Sandy says, "This is the second time around, for all of us."

"At least yours aren't down highway 71, every time they get a chance," Belinda says speaking of Kim.
She has been sneaking down to Columbus to see Bruce. That was, until Sam and Belinda found out and took her Nissan Sentra.
"She wasn't happy about that, *at all*. But she'll get over it," Belinda says with a smile.

"She'll just sign a scholarship in the spring and go right on," Sandy laughs, "Like Trisha did. Except she was going a little farther down that same highway."

"Well she can go, *then*," Belinda says, "At least then, she will be where she's *suppose* to be."
They laugh and have a great day at their new jobs. They love their store.

The crew mothers are all working full time in their own businesses. Except Pearl. She's still fulltime at East General but she works with Jo at *Big Mama's House* most days, before going to the hospital. She helps out at whichever business needs her, when she's not at the hospital. All of their grandparents and most of the fathers, run *The Crews House of Soul Food*.

But the latest news is, big mama and poppa are moving back to Cleveland so that they can join their best friends in the restaurant and catering business. As for now, Chill and Renee help with the daily hot meal deliveries. Along with Jason, who runs his own real estate business from his
118

TIME TO LOVE-RELOADED-TIME WILL REVEAL 3

home. This leaves him with very flexible hours to help out, whenever or wherever they need him. He'll get an office at CrewLand, once Ebony graduates and opens her Real Estate office in the future strip. As for now, all of the businesses are fully staffed and still turning great profits.

With T-baby and Rich still away at college, Sandy and Anna alternate bringing Rich III to *Granny's House* each morning before opening up their shops. He isn't able to move to Cincinnati. Not with basketball and football seasons still going strong.

"Sandy, we may as well get use to it," Anna says, "All of our kids seem to be heading off into other careers, first," Anna says, "*Pro* leagues."

"I know that's right, girl," Sandy agrees, "But they'll always have these businesses to fall back on. I still want Trisha to play in the *WNBA*."
All the parents are very proud of their offspring's entrepreneurial efforts.

"It's great to see them all doing so well," Anna adds.

"Yes *and* legal," Sandy adds with a smile.

Late October marks the start of basketball and Ajay's 1st NBA season. Miami will be playing the Cleveland Cavaliers, Thanksgiving week. Ebony and T-baby's season will start the week of Thanksgiving. June and Rich's football team is doing well, again this year. They expect to qualify for post season play again in January. Bre's team is expected to do very well for her senior season. Bruce and the Ohio State team are having a winning season too. Kim is cheering for football. She made the girls basketball team at MLK. They're expected to advance to the State tournament. Reaper, Jesse and Sam's, MLK football team are definitely going to the state tournament. They're expected to win it. They're also trying to break the record of wins set during June and Rich's senior year.

Richard Jewell, the man who was arrested for the Olympic bombing back in July, while the crew was there, was vindicated this month. Eric Robert Rudolph pleads guilty to the bombing. Rudolph will get 4 life sentences plus 120 years, for this terrorist act. Which to date, is still not called a terrorist act. *Why not?*

The October celebration includes 22 year anniversaries for Brian and Brenda James Sr, as well as Sam and Belinda Logan Sr. Birthdays include Stoney's 27th and Rob makes 26. Rich turned 21 and Greg Jr made sixteen. The big kids party will be at the newly opened *Big Mama's House*, for Archie Jr, who will turn 11. He has already moved up to play basketball for 9th grade because he's just that good. He wants to be like Ajay. CJ
119

turns 5, down in Atlanta. She receives another gift from her grandfather, Chester Lee. Little Jerica turns 2 and has her party at *Granny's House,* for the five and under crew.

The crew think about Tupac's death again, as November rolls by. They decide to have another tribute party to him, Thanksgiving weekend. They still have Bone Thugs n Harmony performing.

"Thanksgiving week is finally here," Ebony says as the Natty crew prepare to leave for Cleveland.

"Yes Lord. It's about time we get to go home again," T-baby adds. Her and Rich haven't seen their son in almost a month. Ebony hasn't seen Ajay since the weekend Tupac died. She's handling the separation, much better than she ever believed she would.

"It's because you still got us," Tank says with a chuckle.

"Yes. We're not gonna let you get too lonely," Rebbie adds as they load their bags into the cars and head off for Cleveland.

"My baby bought a ninety seven Grand Cherokee. They got it at the detail shop," Ebony says as they're driving up highway 71, "I can't wait to see what they did to it."
Ajay owns 3 vehicles. He still has the 64 Chevy convertible, which stays in the shed at his parents house, covered up. He has the 78 Cadillac Seville, in Miami. He plans to ship it home and ship the Jeep to Miami, this month. The Natty crew are on the road enjoying conversation, when T-baby alerts them on a passage of time none of them had even thought about.

"Y'all know who got out, last week, right?" T-baby asks.

"Who?" Rebbie asks.

"Tameka," she answers.

"That's *right*," Rebbie says, "She *was* suppose to get out, this year."

"Uh huh. A lot has changed since she got locked up," June says.

"We grew up," Ebony adds with a laugh.

"I don't even care about fucking with her anymore," T-baby says.

"I know kid, right? We're past all that stuff," Rebbie says, "Why did you mention it anyway?"

"Mama said she came to the restaurant looking for a job."

"Really?" Rich asks, "Did they hire her?"

"Papa called ma and asked her, *if* she thought it would be cool and she called me," T-baby says, "I told her I didn't care if they give her a job. But watch her."

"That's real big of you, baby," Rich says, "You really must be over the shit she did?"

120

TIME TO LOVE-RELOADED-TIME WILL REVEAL 3

"Yes I am. And the shit you did *too*," T-baby says, "As far as revenge goes, we got too much to lose now."

"I'm not," Rich says, "But if you don't mind it. I don't mine it." They drive on in Rich's Caprice. Nina and Tank are ahead of them, in her Camry, with Jerica sleeping on the backseat.

}*Pittsburgh{*

Angel calls Alana tonight. This time she has a plan of how they're going to contact Ajay and Tank, for Thanksgiving and beyond.

"I heard our girl Tameka is gonna be working at the restaurant," Angel says.

"No *shit*?!" Alana yells, not believing Angel.

"I heard that shit from a bitch that live in my mama's building," Angel tells her, "And your girl Gloria, who use to run with Anita and Samantha. She got a baby daddy that's a damn guard, on the next tier. She came to see him. I was on laundry detail. She told me that shit too. But Shaniqua, from mama's building, got a lover on my cell block. She told her to tell me, Ebony's grandfather is hiring Tameka. But Alana, that's T-baby's grandfather too."

"Damn," Alana says, "How that bitch get in, like that?"

"She must still be *fuckin* Rich, home girl," Angel says, "*See*. That marriage shit don't mean nothing."

"Well that bitch is gonna hook shit up for us too, then," Alana says, "As soon as my probation and shit is up, I'm moving back to Cleveland."

"What about your white girlfriend?" Angel ask as she giggles.

"Farah is not my girlfriend," she says, "I mean, we did experiment and all. And yes, the shit was good. But me and her got to have some dick in our lives, so we're gonna keep a boy on the side."

They laugh and further discuss their plot to reenter the crews lives. Even though they barely escaped with their own lives, the 1st time around.

}*Cleveland{*

Ajay arrives with the Miami Heat, on Wednesday evening. He comes by CrewLand Mall and brings his entire team to eat at *The Crews House of Soul Food.* They have a great time, love the food and consume a lot of it. They're going to have Thanksgiving dinner at the restaurant tomorrow, where the crew's family are going to gather this year, as well.

Big mama and poppa are in Cleveland for Thanksgiving. She gets right in there with her crew and puts together a wonderful Thanksgiving

121

dinner. The crew and the Miami Heat eat as much as they can hold. After a filling dinner, Brian Sr and Rich Sr take Ajay to Crew Details to see his new Jeep. He absolutely loves it.

"You're shipping it out Monday?" Ajay asks.

"Yea. We got the paperwork ready to go," Brian Sr says.

"I can't wait to drive it again," Ajay says, "I'm gonna take my girl for a ride in it, while I'm home. See if she likes it."

"She'll like it," Rich Sr says, "It's got everything in it but a kitchen sink and toilet."

They all laugh.

Even though the Heat are staying at the Fillmore Hotel, Ajay is allowed to stay at his family's home, during this stop. Ebony stays with him. She's staying at Jo's house and sleeping in Ajay's room since it's completely redecorated. She never even sat on his old bed again. Not since his 15th birthday. But she'll be sleeping in his room, all night. Something she has *never* done. The game is Friday night and a celebration will follow.

"Time flies, don't it?" Ajay says as they're driving in his new jeep.

"Yes it does. But it seem like it's creeping when you're away."

"We'll be together for good, before you know it, baby," he tries.

"Me and my girls was talking about doing the summer semester, next year. So we can come on out," she tells him.

"That's good, baby," he says, "Can you handle that?"

"I have too. I wanna hurry up and get out, so I can be with you," she says, "Especially since we'll be getting married, next winter. Then we can graduate in May ninety eight, on time and not have to carry a full class schedule our last semester."

"That works for me," he says, "Then we can start on our family, right? Since you're not playing in the league."

"Right and right," she says.

"Good. Because I'm done designing our home," he says.

"The one you started in seventh grade?" she asks as she giggles.

"Yep. The same one."

They both crack up laughing.

Papa hires Tameka Robinson as a food server for the restaurant. She has been on her best behavior, so far. She hasn't inquired about Rich, at all. Either she knows not too or maybe she really isn't interested. She hasn't given the crew any trouble. Prison has really changed her. Still, the younger females in the crew aren't that forgiving.

122

TIME TO LOVE-RELOADED-TIME WILL REVEAL 3

The 1st Wednesday of December, as Tameka finishes her shift and leaves the restaurant, she's confronted by Kim, Brittany, Erica, Roo and Pam. They're waiting when she comes through the parking lot, heading to the bus stop.

"You're the bitch who killed my brother's baby?" Roo asks.

Tameka is quiet. She continues walking, trying to make it to the bus stop.

"Bitch, you can't hear!?" Kim yells at her.

"I don't want beef with y'all," Tameka says, "I have a curfew. I'm just trying to make it home, on time."

"T-baby is my first cousin," Kim says, "She might let you make it but I don't have too."

"I don't wanna fight with y'all," she says, "Please leave me alone."

"No baby. See it's not that simple. When you fuck with the crew," Erica says, "The crew fucks with you, *way* worse."

"I work for the crew now," she tries, "I need my job."

"I need that ass too," Kim say as she punches Tameka.

Tameka doesn't try to fight back. She tries to run but the 5 girls have her surrounded. They beat her down, then run to Kim's car, jump in and speed away. Tameka goes back to the restaurant and reports them to papa.

"I'll take care of it," he says, "You won't have anymore trouble out of them."

Papa drives her home, then go find the girls. He tells each of their parents what they've done. The girls are punished. They won't attend anymore celebrations, for 2 months. As it is, they aren't allowed to be in the club during the celebration because they aren't 18. But once they became crew, they was allowed to hang out in the upstairs area which contains Chill and Renee's offices. From there, they had a full view of the club. But now they aren't allowed to go at all. They're very disappointed. Especially Ruthie, who is 1 of the December birthdays. To add insult to injury, Anna tells her she has to be a part of the big kids celebration at *Big Mama's House,* instead. The other 4 girls will have to attend with her. Their parents know that's the best punishment for them. After waiting to turn 13, to be allowed to attend events with the crew. Making them go to the *kiddy party* is the best form of punishment. Not to mention they can't go anywhere except school and their games. Kim can't drive her car for 2 more months. She's really mad because she'd just gotten her driving privileges back, the previous Sunday. Their plans will be further crushed before any good news comes.

Chill plans to renovate the upstairs so it won't be available for the underage crew, after 6 months, anyway. With the growing income levels of

123

many crew members, they want to make the club much more upscale. They're adding a 3rd floor which will contain the offices and VIP. The 2nd floor will convert to a full floor, with exotic dancing and card lounge for card game tournaments. The 1st *and* 2nd generations love that idea. These additions will start immediately after the 1st of the year. The crew continue to make upward strides. Still that street life they keep trying to pull away from, isn't releasing them so easy. The better things get financially, the more accessible they seem to be.

The December celebration is held on Ebony's 21st birthday, Christmas day. Ajay isn't going to be able to come because his team is on the road. But leading up to the celebration, Ebony, Nina, Rebbie and T-baby decide to show their maturity. They have a long talk with Kim, Erica, Brittany, Roo and Pam. The foursome tell them they are over Tameka and they should let it go too.

"She's paid her debt to society. I don't care about her anymore," T-baby says, "She can't fuck with me and Richard, so just let her be."

"Y'all have to stop going after other people," Nina says.

"We didn't do it like that," Rebbie says.

"We let it come to us," Ebony adds, "Then we handled business."

"We have to put it down for y'all," Nina says, "Like Lynn and Renee and the older girls did for us."

"They kept us on point, for sho," T-baby says.

"Y'all have our cell numbers," Ebony says, "Call us. Call Renee and Tonya. Whatever y'all have to do."

"But get your shit right," Rebbie says.

"Represent crew the right way, all the time," Ebony adds.

The 5 girls say they understand and are through with it too.

Roo turned 15, this month while Nina and Ebony make 21. Lil Chill turns 13 and gets crewed up. They're all growing up. There are so many changes on the horizon. Some they're ready to accept and some they aren't. But with Chill and Renee's son being initiated, they have another rule to adhere too. Another long standing one. So before leaving for the celebration, they talk at Chill's house.

"This year, I plan to retire from the active crew," Chill says.

"Yes, y'all," Renee adds, "Our son is crew. We have to fall back."

"Jr will be the active head, from now on," Chill says, "I'm still gonna party with y'all. But until we get a separate facility in place for these minors," he says with a smile, "We'll play the background."

The crew are saddened by this news, as they leave for the club. But they

124

TIME TO LOVE-RELOADED-TIME WILL REVEAL 3

know Chill and Renee are getting older. They'll all fall back, at 30 years old. Chill and Renee are only 27 but they have a 13 year old. That's the way the rules have always been. All of their parents had done the same, in the past. It isn't going to be any different for these parents or anyone else in the crew.

As soon as things get underway and popping, Ajay calls the club. He talks with his fiancée, last and longest.
"Happy birthday and Anniversary. And Merry Christmas, baby."
"It's been seven years since we spent Christmas day apart," Ebony says sadly.
"I know. It's hard. But we have to look at the big picture."
"You're right," she says, "But it's still not easy."
"No it's not. But in a year, this will *really* be our season," he says, "And I'll see you before New Years, right?"
"Oh it will be, for sure. And you definitely will," she says, "I'll be in Miami, Sunday for sure. To change the scenery."
They laugh.
"Cool. That gives me something to look forward too," he says.
"A Happy New Year!" she screams.
"Yes and we can bring it in, together," he says, "When do you have to be back at UC?"
"On the third. We have a game on the fourth," she says.
"So do we," he says.
"You know what, baby?" she asks.
"What's that?"
"The more things change…," she starts.
"…The more things stay the same, ha?" he finishes.

REST IN PEACE TO:
TUPAC AMARU SHAKUR
SEPTEMBER 13, 1996
We pray for your family in this time of grief.
The entire Hip Hop Nation grieves with you.
We loved him like family.
He will live on with this crew eternally and will never, ever
be duplicated and never forgotten!
He will be mourned forever!

125

TIME TO LOVE-RELOADED-TIME WILL REVEAL 3

CHAPTER 28

THE REVELATION

Tank makes 22 on the same day of the January Celebration. The year is 1997. Tank, Rich, June plus Bre, down at Tech, are looking forward to graduating from college, this May. 19 year-old Bruce and Ohio State won their bowl game, earlier this month. He enjoyed lots of success. And he garnered many awards during his freshmen season including, Rookie of the year. Jb is already working contract options for Bruce's future. Right along with June, Rich and Tank. Bre doesn't wish to play pro ball, after college. She's going to Officer's Training School after graduation.

Jesse is 16 years-old. During his sophomore football season, they won the state title. They beat Rich and June's record by 1 game. Which left him, Greg Jr and Reaper thrilled. They're already being recruited by colleges but Reaper is determined to make a career in music. That's all he talks about. He's scheduled to open for the Bone Thugs N Harmony/Mo Thugs concert, this February, in the *Gund arena*. His parents want him to go to college, even if he doesn't want to play sports.

This month's major announcement comes from big John Brown. After nearly 27 years of driving cross country, he's retiring from the long hauls. Starting in February, he's going to drive locally and open his own company. He owns 5 rigs now, though his goal was three. He wanted to own 1 for each of his sons. With his own trucking service, he'll do all of the deliveries for Crew Enterprises, as well as some of the local supermarkets. Pearl is just happy she'll have him at home, every night. John is also able to do any repairs for Crew Enterprises. He's a jack-of-all-trades, so to speak. He knows carpentry, auto repair and plumbing. Just like most of the men in this crew, their fathers had taught them many trades to fall back on. And they're going to put them to good use, by helping with the building of additional mall space and the renovations of the club.

Today, February 21, 1997, Rebbie's grandparents Charles and Annabelle Wilson, have been married for 45 years. The crew have a party scheduled for tonight. Erica is happy her punishment has ended, so she can join in the festivities upstairs at the spot, for a change. Her and Sam Jr have finally made 16.

June and Rich win the bowl game in New Orleans, again this year.

They'll be entering the draft next month, with Jb as their agent. He has sweet deals in the works for both of them. No matter what team drafts them, they're sure to go 1st round. As a track star, Tank has been courted by the league. But he's already said he's happier, just working at home in *their* businesses, so he can raise his daughter.

"I just want season tickets from y'all, just like Ajay did for me," he says and laughs while June and Rich promise him he'll get them.

"No matter where we are. You're getting tickets," June promises.

"A plane ticket to the game too," Rich adds.

With a little pressure from Pearl and Jo, Tank and Nina have decided to remain in Cleveland, instead of moving to Atlanta. They've acquired some property from Jason Carr, by way of Mr. Parkwood. They are building a home. It isn't far from the street where they both grew up, in Shaker Heights. But it's far enough away, that they'll have to drive.

"I want Jerica to have the same life we did, without all the illegal stuff," Tank says as everyone laughs.

"Man, you've grown up," Chill says.

Him and Renee are still heading the meetings. The crew aren't willing to let them out of their leadership roles, too easily.

"Since I'll be here full time, after May," Tanks says, "We're gonna do an arcade and dance club when I get back up here. That'll be for the under age crew. We'll have a snack bar and video game tournaments. Then they won't have to be at the main club, at all. I'll manage that one."

"How about we design it exactly like the adult one?" Renee offers, "And instead of an exotic club on the second floor, that's where the arcade can be. *And* a tutoring room, where the adult card lounge is in the main club."

"Yes and the first floor for dancing," Nina says, "Just like the big spot. The third floor VIP, over looking the other two."

"And offices on the third floor, in both," Tank adds, "But we need concessions in the kid's spot, where the bars are in the main club."

"Oh for sure. Because they won't be able to buy from the bar and grill, like the older crowd because of the alcohol," Renee adds speaking of another business they're opening, now that John has retired from the road.

"We're going to lock this muthafucka *down*," Chill adds as they all laugh.

Then him and Renee smile. For them, it's their crew's way of saying they don't want them to *ever* retire. By doing a separate club for Lil Kenny and

127

his crew to go to, says they still want them around. Chill and Renee really didn't want to retire, no more than any one else wanted them too. So they're pleased with the new proposal. The entire family approves of it too.

"The crew will always change, for the better of the crew," papa says when they call and tell him.

As the close of the college basketball season draws near, Ebony, T-baby and their UC team plan to get an NCAA nod. They're favored to go to the big dance. T-baby is even more excited because now that Rich's season is over, they can bring their son to Cincinnati to live. He's returning with them on Monday, March 10th.

Ajay and the Heat seem playoff bound, at this point. March is a busy month for the crew, with a lot of major things happening.

John drives 1 more road trip to Houston. The 1st week of March, John, his brother Greg, Al and Brian Sr move big mama and poppa, back to Cleveland. They're going to live with papa and become an intricate part of the restaurant. Big mama will be in charge of planning the menus. She's looking forward to cooking her famous recipes, alongside of her friends. She's fully recovered from her bouts with breast cancer and is more than ready to move back. Her 1st granddaughter is getting married, this year. And with a wedding as large as this 1 is suppose to be, they're going to start preparations, this spring. Ron, Carolyn and their 3 children bought the Houston property from poppa and big mama.

"I want to keep it in the family," poppa says, "And they're family." Ebony is so excited to have big mama in Cleveland.

"Now you can *really* help us plan our wedding," she says.

"Baby girl, I wouldn't miss that for the world," big mama tells her.

]March 8, 1997[

Ajay is playing in Cleveland tonight. Him and Ebony are having a nice conversation, as they prepare to leave for Gund Arena.

"We're gonna miss the Soul Train awards," he says, "But I'm taping it."
His entire crew and any family who aren't working, are going to his game. Ebony's team doesn't start their conference play until Wednesday, which is the reason she's home.

"Will you be able to make it to one of my games, before the season ends?" she asks.

"I don't know yet," he says, "If not, I'll catch you in North Carolina at the NCAA tournament."

128

His professional schedule is tight and he's always on the go. They haven't seen each other since the 1st Friday of the year.

"It's gonna be alright, baby girl," he says, "You and me, we're gonna be alright. And I'm so glad I get to see big mama when I come home now. That's *still* my dog."

They laugh hard.

The Heat win and eat at *The Crews House of Soul Food* again. The grandparents go all out on the menu again.

"We got authentic big mama's soul food in here, now," Chill says.

Ebony and Ajay go straight to mama Jo's house, after they eat. They turn off their phones and go to bed. Tank and Nina are staying at Pearl's until their home is finished. The younger crew have command of the apartment at the U. Ajay doesn't want to try sleeping out there. Not with all the traffic they have, in and out.

The following morning when Ajay and Ebony wake up, they're planning to take a shower, then watch the video tape of the Soul Train awards. Ajay has gotten up and gone straight to the bathroom. While Ebony takes over his pillow and his side of the bed. She's feeling lazy as she grabs the remote and turns on the TV. That's when she see some very disturbing news. She notices a ticker scrolling across the bottom of the TV scene and calls Ajay, to come back and see it. He does.

"Ah man," he says as his face goes sad, "Another legend, Gone."

Christopher Wallace aka *The Notorious B.I.G* had been murdered in Los Angeles. They call Rob and Jan, immediately.

"We went to the awards," Rob says, "We couldn't even get into that after party. Because it is too packed with major *celebs*. So we went to another one."

"We heard about it, right after it happened," Jan adds, "He got shot while riding in a suburban with his crew. He died at Cedar Sinai, later. That tore me up when I got the news, y'all."

She's on the other extension. She starts to cry while she's talking about it. They can tell by her voice, she's been crying a lot. B.I.G. is her favorite rapper. She feels like he was the greatest of all time and Rob agrees.

"He was definitely original," Ajay says, "This is fucked up."

"First *Eazy*. Then *Pac*," Ebony says, "Now *Biggie*. What's the world coming too? Hip Hop will never be the same for me."

"I wonder how our hometown thugs are holding up?" Ajay offers, "They were friends with all three of them."

"This is a sad day for Hip Hop," Rob adds.

129

TIME TO LOVE-RELOADED-TIME WILL REVEAL 3

The March celebration has a light attendance. Ajay, Ebony and T-baby, all have games on the road where Nina is cheering. Rich, June and Rebbie are in New York at the NFL draft with Jb and their parents.

June goes to the Baltimore Ravens at 29 million for 5 years. Rich gets selected by the New York Jets at 20 million for 5 years.

Later this month, Nina and Tank celebrate 1 year of marriage. Their new home is almost finished but not until early June.

In April, Lynn celebrates her 24th birthday, down in Atlanta. Her and Jb are looking forward to the birth of their son. Her due date is April 24th. Pearl and Jo plan to be in Atlanta for the birth of their 2nd grandchild and 1st grandson. Jo is starting to worry because Lynn isn't closer to her and home.

"Lynn, I wished you lived closer," Jo says during 1 of their many phone calls. She adds, "So I can be there to help you."

"I know, ma," Lynn says, "But we really like living down south."

"I'll never get to see my *only* grandson."

"Ma, we visit Cleveland, at least once a month," Lynn offers, "You'll get to see him."

"Pearl and I will be there on the twenty first," Jo says, "And we're staying until he arrives. Alright?"

"Okay. That sounds perfect," Lynn says as she gasps for breath. She's miserable, at this point. She's just tired of being pregnant.

"I have three weeks to go until I'm due. I'm really nervous."

"Lynora, there's nothing to be nervous about," Jo says, "The baby does all of the work, really. You just need to push when your doctor tells you too. That's about it."

"But Nina says it hurts, a lot," she tries.

"Every pregnancy is different," she says, "You may have an easier time, then she did. Or you may have a harder time. You can never predict how it's gonna go."

June and Rebbie are going to Dr. Weston, every week. Their due in less than a month. Rebbie has gotten all of her classes in order. She'll have time to finish the semester before the baby comes. Unless she comes early. Their ultrasound revealed they're having a baby girl. Rena and Brenda have bought so many things for their new granddaughter, already. And her Cincinnati nursery room is packed to the hilt, just waiting for her arrival.

130

TIME TO LOVE-RELOADED-TIME WILL REVEAL 3

Ebony and T-baby's team advance to the sweet 16 before they're eliminated by *Stanford*. Bre and her Tech team lost in the 1st round. Ajay and the Heat are in the playoffs, best of 5 series. They lead 2-1 and will play game 4, tomorrow in Miami. Ebony wishes she could go but she has to study for her finals. Ajay made her promise she would maintain the Dean's list, this year too. They haven't seen each other since mid-March, when he'd shown up in Durham for her 1st and 2nd round games. Even then, they didn't have much quality time. He had to leave for Detroit, almost immediately after her win which advanced them to the sweet 16. They survive on phone calls, at every break they each get.

"I miss you, baby," she says as they share a brief mobile call.

"I miss you too, baby girl," he says, "But if we keep winning. You can come see me play after your semester ends. If we don't, I'll be home shortly afterwards. Okay?"

"Okay. As if I have much of a choice."

He had been voted to the All-Rookie team at the all-star break. He was also in the 3-point shootout, where he was 4th runner up. The Heat win their 1st round and advance to play the *Charlotte Hornets*. While Ajay focuses on the new series while missing everybody at home, Ebony studies at UC and aces her finals. Then she starts the preparations for their big wedding day.

While Ebony is getting ready to become Ajay's wife, Angel is in prison making moves to foil Ajay's life plan. And still, there are more additions for the crew.

"Hey, Ajay. What's up, bro?" Lynn asks from *Grady* hospital in Atlanta.

"Not much. Just getting ready to pull this series with Charlotte, even at one," he says, "What's good with you?"

"I just wanted to call and tell you that you're a new uncle."

"Ah *man*! I wanted to be there, sis," he says.

"I know. But we couldn't wait for you to finish playing," Lynn says and giggles, "He just decided to come on today."

"You know I'm about to go and buy him a lot of stuff. I'll send it out to you," he says.

"When are you coming to see him?" Lynn asks.

"Before I go to Cleveland," he says, "I have to get Ebony a ticket, today. So she can meet me for game three, in Miami. While she's in Miami, she can get us tickets to Atlanta."

"Seems like she's really doing well, with this separation thing."

"Not really. It's just that we've both been busy, these last two

131

months," he says, "Now that her semester is ending, she's ready to come see me. And I'm ready to see her too," he adds and laughs.

"That's what I'm talking about, brother," Lynn says as she smiles, "Are you still keeping those groupies at bay?"

She knows her brother loves Ebony and Ebony loves him. He has also told her about all the women who have been approaching him, now that he's an NBA All-Star. But he's been *pretty close* to faithful. He hasn't fallen for the gold diggers and traps, he's been up against since coming into the league.

"You know I'm use to being sought after," he says and they share another laugh.

They talk for much of the early morning, before he has to go to a team meeting at 7am.

Jb has barely lost sight of his new son, since his birth. He's been holding him, nearly the whole 2 hours of his life.

NAME: John Brown III
BORN: May 12, 1997
TIME: 4:15AM
WEIGHT:8lbs 6ounces
HEIGHT:25 Inches

Jo, Al, Pearl and John are in Atlanta for the delivery. They are 4 very proud grandparents.

"Mama, he's a big boy, right?" Jb asks.

"Yes," Pearl says as she admires her 1st grandson. She's finally gotten a chance to hold him, as she says, "He's almost as big as you were."

"Yea son. You weighed nine pounds and was already two feet long, when you came here," big John adds.

Pearl and Jo call the crew to give everyone the news.

"How is she?" big mama asks, from Cleveland.

"She's doing fine, mama," Pearl says, "She's tired and ready for some sleep. But she did fine."

All the family back in Cleveland make plans to visit Jb and his family, in Atlanta, as soon as possible.

Ajay will be in Cleveland for the May celebration, the same night of Kim's graduation from MLK. Kim signed a full basketball scholarship to Ohio State, last month, where Bruce will be a Sophomore. But before the

132

celebration and after the Charlotte series ends, Ajay and Ebony go to Atlanta with Tank and Nina. Jerica stays in Cleveland with Jo and Pearl, who have returned home.

Ajay and Ebony take lots of presents for their new nephew. They had also brought CJ with them, which makes Bre and Ced, very happy.

"I've been missing my baby," Bre says.

CJ has been staying with Deb and Jackie in Cleveland, until Bre finishes at Tech. Her and Ced will bring CJ back to Cleveland when they return, along with Ajay, Ebony, Tank and Nina for the celebration. Lynn and Jb won't make it this month. Neither will June and Rebbie, as it so happens.

When Rebbie told Ebony, the day before, that she didn't care when her little girl came. Just as long as it was soon. She sure didn't expect she would cause her to loose sleep. For the last 24 hours, Rebbie's been dealing with pain and discomfort. Her labor starts early, the morning of the 23rd.

"Baby, I think my water broke," she says to June, when she wakes him right back up at 2am.

"What?!" he says as he jumps up, still groggy.

"I can't stop peeing, baby," she says.

"Let me call doctor Weston, right now," he says.

First, he grabs the clock radio and starts trying to dial it. Rebbie takes it out of his hand and replaces it with his cell phone, after she starts the call.

"It's ringing, baby," she says.

She's in pain again as she gets up out of bed and goes to the bathroom.

"*She said for us to head to the hospital!*" June shouts through the bathroom door.

"Call, mama," Rebbie tells him.

They've been staying at Jr and Tonya's home, while designing their new house, right next door to Tank and Nina's.

"I am," June says, "That's who I'm calling, now. And mama too."

"Are you sure you're not setting the alarm?" she asks, still trying to be humorous even though she's in pain.

He doesn't offer an answer. He just laughs. Then after he's off the phone, he gets her bag and puts it in the car.

"Take your time, baby," he says, "I got the car ready to go."

She comes out and gets into the Camry. They head for East General.

"I see you decided to bring my car," she says with a smirk.

"I didn't want all that water in the *Legend*," he says with a smile.

He's nervous but he isn't so gone that he doesn't think about his car.

What man ever is, that nervous?

133

"Whatever," she says.

She rolls her eyes at him, right before another contraction hits. He tries to help her with her breathing but she's screaming so loud, he just drives on to the hospital in silence.

Rena and Brenda arrive at the hospital, just after them. Ebony, Nina and T-baby arrive within the hour.

"How are you, kid?" Nina asks.

Rebbie isn't in the mood to talk. Her girls stay with her while Rena goes to call Archie Sr to tell him how Rebbie's doing. He's getting ready to come to the hospital. She tells him, Rebbie has been having painful contractions but she hasn't dilated past 4 centimeters. Big Archie heads to the hospital and Brian Sr comes with him. They arrive later in the morning, hoping the baby will be already born. Archie doesn't want to see his daughter in pain and Brian Sr doesn't want to witness his son pass out.

"She's been in active labor for 4 hours. She isn't progressing. Doctor Weston is going to have to take it," Brenda tells her husband.

Rebbie can't go any longer without dilating. Her water is long gone when Dr. Weston takes her to surgery. She gives birth to a beautiful baby girl on the 23rd day of May. She had to have a C-section delivery. Proud father big June, has *Baltimore Ravens* cigars for everyone. Even the hospital staff members get one. He also has *Baltimore Ravens* paraphernalia all over Rebbie's room, before she's even moved to it.

NAME: Orian Chanel James [*O-Ryan*]
BORN: May 23, 1997
TIME:7:02AM
WEIGHT:8lbs 9ounces
HEIGHT:20 Inches

"Man, this hurts," Rebbie says of her fresh C-section cut.

It's noon and she's been moved to her private room. She's chatting it up with her girls. They leave everyone else admiring lil Orian Chanel James, so they can have foursome time.

"Kid, just rest, okay?" Ebony suggests, "We're gonna be here and we can get whatever it is you need."

June has gone back to the nursery with Ajay, Tank and Rich.

"Man, y'all trying to show me up, ha?" Ajay asks as he looks at little Orian.

134

TIME TO LOVE-RELOADED-TIME WILL REVEAL 3

He has that longing he had when he saw Jerica, Rich III and John III.
"You're gonna have to get it right, dog," Tank says as they laugh.
Ajay smiles, only briefly. He's thinking about Ebony, who most likely feels the same way he does. All of her girls have babies and all of her girls are married. She's still childless and only engaged. He had already decided when they do get married, he's going to make sure it's the most special day of her life. And they'll start on their family, right away. But before any of that can happen, they have to know each other, completely. They have to be open and honest about everything. He needs to know why does him putting his finger in her, cause such a dramatic reaction. They've been a couple for 10 years. They have beaten down 1 conflict after another. But that one thing still exist. He's going to fix it before they wed. She had nightmares before Raymond White attacked her. Those nightmares have became more severe since the attempt on her life which took the life of their 1st born. His protective instinct makes it mandatory that he make it go away. At this point, it doesn't even matter what it is. Nothing can make him not want her or take care of her. *Nothing.* Besides, he has an issue of his own that he wants to get off of his chest. So they really need to talk. They need some alone time. This weekend is as good of a time as any. Because he's more anxious than ever to be her husband and a father. He's confident that she's still just as eager to be his wife and the mother of his children.

He leaves the hospital with only 1 thing on his mind. His future bride and her peace of mind. He rents a suite at the Fillmore Hotel, for a very special weekend. It has to be the perfect setting. He arranges with the concierge to have champagne, strawberries and a special candle-lit dinner.
"What time would you like this, sir," the concierge asks.
"Eight pm."

When they leave the hospital, Ebony, T-baby and Nina go shopping for Rebbie and Orian. They take all of the gifts to Jr and Tonya's house. June and Rebbie will stay on there until their home is finished. Their home will be finished by Rebbie's birthday. Rich and T-baby have a home going up, across the street from Rebbie and Nina. It'll be ready in July. Rich and June will be in NFL training camps, by then. Them and Tank graduate from UC this July, with new homes to move into. They ride by the site of the new homes, after leaving Jr's. Ebony picks out a spot for her and Ajay's home, then they head back to the hospital to have lunch with Rebbie.

Welcome to the world, John Brown III & Orian Chanel James.

135

TIME TO LOVE-RELOADED-TIME WILL REVEAL 3

Ajay visits Chill, at The Chill Spot, as he's going over last nights reports, while Ebony spends time with her girls. While he's there, Chill tells him about the many calls they still receive at the club, from Angel.

"You've *gotta* be kidding," Ajay says, "*Still?* Since the first time?"

"Every time something major happens with you or this crew," Chill says, "She calls here. Ajay, I got some folks keeping tabs on her, inside. She's really trying to find someone who can get to you."

"Get to me, how?" he asks.

"The bitch still wants you and she still wants to get rid of Ebony."

"Then why don't we just get rid of her?" Ajay asks.

"Do you really wanna do that?"

"She still wants to kill my wife," he says, "Hell fuck yea, I do."

"She ain't got no power," Chill says, "But I'll keep tabs on it. If she gets out of hand, I'll have her *and* the wannabe lovers, knocked off. They got her fooled like they can fuck with crew, just to fuck her. How's that?"

"Perfect," Ajay says, "Until then, don't mention that bitch to me. Unless it's the killing hour."

"Got it."

As afternoon turns to late afternoon, Ajay calls Ebony on her cell phone. He has plans for them, tonight. Not even the anger he has about Angel still scheming, can take his mind off of making sure Ebony is secure.

"Where are you, baby?" he asks.

"I'm back at the hospital with Rebbie."

"Do you have plans for tonight?"

"I'm spending it with you. I don't know where," she smiles, "Do you wanna stay at mama's tonight? Or mama Jo's?"

"Neither," he says, "I've got something else in mind."

"What are you up too, baby?" she asks as she giggles.

"Just keeping a smile on my baby's face," he says, "I'll pick you up at seven thirty, from mama P's house. Alright? And wear something sexy." She smiles. She has no idea what he has planned but she has butterflies. She knows with her man planning it, it'll be a very special night. She can't wait.

He picks her up, promptly at 7:30. By 8pm sharp, they're being served dinner in their suite at the Fillmore. After signing an autograph for the room service attendant and giving him a healthy tip, Ajay closes the door and locks it.

"We won't be leaving here until tomorrow night, baby girl,"

136

he says, "The next twenty four hours of your time, belong to me."

"I have no problems with that," she says and smiles.

They eat dinner over very stimulating wedding conversation. He's trying to find out what would be the perfect wedding for her.

"I want a rainbow wedding," she says.

"What's that?"

"I want all the colors *of the rainbow* to be our wedding colors."

"Okay. What else?" he asks as he smiles.

"I want mama Rena to sing a song. Daddy and of course, my girls *have* to sing something."

He's taking mental notes of all the special request she makes. Unbeknownst to Ebony, he had the opportunity to meet *Mariah Carey* after a *Knicks* game. He was surprised to find out, she is a fan of his. She told him she has a home in Miami and has kept up with his accomplishments since he was at UC. They exchanged contact information, the same night. Since then, he's told Mariah about Ebony and how much she loves her music. He also told her about the upcoming nuptials and that it would be a perfect gift to Ebony, if she could somehow manage to sing at their wedding. Mariah told him she would definitely try to fit it into her schedule. If she can do a song, that will be his special gift to his new bride. But it will be a surprise for her, as well.

"How many people are we inviting?" he asks.

"I don't even know," she says, "Mama and big mama have ordered a thousand invitations."

"That's big," he says.

"Is that *too* many, Anthony?" she asks.

"No. Not if that's what you want," he says, "Just as long as you're there. I don't care who else show up," he adds and they both laugh.

"I'm gonna design the program and I want it to have all the colors of the wedding," she says with a smile, "It's gonna be *so* pretty."

"Whatever you want, baby girl. Just remember that," he says, before asking her, "How do you feel about all of your girls having babies now and we don't have one?"

"It's a little sad but I love all the new babies. I wanna baby sit for each of them, every chance I get."

"I really do want kids, baby," he says, "After seeing Jerica, then lil Rich, lil John and now, Orian," he says, "I really feel like somebody's missing from that crew."

"I know what you mean," she says as she looks into his eyes, "But

137

we've decided to wait until after we're married, through with school and have our home finished. I'm willing to stick to that."

"They're having a hard time trying to spend *quality* time with each other and the babies," he says, "They don't get to see the kids, that much."

"That's true and I don't wanna ever have to leave our kids."

"I don't want to have to be away from you or our baby, when it does come," he says, "I'm already in Miami. I didn't want you to be at Natty and our child be here, like they have to do. That's why I really know we should wait and that's why I waited."

"Me too," she agrees.

"I want to include Terrell and aunt Jessica," he says. Then he jokes, "So he can see what he missed out on."

She giggles at him and says, "He knew then that I didn't like him. You're the only boy I've liked, in my whole life. So this really is a fairy tale. And I agree," she says with a smile, "I want them to be apart of our special day. I know big Al would like that too."

"Then it's set," he says, "A thousand people."

"Anthony, you're a celebrity," she says, "You have so many colleagues, sponsors, teams and crew too. It could be more."

"I might pass out, up there," he says and laughs, "What then?"

"We'll revive you," she says as she laughs too. Then she says, "And we'll keep right on going. I'm marrying you and you don't wanna be on TV fainting. That's really not gangster, baby."

They laugh hard. He gives her a kiss, then he stares at her for a few seconds. She smiles shyly. He admires her gorgeous smile with that little hint of innocence. He absolutely loves and adores this woman. And he will go through fire to make her happy.

"So what colors will we have?" he asks.

"I want gold, blue, red, green. Your favorite color *purple* and of course, white for us," she says, "Purple will be the base color for the big crew. Lavender for the junior crew. Pastels, like bright yellow, baby blue, pink and mint for the junior party. And you know April and Yolanda have to be bridesmaids. It's gonna be a big event."

He smiles at her and says, "It's gonna be big, anyway. A thousand people."

"Since it's going to be on New Year's Eve, what time should we start the ceremony?" she asks.

"At least by four o'clock," he says, "So we can be done with our part of the reception, two hours before midnight. I want to bring in the New Year with my new wife, alone. That's my *only* demand."

138

TIME TO LOVE-RELOADED-TIME WILL REVEAL 3

She smiles and says, "That sounds perfect."

"So where are we going on our honeymoon?" he asks.

"Baby, I'm leaving that up to you," she says, "Since the bride gets to plan the wedding. I think the groom should plan the honeymoon. Especially my *ever ready* groom."

"Alright. I got that. But it's gonna be a surprise," he says, "We're doing something different for our honeymoon. We can take the cruise when it's warmer."

"Okay. It'll be *too cold* to be on a ship, in January," she says with a smile.

"As long as you bring that smile with you. I'm gonna stay warm."

He gets up and walks over to her side of the table and reaches for her hand. "Dance with me," he says.

She takes his hand and they dance in the middle of the room. He plants several kisses on her face before moving in for a long passionate kiss.

"I love you so much, baby girl," he says effortlessly.

"That sounds so good when you say it," she says with a smile, as she looks into his eyes.

He use to find it hard to say, I love you. But he has said it to her, a lot over the phone, since first going to college in Cincinnati and even more since being drafted to Miami. He has become very comfortable, not only saying it to her but also showing her how much he loves her. They continue to dance as he leads her to the bedroom, undressing himself and her, along the way. By the time they arrive at the foot of the bed, they're totally nude. He's going to work his way to finding out the cause of her trauma and he knows he's going to have to go there, just once more. As he lays her down, ever so gently, he gives her body kisses as her breathing increases.

"I know you and your girls been talking about the *Red Light Special*. But I'm still saving that for the honeymoon."

She smiles as they reminisce about the time, 2 years ago, when her and her girls were practicing to perform the song, at 1 of their celebrations. She was singing it at his apartment and it caught his attention. She remembers not even knowing what the song meant and him having to explain it to her. She also remembers how embarrassed she was after learning that she had been singing a song about something, she knew absolutely nothing about.

"You will though," he says to her, "We're gonna teach each other. But not until after we get married."

He continues kissing her neck and breast, while his fingers probe her body. They have to discuss her sensitivity issue. He's going to get it out front and

139

hopefully, get it over with forever, tonight. He loves her and she loves him. He wants her to know she can tell him anything. That's 1 of the things he can't rest until he knows. He continues kissing her as he rubs her clitoris, vigorously. He eases 1 finger inside of her and she rejects him, as he'd expected. But he didn't realize how quickly it would unfold. But it does. Tonight, she has a full recollection of the incident she had once blocked out. It has been coming back to her in large portions since her car accident. This time, she remembers it all. And this time, he wants to know what caused it and he wants to know now.

"I just don't like it," she tries, like she has tried before but he can see something different in her eyes.

He can tell she's disturb by the memory. He knows she has a real reason because she's trembling. Like she did the first days and weeks after the Raymond attack. But now, she just doesn't *want* to tell him because she doesn't think he'll understand or love her anymore. He won't accept that answer. Not this time. He wants her to be free. To not be afraid of going to sleep or of his intimate touch. He wants to know the story behind it. He has to know it now.

"Baby, we're getting married, seven months from now," he says, "I don't want there to be any secrets between us."

"There aren't any secrets between us," she tries again.

This time he lifts her chin, pulls her face to his and looks into her eyes.

"Then tell me what is it about me putting my finger inside you, that makes you freak out. Please, baby," he says desperately, "Let me know what it is, so I can help you."

"I don't know if I should tell you or if I *can* tell you," she says, "You may not like me after you hear it."

Now he really wants to know and he isn't going to sleep until he does.

"Try me," he says, "Just tell me, baby. *Please*. Because I know it's something. Chill and my daddy know you're uncomfortable with it. But I don't know. I'm your man. I love you, Ebony. Please don't shut me out."

"Okay, baby. I'll tell you," she starts, "But promise me you want leave me after I do."

"Nothing can make me leave you," he says, "I know you're not a boy. I've been down there, already. That's the only thing that could've changed my mind about you, before we was intimate. So just say it."

"You're not the first man that touched me," she says bluntly.

He's confused now but more concerned. Who's been intimate with his girl?

"Who?" he asks.

140

TIME TO LOVE-RELOADED-TIME WILL REVEAL 3

She begins to tell him the story of the tragedy that happened to her at big Paul's house, when she was 6 years old. It was on the day that Neal Palmer was killed. Neal Palmer was a male friend of her parent's crew. He still lived with his parents in the house that use to be on the other side of big John and Pearl. It's a vacant lot now. Owned by big John and Pearl. Neal Palmer use to attend their parties, card games, cookouts and all but he was never crew. He hung around because he always wanted to be crew. No one ever allowed him membership, much like the Cleveland whores, the 4 admirers, Eddie, Jake and the Raymond's of the present crew's reign.

"Do you remember when Chill went to training school for killing Mr. Neal?"

"Yea. He was beating up Chill. Chill got big Paul's gun and shot his ass," Ajay says, assuming the story he got back in 1982 was the real one. But he's about to find out what *really* happened.

He says, "Just lay back, relax and tell me."

She lays down next to him. They both stare at the ceiling fan and she begins the unveiling.

"Early that day, I went over big Paul's house to get Chill to play basketball with me," she says, "You know he use to teach me how to shoot. Before I started playing basketball with you, right?"

"Right."

"Well when I went inside the house, Chill was upstairs getting ready to take a shower. Big Paul and your dad had just went to the store to get some more drinks. Mister Neal was waiting for them, so they could play domino's. I went in the kitchen to get a freezer cup, like we all use to do. Mister Neal followed me in there. He started talking to me. He gave me some money for candy. He ask me for a thank you hug. I gave him a hug. But he kept holding me for a long, long time," she says as her voice cracks.

Ajay can already tell this story is going to anger him. Not at her. But he's already feeling anger as he urges her to continue.

"Then he was telling me, I was a pretty little girl and all of that stuff. He started rubbing my hair with his hand and touching my legs. And ...., and then he put his hand in my shorts. I was so scared. But he kept telling me......, it was okay.. he was my *special* friend and he always gives me money to buy candy," she can barely speak, at this point, as the tears come.

Ajay feels the sting of tears in his eyes and more anger in his heart. He rolls over on his side and looks directly at her. She has gone so deep into the past that she doesn't even notice when he moves. He knows this is her first full recollection of this event since elementary school. Because even after the

141

Raymond attack, she didn't turn pale. In this memory, she's a defenseless little kid. Blind to the cruel motherfuckers of the world, who ally themselves with pillars of the community and the wholesome folks. So they can prey on some unsuspecting child. Ajay watches Ebony as she clinches her knees together. Tightening the muscles in her thighs and in her jaws, as they lay on the bed together. She's wringing wet with sweat and wiping her hands together as if there's dirt there that only she can see and can't rub off. Even when he reaches and takes her hands into his and kisses her cheek, she doesn't acknowledge it. She has gone back there. He can see it in her eyes. This had been a very traumatic experience for her. One she had completely locked out in an attempt to have a normal life with him. She had just recently recalled it. He can tell by the pain on her face and in her eyes, she wishes she could've left it buried. But it wouldn't stay there. It couldn't stay there. The trauma of loosing their baby had caused her to revisit the worst tragedy of her life. This 1 marred her innocence and shattered her ability to be completely open with males. Or intimately free. Ajay wishes he could just hold her and let her cry herself to sleep. But not now. Not tonight. He wants to know the whole story so they can bury it once and for all, together. The same way they had done with her most recent vile natured waste of an egg and sperm union, Raymond White.

"It's okay, baby. Just go on," he says as he tries to reassure her.

"I told him, my daddy said…, never let nobody touch my private. But he said my daddy………, just didn't want me to have friends and he was my friend. He was touching my private……, his fingers and then……, he,…..,he…..., he tried to put his finger in me…., it hurt…," she says as she cries harder and he holds her close to him.

He encourages her to breath and take her time. After a few minutes, she's able to continue. She rolls over into him and puts her ear next to his heart. She says, "I pulled away and I ran upstairs to Chill's room and locked the door. The same room that you use to sleep in. You know that was Chill's room before big Paul died," she says as he listens intensely without saying a word and his heart breaks as she goes on.

"Mister Neal came upstairs to try to find me but then Chill was coming out of the bathroom. He came to his bedroom door and it was locked. I could hear him asking *'How did my door get locked?'* That's how mister Neal knew I was in there. He told Chill I was in there and that I had come over and come up the stairs. So….., Chill starts knocking on the door and calling my name. At first………., I didn't open it because I was just……, just scared. Then,………….., I opened the door. Chill and mister Neal was

142

both standing there. I start crying, loud," she says as she can barely breath. "Hold on a minute, baby girl. Take your time. Okay?" he says, "It's alright. Nobody can hurt you now. *Nobody* is gonna hurt you again." She continues, "Chill was asking me what was wrong with me. Mister Neal was telling him to send me back downstairs, so he could get dressed. But Chill told him no. He told him I wasn't gonna go downstairs and he already had on his shorts, so it was okay if I stayed in there with him. He told mister Neal to leave because I seem to be scared with both of them there. Mister Neal looked at me, real mean like. Then he put his finger over his mouth, trying to tell me not to tell Chill. Then he slowly leaves the room but he kept looking back at me, *real* mean. Chill was putting on his shirt, so..., he didn't see him doing that. I was still crying and Chill wanted to know what was wrong with me. Finally, I just told him after I stopped crying, a little bit. I just told him. I remember Chill got so mad. But big Paul wasn't back yet. Chill told me to stay in his room while he went downstairs. I could hear him cursing at mister Neal." She looks up at Ajay, then continues, "Baby, that made me happy because Chill was taking up for me. He was fussing with mister Neal. Then mister Neal got mad at him and...., called him a little bitch. That must be how the fight started because I could hear them fighting. They was scuffling. I came out of that room and I ran downstairs. Mister Neal was beating Chill up, real bad. I didn't know what to do," she says as she cries uncontrollably.

Ajay allows her get it out but holds her tighter. She's now wedged so close to him that he's shaking from her body trembling. He wipes her face, looks into her eyes and ask if she's okay. She nods her head and goes on. Now she just wants this monkey off of her back. She wants him to know, so he can protect her from even the memory of it.

"Chill is like my big brother and I didn't want him to get hurt, no more. So, so I remember he......, he had showed me where big Paul keep one of his guns. In the living room closet. I ran and got it. I wanted to give it to Chill but mister Neal had him pinned down on the floor......, just beating him," she says, "I couldn't help him. I was so scared......., if mister Neal beat him up, so bad that he couldn't get up. Then mister Neal would......, he would hurt me again," she says.

"But Chill did get up, right?" he asks, trying to help her along, "He did get to the gun and he shot him, so he couldn't hurt you no more. It's okay."

"No Anthony! You don't know what happened!" she yells all of a sudden, as he looks at her for clarity.

143

TIME TO LOVE-RELOADED-TIME WILL REVEAL 3

"Chill didn't shoot mister Neal! I did!" she yells as she continues to cry. He still holds her close to him and she continues to tremble.

"Baby girl, it's okay," he says as he tries to comfort her. He starts to cry himself, as he says, "You did what you had to do. Chill was being hurt because he was *protecting you* from being hurt. You *protected him.* That's *all* you did."

She can't speak as she lays in his arms and they both cry. Ajay is so angry. He knows Mr. Neal is already dead. He knows he had been killed that day. But he had no idea that Chill hadn't been the one to shoot him.

"So my daddy know the truth too, ha?" he asks.

"Yes. Right after I shot the gun," she starts again, "That's when big Al and big Paul had just walked in the house with their bags. Mister Neal fell on top of Chill, then everything really got crazy. They was asking us what happened. But they both saw me with the gun. They knew that I had shot it because they was in the house," she says, "Big Al wanted to know what had happened and he was asking me. While big Paul helped Chill get up and he was asking Chill what was going on. Then Chill told them the whole thing. They got mad. *Real* mad. Madder than Chill was. Mister Neal was laying there but he was still talking and saying that I shot him. And telling big Paul and big Al that they're bad ass kids was fighting him and had the nerve to shoot him. He wasn't even close to dead but big Paul and big Al......, they had finished killing him. They beat him, so bad and choked the rest of his life, ..., and breath, out of him," she finishes.

Ajay is stunned but proud. And in a way, pleased. All of his life he had known his own father was protective of Ebony and he didn't really know why. But that made him feel like he had to be too. He knew John was on the road, all the time and had asked Al to look out for his family while he was away. He thought his father was extra protective of her because she was a girl. He had no idea his father knew more about her, then even *he* did. Now he understands what his father meant when he said, '*she's gone through something in her young life that you might not be ready to accept or really understand.*' His father knew how he was about her being true to him and only touched by him. Al didn't think he was mature enough to be able to be compassionate and understand that this wasn't her fault. He isn't even sure if he could've understood it, back then. But he certainly does now. He's so proud of his father, right now. He did then, what Ajay wishes he could do now. Beat the shit out of this monster who was trying to steal his future. This *wasn't* her fault. She was just a little girl. As far as he's concerned, she's still his girl and *only* his. He's the only 1 that she has ever *allowed* to

144

touch her. There are still some things he wants to know. They both have managed to wipe back some tears. She still sobs, slightly but he can see that she's coming out of it. She'll have relief from that horrible day. In a way, he feels like he's protecting her right now by helping her to cleanse.

"Ebony, I love you," he says suddenly, as he looks into her eyes, "Hearing that don't change *anything* about us. If anything, it makes me feel closer to you. I just wish I would've been there to protect you, then."

"But you was almost eight," she says.

"I was doing big boy things, at eight," he says as he explains some of the things his father had told him when he 1st found out they were a couple. "It all makes perfect sense to me now," he says, "But how did Chill end up going to jail? Why didn't daddy and Paul go?"

"Big Paul and big Al sat me and Chill down. They explained to us how they would say it had all happened," she starts again, as she tells him the story that Al and Paul had told the police. "Big Al told me that he didn't want anybody to know that I'd been hurt like that. He said he didn't want nobody but the people in that house to know what *really* happened. They told me and Chill, they was gonna tell the police they had got in an argument over the dominoes game before going to the store. Him, Paul and mister Neal-"

"You don't have to call that muthafucka *mister,* no more, baby. He wasn't a man. He definitely don't deserve respect from you," Ajay says.

"Okay. Big Al, big Paul and ...., Neal had got into a fight over the game before big Al and big Paul went to the store. Chill had come in from playing basketball with me while they was arguing. And after they left, mister, I mean...., Neal had said something to Chill and Chill, knowing that his daddy had just argued with him, started arguing with him too. But Neal had jumped on Chill. They said that....., Chill and Neal got into a fight and that Neal had beat Chill up, pretty bad. Big Al and big Paul had come back from the store while Neal was beating up Chill. Al and Paul started to fight Neal to protect Chill but Chill was still angry. And he went to the closet and got the gun and shot Neal. They didn't think he would get any time because he was thirteen. But eventually, he did. I remember mister Wheeler was able to get him sent to a training school for young boys. Where he could still have school and all. And he wouldn't miss out on his education. He had to go there, for like-"

"Nine months," Ajay interrupts, "I know he went for nine months."

"Yes," she says, "And he never told the truth about it. He just went

145

and did his time. His nine months and said nothing. *My* time, really."

"Baby, you didn't have any time to do," Ajay says.

"If they had told the police what had really happened. Then Chill wouldn't have gotten any time, though," she says.

"Yeah but Paul would've," he says, "A lot of it and daddy too."

"I know, ha?"

He dries away the few tears that remain on her cheeks.

"So my daddy protected you and you protected him too, for all of these years," he says, "Nobody knows about what really happened except you, Chill, daddy, Neal and big Paul?"

"And you," she says, "But I had blocked it out until after I shot Raymond. Then I start seeing images of it. But it still didn't make sense to me. Not until after the accident. When I was out, I dreamed about it. That's why it hurt extra when I woke up and our baby was gone. It was like losing my innocence, all over again. I remember. I felt like I died then. I could see me in my dream, watching you on a plane. Then I saw me as a little girl, you as a little boy. Then both of us grown up, like older. I guess God put that there for a reason."

"So you would fight to stay alive, for me." he says as she looks at him, "I would've destroyed myself if you would've died, that day," he admits, "I know I would have. I was already thinking about it before I got there and saw you."

"I wasn't ready to go," she says, "Because I still had this secret that you didn't know." They look at each other.

"Paul and Neal are both dead now," he adds, "What about big John and mama P?"

"They don't know about it, still," she says, "If they do, they never said anything to me about it. Big Al probably never said anything. He just made sure you was good to me and patient. And Chill did too. But mama and daddy never said nothing."

"Well they wouldn't have, anyway. I don't think so," he says as he's digesting this revelation well. "I'll never leave you, Ebony," he says, "Never. And there's no way I would blame you for Neal or Raymond."

She finally smiles at him. She's relieved to know that her being abused as a child doesn't change his feelings about her. She had never understood that it really wasn't her fault. She felt like she should've known better than to go around Neal. But he wasn't a stranger. He attended all of their celebrations, parties, events and her church too. Anthony doesn't blame her. No one had. She can be okay now.

146

"Knowing about it, don't make you feel like you wasn't the first one to touch me though?" she asks.

"No."

"It doesn't change your mind about me? *Us?*" she asks.

"How *could* it?" he asks, "I've always protected you, haven't I?"

"Yes," she says, "You always do."

"And I always will," he says, "My daddy got it started."

He takes in all that she has just told him. He feels sad to know that she had been abused as a child and it definitely explains why she was always so withdrawn from everyone, for so long, back then. And she was always considered a special little girl. That's what his daddy always said. That's what made him notice her and start to like her. It's true. She is special. She's even more special to him, at this moment. He kisses her and asks, "When we was in the hotel room, after you shot Raymond, you said, *I feel like I've been here before.*"

"Yes," she says, "That's what I was talking about. I was gonna try and tell you then. But I couldn't get all my thoughts together. It all came back to me, after I died down in cliff ridge. I didn't remember it before that day. But I always knew I couldn't stand to be fingered like-"

"I won't do that to you, baby girl," he says, "Now that I know the reason. I'm sorry I ever tried too."

"Anthony, I want to be free with you," she says, "Remember what you did after Raymond?" she asks, "He put his mouth on my breast and I had to learn to get over that and I did with you. Cause you're the person who's suppose to help me to overcome things like this. That's why God let me trust you, so I could let you get close to me."

"Uh huh," he says, "But this ain't the same thing, baby."

" It is *too*, the same thing," she says, "It's directly related to that. I don't want to be haunted by him either, Anthony. I just don't want him to interfere with our lives. Not our sex lives. Nothing or nobody. Okay? Before I'm a wife and a mother," she says, "I just want to be free of it and you're the only one who can help me do that. Because I care so much about how you feel and what you say. Okay?"

He says, "Okay. But for now, I'm not gonna do it until you say it's okay."

"Alright, Anthony," she says, "I'm really glad I told you."

"I am too," he says, "I really wish I could go and dig his ass up and fuck him up, some more."

She laughs for the first time in hours, as she hugs and kisses him.

"Thank you," she says, "Thank you for showing me that a man can

147

love a woman and make her feel good about it," she says, "And it doesn't have to be something that makes her feel dirty. I've met women *and* girls, who have no idea what that feels like. I'm blessed."

"I did that?" he asks as he smiles.

"Yes you did that, baby," she says, "From day one, you did and you still do. You always let me know that sex is about me and how I feel when we're doing it. And I know that you care about me, as a person. I am *so* blessed."

They lay in each others arms, for a long time. Just talking and making plans for their life together.

She initiates sex in a way that he finds so sensuous. He's very turned on by her uninhibited actions. She takes his hand and places it on the part of her body that she wants him to touch. All of this, while making eye contact with him. Proving and showing him that she feels completely free, honest and okay with their intimacy. He realizes he has broken down the last wall that was up between them, for over 15 years. She sexes him good. He realizes that back when they was 6 and 8, and she treated him mean and said she *"couldn't stand him,"*. It wasn't because she didn't like him. It was because she probably thought he wanted to touch her like Neal had and she was afraid of that. How special he must be to her, for her to allow him the pleasure of touching her and becoming intimate with her, after what she has endured. He knows he has to love her forever. And it's going to be *only* his pleasure to do so.

He thought Chill had been the 1 to kill Neal, 2 weeks before Chill had turned 14. But in fact, it had been Ebony who shot him. Ebony had killed the 2 men, in her life, who had hurt her. Neal would have died anyway. Even if he hadn't been choked out. He was shot in the heart. Ajay knows she can kill to protect herself. He definitely knows he doesn't want to hurt her. *Ever.* He's even feeling more guilty for all of the Angel's, Debra Whitman's and Darlene's that she had to endure because of his selfishness. And still, with all that she had overcome to be with him, she still loves him unconditionally.

"Baby, you know what big mama always says right?" he asks.

"What's that?"

"Whatever don't kill you, makes you stronger," he says.

"Yes," she says with a huge smile.

"We're still living, baby girl," he says.

"And stronger than ever," she says as she nestles in his arms and goes fast asleep.

148

He watches her as she sleeps peacefully, for a change. While watching over her, he thinks of the things that he sees differently since her revelation. Then he picks up the phone and calls Chill.

"Hello," Chill answers.

"Hey man. Do me a favor?" Ajay asks Chill.

"Anything," Chill says.

"Call daddy, on three way," he says.

"Hold on," Chill says as he gets big Al on a 3-way phone hook up.

"Hello," Al says.

"Hey pops. What's up?" Ajay asks Al.

"Nothing much, son," Al says, "What's up with you?"

"I got your other son on the phone too. I'm downtown with Ebony, at the Fillmore, first of all," he says, "In case y'all are looking for us."

"Well, son. I'm happy for you. What's going on Kenny?" Al ask as he and Chill laugh first. Then Ajay laughs too.

"I just wanted to tell both of y'all thanks and I love you," he says.

"Wow," Chill says, "We know that already, man. But that's it?"

"Yea, that's it," Ajay says.

"What's *really* going on, man," Chill asks.

"She told him, Kenny," Al says.

Chill thinks for a few seconds, then he responds.

"Oh, okay! Now I get it," Chill says, "How do you feel now, bro?"

"I'm feeling like my whole life changed tonight," he says, "A lot of the things I thought I knew. I found out, I didn't. But now I know what I have to do. I understand why and I know, without a doubt I'm the man. I just had to call. I wanna tell both of you how much I appreciate all the things y'all have done for me and baby girl. And I know why y'all did it."

"Well, son. Now can you understand why I never wanted you to hurt her?" Al asks.

"Yes sir, I do," he says.

"I knew you liked her, son," Al says, "It was never a doubt, in my mind, from day one. How could you *not*? From the time you was five years old, I knew you was not going to be satisfied until you had her as your girlfriend," Al says, "John and me, we use to talk about it, all the time. It was a joint decision between he and I, for me to take on his father role when he was away. He knew she would like you too. Or at least, he wanted her too. Your mama and Pearl, they couldn't even think of y'all like that, back then. But I told John I'd groom you to be the man for her. I always saw her as my future daughter in law," Al says, "Did you know that?"

149

"No I didn't. I knew you always said she was precious and special," he says.

"And now you know why I always stayed on you about being real with her?" Chill asks.

"Yes, brother," Ajay says and smiles, "You did and I do."

"You know it all," Al says, "And still, I'll never mention it."

"Me either," Chill says, "But I'd do it again tomorrow, if I have too. That's what drove me mad about Raymond. Me knowing what she had come out of, to grow into a respectable young lady. And to know love and loyalty. She had blocked this shit out. I really believe that."

"She had," Ajay says, "She told me she had. It started coming back after Raymond. Then *all* the way back, after the car accident."

"I wanted his ass to pay for trying to take her innocence," Chill says, "She's rare. All of our girls in this family are wholesome," he says, "I have to do my part to keep it that way. Y'all feel that?"
They all agree and Chill says, "I'll take all of this to my grave. I'd do it again, to protect her, my brother."

"So will I, son," Al says.

"That's my job now," Ajay says, "And I'm not gonna slack on it. Not at all."

"I'm proud of you, Ant," Al says, "You've turned out exactly like I wanted and dreamed about. You're alright with me, you know that?"

"And me too," Chill says and laughs.

"I know y'all have our backs," Ajay says, "And we will definitely be alright!"
They hang up and he falls asleep, holding Ebony tight in his arms.

REST IN PEACE TO:

CHRISTOPHER "B.I.G." WALLACE
MARCH 9, 1997

We pray for your family in this time of grief.
The Hip Hop Nation grieves and will keep your name alive.
There will never be another NOTORIOUS B.I.G.

150

CHAPTER 28

……..THE MORE THINGS STAY THE SAME!

Ebony sleeps in on Saturday morning, until Ajay wakes her to say breakfast has arrived.

"What time is it?" she asks.

"Ten o'clock," he answers and smiles, "Get up, so you can have some breakfast. You slept *good*. The best I've seen you sleep, in awhile."

"I really did. I didn't even have *one* nightmare, all night," she says and smiles back, "It's been awhile since I could say that."

"Now I know it was because you was worried about how I would feel."

"I'm sorry I put you through that. Getting elbowed and all."

"It's all good," he says, "I go in the paint, a lot. You know when I cross over and drive the lane? I get bowed hard. I'm use to it."

They laugh as she gets out of bed and follows him into the bathroom for their dailies.

"They have everything in here, baby," she says as she surveys the bathroom, more carefully this time.

"That's how it is when you stay in a plush hotel," he says, smiling as he turns on the water for his sink.

He washes his face and brushes his teeth, along side of her, in the matching sinks as they stare at each other in the wall length mirror.

"I'm setting up our master bathroom just like this," he says, "With *his and her* everything."

"So are we getting a house in Cleveland or Miami?" she asks.

"Probably both," he says, "What do you think? Do you like the condo. Or would you rather look at a house?"

"I want to build the dream house in Cleveland. Out by the crew," she says, "You told me to look for a spot and I did. Do you *really* still have the house you was drawing when we was growing up? French Country style, as you called it."

"Yep. It was in my closet at mama's," he says, "With the master suite, ten bedrooms and a six car garage. Yes indeed, baby. I can afford it too." They both laugh. Then he says, "Big Archie doing the blueprints and I'm adding some more too it. It's a surprise." He chuckles.

TIME TO LOVE-RELOADED-TIME WILL REVEAL 3

"I always knew you would be able to get that house," she says as she smiles. "You've always been a hustler, baby. But for when we're in Miami, the condo *is* pretty big. We can just stay there."

"What about the kids?" he asks and laughs, "The condo is three bedrooms with bad scenery."

"We've got time before the kids come," she says, "Let's see how the Miami thing works out. The scenery isn't a factor. I'll make sure security do the job they get paid for, if I live there *with* children."

"That's my girl," he says, "Always thinking logically."

"I have my moments," she says and they laugh. And as they head over to the table for breakfast, she adds, "This is the life."

"It gets lonely though," he says with a sad look on his face.

"Not for long, baby," she says, "Soon, I'll be with you and you won't have to be by yourself or depend on the scenery either."

"No scenery or otherwise, has ever, nor will they ever have the benefit of laying me, where I lay my head," he says, "I was young and dumb when I took Anita to my room," he says with a laugh, "Not since then has that happened. And I redecorated it."

"Thank you, Chill," she says as she laughs.

"And me too, baby," he laughs, "I caught on, a long time ago."

"I have to admit. Nothing like that happened again," she says, "But the living situation-"

"Yea. But when I'm on the road, after the kids," he says, "You won't be able to travel with me, as much."

He cuts her off on the Darlene part. He'd rather not be reminded. She knows he did it, conscientiously too. They both laugh again.

"Okay. But don't be negative about the future things," she says, "Haven't we always managed to be together?"

"Yes we have," he says with a smile.

They eat their hearty breakfast, then shower. After they're dressed he says, "I need to talk to you too."

"About what?" she asks as they sit back down at the table.

He has 2 things he's battling with telling her. One has haunted him since he was a young teen. The other happened early in his sophomore year, at UC. But he's not ready to divulge that 1 because *she's* still attending there. It's a matter of something 1 of her teammates had done and still acts on. But he knows if he tell her, it's going to cause a riff within her team. She has enough to deal with, just getting though this year without him there. He isn't going to make it any harder. He'll tell her. But after she's done at UC.

152

TIME TO LOVE-RELOADED-TIME WILL REVEAL 3

They've talked sexual assaults enough, for 1 outing. For now, he's going to purge himself of, at least the teenage secret.

"Since you came clean, last night," he says, "I need to do the same."

"What do you have to come clean about?" she asks.

"A couple of things," he says.

"Like what," she probes.

"Cocaine," he admits.

"What about it?"

"I use to use it," he admits.

"*What*? *When*?"

"Nineteen Eighty nine. Jb's party and my fifteenth birthday?"

"Yes. Especially yours," she says as she reminisces about that *hell-of-a-night* when he had been sexually overbearing with her.

"I was on it, that night. *Bad*. And that day I was in my room with Anita and-"

"Baby, are you *serious*?"

"As a heart attack. The day I got shot, I was feigning for it," he admits, "That's why my temper was so short with Tim. I was easily irritated when I was on that shit. And more irritated when I didn't use it," he says. "But I wouldn't use, that day. I'd promised Chill and my pops, I wouldn't ruin my scholarship or my shot at this NBA league. Coach Booker knew about it and so did mister Parkwood. All of them helped me to get clean. That's why pops didn't feel I would be understanding about the issue that we discussed last night. Cocaine users are not patient, baby. That's how they knew I wanted *you*. Because I was patient with you and I quit for you."

"When did you start doing it?"

"Right after big Paul got killed," he admits, "Chill was using it then *too*. We all started doing it. Renee helped Chill kick when she made him go to a treatment clinic. Because lil Kenny found his stash and was all in it."

"Oh baby, no!"

"Yes. He stopped *that day* and never used again," he says, "But me, Jr and Rich, we was still experimenting with it. All of that crazy shit we was doing. Jr fucking with Angie, bringing her around the crew and hurting Tonya, before you went to Houston. Rich fighting T-baby, running with all them ho's and me, just acting like I didn't give a fuck about nothing. Living with Darlene. Like that wasn't gonna hurt you......, and my whole family," he says slowly, "It was worse when you went down south. I didn't wanna miss you. But I did. It just seemed like that powder, it just numb the pain.

153

It just seemed like it made it easier to deal with it because I was stoned out of my mind and my senses felt numb."

"What about after Chill's wedding, at their house. When you was going off about Raymond and saying some real mean things?" she asks, "That didn't even seem like you. Not with how sensitive your was with me, in Houston, at the hospital."

"Baby, I was on it for five years," he says, "Just not *everyday*, the whole five years," he admits, "During the times when I acted like someone else and act-"

"At MLK, that day in the gym?" she asks.

"When I just took it?" he asks and she nods. "Hell yea. That shit made me feel invincible," he tells her.

"I knew something else was either on your mind or controlling it," she says, "But that's why I stayed. I knew it wasn't you. My girls use to be like, *'just stop going around him and he can't do things to you.'* But my heart wanted you and told me that you needed me, even more. So I could never just leave you. Even when it *was* bad. I knew you liked to smoke weed, a lot, though. But I never knew about this. What was in your room? When mama Jo went off on you that time, when you moved out?" she asks.

"I had my crack stash in my pants pocket. But I was selling that," he says, "We all did that but we wasn't using it. Most of us, never used it."

"Most of y'all?"

"I never did crack. Ever," he says, "And I never wanted too. Just weed, powder, ecstasy," he reveals.

"What's that?" she asks, "That sex pill?"

"Yes," he says, "But I've taken that with you, a few times. But either way, your sex was still the best," he says as he smiles, "I don't need no additives or enhancements with you. It's all natural."

"You're really good at what you do," she say as she smiles.

"Uh huh and you make me better," he says, "I don't need drugs to get up for you."

"Who did?"

"Did what?" he asks, "Needed drugs to get it up?"

"No," she say as she laughs, "Who did crack?"

"Just know that I didn't, okay?" he says, "I'm not gonna go in on nobody else. I just wanna give you *my* confessions."

"Big Al knew about it?"

"Yea, he knew. See, pops been there too, baby," he says, "He had a problem with it when he was in the game. He knew I was on it, before I
154

ever admitted it to him. He came to me and told me he knew."

"Baby, I never knew," she says, "I never even had a clue."

"You didn't know what to look for," he says, "Plus I always had Cheese. So it's not like I was stealing or no shit like that, to support my habit. We had it already. That's what we cook the crack with. But I was the one who got Anita strung out on that rock," he admits. "Andre and Joe, both on that rock too, That's kind of because of me too. But that's why they did what they did to them hoes from Houston. Because they wanted some more drugs and they gave them their money to get weed and base. And them hoes didn't go with them. They was suppose to score from me, so we brought the girls with us to meet them. They got money from them to pay me but Sonya and Shuntay didn't get the rocks for them nor did they go with them. They stayed with us. That's when me, Stoney and Rob ran the,... Well you know the tr... You know that part."

She sits and listens to her man as he confesses his sins. In a lot of ways, knowing what she knows now about the cocaine use, she knows 1 thing is for sure. That it hadn't been Anthony who caused any of the bad memories, she's had in their 10 year relationship. Not that guy who treated her mean, on several occasions. The guy who seemed to be in another world, at times. When he had sex with her. The guy who initially ignored her accepting a prom date with BJ, in high school. Then turned almost confrontational when she didn't give in to him in the gym, without questioning him, first.

"I will always be a recovering addict, Ebony," he says, "I just stay away from temptation, as much as possible."

"How long have you been clean?" she asks.

"The day after I found out you was pregnant, I asked coach Booker to get me some help and he did," he starts, "It was hard to kick but I just kept talking to you. I was worried about whether it had affected the baby or not. You was so positive and happy," he says, "I didn't wanna fuck that up. Every time something bad happened, I wanted to use. Every time I was missing you and home and the crew, I wanted to use. But I didn't. That day I found out you was in the accident in your car, I prayed, *so* much. I was on my way to get high when I found out about it. I knew I had to come on home to see about you. I thought you was dead," he says slowly, as he goes into a blank stare, "I was gonna do a lot of it and try to check out. I wanted to be dead too. Honestly."

He looks into her eyes as she moves closer to him, so she can hold his hands. He continues, "Then I, I kept calling your cell phone and Jacobson finally answered. He told me you was at the bottom of the Cliff. Then he told me

155

….., you was still alive," he says as his speech gets slower, "I was gonna blow some but….., coach Booker got to me, first. He kept talking to me. He already knew and….., he just knew…., he knew I was gonna go off and …, do something stupid. So he stayed with me. He got me to Parkwood and got me home. To you." She grips his hands tight and he continues, "I promised God, *that* day, that if he let you survive, I would treat you the way you deserved to be treated. That's what I've been trying to do."

"You was worried about if the baby would've had it in her system?" she asks.

"Yes and when Angel got sentenced and you said God has a plan for us and his script is already written. The only way I could find to justify God letting something like that happen to you, instead of to me, was him putting Angel there to do it. To show me how my doing you wrong almost cost you your life. And two, to take my child away that I had probably affected. I was doing a lot of it. I know she would've been affected somehow. Some way. It could've been a little or a whole lot."

She gets up, goes to him and sits on his lap. Then she gives him a tight hug.

"Do you ever think about doing it lately?" she asks.

"No. I know what I have now and what I want. But I see a lot of people doing it, baby," he says, "In the NBA, at the parties and in the VIP sections, at the clubs. I just leave and go to my condo, if we're in Miami. Or I go back to my hotel room and call you or somebody at home. Just so I can get my mind off of it," he admits. "It works because I don't even have the desire to do it, anymore. I'm glad about that. But I do think that might be the reason God took my first born. Because I was using during that time and our baby could've been affected. It kills me. I don't ever want to use again, Ebony. I wanna live. I wanna live with you. I want you with me, for the rest of my life. You've saved my life, *so many times,* woman. And you never even knew it. I just really want you to know that," he continues, "Part of the reason why I was so hard on you was because I needed you to stay straight with me. To save me."

"I'm here for you, Anthony. I always have been. No matter what," she says, "We've got a beautiful life ahead of us. You don't have any reason to be worried about me and you. I forgive you, baby. I love you. I've always loved you. I loved you then, I love you now and I will love you for the rest of my life. I have no doubts. No fears. I believe in you because I know you really want me to be happy." She smiles.

"I'm hornier than a *muafucka*," he says suddenly, as they laugh but he isn't done. "I know you love me. I've always known that," he says, "But

156

I had to return that love in order for us to be one hundred percent. That's what I plan to do."

"You have and you always will," she says with a smile, "Do you know how I knew that *then* and how I still know now?"

"How do you know, baby?" he asks as he looks into her eyes.

"Because even during all of that turmoil. The one thing you never wanted to do, was to see me unhappy," she says, "You using cocaine, will hurt you and if you're hurting, there's *no way* I can be happy."

He wanted to confess that 1 other thing about her teammate at UC. But she still has to go back there and play with her. Plus he feels so vulnerable about saying anything about it. He'll find a way to tell her soon. Either that or he'll learn to suppress it for years, like she had done with Neal.

She sits on his lap at the table, as they hug and kiss. They have been completely open, honest and forthcoming with each other, about the times and things in their lives, up until this moment. She even knows about the 3 groupies he'd had group sex with, since he was drafted. He told her about them when she visited with him during the playoffs. She doesn't care about any of them. Not Angel or Anita. Nor Darlene. None of them matter. She's his better half. He's just told her, *she's* his reason for living and succeeding in life.

"Nothing can come between us, baby," she says, "Nothing or no one. Ever again."

"No one ever has. Except me. I won't do it again, though. You deserve the best that I have," he says, "And I'm gonna give you my best."

They spend most of the day together, at the hotel. Then later, they go shopping for gear to wear to the celebration tonight. But before going to the celebration, they call and check on Rebbie, June and Orian.

Rebbie tells Ebony she's being discharged, Monday morning.

"We'll see y'all then," Ebony says.

"Okay kid," Rebbie says with a smile.

"See ya," Ebony says.

"In a minute."

All of their parents are at the celebration, tonight. Debbie and Brad Sr remind everyone about Bre's graduation from Tech, on Saturday. Most of Chill's original crew are going, along with Debbie and Brad Sr. Bruce is flying down from Ohio State and bringing Kim. Jackie and Jason are taking CJ to see her mother graduate.

157

The parents run Crew Enterprises and keep the minor children while the crew are in Atlanta. June and Rebbie aren't able to travel, though they want too. Dr. Weston wouldn't allow Rebbie to fly, so soon after giving birth. Jr and Tonya go but Brad III stays with Rebbie, June and Orian because schools don't let out for summer until June 3rd.

While in Atlanta, the crew go out to the site of their southern business venture, set to open in June of 1998. Ajay, June and Rich have invested some of their professional salaries into the venture, along with Jb and Lynn. There will be a strip mall called, *The Crew Complex*. It will include a new club which they name, *The Dirty South Chill Spot*. The complex will house the 3 story club designed exactly like the adult club in Cleveland. There is an elite restaurant, *Southern Exposure*. It's upscale with *by reservation only,* seating. There's a sports bar and grill, *Crews Hideaway*. Down the block and still on the same property, is a spacious game room and arcade named, *Crew Kids Sports Arena*. It's set up with a large multi-purpose room, like the one in Cleveland. But this 1 has an all purpose gymnasium with a weight room and a basketball court, complete with bleachers. Plus a fully loaded arcade with all of the popular games. *Crew Kids Sports Arena* is an arcade and gym combined, for the Atlanta business. In Cleveland, *The Spot II* doesn't have a gym because Ajay will be building his sports complex, in the very near future.

"That office space on the far end is where I'm gonna set up my southern sports agency office," Jb says.

"Do you still need staff for all of these venues?" Chill asks.

"I've got thirty interviewed and on file, so far," he says, "I wanna hire new graduates and college students, mostly. We can employ some high school students, in the arena, since there won't be any alcohol served there. We can employ sixteen and up."

"Will somebody have to move here to help out?" Ajay asks.

"Jan and Rob are in the process of relocating here, so Rob can get his new record label jumped off," Chill says.

"That's right and that space over there, next to the bar and grill, is for his studio," Ajay says, "Ebony and I we'll be close enough to help out too. But not until she graduates."

"We got folks coming in from H-town," Lynn says.

"Wayne and his girl, Courtney, are coming down to help with the opening," Renee says, "And David, Charles, April and Yolanda from Houston. Terrell is moving here, in the next few months, with his girl, to help run the club and the studio with Rob."

158

TIME TO LOVE-RELOADED-TIME WILL REVEAL 3

"Shantel Jacobson is suppose to be moving to Atlanta to play ball, after graduation," Ebony says, "I'm sure she would like to supplement her income and invest too. I'll mention it when we go back for preseason."

"Cedric will be helping out until he moves to Sacramento with Bre, in August," Lynn says. After Bre's graduation, she's moving to McClellan Air Force Base for Officer's Training School [OTS]. CJ will be closer to her grandfather, Chester Lee, when she makes that move west.

"We'll definitely have enough businesses for every member of the crew to have something to fall back on," Jr says.

"And then some," Ajay offers.

****

The 1st Monday in June, the foursome start their summer semester at UC. Ajay is staying in Cincinnati until he has to report to camp in August. He stays in shape by practicing with his Natty team. He avoids being in the presence of the women's team, the entire stay.

June and Rich report back to their rookie camps. They'll return in 3 weeks to graduate, along with Tank.

Orian, Rich III and Jerica will stay in Cleveland while the foursome go to summer school and Rich and June go to training camps.

John III is in Cleveland while Lynn finishes OTS and Jb works with his sports clients. They get the final paperwork done for The Crew Complex business venture, which keeps them all on the go. Lynn will graduate OTS in early December, before Ajay and Ebony's wedding.

Tank and Nina's home is ready for occupancy by the 30th of July. It's the weekend and the Natty crew are home to help get things moved into the new house. They work, tirelessly. All night, Friday and most of the day, Saturday. With help from several of the crew, they manage to get everything arranged the way Nina wants it.

"Damn, I'm tired," Ajay says.

"I'm just glad it's all done," Tank says as he hands Ajay a beer. Chill and Jr are the last of the crew to leave. They have to go open up the club. T-baby and Rebbie go and get Rich III and Orian from Sandy and Rena. Ebony gets John III from Pearl. Nina has already brought Jerica to see her new home. The foursome, the kids and Ajay will stay at Nina and

159

TIME TO LOVE-RELOADED-TIME WILL REVEAL 3

Tank's home tonight. Nina and Tank want to be their host in their new 5 bedroom, 5 and half bath home, this weekend.

"But me and Ajay are going to the club tonight," Tank says, "I need to check out the new spot site too."

"I figured that much out, when Chill and Junior left," Nina says with a sly smile.

"That's alright," Ebony says, "We'll stay home with the kids, *this* time."

"That's it, baby," Ajay says with a kiss, "Get you some practice." They all laugh.

After Tank and Ajay dress and leave for the club, Nina orders pizza. Ebony has rented some movies for the ladies and some for the kids.

"What movies did you get, Ebony?" Rebbie asks.

"I got *Set It Off*, *Jason's Lyric*, *Mississippi Burning*. And *The Lion King,* for the kids," she says as they laugh, "Something for every mood."

"We got a two year old, a one year old, a one month old and a three week old," Nina says.

"We got our hands full, is what we got," T-baby says.

"And homework too," Rebbie adds.

"Our club days are over," Ebony offers.

"No they're not," Nina says, "When June and Rich come back for graduation. The two of them, Ajay and Jeremy are gonna baby-sit, so we can go to the club."

"Oh yes. So Anthony can get some practice too," Ebony says as they laugh again.

"They won't even be here for our first year anniversary," T-baby says with a solemn look on her face.

"I know, Tee," Rebbie says, "But we're gonna make up for it in July, when they come home."

"I'll baby-sit while y'all go celebrate," Ebony says.

"And I'll help," Nina adds, "We can keep them, right here. Like they are, *right* now."

She makes funny faces at Orian and John III, as they sit in their carrier seats. Jerica and Rich III are already trying to pull her vases off of her coffee table.

"We've got some terrible one's and two's action happening, up in here," T-baby says as she gets Rich III and Jerica and put them in Jerica's playpen together.

160

TIME TO LOVE-RELOADED-TIME WILL REVEAL 3

The Spot is jumping and Ajay has a constant line of fans wanting autographs. He signs each and every 1 of them, before going upstairs to VIP. The renovations and additions are done and the club is top-of-the-line. There are celebrities in the crew now. For privacy, VIP became *necessary*. The junior crew use to hang out on the 2nd floor, when it was just offices. That's the exotic dance or strip club, now. The 3rd floor is VIP. Renee and Chill's offices are there also. The Junior crew can no longer go up there to hang out. This is only a short term problem. Their kid's club or *The Spot II*, opens 4th of July weekend. It's located directly across from *The Chill Spot*, in the new strip mall. It's housed between *Big Mama's House* and the future Bar-n-Grill. The bar and grill will carry Stoney's name and will be run by the best grill men in the crew, Al and John.

But for now, the junior crew hang out at the U, at Reaper's apartment. Ajay left it fully furnished for Bruce, when he moved out. When Bruce went to college, the next oldest junior crew male, Reaper, took it over. Bruce and Kim stay there with Reaper, now that it's summer. Brittany stays, every chance she gets. But Brenda or Brian Sr are always coming out there to take her home. No matter how many times they come to get her, she still insist on trying to spend the night. She reminds the crew of Ebony and Nina, a few years ago.

"It's too bad mama don't still live in Houston because I would be sending your butt down there to stay. Just like Ebony did," Brenda has said to Brittany, on several occasions, "Now I see where Pearl was coming from. But then Reaper would just move down there and mama wouldn't mind."

Big June calls Rebbie on his 22nd birthday to remind her to get with the builders and get the keys for their new home.

"They're suppose to put all the doors up, next week," he says.

"It's looking so good in there," Rebbie says to him, "It won't be long before we can move in."

Chill is 28 and Ally has made 14. Her and Steven are inseparable, these days. They've spent a lot of time at the U. They got busted together, the night of the May celebration, by their mothers. It was a scene reminiscent of Ajay and Ebony, 8 years ago, at the motel. But Ally and Steven was trying to sneak off to Ohio State with Kim and Bruce. It got so heated, that Rebbie traveled back home from summer school to talk to her little sister.

Renee and Chill, Jr and Tonya have been married 6 years. Jb and Lynn, Jan and Rob, Ced and Bre celebrate 2 years. Rebbie and June, Rich and Trisha married 1 year have to celebrate in July, because of *NFL* camps.

161

TIME TO LOVE-RELOADED-TIME WILL REVEAL 3

Papa is honored again for him and Granny's 44th anniversary. But lately, 1 of the church lady's, Mrs. Ida Mae Graves had taken a liking to Papa Brown. John Sr and Greg Sr are very vocal against it. While Pearl and Sandy think it's kind of cute. They don't want him to be lonely.

The 4th of July celebration is finally here. The junior crew are excited to have their own club, *The Spot II*. Nestled next to it, is an after hours grill, owned by crew. The grill opens up at 10pm, when *The Crews House of Soul Food* closes. The crew named the grill, *Stoney's Sports bar-n-grill*. It's closing time will be 4am. They'll catch the hungry crowds, leaving the adult club. Tank manages the kids club. He has the undergraduates on staff. The kids spot has concessions, as well. John and Al run Stoney's. This gives them more opportunities to show off their grilling skills. They're the main 2 who always claimed to be the masters of the grill, every 4th of July and cookout. The other fathers have bowed out of that contest, by now.

Ajay is just as focused on his future going smoothly, as he is on keeping his jump shot *wet*. He hooks Mr. Parkwood up with Jason Carr and buys up all of the remaining property in and around their CrewLand mall area, in preparation for new businesses of the near future. He also puts the money up for the 3rd strip mall. Ebony is majoring in Real Estate banking and Investment Strategies. He wants to make her transition into her new job and office, effortless and with plenty of projects for her to come onboard with, as soon as she gets her degree. T-baby is majoring in Finance Law and Accounting, Rebbie in fine arts while for Mrs. Nina Brown, Cosmetology and Business Management is the degree she seeks. When they finish at UC, they're offices will be housed at the third property. His plans show the newest strip mall to be just north of the other 2. Once it's completed, the CrewLand mall will take on a U shape. Ajay owns the land just south of these structures, as well. If they decide to go with a completed square, they'll already have the property in the family. Next, he acquires 50 acres, including the spot Ebony picked out in the prime area off Cliff View, where Tank, Rich and June have their homes. However, Ajay buys the remainder of the property in the section. This assures him, no one else will live in their neighborhood but them and those they sell too. Ebony will be in charge of all future Real Estate transactions for these properties, as well. Him and Ebony's domain will be located directly behind Rich and T-baby's home. But with the size of their property, the home will be around the bend and 2 blocks away. They had taken the drawings he'd done as a 7th grader
162

TIME TO LOVE-RELOADED-TIME WILL REVEAL 3

and had big Archie, a drafting major and Jr, an architect major, to perfect the plan for their abode. It will be a 3-story, split-level, French Country and Castle styled, 9000sqft mansion. With a double stair Foyer, 2 elevators, 14 fireplaces and a 2-story Living room. A Family and play room with floor to ceiling windows. The Library, with a catwalk and bookshelves above, leads into a spacious master suite with a powder room and his and her walk-in closets. A separate master bathroom with a large elevated Jacuzzi, sitting in a window-seated bay window, overlooking the view of the garden terrace outside of their master suite. There are 10 other bedrooms. 5 on the 2nd floor, 2 on the 3rd and 2 in the basement. 6 full baths. The largest 1 is the master bath. Then 2 on the 2nd floor, 1 on the 3rd and 1 in the basement. Five ½ baths. 1 at the foyer, 2 next to the Veranda and patio, 1 on the 3rd floor. The last bedroom, full bath and 4th ½ bath will be above their dual 3-car garages and will double as a servants quarters. It has a living room and kitchen. This space will go to their 1st born son when he joins the crew, as per Ajay's word. It's similar to the 3rd floor suite which has no kitchen. The main kitchen, where Ebony will prepare the family meals, will be State-of-the-art. There's a smaller one on the Veranda which opens to the backyard. They have a half court next to the basement and a full court out past the lawn. A swimming pool, inside and out. An in-ground Jacuzzi, exercise room and a basement party room. A sitting room, office and study, on each floor. A home theater, family dining room and breakfast nook. A billiard room next to the door of the basement with a bar, wine cellar and beautiful flower gardens, next to each entrance. The Estate has a restaurant size dining room attached, for family holidays. A garage for a boat and 2 ATV's, will be next to the man-made lake where they'll have 4 gazebo's. Ajay will add a gazebo for each of the foursome couples and 4 bridges with walkways to each couples home. Behind Ajay's home, there will be a fully functioning 4 bedroom, 3 full bath, guest house. He said that's where guest can stay, after they fill all the bedrooms in the main house with kids. He wants at least 5. Ebony isn't trying to negotiate. She wants a lot of kids too. They give uncle Greg's construction team the go ahead on all projects and leave their fathers to see after them, while they tend to their career and classes. Ajay also requested that all of his outside stairs, steps, drives and driveways, be made of marble with extra shine, so they look wet at all times.

Ebony's in Natty when she gets a call from Mr. Parkwood. What he tells her is going to serve a triple purpose for her man. It's Ajay's 23rd birthday and she's made him a special dinner at the house in Cincinnati.
163

TIME TO LOVE-RELOADED-TIME WILL REVEAL 3

When Ajay arrives, Tank, Nina, Rebbie and T-baby have gone to Cleveland, so Ajay and Ebony have the Natty mansion to themselves.

"Baby, my probation ends Monday," he says while they're eating.

"I remember," she says, "That's why I planned a special weekend for you."

"Oh yea? What else do you have for me?" he asks as he smiles.

"It's a surprise, baby," she says.

"You know I don't like surprises," he says with a grin.

"Well that's *too* bad. Because I'm not telling you," she says, "You're just gonna have to wait."

She has found out from Mr. Parkwood and coach Booker, that Ajay will receive a key to the city of Cincinnati. He had received 1 in Cleveland, in 1992. They're sponsoring a gala in his honor, at the campus arena. His crew and family are coming for the celebration, on Sunday night. But as they dine, this Saturday afternoon, Ajay has a surprise of his own, for Ebony.

"Baby, I got something I want you to watch," he says with a sly grin, as he puts a DVD in the player and lets it play.

She laughs instantly, as she says, "Oh my *God*! You *kept* this. I forgot all about it. I forgot I taped it. That's your fault."

It's the recording of her striptease, before he went to the NBA Combine meeting in New York. What she didn't realize is that the camera recorded the entire evening and the next morning too. On the DVD, which he dubbed himself, is not only her striptease. It had recorded them making love, leaning over the counter, on the chair and when they worked it out on the couch. While she was sleeping, it recorded Ajay get up off the couch and turn the camera off. Then him walking back to the couch, 5 hours later.

"You started it back, baby?" she asks with a shy grin.

"Uh huh," he says as he chuckles.

It had recorded their late morning session and when they set their wedding date. It had their entire conversation, before church.

"I didn't know it was still recording," she says, "I was suppose to turn it off after the dance part. But you wouldn't keep your hands off the dancer. You just couldn't wait."

"Nah, I couldn't," he says, "I don't do *real* well with teasing. And there was no way in *hell* I was leaving Cleveland without that camera," he says and laughs, "I got the whole kit, tripod bag and all."

"It was *your* camera. I'm glad you got it, though," she says, "Because I didn't even think about it when we left for church, that morning. We was running late for little lil Rich's christening."

164

"I know, baby. I got it," he says, "Because if I wouldn't have, it's no telling who would be selling this motherfucker, by now," he says, *"For fifty nine, ninety five!"* They laugh at his *Menace to Society* reference.
"I've been watching it, in Miami," he says, "It turns me on."
"I feel you," she says, "It's turning me on, right now."
"Well come here and let me help you with that," he offers and they turn in for the remainder of the day.

On Sunday, they attend Ajay's surprise gala. Officer Jacobson is there, as well as George Wheeler, Dr Weston, Aunt Jessica and Terrell. The gala is covered by many media outlets, including *ESPN*.
"My baby is a celebrity," Ebony whispers to Ajay as they share a slow dance during the gala, "You're a talented star."
"My baby is a talented star too," he whispers in her ear, referring to their DVD recording. "You deserve an Oscar, baby girl. If they see that DVD, you'll be getting a whole set of keys."
They both laugh and continue to dance. The gala is a big success and raises lots of money for Ajay's *Boys and Girl's club* charities of Ohio.

}July 18{
Friday is graduation time for June, Rich and Tank. June and Rich arrive in Cincinnati to find all of their families there for the ceremony. Afterwards, everybody drives back to Cleveland. Instead of a normal crew celebration, everyone helps Rich and T-baby move into their 6 bedroom, 5 bath home. Ajay and Ebony are staying at Tank and Nina's, this weekend. June and Rebbie are staying with T-baby and Rich, who's house is directly across the street from Nina and Tank's. June and Rebbie's house, which will be ready in 2 weeks, is next door to Nina and Tank.
On Saturday, the foursome go shopping for more summer outfits. They pick up something to wear to *The Spot* tonight, then they return to their Cliff View community, which still hasn't been named. The foursome are going out this weekend, as planned. The guys will watch the kids. Ajay is going to keep John III at Tank's house. Rich and June are at Rich's house with Rich III and Orian. They'll get together at Tank's house, before the ladies leave.
Nina and Ebony are in Nina's bedroom getting dressed while Ajay and Tank play with John III and Jerica in the family room. The guys are going to play dominoes, once Rich and June come over with Rich III and Orian. When Nina and Ebony are dressed, they come into the family room,
165

modeling their outfits and let their men know they're ready to leave.

"You look beautiful," Ajay says to Ebony.

"Thanks, baby," she says and smiles.

"My wife looks better, though," Tank says as he grabs Nina around her waist and she giggles.

"Bullshit," Ajay says, "Your sister looks like a goddess."

They all laugh. Ajay and Tank are listening to a CD titled, *Based on A True Story*. It's from a popular Miami rapper known as *Trick Daddy*. Ajay heard of him since moving to Miami.

"This brother is large in Miami," Ajay says, "*Uncle Luke* put him on. He's gonna blow, real soon. He's *got* too."

"I like this," Tank says and orders an edited copy for *The Spot II*.

The ladies prepare to go meet T-baby and Rebbie. Ebony is driving them in Ajay's Grand Cherokee.

"We're leaving," Nina says as she dances to Trick Daddy's CD.

She kisses Tank and Jerica. Ebony gets the keys from Ajay, then kisses him, John III and Jerica.

"It's early to be leaving for the spot," Ajay says, "Y'all are VIP and valet. You don't have to worry about standing on line."

Him and Tank laugh at his joke. He's about to say more but T-baby and Rebbie come over. Rich and June have come with them and brought their kids, so he decides against it. The ladies double check all of the supplies for the babies and make sure their men have ample food and snacks for the evening. Then they leave.

What their guys don't know, is they haven't put on the outfits they plan to wear. After leaving Nina's, they go to Pearl's house to change. Each of them have a bag which contains the skimpy outfits they plan to wear. They go to Ebony's room to change, knowing Pearl is going to be over at Brenda's house and won't be a thorn in their sides.

"Y'all, we're gonna get in trouble. I know it," Ebony says.

"Girl, we're grown," T-baby says, "Besides, all we have to do is come back here and put back on the other clothes, before we go home. If *you* want too."

"I don't know about this," Ebony says, "Anthony hates for me to wear a lot of make up. And if he sees me in these kind of clothes, he's gonna burst something, wide open. Hopefully not my dome."

They all laugh. They're wearing halter styled tops which allow maximum cleavage. More so, in Ebony's case. She has the largest breast. They wear very short hip hugger shorts which barely cover their *assets*.

166

TIME TO LOVE-RELOADED-TIME WILL REVEAL 3

"I'm not comfortable wearing this," Ebony tries.

"We got on the *same* thing," Nina says, "Just different colors."

"What if they find out?" Ebony tries, "I'm hanging out of mine."

"We'll be already in the club by then," T-baby says, "What are they gonna do? Leave the kids and come get us?"

"*Yes*," Ebony says, "Anthony will. In a New York minute."

Rebbie agrees with Ebony but as usual, Nina and T-baby insist they can make it work.

"One for one," Nina says.

"And all for all," they say together.

"But I don't have to like it," Ebony adds as they giggle.

They come downstairs to leave. Big John, who's preparing to go open up the bar and grill, sees them and protest, immediately.

"Baby girl, what in this world are you wearing?" he asks.

"These are our matching outfits, daddy," she tries.

"You must've left most of it at the store," he says as he frowns.

The ladies laugh and go on out the door. They load into the Grand Cherokee and head to the club, as John go next door to get Al.

"Man, I wish you could've seen what our daughters just left here wearing," he says to Al.

"What?" he asks and John describes the outfits.

"I know the guys aren't okay with them wearing that sort of shit," he says, "That's about why they came out here to change."

"I think we should find out," John suggests, as him and Al take a detour to Cliff View and directly to Tank and Nina's house.

They arrive to find all 4 guys and 4 kids. The guys are playing dominoes and the kids are napping.

"Hey man, what's up with y'all?" Tank asks as he opens the door.

"You babysitting tonight, ha?" Al asks.

"Yea. It's the wives turn to go out," Ajay says with a smile.

That's the last time he's going to smile, for a few hours. They're all buzzing from drinking *Hennessy* and *Crown Royal*.

"Y'all about to go open up Stoney's?" June asks.

"We was leaving to go down there," John says, "But I witnessed something I didn't agree with and I wanted to come by and hear your side of it," John says, looking directly at Ajay.

"What's going on?" Rich asks.

" I just saw the girls, by the house," John starts, "They left there in some pretty skimpy clothes. I don't think that's appropriate-"

167

"What skimpy clothes?" Tank asks and once again, John gives a description of what the 4 ladies have on.

"I turned my daughter over to you," John says to Ajay, "I hope you're not gonna let her go out looking like no tramp."

Ajay is already looking for some car keys and has been, since John said, "*I just saw the girls by the house.*"

"I'll drive, man," June says as he pulls his keys from his pocket.

"They played us," Rich says, "I don't believe this shit."

"I told Ree Ree not to wear that shit," June says, "She must've put it in a bag before she left."

"Can y'all stay here until we go handle this?" Ajay asks.

"No problem," John says as he shakes Ajay's hand.

Then he pours a *Crown on the rocks* for Al and himself, from 1 of the large bottles.

"Oh yea," Tank says, "Help yourselves to the drink and food, if you want too. Just make yourselves at home. We'll be back shortly."

They leave.

Meanwhile, the foursome are arriving at *The Chill Spot*. They've already been valet parked and are making their way to the velvet rope.

"Baby girl! What the hell are y'all wearing?!" Renee asks, chopping into them as soon as they walk up to the VIP entrance.

"We got matching outfits," Ebony answers.

"Where's the rest of it?" Renee asks, "Ajay is gonna tear this whole strip up, if he sees you in that. I know he don't know you have it on."

"No, sis," Nina says, "None of them know."

"If Kenny or Jr see y'all, they will," she offers, "You know this."

"They got the kids, though," T-baby says, "We're gonna have to fuss later. But for now, *we're in the house!*" She sings.

They make their way pass the velvet rope and into the VIP lounge. They attract major unwanted attention, right away. Guys are closing in as they walk through a bottle neck of overzealous fellows.

"I can't have nobody groping and grabbing on me," Ebony says, "I told y'all we shouldn't have this on." She peels guys hands away from her and complain. "Don't touch me!" she yells to 1 patron.

"Ebony, put them in their place," T-baby says.

"Tell them you're married," Nina says, "They'll leave you alone."

"Well, it didn't work on him," Rebbie says as she rolls her eyes at an annoying male patron, who insist on following her.

"Why can't we wear what we want without being harassed?"

168

Ebony asks as she pulls away from yet another male patron, "Do you *mind*? Please don't touch me," she says, "I have a husband. He's the only one who's gonna touch me."

"Not if he's not here," another male patron says.

They continue their struggle to be left alone, only 10 minutes into their club night. That's the same amount of time it takes for their guys to get there. Ajay doesn't even wait until he's there. He calls Chill, on the way.

"What's up, man?" Chill asks, answering his cell phone.

"Yo, bro. You see baby girl and her crew, out there?" Ajay asks.

"Nah. I haven't seen them yet," Chill says, "They probably went through VIP. Renee on that door. I'm checking the bar backs, right now."

He calls Renee on her radio.

"*Baby, have you seen the foursome up there?*" he asks.

"*Yes baby. They're up here,*" she says, "*what's up?*"

Knowing full well, what's most likely up.

"They're in VIP, m-," Chill says but Ajay had hung up when he spotted his Grand Cherokee in valet parking.

Him, Tank, June and Rich are at the VIP entrance before Renee can warn the foursome. Ajay has a trench coat draped over his arm.

"What's up, crew?" Renee asks as she opens the velvet rope, "I told them y'all was gonna loose, it if y'all found out!"

She teases them as they pass and barely mumble hello. She knows all 4 are angry and looking for their ladies. When they make it into the lounge, Ajay surveys the room. There are fans seeking autographs from him, June and Rich. Ajay has Tonya to come up and organize something for later tonight. But right now, he's here on an urgent matter. Tonya tells the fans they'll sign autographs later, on the 2nd floor. Ajay continues his search for Ebony. He sees T-baby, trying unsuccessfully to shed some overly aggressive male. He points her out to Rich and Rich goes directly to her.

"Nigga get the fuck out of my wife's face," Rich says to the male. Then he demands that T-baby come with him and she does.

Nina is dealing with another obnoxious guy, who's trying to get way too close to her. Tank goes to get her.

"Let's go, Nina boo," Tank says.

"Hey man. I was here first!" the male patron yells.

"You wanna stay here!?" Tank yells back.

The male decides to back off. But not without some harsh words.

"Nigga how you want it?" Tank asks as his crew closes in.

The male notices Ajay and June move over and stand with Tank. That's

169

when he realizes who they are and backs all the way off. Tank grab Nina's hand and brings her with him. June and Ajay don't see Rebbie or Ebony. Ajay is loosing patience and thinking the worst.
Somebody has her hemmed up, somewhere.

Then he notices a huddle of guys at the ladies restroom doors. They're acting as if they're plotting on going inside. He sends a VIP waitress in to tell Ebony and Rebbie, their girls need them. As him and June make their way to the doors of the ladies room. They stand directly in front of them. Chill has been informed of the situation and comes upstairs to assist his crew. Ajay grows more impatient while waiting and hearing these males discussing his woman's assets and what they plan to do with them. So he hands Chill the coat, then barges into the bathroom. June goes in behind him. Chill and security discourage a few other male patrons, who was trying to do the same. June sees Rebbie as soon as he enters.

"What *the*?!" he yells and 2 females escape the restroom quickly. Rebbie calls for Ebony to come out of the stall where she's been hiding. The waitress had told her Ajay was in the club. After hearing June inside the bathroom, she knows Ajay's in there too. She can smell his cologne. June takes Rebbie out with him, on Ajay's request. He sends the waitress out too. Leaving him alone in the bathroom with Ebony. He pushes on the stall door but it's locked.

"Open it, baby girl," he says and his voice is fresh out of patience. She opens the latch. He pushes the door open and sees her.

"Oh *hell* no!" he yells, in a tone that startles her. "Come here. I know you know better than this. My wife don't dress, like *this*."
His tone is a mixture of anger and disbelief, sprinkled with disappointment. She reluctantly comes out of the stall. He escorts her out of the bathroom. The 1st person she sees is Chill. He frowns and shakes his head, then wraps the coat around her.

"That's not even you, baby girl," Chill says.
Ajay leads her out of VIP, through the lobby and to the elevator in front of him. Chill escorts them down to valet where Ajay's vehicle is already waiting. Rich and T-baby are in it. Tank, Nina, Rebbie and June are in June's Legend, waiting to pull off. Ajay opens the passenger door for Ebony to get in. She does. He closes the door, goes around and gets in. They leave. Chill and Renee think it's cute but they know the guys are upset. The 2 vehicles leave the CrewLand Mall, heading to Cliff View.

"*What*?" Nina asks Tank as June drives.

170

TIME TO LOVE-RELOADED-TIME WILL REVEAL 3

Tank nor June say anything. Neither does Rebbie. In Ajay's Grand Cherokee, he says nothing to Ebony. She doesn't dare speak. T-baby remains quiet. She doesn't want to make it worse for Ebony. But she's going to let Rich have it when they get home. Both vehicles arrive back at Tank's home, in silence. The 4 couples get out and go inside. John and Al are pleased the guys have brought them back.

"Big John, you snitched on us?" Nina asks her father-in-law.

"Hell yea, he did," Al says, "Nina, you have better sense than that. You're a married woman and a mother."

She doesn't respond. She knows her father is right. John and Al kiss the grandkids goodnight and leave for Stoney's. T-baby and Rebbie go get their babies, then follow June and Rich across the street. Tank and Nina go into their bedroom to talk, leaving Ebony alone in the kitchen with Ajay.

He sits down at the bar and pours himself a drink of Hennessy. He's eerily quiet as Ebony stands next to him. Studying what her next move should be. He drinks his Hennessy, straight down and pours another, quickly.

He finally says, "Go in there and take that off. Put on your nightgown and wash that makeup off your face, please," he says in a chilling whisper.

Immediately, she does what he tells her to do. Meanwhile, Tank and Nina argue, loudly.

"You're not wearing that type shit, *nowhere*, baby!" Tank yells.

"Jeremy! Why not?!" she yells back, a bit louder than he had.

They're voices continue to rise. They're in their master bedroom and can be heard, all over the house. Tanks patience is completely gone, as he asks, "What was y'all gonna do? A fucking rap video!?! Woman you better go back there and come up *outta* that shit, right now!" he says bluntly.

"There's nothing wrong with these outfits," she tries with less bass in her voice, this time.

"That's nothing a man wanna see his woman in, in public!" Tank yells, "Now if you can get some bed clothes that look like that, I'm wit it. But get your ass in there and take that shit off!"

She throws her hands up and retreats to her dressing room, where she quickly changes into her robe and returns.

"Is this better?" she asks, "This is how you want me to look, all the time, ha?"

"Baby, you know I don't have a problem with you going to the club. But you're not gonna be going out there or nowhere else, like that," he says, "You feel me?"

171

"Okay, baby," she says, "I was wrong and I'm sorry."
She gives him a kiss. He accepts it. But he isn't over being angry, just yet.

Ajay gets up from the bar and joins Ebony in their suite. She has washed the makeup off and put on her nightshirt. She sits on the bed, waiting for him to say his peace. As he comes into the room, she looks down at the floor. She feels disgraced. He comes over and sits next to her.

"You disappointed me, tonight, baby," he starts, "You really wanna make me feel like I can't trust you?"

"No," she says, keeping her answers short.

"Well that's what you're doing," he says calmly, "If you wanna go out, that's fine. But you're not going out anywhere in that kind of shit you had on. Do you understand me?"

"Yes, baby," she whispers as she pulls at her nightshirt.

"Why did you try to defy me?" he asks, "You knew somebody would tell me."

"Yes but-"

"But what? You didn't care if I didn't like it?"

"Yes I care," she whispers as she's embarrassed now.

"Then why didn't you put it on while you was here?" he asks.
She doesn't answer. "Because you knew I would object to it, that's why," he says, answering his own question. "You had that makeup painted all over your face. With your breast hanging out, ass hanging all out," he says, his voice starting to rise. "What the fuck was on your mind?"
His voice rises a little more as he looks at her. She still doesn't say a word. "Do you hear me talking to you?" he asks, his voice is impatient now.

"I'm sorry, baby," she says, looking at him for the 1st time.
She can see the disappointment and uncertainty in his eyes.
She says, "I just wanted to be like my girls."

"Your girls ain't like that, either," he says, surprising her. "They got husbands and babies at home that love them. They was doing the same damn thing you was doing. Being muthafuckin' defiant."

"Okay," she says as she feels the sting of tears in her eyes.
She could never stand for him to be mad at her. He reaches for her chin and she flinches.

"What the *hell* are you jumping for?" he asks.

"I don't know," she says, looking at him, "I thought you was gonna slap me."

"*What?*" he asks, "Slap you? Baby girl, gone wit that. You know I

172

don't hit you. I have never hit you, have I? *Ever?*"

"I just thought-"

"I get mad as fuck, sometimes. But I have never hit you nor have I threatened to hit you," he says.

"Maybe I thought I deserved it," she says.

"Don't ever say that," he says, "No woman deserves that. I'm a man. Now, are you a woman?"

"Yes."

"Are you *my* woman?" he asks.

"*Yes.*"

"Do you want to remain *my* woman?" he asks.

"Yes, Anthony," she answers as she looks at him.

"Then listen to your man, alright?"

"Okay."

"That shit you had on tonight," he says, "That's *ho* shit. You're way to pretty and intelligent to be putting yourself out there, like you did tonight. Did you see how them niggaz was acting?"

"Yes. I wanted to leave. That's why me and Rebbie went to the bathroom," she admits, "To get away from them."

"They was fixing to come in there," he says, "They was outside the door getting their courage up. Do you know they was swapping condoms, outside of that door?"

She looks at him with fear in her eyes. She's envisioning her and her girls being assaulted, inside of their own club.

"You know what guys do with condoms," he says, "When guys see girls dressed like they *don't want any clothes* on their bodies. Our first mind is to get them off, as quick as possible."

"I wanted to leave, baby," she says, "I didn't even wanna wear it."

"Okay, look here," he finally says. "I can see that you know what you did was wrong. So I'm not gonna grill you about it, no more. But you better be good to me, from now on. You've given me chances, so you get one," he says with a smile, as he pulls her chin to him and kisses her lips. Then he asks, "That's much better than a slap, right?"

"Yes," she says as she smiles.

She's surprised. She expected him to go off on her, for hours, about trying to be sneaky. But he isn't going to do that.

"Anthony, I'm sorry I did that," she says as she turns her knees toward him. "I mean it. I knew you was gonna be upset. But we said *one for one and all for all* and we just went on with it-"

173

"I know y'all tight, like that," he says, "That's not something either of you would do alone. But together, y'all lose your minds," he says as he chuckles. "It's okay, this time. Because it ended well. I don't want some guy to hurt you because you're looking like a female who wants his attention. No more ho gear. Because your crew can't always be there to keep those type of guys off of you. You got it?"

"Yes," she says, "I got it."

"And not that make up shit, either," he says, "You look so much better without all that. Ebony, you don't need to wear makeup."

"Baby?" she starts, "I thought you said you liked *Lil Kim* and *Foxy Brown*."

"Yea, I do. But *Lil Kim and Foxy Brown* ain't my fiancée," he says, "*Ebony* Brown is. Do you hear me? You are. They may not even be like that. That may be a front or an image."

"We really wanted to go out and we just messed it all up," she says.

"I tell you what. I'll give you a chance to make it up to me."

"How?" she asks with a smile.

"Well, we called the mama's, on our way to the club. We asked if they would keep the kids tonight," he says with a smile. "They said yes. So you need to get dressed again. This time, I'm picking the outfit."

"Okay."

"We're gonna take y'all out and show y'all how to act," he says with a slight smile.

Then she hears the door bell ring. It's Pearl and Jo, letting themselves in. They're here to baby sit. Rena, Anna, Brenda and Sandy have gone to T-baby's house to get their grandkids.

"We came to rescue our babies!" Pearl yells.

"That's right," Jo agrees.

They go straight to the nursery to get John III and Jerica. Tank and Ajay help them put the babies gear in the van. Rich and June are coming across the street. They help Anna, Sandy, Brenda and Rena pack their kids stuff into the other van.

"Baby girl, baby girl, baby girl. What's up now?" Pearl asks with that *I-told-you-so expression* on her face.

"What's wrong with you?" Ebony asks as she tries to hide her smile behind her hand.

"Oh there's nothing wrong with me," her mother answers, "You got yourself a good man, right here. That's all. You spent all of these years trying to convince me that he was good. Now you wanna turn *bad*? Ajay

174

ain't even going for that, little Ella. You better know that, girlfriend."
She giggles and kisses Ajay on the cheek. Then she thanks him for looking out for Ebony, once again. Jo, Sandy, and Rena do the same with Tank, Rich and June.

"Thank God, we have some good son-in-laws," Sandy says as they climb back into the vans.

"So y'all just gonna kidnap our kids, like this?" Nina says with a smile.

"Yes we are. And don't come looking for them for, at least a week. Or until y'all learn how to act," Jo says, "We got them and we're gone."
Then as suddenly as they came, their mothers leave with the babies. Ajay tells his boys the plan and they implement it quickly.

"Now men. Let's get these beautiful women dressed in something appropriate," Ajay says, "And show them a good time."
He taps Ebony on the behind and points to the door. Rich goes home to help his wife get dressed. June has already picked out Rebbie's outfit. Tank and Nina are in their room. Ajay and Ebony go back to their suite.

"Let me see what else you bought," he says, "We can pick something for you to wear, okay?"

"Okay," she says as she lays all the outfits out, 1 at a time.

"Not that one. Not that, either," he says, "Hold up a minute."
He looks through all of the outfits she bought. Finally, he picks out 1 which he deems appropriate.

"Wear this one," he says, handing her a *FUBU* denim pants outfit.

"Anthony, I don't wanna wear that tonight," she tries.
Nina and Tank enter the room. They're having a similar conversation.

"We was saving those for Ree Ree birthday party," Ebony tries.

"That's the only outfit in here that's gonna work for you," Ajay says, "If you can't wear this one, then you and your man can stay here."
He's serious and she knows it. She goes into the dressing room, takes off the nightshirt and puts on the pantsuit. Nina does the same. Then the phone rings. It's June calling to say they're ready to go.

"Pull on over here, man," Tank says, "We're still waiting on baby and twin to finish dressing."
When they come in, Ajay and Tank smile. June and Rich have picked out the same denim outfits for their ladies to wear. The ladies are still in matching outfits of different colors and they look sexy and classy.

"You can leave the rest of these outfits with me," Ajay says to Ebony, "We're returning them all, before I leave here. And I'd better not
175

have nobody telling me, you up here wearing that ho shit, *ever* again."

"Okay, baby," she says as she giggles, "I understand."

Ajay had been truly agitated and she knows it. She's leaving well enough alone about the outfit's the guys chose. T-baby and Rebbie come inside as her and Nina finish changing. They're still slightly irritated with their husbands and so is Nina. Her girls are still trying to make their points but Ebony remains quiet. She wants to go out with all of them and she knows if her and Ajay have to discuss it any further, then they won't be going out at all. They smile at each other as they go out to load up. The 4 couples take the Grand Cherokee and the Legend and head back to *The Chill Spot*. They arrive back at valet parking, just past midnight and go back through the VIP entrance.

"Much better, sister!" Renee yells, "I see y'all got some wanted company now, ha?" She's laughing as she lets them pass *the velvet rope.*

"That's what I'm talking about!" Chill yells, as soon as he sees the 8 of them come back in.

"Y'all have a good time," Renee adds, "I'm sure y'all can now!"

Enjoy themselves, they do. 1st order of business is Ajay, Rich and June sign autographs for an hour. Then they get to the VIP party. Before long, they're back downstairs on the main dance floor, partying like they use too back at Chill and Renee's house. Ebony and Ajay are dancing. She pulls him close to her.

With a bright smile she says, "The more things change…,"

"……..the more things stay the same!" he yells, as he finishes her sentence.

Jan and Rob are home, the 1st weekend in August. They help June and Rebbie settle into their 6 bedroom and 5 bathroom home, next door to Tank and Nina. Jan and Rob are in the process of relocating to Atlanta. They've purchased a home in Smyrna, in the same neighborhood Jb and Lynn live in. They'll be Atlanta residents by the end of the month. Jan has already switched to Georgia Tech's med school program, where she'll continue her graduate studies in 2 weeks. She's going to be a pediatrician and a good one, at that. She was always the patient 1, in the crew and extremely bright.

For the August celebration and Rebbie's 21st birthday, their husbands get them very gorgeous and appropriate outfits to wear. They look sexy and mature. Jr will turn 26 on the 14th. Jan is going to celebrate her 23rd birthday, down in Atlanta. To help make their transition as

176

TIME TO LOVE-RELOADED-TIME WILL REVEAL 3

smooth as possible, Jb and Lynn have come home to help. They're also
taking John III back to Atlanta, despite protest from Jo and Pearl.
"Ma, he's been here for two months," Lynn says, "I miss my baby."
"I know, Lynora. But y'all have to work, *so* much," Jo says.
"Ma, we'll manage," she says.
"I don't want y'all to *just* manage when it comes to my only
grandson," Pearl tries, "He's a Prince. A future king."
They all agree and share a laugh as Pearl asks, "Aren't Cedric and CJ
moving to California when they leave here, this time?"
"Yes ma," Jb says as he plays with his son. He says, "Bre's trying
to get CJ stuff shipped out by Monday, so she'll have it in a week or so."
"Bre's home this weekend too, isn't she?" Jo asks.
"Yes. Her and Ced are at mama Deb's with CJ," Lynn answers.
"Lord. Y'all taking all the babies," Pearl says.
"Tank is gonna be here with Jerica," Jb says, "Orian and lil Rich
are gonna be here too. Y'all are gonna have plenty of babies to slobber all
over," he says with a smile.
He's making farting sounds with his mouth, on his son's stomach. John III
loves it and appears to have missed it a lot.
June and Rich are back home, only for a weekend. They have to
report back for a preseason game, by Tuesday. T-baby and Rebbie have a
special dinner for 4, at Rich and T-baby's house, before the guys leave.
Their summer semester ended last Friday. The fall semester starts in 2
weeks at UC. Ajay will be reporting to preseason camp on Tuesday, as well.
Kim is so excited to begin her freshman year at Ohio State, where
Bruce will be a sophomore this season. He's home for the celebration too.
He's happy to be moving Kim, back with him. Their alumni have rented a
condo for the 2 of them. The entire junior crew seem trilled with this bit of
news. Their parents have already threatened to have the condo taken away,
if they have any trouble with them going down that highway without them
giving permission.
The August celebration is the 1st in months, in which every single
member of the crew attend. Chill, Renee, Rob and Jan are there with Jr,
Tonya, Jb and Lynn. They party with Ajay and Ebony plus Ced, Bre, Tank
and Nina. June and Rebbie are glad to be back in the party where Rich, T-
baby, Bruce and Kim have a couples dance contest. Their junior crew of
Reaper, Brittany, Greg Jr and Erica plus Jesse, Roo, Sam Jr and Pam at
The Spot II, think their party is hotter than the 1 at the adult club. Steven,
Ally, lil Kenny and Chaundra agree with them that their party is hotter.
177

TIME TO LOVE-RELOADED-TIME WILL REVEAL 3

The fact is both parties are equally hot. The active crew is double the size it was in 1989. They are 32 strong now and they never forget to include Stoney. They've formally inducted Arthur, Wayne, Kilo and Justine into the crew. Though Arthur was made legit by the fathers, years ago. Terrell, who is in Cleveland tonight, is officially inducted. He's a permanent fixture around the crew, nowadays. That makes Al happy and Ajay too. He has stopped grilling him about trying to like Ebony when they were children. He's going to make sure him and Terrell are permanent parts of each others lives. He's going to encourage his father to do the same with his aunt Jessica. Charlotte will be the only new member of the crew, this year. She'll turn 13, November 3rd. Brandon, 1 of the twins, already has his eyes on her. She's older than him but he doesn't care because she likes him too.

Tuesday after Labor day is the start of school. Shannon the Reaper is a senior. He has signed a record deal with Rob's label which is partnered with 1 of the hottest record labels in Atlanta. The 99 crew are all juniors. Erica is captain for the football cheerleaders. Brittany has signed to Rob's label too. She's a junior homecoming maid, this year. Jesse is starting wide receiver. Sam Jr lettered in Track and has offers to CSU. Greg Jr is starting QB. He broke every QB record at MLK and still has a year to go. Ruthie and Pam are sophomores and homecoming maids. The 2 of them and Chaundra are high honor students, each year. Ally, Steven and Chaundra are freshman. Kenny Jr is an 8th grade football standout, who moved up to play with MLK. Charlotte is 7th grade and captain of her basketball cheering squad. Archie Jr is a 6th grader. He moved up to play basketball for the 8th grade team. He's the next crew going to the NBA. The twins are 5th graders. Brad III starts 1st grade while CJ starts kindergarten in Sacramento. Destiny is 4 years old and attends at *Granny's house,* where Jerica, Rich III and Orian attend. Jerica will be 3 this October. Lil Rich will be 2 on the last day of this month. Orian is 3 months. Lil John is 3 and a half months and has an in-home sitter in Atlanta.

Cedric bought Bre a 98 Acura Legend for her 23rd birthday once at McClellan. She's happy to have her daughter in their own home. Rob's 1st purchase in Atlanta is a 98 Lexus Sedan. He's got his record label kicked off with major distribution. Reaper is the 1st artist he'll release.

When the New York Jets play their 1st game, in Pittsburgh, Rich surprises T-baby with a 98 Mercedes Benz 300. It was suppose to be his but he wants her to drive it until he buys her one. She's fine driving her and Rich III around in a Benz, for the time being. By Rich III's 2nd birthday, Ebony and Ajay's wedding invitations are mailed out.

178

TIME TO LOVE-RELOADED-TIME WILL REVEAL 3

MR. AND MRS. JOHN & PEARLINE BROWN, SR.

REQUEST THE HONOR OF YOUR PRESENCE

AT THE WEDDING CEREMONY OF THEIR DAUGHTER

MISS EBONY ELOISE "BABY GIRL" BROWN

TO

MR ANTHONY DEVANTE' "AJAY" JACKSON

OF THE MIAMI HEAT,

THE SON OF

MR. AND MRS. ALLEN & JOANNA JACKSON, JR.

ON

DECEMBER 31, 1997
AT

THE FIRST BAPTIST CHURCH OF CLEVELAND OHIO
PASTOR LARRY E. TUCKER, OFFICIATING

TIME-4:00PM

PLEASE RSVP
FOR
SEATING WILL BE LIMITED

RECEPTION WILL FOLLOW AT: THE CHILL SPOT
BRIDAL AND GIFT REGISTRY:
MACY'S
DILLARD'S
NEIMAN-MARCUS
SAKS FIFTH AVENUE

179

TIME TO LOVE-RELOADED-TIME WILL REVEAL 3

CHAPTER   30

LET NO ONE PUT ASUNDER

}OCTOBER 4{

There's so much to do on this celebration day, in preparation for the big year end wedding. The crew are home and the Houston crew are in town. But before they can focus on the celebration, they have to do wedding stuff. They have sizing and fittings to take care of. Yolanda, April, Terrell and Jarvis are new to the crew wedding family, so they have to have their measurements taken. The entire wedding party has to come in today. Rena, Sandy and Belinda have them scheduled throughout the morning. The girls will come by *Crew Gear and Alterations,* at scheduled times, to be measured for their bridesmaids dresses and the guys, for their Tuxedo's.

Ebony, Pearl and big mama are there, very early. Ebony had been measured for her wedding gown in July. Today is her 1st fitting. No one else is allowed to see her gown except the women present now. It's look and design will be kept secret until she walks down the aisle, on her big day. A description will be given to the media for the newspapers and TV coverage. But not until the week of the wedding. This is something big mama, Jo and Pearl requested. This wedding is already being billed as *The Royal Wedding of Ohio* by the UC alumni and many sports and crew fans. The bride and groom have been titled *Mr. and Mrs. Ohio Basketball,* since both was the #1 players in the state as senior high school graduates. The University of Cincinnati has released a full court press on media outlets for this event.

"It's free publicity for the university," Ebony says as she models, "They say it's helping with recruiting too. I don't know how."

"Ebony, does that feel too loose on you?" Sandy asks.

"A little but-"

"There are *no* butts," aunt Sandy says, "This is the bodice of your wedding gown. It has to be perfect."

"Okay. Take it in some," Ebony says and smiles.

"She's got such a tiny waist," big mama says as she admires Ebony, who models the 1st cut of her gown.

"And she has these breast, hips and butt that they have to get around too," Pearl says and laughs. The she adds, "Just like her mama."

"She's a sister," Belinda offers, "We come like that. *Standard.*"

They all giggle as Ebony steps out of her gown and gives it to Sandy.

"That's what Ajay likes, isn't it baby girl?" Rena asks with a smile and Ebony blushes instantly, not offering a comment.

"She's beautiful, inside and out," big mama says, "He can't help but to love all of her."

Ebony is done for today. Sandy takes the bodice and puts it back in it's special bag and zips it up. The Matrons of honor; Nina, Rebbie and T-baby come in. They have their kids and they all have to be fitted.

"We're wearing purple, right Eb?" Rebbie asks.

"Yes, kid," Ebony answers, "And your husbands will have on purple bowties and cummerbunds, with *their* white tuxedo's."

"They're the best men, right?" Belinda asks making a notation on her notepad.

"They sure are!" her girls say in unison as they giggle.

"The *best* man is getting married," Ebony offers with a smile.

They all laugh. Jerica will be 1 of the 3 flower girls. Rena takes her measurements and Orian's also. She's the *honorary* flower girl.

"My baby needs a pretty little dress too," Rena adds while she measures her granddaughter, Orian.

Sandy measures Rich III for his ring bearer tuxedo as Renee and Tonya stroll in with Destiny and lil Brad, in tow.

"We're ready for our close up, *mister De'Mille!*" Renee yells in a dramatic voice, then she giggles.

Her and Tonya are 2 of the 8 senior bridesmaids. Destiny will be the junior bride and Brad III is the junior groom.

"We got Bre, CJ and Janice, last night," Belinda says.

CJ will be the 3rd flower girl.

When Lynn arrives, she brings John III, Yolanda, April, Erica and Pam with her. Erica and Pam are 2 of the 7, junior bridesmaids.

"Let's see, we've got Ebony, T-baby, Nina, Ree Ree and Renee. Tonya, Jan, Yolanda, April, Lynn and Bre," Sandy says.

"We're still waiting on Kim," Rena offers, "And that will be all of the senior ladies."

Kim comes in, a few minutes later, with Roo, Ally, Chaundra, Charlotte and Brittany. Brenda brings Brina and Brandon by, on her way to open up *Granny's House*, for the day.

"That's all the girls, right?" Pearl asks.

"Yes," Belinda says, "Plus we've already got John III, Rich III, Brad III and Brandon."

"All of those thirds, keep this family growing," big mama says with

181

a smile, "Okay ladies. You're all done for today. Your first fitting is November eighth and don't forget."

They show Ebony samples for her reception and honeymoon attire, before she's excused. All of the mothers will wear similar dresses in a cream color. The ushers, host and hostesses will wear tan.

The guys start to file in and the shop is getting crowded. Ajay goes straight to his bride-to-be and gives her a kiss.

"Are you done?" he asks.

"Yes. For today, at least," Ebony answers with a smile.

"You ladies can go, so we can get the guys in here," Sandy suggests. Ajay, Tank, June and Rich have strolled in with Jb, Chill, Jr, Ced and Rob, right behind them.

"All we need from the guys are measurements for the bridal shop," Pearl says.

"Ajay, don't you look very handsome, this morning," big mama says with a bright smile.

"Thank you, gorgeous," he says, giving her a kiss on the cheek. "How are all you beautiful folks doing this morning? Good, I hope."

He's such a cut up.

"*Just fine,*" or "*Good and you,*" echoes throughout out the store.

"You could've asked me that, this morning," Nina says with a smile. She adds, "You stayed at my house, last night."

She never passes on an opportunity for a bit of sibling rivalry with her only brother.

"Be quiet, girl," Ajay says and smiles as Sandy measures him.

He isn't going to let Nina get a pass. Still, they've been closer than ever, these days.

"Big mama, you don't think I look handsome this morning too?" Chill asks with a smile as he kisses her on the cheek.

"Of course I do, Kenny," big mama answers, "All of my young fellows look debonair, as always."

Ajay turns his attention back to his bride. He has a special appointment for them today.

"Baby, you wanna meet me for lunch?" he asks.

"Of course I do. What time?"

"As soon as I finish up here," he says, "All you ladies go over to the restaurant. We'll meet there." The ladies leave. Then turning to Pearl, Ajay adds, "Terrell and Jarvis will be in around three. We're picking them up from the airport, after we eat lunch."

182

TIME TO LOVE-RELOADED-TIME WILL REVEAL 3

Pearl smiles at him. She's probably just as excited as him and Ebony are, about this wedding day.

"I wanna talk with you, later," Pearl says to Ajay, "No hurry. But before the wedding."

He tells her they'll do it soon. Bruce, Reaper, Greg Jr, Jesse and Steven come in, just as Rena is finishing up the 1st set of guys.

"I'll take these," Sandy says.

Belinda measures her son Sam Jr, lil Kenny and Archie Jr, when big Sam brings them in.

"All we have left now are the father's and husbands," big mama says.

"I got big Sam, already," Belinda says.

"That went a lot smoother than I expected it would," Pearl says.

"That's because this is your *first time* being *mother* of the bride," Sandy says, "It's a lot more work for the bride's side. I'm so glad I have two sons and a grandson left to go." They all laugh.

"But you'll still have to sew them all," Rena says and smiles.

"That's true," Sandy agrees, "But my pockets get a break."

"I knew they would all get in here, on time," big mama says of the 3rd and 4th generations. "They're all my babies."

After Terrell and Jarvis measurements are done, Ajay and Ebony hook them up with Tank. Then they go to the construction site of their new home. The builders started on theirs, immediately after finishing June and Rebbie's home, back in July.

"I added a little bit more to the plans, baby," Ajay says.

"How? What changes did you make?"

"Everything that was there is still there. But I had them to add another office on the second floor. Plus a pool house over there," he says, pointing to the freshly poured concrete slab behind the main house structure. "I was hoping big mama and poppa would stay in the guest house, though. So she won't be all the way in the point when you need her."

"Have you mentioned it to them yet?" she asks.

"No, not yet. I'm gonna wait until it's finished and decorated," he says, "Big mama will want to be closer to you, when you *do* have a baby."

"Yes, that's true," she agrees, "The pool house looks big too," she says, looking at the blueprints.

"It's the same size as a regular, one family home," he tells her, "It's smaller than the guest house. It has three bedrooms and two and a half
183

baths. The guest house master bathroom has a Jacuzzi tub plus a regular tub. Just like our master bath but smaller. I'm having it done with handicap access, just like our house. So when they get older, it won't be hard to access and move around in it."

"I see the handicap ramps, all over the property," she says with a smile. Then she adds, "Even our house has the ramps."

"This is your house. And you never know when someone in a wheelchair may need access," he says, "Eventually, I want us to make a whole section in this community, for the first crew. So we can keep an eye on them, all the time. We can take a section of our land and build four more homes and still not have anyone *directly* next door."

"This isn't gonna be a house," she says as she smiles, "This is an Estate." They smile at each other.

"Plenty of room for us to get buck wild in, ha?" he asks with a kiss on her cheek. "I added an awards room, next to the billiards room."
She smiles in agreement. She loves looking at the plans for their house. She looks at the structures which have been completed, so far. She can see their estate shaping up, already. The individual wall structures are already up and so are the enormous ceiling rafters.

"All this big space, over here, is our bedroom, bathroom, main study, office and the two story library," he says.

"So you wanna have two study rooms or offices?" she asks.

"Yes. One on the second floor too," he says, "For when our kids are small. Then we can work on our projects and be close enough to them, if they wake up or whatever."

"And it can be their study room, when they get big," she says.

"*Exactly*."

"You thought of everything in this house, you designed fifteen years ago. Didn't you, baby?" she asks with a smile.

"I knew who and what I wanted, *way* back then," he say as he gives her a sweet kiss.
Then he heads off to talk with uncle Greg, the foreman, while she continues her walk through the massive structure.

"This place is gonna be *humungous*," she thinks out loud.
1 of the laborers agrees and says, "That's an understatement, ma'am."
Ajay has invested his money, well. He's known for always thinking ahead. Not only for himself but for Ebony and their future kids. With the residuals he earns from their businesses, he has arranged to have both their parents homes renovated. This will be their anniversary gifts from him and Ebony,
184

next year. Their renovations will begin, as soon as Ebony and Ajay's home is complete. All the parents and grandparents will eventually receive the upgrades, remodeling or a new home. Thanks to the crews entrepreneurial efforts. Chill's crew and probably the younger crew too, will eventually build in this new community.

Chill and Jr are the next to build in *Jackson Heights,* the name they've chosen for their new gated community. The entry road, *CrewLand drive,* is 4 lanes. 2 to enter and 2 to exit. Of course, it's a secured upscale community. The security gate is nestled between the double lanes, military base style. Only the gates are much fancier and the booth is a replica of a small home. The main lanes wind around into a curve and come to a U-shape. At the base of the U-shape is the front of Ajay and Ebony's property. The driveway and rooftops will be viewable from the street. The 1st right, after entering the security gate, is *Payne's Lane.* Down that road is where Chill and Renee's new home will be erected. The 1st left, after entering the gate, leads to *Wilson's way,* where Jr and Tonya's new home will be built. *CrewLand Drive* is where Nina, Rebbie, T-baby and their husband's homes are finished and occupied. From Rich's backyard, you can view the rear of Ebony and Ajay's home. A large median, which separates the 4-lane road, starts at the booth and runs the full length of CrewLand drive, with intersections every 30 yards. Landscapers work daily. Planting trees, hedges and flowers to beautify the area. Outside of the security gate and booth, sits a large marble and granite sign that will display the name, *Jackson Heights.* Several ponds are being dug out and there are still acres of undeveloped land for future crew, when they're ready to build. Ebony will handle the land sales for Ajay, who owns the balance of the land.

"When you open your real estate office, in June," he says, "You'll be in charge of selling the land to our crew. As of right now, we own the rest of this. As far back and to the sides, as your eyes can see."
She's blown away. Their mansion and private property alone, sits on 75 acres. The total acreage he purchased is 250 and he's planning to buy more.
"We can add sports fields, a main pool and a big park in the very center, if you wanna do that later," he offers, "So all the kids can have a safe place to come together and the daycares can do field trips here too."
"I think we should," she says, "I know the crew are down for that."

}Miami, Friday October 10{
"How was your flight, baby?" Ajay asks Ebony as they head to the Miami condo.
185

TIME TO LOVE-RELOADED-TIME WILL REVEAL 3

"It was alright," she says, "But I still don't like to fly, though."
She's visiting him, this weekend. He has a preseason game tonight against Orlando.

"I've already set up the honeymoon, baby," he says.

"So are you gonna tell me where we're going?" she asks.

"Uh uh."

"How am I gonna know what to bring?" she asks as she smiles.

"You're not gonna be dressed," he says and chuckles, "Well, not for the first twenty four hours, you're not."

"Okay. But what about going and coming?"

"There will be a lot of that," he says and laughs.

"*Anthony*," she says, in her impatient voice.

"I know your sizes, baby," he says, "I'm paying for the honeymoon and everything you need for it. And there won't be any *ho* gear involved. Auntie Rena, Sandy and Belinda will have your bags already packed and waiting. Along with the clothes they're making for you to wear to the honeymoon. It's all set, Ebony. The only thing needed is you."

"Alright," she says as she smiles, "It's gonna be perfect."
She's learned to leave well enough alone, when he's in charge of her or her comfort. She trust him, completely. She's been dressing for him and he's been buying her clothes, jewelry and accessories, since she was 12 years old. He definitely knows her sizes, style and her favorites. Furthermore, he knows what looks good to him and she loves to look good *for* him.

Miami wins their scrimmage game, then he takes her out for a nice dinner and a night on the town.

"Miami is a beautiful city," she says.

"Yes it is," he says, "Plus the weather is great. It gets hot down here, though baby. When I came in July. *Damn*."
She believes him. It's 10pm and the temperature is still in the high seventies, in October. Before taking her to his favorite nightspot, he drives her around town. He even shows her some of the places on *Star Island* and *South Beach,* where scenes from the mega popular movie, *Scarface* was filmed. Including Frank Lopez's home, where the infamous scene with the *Goodyear blimp* was shot.

Later at the club, he's approached by a lot of beautiful women. They know him, already. He's a celebrity, of course. And a member of the *Miami Heat*. Everyone knows him, by now. The gold diggers are out in force. He waste no time introducing these hopefuls to Ebony.

186

TIME TO LOVE-RELOADED-TIME WILL REVEAL 3

"This is my lifetime lady, Ebony Brown. Soon to be Jackson," he says, "She's my fiancée."

The women speak to her and smile. But they're not genuine and she knows why. They're after her future husband. Simply because he's rich, famous and good looking. But they don't have the slightest idea about what really makes him tick. It doesn't matter though. He's *so* off the market and has been, for all of his life. He plants wet kisses on her and she giggles, while his groupies walk away frowning as if something in the club smells foul.

Saturday evening, after some light shopping, they go back to the condo to organize their wedding program.

"Are you ready to get organized?" she asks.

"Man, it's starting already, ha?" he asks and laughs.

"What's starting?"

"Are you trying to domesticate me?" he asks.

"No," she say as they laugh.

"You wouldn't rather have your girls help with this?" he asks.

"No. Not this part," she says, "I want you to know everything, baby. I know how you *hate* surprises."

"You've got a point," he says, "Let's do this. I don't wanna show up and find out we're gonna square dance and dosey doe, down the aisle."

They crack up laughing. He's excited too and he already has a pen and pad waiting to take notes. This is an exciting time for both of them. He looks forward to the day she takes his name, just as enthusiastically as she does. She has been writing his name as her own, for a decade. Now that they're actually making it a reality, he wants to make sure it's the magical day that she's dreamed about and he tells her. They smile at each other and proceed.

"Okay. You and I are wearing all white because we're the *bride and groom*," she says in a melodic voice.

"Finally, it's our turn," he says as he smiles and she smiles back. "But I've got sins, though, baby. They might make me wear grime."

"Stop it, Anthony," she says and giggles while he tries not to laugh. She continues with the program. "The senior party's colors are, let's see,... my girls are matrons of honor and their husbands are the best men. They'll wear purple. Renee, Chill, Lynn and Jb will wear gold. Tonya, junior, Bre and Ced will wear blue." She says, "Jan, Rob, Kim and Bruce will wear green. And Yolanda, Jarvis, April and Terrell are gonna wear red."

"Good. Terrell and Jarvis both like red," he says, "That's the big crew. What about the juniors gear? How are they gonna match?"

187

BLACK COFFEE   TIME TO LOVE-RELOADED-TIME WILL REVEAL 3

"They'll have lighter shades, like the senior they stand next too. Or they'll wear pastels," she says.

"Okay," he says, "Let's go."

"Erica, Greg junior, Chaundra and lil Kenny will wear yellow. Roo, Jesse, Brina and Archie Jr will wear baby blue. Pam, Sam junior, Charlotte and Brandon will wear mint. And pink for Ally and Steven."

"Why does Steven have to wear pink, baby girl?" he asks, "And they're having unprotected sex, everyday. Did you know that?"

"That's the color I picked for Ally," she says, "It coordinates with red. And how do you know more about what's happening in Cleveland, than I do. But I'm closer?"

"You can't find a boy friendly color for him to wear?" he asks, "Cause I'm the man. Everything moves through me, after Chill. You know that, baby girl." They laugh.

"Okay. Help me think of a better color," she suggests, "And I knew they got busted. Mama Rena and them, had a *you-me-and-mama-at-the-motel-room* moment. She asked her mama for pills but she said no."

"She told her mama she was doing it. The motel thing did remind me of us," he says, "We've come a long way from that night, baby."

"We sure have," she says, "But mama Rena won't put Ally on the pill. Rebbie has been begging her too. But she said no. Big Archie ain't having it either. But Ally's hotter than Rebbie was. She's the aggressor."

"They gonna have another grandbaby, then," he says, "Because Steven knocking the stuffing off that shit, every chance he gets. And if he don't wanna fuck, she threatens to cut him."

They laugh hard, before she says, "I know. She threatened him the other day and he called T-baby and Rebbie, at school, to talk to her. She admitted to Rebbie that they've been having sex since she was ten."

"That's crazy," he says, "Now we know why she was dying to get to the crew parties. But let's get back to us, baby. The important stuff."

"Okay," she says, "Give me a color suggestion for the young fuckers, that beat all of us, except you, please."

He chuckles at her. She's steadfast and determined to get their program done while giving him some humor, at the same time.

"Let's see," he says, still laughing, "How about lavender?"

"It needs to be a hue of red," she says, "Lavender is the color for the junior maid of honor and junior best man. That's Brittany and Reaper. I know Reaper's not gonna wear pink."

"Steven either, so make it a rose color. Something darker than

188

pink," he suggests, "Rose will still blend with the red, *right*?"

"Yes," she says, "Okay, that works. That works better than pink, actually," she says as she smiles at him and he smiles back, proudly.

"Ally and Steven will wear rose," she says, "I have to call aunt Sandy and tell her, right now. So they can make the changes."

"Wait until we finish the whole thing, before you call," he says.

"Okay. Then next is the junior bride and groom, the flower girls and ring bearers," she says.

"They're all wearing white, *right*?" he asks.

"Yes. You're doing great," she says.

"We've had lots of weddings to learn from," he laughs, "Is that it?"

"Yes, that's it for the wedding party, *itself*. But we need to do the rest of the program. Like how many songs, etcetera," she says as she smiles. She informs him of the songs, she wants. He agrees with each 1. They've always had the same taste in music. 1 of the songs is *Vision of Love* but Ebony is the only 1 comfortable enough with Mariah's high notes, to sing it.

"Can't we just play the record?" he asks and they both laugh. Then he says, "I guess not."

"It's okay if we don't have it, baby," she says, "But I want five songs, so let's decide on one more."

She looks disappointed as she scratches it from her notepad. He already knows he has *Mariah* lined up to sing it for them. Only he doesn't know if she'll make it to the wedding or if she'll sing it at the reception. Either way, he *will* have her there to perform it. He's already told Pearl and big mama about it. This will be a surprise *for Ebony* and his song *to her*. When the programs do come out. Ebony will receive a few dummy copies to approve. But the actual programs will read;

Song to Ebony from Anthony; Vision Of Love by Mariah Carey.

She won't see the real program before the ceremony. She'll be totally and thoroughly surprised when she see 1 of her favorite voices, singing her favorite song to her, at her very own wedding.

"I want mama Rena to sing, *I Feel Good*," she says, "That's my song to you. And poppa got *The OJay's* again. Their gonna sing, *Forever Mine*," she says, "Your parents are gonna sing, *If this world were mine*. Mama, daddy, aunt Sandy and uncle Greg are singing, *Here and Now*, together. Maybe my girls will sing *Vision Of Love* for us."

"How many songs is that?" he asks.

"Five, with Vision of Love."

"Yea, that's enough," he says.

189

He'll arrange for Nina, T-baby and Rebbie to sing background vocals for Mariah, if necessary. But he knows Mariah won't let them down. Not now that she knows how much her music has meant to their relationship.

"Poppa, big mama and papa, already asked me if they can do a poem," she says.

"Okay and they always come wit it too. So that should be tight," he says, "I want grandpa Joshua and Charles to do the prayer."

"And grandma Sally and Annabelle can do the scriptures," she says, before asking, "Are we still writing original vows?"

"*Hell yea,* we are," he says, "And you'd better dig deep, girl."

"Okay," she says and smiles, "That's it for now, baby."

"Good," he says, "Now can you make me that dinner, you was planning to make? And I'll call mama Sandy with that one color change."

"Oh it's starting *already*?" she asks, getting him back for that domesticated comment. "Are you hungry, baby?" she asks laying her head on his stomach. "Oh God! It's growling at me," she says and laughs.

"Because I'm *hungry*," he says, sounding spoiled rotten, "Yes. I'm hungry. Come on. Get up and feed me."

She heads into the kitchen to prepare fried and boiled shrimp, whole ground mullet, potato salad and garden salad, for dinner. He follows her. She pulls the seafood from the fridge and he notices it isn't dressed.

"Baby, you could've gotten that already cleaned," he offers.

"I know. But it's cheaper for me to clean them," she says, "It only takes me fifteen minutes to clean six, big fish and 2 pounds of shrimp."

"You learned that in Houston, didn't you?" he asks with a smile.

"Yes sir, I did," she says and they both laugh.

He's impressed as she flips the large fish over, slices off it's head, cuts the stomach open, rips the guts out and puts them in her trash bowl.

"Wow! My wife, the butcher," he says, making another joke.

"*Southern chef* is what you meant to say," she says with a smile. "*Chef's do that,*" she says, quoting Samantha Cane from this years movie, *The Long Kiss Goodnight* with *Geena Davis* and *Samuel L. Jackson.*

"Big mama taught you how to cook, like her, when you was down there," he says, "You *could* be a chef."

"Poppa taught me how to clean fish and shrimp too," she says, "He use to take me fishing with him and mister George. Fishing is fun. We have to go, sometimes."

"We will. We got a lake and ponds, going on our own property," he says, "Just tell them what kind of fish you want in it." They laugh.
190

TIME TO LOVE-RELOADED-TIME WILL REVEAL 3

"I look forward to teaching our kids how to fish *and* clean them," she says, "But that'll be fresh water fish. We'll get *Brims, Catfish* and *blue gill perch*. And teach them how to pick their own bones out, by age five."

"My wife is *Ellie Mae Clampett*," Ajay says as they laugh, "Still you can get them dressed, if you want. I got *uncle Jed* money. I can afford it."

"I thank you, baby," she says, "But I like to save us money. Whenever or wherever I can. You know me."

"Cool," he says with a smile, "That's why I'm marrying you."
He kisses her, then leaves her to her cooking duties. He goes into their large living room, starts up the fireplace and sits down in his oversized recliner to watch his wall sized television.

"Baby, what song will we dance too?" she asks from the kitchen.

"When?"

"Our first dance, as husband and wife, at the reception," she says for clarity.

"*Voyage to Atlantis*," he says, "Don't you think?"

"Perfect," she says with a huge smile.

"Oh yea and for the honeymoon, we're only gonna have four days and four nights," he says, "Before we have to report back to our teams. I was thinking we can take a short honeymoon after the reception. Then go for two weeks or so, in July."

"Okay, baby," she says, "We can come here if you want too. We'll have privacy, sort of. As long as we can hide from *the scenery*."
He's thinking of something a little more private and somewhere they've never been. He's made reservations for December 31 to January 3rd. They'll head back on the 4th. Then in July, he's taking her to Jamaica and the Virgin Islands for 2 weeks and start working on *their* family.

"Oh yea and on the honeymoon. That's when the red light special starts," he says with a grin, as he peeks into the kitchen to see her reaction. She's giggling and blushing, from ear to ear.

}Cincinnati{

By the 15th, Ebony and T-baby are into the preseason practices of their senior year. They have to represent and go out with a bang. Both of them have been heavily recruited by the new league, the *WNBA*. Neither of them are interested in the league, at this time.

"If we play, that means we'll never see our husbands," Ebony says to coach Sanders.

"It's an option, ladies. I think the two of you could do really well in

191

the league," coach Sanders tells them, "You're *Natty's* best chance." They tell her they'll think about it. But they know they won't. Not much. They want to play together, wherever they would go. And they know, in the WNBA, they wouldn't be afforded the opportunity to choose. And furthermore, with their husbands already playing pro sports, they'll have a difficult enough task just trying to get some quality time with them. If they join the league, they'll be on opposite ends of the country, most of the time.

}*Jackson Heights*{

It's Halloween in *Jackson Heights*. The community is decorated with ghost, goblins and goons, done by their awesome beautification team. For trick or treat, 1st the foursome drive Jerica, Rich III and Orian through Shaker Heights, The Point and Cliff View, then return. Nina, Rebbie and T-baby combine the candy and put it away until they can inspect it. While Ebony takes the candy they all bought to hand out and combines it in a 10 gallon *Rubbermaid* container. With playpen and walkers, they bring the kids outside into Rebbie's heated, 3 car garage. The ladies sit out on the driveway and serve candy, as kids come through their neighborhood looking for treats. All the crew bring their kids. Destiny wins cutest costume, this year. She's dressed as Cinderella.

Charlotte turns 13 and is initiated to the crew. But her, like the rest of the females, is anxious to see how her bridesmaids gown will fit. Today, they have a fitting. Ebony's matrons are planning her bridal shower also. They stay at Nina's while Ebony goes to *Crew Gear and Alterations* alone. Only Pearl, big mama, Sandy, Rena and Belinda have seen her wedding gown. But Pearl wants Jo to come in for the 2nd fitting. It isn't 100% complete when Ebony tries it on. But she gets a pretty good vision of what the final gown will look like.

"It's beautiful, already," Jo says with a smile, "Ant is so excited. I don't know *what* you did, baby girl. But thank you." They all laugh.

"All they have to do is the long train and the veil," big mama says.

"Do you know my husband and your daddy predicted this would happen?" Jo says to Ebony, "You and Ant was babies, then. Three and four years old. My only son, *truly* loves you and I am so happy."

"Anthony told me, big Al said that to him," Ebony says, "But he said, you and mama wasn't ready to hear any of it," she adds with a smile.

"We wasn't," Pearl offers, "Y'all remember that part. But over the years, when y'all tried our patience. They kept us in line."

192

TIME TO LOVE-RELOADED-TIME WILL REVEAL 3

"They wouldn't let us interfere, like we *really* wanted too," Jo adds, "But we thought they was crazy. I knew you was the girl, for Ant. I just didn't think he was going to get himself right."

"And Jo would always tell me that," Pearl says, "She thought, for sure, Ajay was convincing you to do something wrong. But I knew better than that. You know the times when all of you would be out late or at Renee's drinking?"

Pearl cuts her eyes at the ladies. They snicker, signifying the crew hadn't gotten away with anything. They knew. Because they did the same things.

"So many times, me and Pearl wanted them to come with us to make all of you go home," Jo laughs, "But they wouldn't."

"The clincher for me, was when John said it was okay for you to go with Ajay to Cincinnati," Pearl says, "For his seventeenth birthday. I knew he was all for you two being together, then. It was no doubt in my mind that he saw Ajay as his son-in-law." She giggles.

"That didn't shock me," Sandy says, "Ajay was standing up for her, even back then. John knew he could handle things, ha Ebony?"

Ebony blushes and says, "I guess so. I knew he liked me with him, when I got out of his truck to kiss him, before I moved to big mama's."

"You're right about that," Jo says, "I say Pearl and I was quicker to accept *her* boys and *my* girls, together, early in your lives."

"Jb and Lynn didn't leave us much choice, now did they?" Pearl ask as they all laugh again.

"Honestly, Pearl and I thought you and Ant was destined to be single," Jo says, "Because y'all were both *so* head strong."

"That is until *I told the both of you*," big mama sings.

"You sure did," Rena says, "You told us about all of them."

"And she told us about us too," Belinda says as she chuckles, "*And* let our parents know it too."

They all laugh as Ebony steps out of her gown and the ladies take it back into hiding. The wedding party females are showing up.

"The party is *in the house!*" Nina yells as she parades the entire female wedding party in behind her.

"We told you, your matrons had this thang locked?" Rebbie adds.

"Didn't we deliver?" T-baby ask and they all laugh.

Her girls had given her their word that they would get all the females into the shop, at once, for their fittings. So she could see how well her rainbow colors blended.

"I knew my girls would hold me down," Ebony says as she smiles.

193

"Come on in. I have *got* to see y'all in these gowns. Get them on, please. I need to see if my colors are matching up. Anthony said he's gonna be checking for my vision."

She's giddy, as they all try on their dresses. Rena and Sandy pin what needs to be altered. For the most part, they'd cut everyone of the dresses, perfect. April and Yolanda are here from Houston. But the Atlanta and California crew don't make it in, this time.

"We've done dresses for all of them," Belinda says, "We can work theirs without them being here. We've got cuts for them."

"I have at least one girl here, in each color," Ebony says, "That's fine. Y'all look good together. *Okay!*" she yells in excitement.

When they're done with the fittings, she ask them to come with her to *Jackson Heights.* She's going to show them the mansion, Though it isn't completely finished, she wants to show them where they'll stay on the night before the wedding. The guys will stay at Rich, Tank and June's homes. They'll go elsewhere for Ajay's bachelor party.

Ebony and Ajay's Estate will be finished on the 18th of the month. She tells the ladies this, as they arrive at the mansion.

"Ten more days until we can move in," Ebony says as her and all of the females, look around the entire estate.

The entire community has been closed in by a wrought iron fence which stands 15 feet tall. The guard booth at the entrance is fully operational and ready for the security team. Until then, the secured entrance gate keeps the premises protected. The only way to open the huge gate is by keying the password into the box and using a key, at the same time, for entry. Further, all homes have separate iron fences and state-of-the-art security systems. David Jacobson had recommended and installed their security systems. He's going into the private security business after he retires, in 4 weeks. As for now, he moonlights for *Crew Enterprises.* He has 14 officers who work with him. 1 of the officers is Stanley McDaniel, the officer who responded to Stoney's house on that fatal morning, nearly 7 years ago. The crew secured the loan for Jacobson's business venture which is under the *Crew Enterprise* umbrella. He has all the money he needs for extra crew and equipment. Aside from his security staff installing systems for other locations, their only responsibility is the crew. The crew businesses and homes are their only assignments. David Jacobson will man the booth at the Jackson Heights entrance personally, at the crew's request. Ajay and Ebony already feel a special connection with him. Ajay knows he'll do the best job possible when guarding his wife, his future kids, their homes and their entire private
194

TIME TO LOVE-RELOADED-TIME WILL REVEAL 3

community. Jacobson hires additional officers to insure there will be someone assigned to *Jackson Heights* and *The CrewLand Mall,* at all times. They will also secure their parents and grandparents homes. *Jacobson security* will be the number 13 and official Crew Enterprise business, as of the 1st of the year. Jacobson will be on duty in the booth, when the newlyweds return. Ajay has left strict orders that no one enters that gate unannounced or uninvited. Jo and Deb help Jacobson interview additional officers and staff, for a future roster, as they expect the need to arise, sooner than later. Jason Carr helps handle his accounting, along with Renee and Tonya, as they do for the crew. Once T-baby and Ebony finish college and set up in their offices at CrewLand Mall, the accounting and Real Estate will be their jobs, first and foremost.

Ajay is home on the 17th, for the final walk through of him and Ebony's large estate. Before he goes to do the walk through, he meets Pearl at their restaurant for lunch.

"Hey, Ajay," Pearl says, "I'm glad we could talk."

"Finally, ha? No problem, mom-in-law. What's on your mind?" he ask as he turns in their lunch orders and they begin to talk.

"First of all, I wanna say that I'm sorry for all of the years I interfered with you and baby girl," she says.

"It's not a problem," he says, "You wasn't really interfering."

"I've always loved you, like my own. I was just afraid of your tough side. I knew she would like you because you're just like her father. That's what attracted me to John," she says with a smile. "He was always a protector and took no mess from anyone. White, Black or other."

Ajay can't comment, at this point. He just smiles and listens.

"I only wanted to make sure you wasn't gonna go for *just* the tough side. But that you'd take that and turn it into something good," she says, "And you certainly did that."

"I knew you loved me," he says, "I told you that. I never thought you didn't. I knew it was never about you thinking I didn't come from good people or that I wasn't good enough. I even told her that, the day after you and her had the brawl in her room." They look embarrassed, as they reflect on that memory. He continues, "I told her you was one of the fairest people, I know. And that you was only making sure I stayed on my toes. She said you thought I was using her for sex. But mama explained that one."

"I wanted to make her slow down. I guess I just wasn't ready to see her do the exact same things, she'd watched me do," she says and laughs.

195

"Which is being happy with my first love, for the rest of my life. I guess I just wanted to make sure you wasn't going all the way with the street stuff and taking her with you."

"Nah. I never wanted to see one hair on her head, out of place. Call me obsessed, I don't know," he says, "But I have always felt, about her, the same way I feel now. I just had to learn how to love her, then let that love grow into something. So that all of the other people *and parents* could see that it was the real thing. I knew when you fussed at her about me, it was to keep her strong. I told her that too. I wanted us to have a relationship that all the people we loved, was okay with. So I had to get her on that page too. And I didn't want her to defy you or big John. But at the same, it's so hard to tell her no."

They both laugh, as she says, "You did that. We're all okay with this union. You spoil her, more than John and I would. We knew Al and Jo had raised you to know how to treat her, *as crew*. We just worried about her getting pregnant. Like at thirteen and fourteen."

"I was never worried about that," he says, "Not that I didn't think it could happen. But I knew when to, *not* do it. Pops taught me about counting the days, so I wouldn't end up with a kid. Because he knew I wasn't gonna use condoms with the girl that I liked," he says and laughs as Pearl looks at him as if she's in shock.

"You've always been wise for your age, Ajay. I have to give you that," she says, "And it was for that reason alone, that I just let you and Ebony be. I knew she wasn't on the exact same level-"

Their food arrives. He takes this opportunity to defend his girl and bride-to-be, once more.

"She *is,* though. She compliments everything that I am," he says, "If I'm not skilled at it, she is. We're a perfect combination. I can say that with no doubt in my mind. That girl can gut open a fish." They laugh.

He says, "I had to learn to love her, per *you* and big *John's* specifications, that's all. I wanted to make you and him proud of me. And want me to be the man for your princess. Your only daughter. But she's my Queen now and we've got to go and look at our castle, after this lunch is finished."

"A castle, indeed," Pearl says and smiles, "The house is *huge*. But Ajay, we couldn't have asked for a better man for my only daughter."

"Good," he says, "Because I'm the only one you're gonna get."

They laugh and dig in. Both are happy they had this talk and relieved that neither of them harbor any resentment from the past. They finish lunch. Then he meets up with Ebony.

196

TIME TO LOVE-RELOADED-TIME WILL REVEAL 3

They do their blood test and apply for their marriage license. Afterwards, they take physical possession of their estate and get all the keys. Then, with Tank, Nina, T-baby and Rebbie, they set up their security systems. Including the entry gate pass code. After setting the main gate code, Tank, Nina, T-baby and Rebbie go home. Ajay and Ebony go back to their new home.

First, he carries her over the threshold. Then he takes her into his arms and kisses her, for at least a minute.

He says, "It's all ours now, baby. We'll see a lot of changes in this house. We'll start our family here and watch *our* children grow up and fall in love. Well, the boy children," he adds as he chuckles.

She rolls her eyes. They hadn't seen each other since her weekend in Miami.

"You got the nursery done in blue, ha?" she asks, "So now we have to have more than one boy child."

"There's one in pink too," he says, "On the other side of the office. We can walk to that one, through here," he says as he shows her the room on the other side of the 2nd floor office, that he'd added to the plan.

"I had the upstairs office put between the nurseries and connected the three rooms. And when you decorate them," he says, "You can do them however you want too. As long as that room is for boys and this room is for girls."

She smiles big. She loves the mansion. They both do, as they take the elevator downstairs to the master suite. He tells her about the wonderful lunch he had with her mother. She's very happy to know she's been discussed.

"In Cincinnati, on my seventeenth birthday, I can remember when you wasn't about being talked about," he says as he laughs.

"But you and daddy was talking about us like we was-"

"Getting married?" he asks as he finishing her sentence.

"You already knew then, didn't you?" she asks.

"I'm trying to tell you, baby," he says, "I've always known. I knew I wanted to marry you. I just had to get you to like me. When I was fucking around out there, I knew. But I had to learn how to show you, I knew."

She lays her head against his chest as they reach the master suite.

"I'm ready to break this muthafucka in, though," he says as he kisses her again and pulls her closer to him.

"On the carpet?" she asks.

"Hell yea," he says taking her down to the floor.

They officially move, in the next weekend, while his team is in town

197

to play the Cavaliers. Pearl and Jo hire decorators to help out with the large estate. It takes 48 straight hours for the décor team to get it right. But it's truly beautiful when they're finished. Ajay and Ebony love it.

"Now when we come home, we can stay in our *own* house," Ajay says to Ebony, after everyone leaves.

"And baby, we're already use to each other," she says, "We're like old roommates now."

"Yea. We already know how each other shit smells and all that," he says and they crack up laughing.

"Thanks for reminding me to get matches for our bathroom," she say as she can't stop laughing. "You're the one that's goofy. You use always call me that."

"You still are," he says as he plants a wet kiss on her, then smacks her bottom as he follows her through the house and she adds her finishing touches.

All the guys have to be fitted and have their tuxedo's reserved, this weekend also. Ajay doesn't have to remind anyone. Chill does what talking, on the subject, that's done, when he says, "Anyone who don't get their's reserved, need not call me again. *Ever.*"
They laugh all the way to the rental shop.

The crew get together for Thanksgiving. Ajay and June's teams are playing in Detroit, on Thanksgiving day. June's game is at noon. Ajay's game is at 5pm. The crew drive up to Detroit for the games and to have their Thanksgiving dinner. Instead of having the traditional Thanksgiving meal in Cleveland, the grandmothers have arranged to cater dinner for both road teams. They have the banquet rooms, at the team hotels, set up for the dinner. The teams enjoy the meal and seeing all of the crew again.

"You ladies can cater for us, anytime," the teams staff had said.
After Thanksgiving weekend, Tonya, Anna, Debbie and Justine book the salons and spa for the entire wedding party, for the whole week following Christmas. Wedding participants will have 1st dibs. The wedding party will be massaged, pampered and styled, from the 27th through the 30th. The 31st is reserved for Ebony, Nina, Rebbie, T-baby, Pearl, Jo and big Mama. At the Cut Shop, Ajay, Tank, June, Rich, John, Al, poppa and papa have the privileges, on the wedding day. The other groomsmen get 1st dibs from the 27th though the 30th.

Thanksgiving is passed. Ebony and Ajay's sights are on their
198

wedding day.

"It's thirty three days before my wedding," Ebony says to T-baby. Today is the Saturday before their 1st regular season game. They're both excited and full of anticipation about their senior season and Ebony's upcoming nuptials.

"It won't be long now, kid," T-baby says as they both smile.

****

Alana is working on behalf of herself and Angel. She's making nice with her Aunt Darlene, in hopes that she'll agree to host her when she returns to Cleveland in a month or so. After her probation ends. Darlene is just about over the anger she had with Alana for helping Angel to meet and consequently, fuck Ajay. Her latest gift by mail may have helped. By some strange twist of fate, Darlene got an invite to Ebony and Ajay's wedding. It was the idea of the crew 1st and 2nd generations. They want her to witness Ajay, in his true form. They're not worried about her causing a disruption. Because they know she wants to remain alive. She knows this crew well enough to know, if she was to ruin an event, especially 1 this large, her life wouldn't be worth a red cent. She has already promised to be on her best. She has an invite to the bachelor party too. And she knows not to breathe a word of it. All the guest know that if the word gets out, before hand, they lose all invites. That includes The CrewLand Mall, as well. Not even the club. Darlene doesn't even tell Alana. She's going to wait until after the wedding, then show her photo's. She knows Alana still talks to Angel. She isn't interested in letting Angel in on any info. Not until after she's had a chance to fuck Ajay, at his bachelor party. Or at least, suck his dick again.

****

The 1st week of December is time for final month preparations. Big mama and Pearl order all the flowers and decorations for the church, the reception hall and the bridal and bridesmaids bouquets. Plus they order the boutonnieres for all the men in the wedding and corsages for the mothers. On Friday, the wedding programs are picked up from the printer.

"I wish we could've gotten Mariah," Ebony says, "That would've been the perfect day." She dismisses it saying "But I know she's busy." Pearl and big mama say nothing. They know the program she's viewing is the fake one. Just as Ajay has requested, Mariah will be performing at the

199

Wedding. With Nina, Rebbie and T-baby doing background. His team has provided all of the beverages for the reception. The liquor list alone is over 100k. The Heat have ordered top of the line champagnes and premium liquors, as their gift to the bride and groom. *The Crews House of Soul Food* is catering the reception, the bridal shower, the rehearsal dinner and the bachelor party. All of the foods for these events is ordered this week.

December 11th is the final dress fittings for the ladies. All of the dresses are done. Sandy, Belinda and Rena will deliver them to the church, on the morning of the wedding.

"Finally got all of the dresses done," Pearl says to Ebony.

"Twenty days ahead of schedule," big mama adds.

"Only twenty days until my wedding," Ebony says with a smile. She's already starting to feel butterflies.

The following Friday, most of the crew go to Atlanta for Lynn's graduation from Officers training school. They hadn't seen John III, in months. They're surprised to see him, so active.

"Lil John is crawling all over *and* pulling up!" Ebony says.

"He's moving so fast, for seven months," Lynn says.

"He's getting out the way for another one," Jo offers.

"I don't know, from where," Lynn says, adamantly disagreeing with her mother.

After completing OTS, she is a full fledged 2nd lieutenant in the United States Air Force. She'll remain at her present duty station, for the majority of the time. But she will have to travel, intermittently to Washington DC, for briefings. She's in the Security specialist division of Air Force Intelligence and 7th in command at Dobbins AFB.

****

"Ebony, we've got the decorations done," Nina says via cell phone. It's the twenty third and Nina's birthday. The females are prepared for Christmas Day and Ebony's bridal shower. The Christmas party will be held at the club. The shower will be at Ebony and Ajay's home, on the day after Christmas. Tonight however, Ebony and T-baby are on the road playing their final game before Christmas break and Ebony's final game before her wedding day. T-baby will rejoin the team at Penn state, for the December 29th game, after the bridal shower. But coach Sanders excuses
200

Ebony from that game, so she can be rested and prepared for her big day. Her teammate, Katrina Dobbs, is 1 of the few who protests. Claiming that it's because they need Ebony there to win. Ebony can't figure out why Katrina hates her fiancée. But she knows he hates her, *equally.*
The crew are extremely busy, the next week. They have to do Christmas shopping and final week wedding preparations.

It's less than a week before the wedding. It's Christmas day and Ebony turns 22 years old.
"Happy birthday, baby," Ajay says from his cell phone.
He's on the road for Christmas night and will be home tomorrow.
"Merry Christmas, Anthony," she says, "My girls got the house decorated with bridal shower stuff, already."
"Yea. That *is* tomorrow night, ha?" he asks in a sly tone.
"Yes and you can't come to it, baby," she say as she giggles.
"Are y'all gonna have naked men in my house?" he asks.
"I don't think so," she says.
"Well, if Nina, T-baby and Ree Ree in charge of the entertainment. Y'all will," he says in a disapproving tone, "And Lynn is flying in."
"Baby, I don't know what they've got planned," she says, "I'm just the guest of honor. The bride, that's it."
"And don't you forget who the groom is," he warns.
"How could I *ever* do that?" she asks, in a sarcastic tone.
"I'm serious," he says, "Don't you let no man grope all over you and shit."
"I won't, baby," she says, "What time will you get here?"
"I'll be there tonight, as a matter of fact," he says, "I'm trying to get there before midnight. But you don't have to pick me up. Tank already got it handled."
Tank will be at the Christmas party tonight, at *The Spot II.* He's leaving Nina in charge, so he can pick up Ajay and bring him back to *The Chill Spot.* Thus, Ebony can enjoy her party and wait for her man to come to her.
There are parties at *The Chill Spot* and *The Spot II.* Lil Kenny is honored at The Spot II party, for his 14th birthday. Ebony is the honoree at the main club. Ajay makes it in, just before midnight.
"I'm glad you made it before Christmas and my day was over," she says.
"This is your week, baby," he says, "The whole week is yours."
"It's your week too," she says, " I need you with me."

TIME TO LOVE-RELOADED-TIME WILL REVEAL 3

The next day, Ajay is whisked out of his own house in the late morning, by his mother.

"You can't be here. Even while we're setting up," Jo says.

"How are y'all gonna just throw me out of my *own* house, ma?" he asks, after his shower.

"This house belongs to the bride-to-be, *today*," Jo says with a smile, "So move it along."

"What time are y'all gonna be finished?" he asks.

"None of your business. Don't you show up here, either," Jo says.

Ebony feels sad, seeing him leave. Al escorts him out of the front door and takes him to Stoney's, to chill with him, John and the rest of the male crew. It's the 26th day of December. *Ebony's Bridal Shower day!*

All of the females arrive, promptly at 6pm. The guys are suppose to be at the sports bar or the clubs, while the bridal shower takes place. But Ajay is determined to crash the shower. He tries several times, to call Ebony but Pearl, Jo and big mama are in charge of her cell phone. They're answering the house phones, as well. He pleads with big mama to let him speak to Ebony.

She laughs and says, "You wanna persuade her to let you come in here."

Jacobson won't let any of the guys through the entrance gate, prior to nor during the shower. Ajay eventually gives up. But he does have a request for big mama.

He says, "Tell Ebony she'd better call me, as soon as it's over."

Big mama chuckles as they hang up. The bridal shower is underway, with all the females of the wedding party and the family, present and accounted for. They're having a wonderful time touring the house, playing music, sipping wines and daiquiri's. While some are dancing. Then Nina calls everyone to order. It's time to present the bride with her specialty gifts. The 1st to present to Ebony is big mama.

"This is your something old," she says as she gives her a string of pearls which was passed down from Ebony's great-grandmother.

"This is your something new," Pearl says as she hands her a large pair of diamond earrings, from her and John Sr.

"This will be your something borrowed," her soon to be mother-in-law, Jo says as she pins a diamond broche on Ebony's lapel. "This belonged to my mother."

"And here is your something blue," her girls say in unison.

They give her the lingerie set she'll wear under her wedding gown. It's a *Christian Dior,* light blue lacy bra and panty set.

202

Next, she receives a beautiful diamond and pearl bracelet from her female wedding party. She's very pleased with her personal gifts as she becomes emotional. She has to clear her throat to speak.

"Thank you, everybody. I'm all set, now," she says through teary eyes, "Something old, something new, something borrowed and something blue. And something very sparkly too."

She's excited. She has gifts for her female party, as well. Each of the ladies receive a set of diamond and pearl earrings, in the wedding color that she'll wear. Ajay will give the guys cuff links in their wedding color, at his bachelor party, later this week.

"Now it's time for some entertainment!" Nina shouts as they turn the music back up, only as a distraction for Ebony.

The door bell rings. T-baby gets the door, then yells back, "Ebony, are you expecting a delivery!?"

She steps back into the foyer to meet Ebony, who heads to the door.

"No. I'm not. But Anthony might be," she says as she joins T-baby.

"Who's this for?" she ask T-baby and the delivery man.

"This guy says he has a delivery for *you*," T-baby says.

"I have some packages for the bride-to-be," the gentleman, dressed in UPS gear, says, "I just need your signature here, please."

He hands Ebony a clipboard with an invoice attached. She signs the paper. Then the gentleman rolls 3 very large boxes into the family room.

"What in the world is all of this?" aunt Jessica asks, pretending not to know what's going on.

The deliveryman opens, then tears away the cardboard from the 3 boxes. Each box contains a large crate.

"What is it?" Ebony asks as she slowly takes her seat.

He unlatches the hooks on the front of each of the 3 crates. 3 skimpy clad, muscular men burst out of each one. Simultaneously, the deliveryman is tearing away his UPS gear to reveal he's wearing the same skimpy outfit. Ebony realizes she's been had now. Rebbie starts the music and all 4 men start to dance around Ebony. Nina, Rebbie and T-baby laugh at Ebony's shock. They'd hired 4 exotic dancers to perform. The men shake *what they're mama's gave them and daddy's too,* in front of Ebony, for the next 30 minutes. They treat Pearl, Jo and big mama to a lap dance, along with Ebony, of course.

"Oh my God!" Ebony yells, as each dancer takes a turn dancing on her lap. "Anthony is gonna kill me!" she shouts and giggles.

She has never laughed so hard, in her life. After the striptease, the ladies
203

offer the guys a plate of food. The dancers garner plenty of tips for their performance. After eating, the men leave the party and the women continue with their games and fun. Ebony receives many beautiful gifts for herself, as well as for her and Ajay's home. Her matrons help her put all her gifts in the master bedroom, so she can show them to Anthony, later tonight. Belinda takes all of her traditional gifts and puts them together in a special bridal box, for the wedding day. She'll bring this box which contains her something old, something new, something borrowed and something blue. Plus her diamond and pearl bracelet, to the church, along with her wedding gown, accessories and honeymoon attire.

When the shower ends, Ebony and all of her wedding party meet their guys at The Chill Spot and The Spot II. Ajay inquires, several times, about the events of her bridal shower but she isn't allowed to tell him.

"Not until the honeymoon," she says, "But I'll tell you tonight, if you tell me where your bachelor party is gonna be."
He isn't willing to divulge that information, so she keeps her bridal shower events, secret as well.

On Monday, wedding food preparations start at the restaurant. The food for the rehearsal dinner is prepped 1st. The grandmothers have to prepare all of the traditional soul foods for the reception.
Macaroni and cheese, Glazed ham, turkey and fixings, collard greens, cornbread, yams, green beans with potatoes, fried chicken, mashed potatoes, potato salad, cakes, pies and tarts.
They prepare the wedding cake and the large chocolate cake for the groom. Ajay's cake is decorated as a basketball court, complete with 10 players and 3 officials with cheerleaders on the sideline. They make a large chocolate cake for the bachelor party, as well. This cake is shaped like a *Black woman*, from the neck to the thighs. The rehearsal dinner meal will be;
Steak, baked potatoes, mixed vegetables, tossed salads, rolls and red velvet cake with iced tea to drink.

The wedding rehearsal is the next day. The wedding party are in town and counted. Many guest have already started to arrive, with more in route. The UC teams come in on Tuesday, as Ebony and Ajay spend their last morning together, as singles. After the rehearsal dinner, they won't see each other again until they stand at the alter, tomorrow afternoon.

His Miami teammates arrive during the rehearsal. They're staying at Tank, June and Rich's homes, with the male wedding participants. This is the plan for all of the men, as far as Ebony knows. All of the ladies finish
204

up their spa, hair and nail appointments, while the men are getting massages, haircuts, trims and such. Then they all meet at the church, for rehearsal. They do a lot of clowning around, as they're known to do. It takes 2 hours but eventually, everyone hits their mark perfectly, before Belinda and her coordinators allow anyone to leave.

"Everything is ready for tonight," June says to Ajay, about his bachelor party, as they file out of the rehearsal.

Ajay pulls Ebony to him.

"Tell me again, *why* we can't sleep together tonight?" he says and smiles.

"Because it's bad luck," she answers as she smiles back.

"How is *that*, bad luck?" he jokes.

"You know why, so stop trying to mess with her mind," Lynn interrupts as they laugh.

Ebony gives Anthony a passionate kiss, before releasing him to his best men and teammates.

"Save it for the honeymoon," Tank says as they all laugh again.

They finally leave the church and go their separate ways.

Tonight, all of the females in the wedding party, 24 including Ebony, are at her and Anthony's home. After they're all relaxing in the family room, sipping wine and bonding, Ebony has a surprise to reveal.

"I know where the bachelor party is," she says.

"Where at, baby girl? Let's go crash it!" Bre yells.

"We have to get into this one, y'all," Renee says as she giggles.

"Because we're zero for four," Tonya says and laughs too.

"Where is it, Ebony?" Lynn presses.

"The civic center grand ballroom," she says.

"How did you find out?" T-baby asks.

"As we were leaving the church, I overheard one of his teammates asking papa, how do they get there," she says, "Why would they need to know that?"

"Are they staying there?" Erica asks.

"All the teams are staying out here," she says, "With the crew."

"Civic center has nothing to do with the wedding," Rebbie offers.

"The reception either," T-baby adds and laughs.

"Ebony comes through again," Nina says and laughs.

"So we're going. Now let's discuss the terms," Renee says.

"We're gonna wait until about ten, before we go," Jan says.

"We'll be out of there before twelve, though," Nina adds.

205

TIME TO LOVE-RELOADED-TIME WILL REVEAL 3

"Now y'all know that they can't see each other after midnight. Or it's bad luck," Rebbie says.

"It's funny because I just told him that, at rehearsal," Ebony says, "But he's not superstitious."

"Oh, wait a minute. Let me guess," Nina says with a smile, "He was trying to get some?"

"Duh!" Lynn offers as they laugh, then get back to the plan of crashing Ajay's bachelor party.

"That's why we're going at ten," Jan says, "We'll be out of there before twelve."
The ladies are bubbling with excitement, over the thought of finally finding 1 of their guys bachelor parties.

At the civic center, the bachelor party is well underway. The guys have packed so many skimpy clad females into the ballroom, it looks more like a Hugh Hefner event. The waitresses all wear bunny tails and corset's with bunny ears. Roc is in attendance. So is Darlene. Alana had been invited, at the last minute by Kilo, at the crews request. The option is to have as many lose women as possible. Samantha, Nicole, Angie, Tameka and Gloria are in the building too. Anita is missing in action. She's been in jail for 6 months, on many shoplifting convictions. Unbeknownst to Ebony, Sonya, Shuntay and Tina are in town from Houston and are in attendance too. Some guys in Ron's crew brought them. Specifically for the bachelor party. Ajay doesn't particularly like the guest list. But he's the honoree. Not the coordinator. He didn't have control of who got invited.

"My man! Are you ready for some football?!" Chill yells over the microphone, from the stage.
That's the cue for the exotic dancers to rush the room. 11 of them are dressed like the Cleveland Browns cheerleaders when they run into the room, complete with pom-poms. Then there are 11 more girls in *Browns* team jerseys. They do a simulated football huddle, then they break out of the huddle to the line of scrimmage and line up in the 3-point stance. All of their thongs are visible. The room roars with cheers, as they snap the ball. 1 dancer goes out for a reception. When she catches the ball and gets tackled, the tackler starts to grind on top of her and the guys love it. Then the music starts and the striptease begins, for all 22 girls. Each girl has her turn with Ajay. He's all smiles as he sits on his grooms throne, surrounded by the male wedding participants, his Miami and UC teammates.

One dancer named Josie tries to put her nipple in his mouth but he

206

TIME TO LOVE-RELOADED-TIME WILL REVEAL 3

declines. However, Jarvis takes advantage of the opportunity when it's presented to him. So does several of the other guys. Like Rich and June, who are a bit overzealous with the dancers, from Ajay's perspective. He warns them to calm down before word gets back to their wives. Instead, they try to convince him to participate.

"You know this is your last chance to hit something," June says, passing Ajay another Hennessy on the rocks.

"I know," he says, "But I don't know about all that."

"Roc is here, man," Rich says as he's feeling up a dancer named Regina. "You know she's wit it."

Chill listens to the conversations and laughs. He's confident that whatever Ajay does, he'll be discreet. All of the past husbands-to-be in the crew had their last flings, at their bachelor parties. Darlene is hoping she'll be the chosen one. She'll be thoroughly disappointed.

Ebony and her crew show up, promptly at 10pm. The party is in full swing. She tries to get in but Stanley McDaniel is on the door.

"Ebony, I can't allow y'all to go in," he says with a smile.

Renee offers him money to let them in. But Chill has paid him much more, to keep them out.

"We'll double whatever they paid you," Lynn tries but McDaniel will not allow them in.

However, he does send 1 of their security guys inside to alert the men that their ladies are here. Ajay and most of the crew come to the doors.

"Baby, what are you doing down here?" he asks with a pleasant smile and he doesn't seem shocked at all that she's found his party.

"I wanna know who's in there," Ebony says, trying to look past McDaniel but he doesn't allow her to see inside.

"You know you can't come in here," Tank says to Nina.

"Oh and why not? We found it," Nina says.

"I found your shower too but I couldn't go in it," Tank replies as him and his wife engage in a tit-for-tat while Ebony and Ajay engage in a long wet kiss.

"Don't let her sway you, man," Chill says as Ajay laughs and continues kissing his bride-to-be.

"Y'all need to go home," Rich says to T-baby.

"We're in, baby. I wanna see what tramps are in there," she says.

Ebony and Ajay are concerned only with each other, as the others focus on who is and isn't going to go inside.

207

"I'm missing you, already," she says, "I don't know how I'm gonna sleep without you."

"Do you feel how hard my dick is?" he whispers in her ear.

"Yes. That's mine and I want it," she says as she looks around to find a private spot for them to duck in too.

"That office, down there, is empty," he says as they head down the hall before Chill calls him.

"Ajay, where you going, man?" he's laughing as he asks.

Ajay tries to explain that they're going to talk, where they can hear each other but Chill, Tank and the crew convince him to come back to his party.

"You've got a bachelor party going on," Tank says, "Save that for the honeymoon. Twin is trying to be slick, bro. Don't fall for it."

They eventually get him to tell Ebony, she has to leave and take her girls with her. She pleads with him but to no avail. It's getting closer to midnight and her girls tell her to come on and, "Let's just go."

Her and the females go back to her house and remain there for the rest of the night. They men continue the party, after they leave. June and Rich are over doing it with the ladies and insisting that Ajay partake in the buffet of women, who are more than willing to be his last fling. Rich is adamant about it.

"Man, are you gonna get you one or what?" he asks Ajay.

By now, Rich has already been fooling around with several of the dancers. But none of them have engaged with any of the females from their past. They know that would definitely get back to their wives. Bruce and the younger crew have all engaged in sexual activity with 1 woman or another, by parties end. Ajay allowed Roc to touch him and give him oral gratification. But he didn't have intercourse with anyone. However, the other guys did. They party until 3am before shutting it down.

"Son, you need to get some rest for your big day, later today," Al suggest as they leave the civic center.

The men are sleeping at Jackson Heights. Ajay calls his house, on the way.

"Hello," Ebony answers.

She's still awake and nervous about the wedding. She's wondering will everything go smoothly. She's also missing her man.

"What's up, baby?" Ajay asks.

"Hey," she asks, "Where are you?"

"On my way back out there," he says, "Meet me on the bedroom patio and let me in, so I can tightening my pussy up before we go to the church."

208

TIME TO LOVE-RELOADED-TIME WILL REVEAL 3

"I would love to do that," she says, "But it's bad luck, isn't it?"

"I wanna see you, in a major way," he says with a smile.

"You can't come here, Ant," Jo interrupts, as she picks up the other extension. *"You'll have to wait to see her at the church. Now go on and go to bed and tell Allen to go to bed too. I hear him giggling in the background."* She demands Ajay hang up the phone and not call back, because, *"Baby girl needs to try and get some sleep and so do you and your father,"* Jo says as she giggles. Ajay gives up and hangs up the phone.

Ebony tosses and turns, all night, as she's much to excited to sleep. She thinks about all of the nights she laid in her bed in Shaker Heights, dreaming of the day her and Anthony would get married. Now she has less than 12 hours to go before she'll be, Mrs. Anthony Devante' Jackson! They have a whole day planned, for just the 2 of them and those who love them. According to their newspapers and news stations, it's a big event.

"I love you, so much, Anthony. This is the best time of my life, baby," she thinks out loud.

She manages to doze off, just before sunlight. It's finally New Year's Eve!

}*The Big day!{*

"It's your wedding day, baby!" big mama says as she enters Ebony's bedroom to wake her.

Following big mama are Michelle and another of Arthur's assistants, who are there to video and take pictures of every move she makes, for this entire day. She opens her eyes and speaks to all 3 of the ladies in her room, as she rolls over and looks at the clock.

"Did she snap a picture while I was sleeping?" she asks big mama.

"I do think she did, baby," big mama answers with a smile, "We need to get moving."

"Okay but I have to call my baby, first," she says.

They have to get ready for their appointments at the salon. But Ebony calls Ajay, first thing, before getting out of bed.

"Good morning, baby," she says.

"It is, now," Ajay says, "Do you have folks snapping pictures in your face?"

"Yes. While I was still sleeping too," she says with a smile.

"What? A man is in my bedroom?" he asks.

"No," she quickly conveys, "There are two ladies taking pictures of everything I do. Maybe I should pick my nose."

209

They laugh as he tells her that he has already tried that and yes, they did take a picture of that too.

"Arthur just let me know, that he knows me well enough not to send a man into my house," he says as he laughs, "I was about to injure the photographer, baby."

"No. Don't do that," she says, "We need our wedding pictures and video."

"I let him make it," he says, "I'm getting my braids freshened up."

"I can't wait to see you," she says, "I know you're looking good."

"I heard you're gonna look like a princess," he says, "My mama has been bragging on you."

"Big mama and mama Belinda are rushing me," she says, "I still have to get my hair and stuff done."

"Aunt Rena and aunt Anna, over here, with that too," he says as he chuckles, "I have to go, lovely."

"I'll see you at the church, baby," she says.

"For sho. I missed you last night, girl," he says.

"We can make up for it tonight," she tells him.

"You'd better believe, I will. For twenty four hours too," he says, "No sunshine."

"Okay," she says.

They hang up after being told, over and over. Arthur and his photography crews had arrived early to catch the pre-wedding activity. They have been filming and photographing, all of the events of this gala. Except the bridal shower and bachelor party. Ebony and Ajay had private and separate photographers for those events. To keep all episodes private until they're ready to share them. The 1st picture snapped, was of the wedding announcement on September 30, before they were sent out. The photo taking continues, as she has breakfast, heads to CrewLand mall and the spa, for a massage and facial. She goes to Crew Cuts and Styles where Ajay has just left, after his braids are done. She can smell his cologne.

"Here's the bride," Justine says as Ebony comes into the salon with Nina, T-baby, Rebbie, Pearl, Jo and big mama.

Today is their day only, on the salon side of Crew Cuts.

"My baby was just here," she says, "I can smell him."

They all giggle as Tonya brings her over to her chair.

"Let's get you going," Tonya says as Ebony sits at her station. Matthew Johnson, Tonya's professor from CSU, is doing Ebony's hair for her wedding day. Another gift from her bridesmaids. Matthew is the best

210

stylist in the Ohio area and a close friend of Jr and Tonya. Nina is getting styled today. But first, she has to style her mother Jo, Tonya and Pearl before she can get her do. Tonya will do Nina and big mama's hair. Justine does Rebbie and T-baby's hair, then her, Tonya and Nina do all of their nails. They're all gorgeous now but hungry. Debbie enters the salon to coordinate the next move.

"It's time to go take our baths and go to the church. Ebony, we've got lunch for everybody," she says, "It's already at the house."

"Did you take Anthony something to eat?" she asks.

"Yes ma'am, we did," Debbie says with laugh, "You're always looking out for my nephew, aren't you girl?"

"Yes, that's my job," she says with a smile.

Tonya and Justine close the salon for the rest of the day and tomorrow. Matthew accompanies them to the house. He'll be at Ebony's side until she walks down the aisle, making certain her style is picture perfect all day.

All of the crew businesses close at noon. All of the wedding attendants are attending to their specific duties. Sandy, Belinda and Rena have taken all the dresses, tuxedo's and accessories plus Ebony and Ajay's suitcases, to the church.

Arthur and his Omega's set up his equipment at the church and at *The Chill Spot*. Rob and Jr get Bone and the Mo Thugs Family equipment set up for the reception, where they'll perform. Ajay gets a call from *Mariah*'s camp confirming she's in town. *The OJay's* and *Levert* are at papa's house, where big mama has made a special meal for them.

All of the wedding participants are at the church to get dressed by 1pm. The food is being delivered to *The Chill Spot*. The wedding performers are set up in their private rooms in the church's annex. Tonya, Nina, Lynn and Justine do all the females makeup.

"Don't do too much, Lynn," Ebony says.

"Oh, I know. I know my brother don't like it caked on," she says as she laughs. "I got it covered, baby girl. You're gonna be radiant when you walk down that aisle, sis." Lynn says as she gives her a wink and a nod, then they both laugh.

It's 3pm when she's zipped into her wedding gown for the final time. Arthur's assistants have taken every picture imaginable, of the females. Arthur has gotten every money shot available of the males. Ajay calls Ebony's cell phone, from his section in the church.

211

TIME TO LOVE-RELOADED-TIME WILL REVEAL 3

"You ready to do this, baby?" he asks.
"Yes, Anthony," she says, "I am so nervous."
"Me too but I can't wait until I see you," he says with a longing in his voice.
"Me either," she says, "It's time to get started. Aunt Sandy is lining up all the girls, right now."
"I know. I have to get ready to walk in," he says, "I'll see ya."
"In a minute," she says and they hang up.

Ebony has large butterflies now or small birds. But she can't wait to see her man at the alter. Their wedding day is finally here. In just a short time from now, she will be Mrs. Anthony Devante' Jackson!
Many guest arrive. They're lined up outside and around the church. The ushers hand out the wedding tokens, to all the guest, as they file in to be seated.
Wedding tokens include; Rainbow confetti bags, the wedding program, the keepsake scrolls and an autographed rainbow colored stainless steel key chain with *Mr. And Mrs. Anthony D. Jackson. Wednesday December 31, 1997,* engraved on them. Every wedding guest receives one.
It's a full house with everyone from their teams past and present. And from Houston to Miami. Their doctors, attorneys, coaches, alumni, family, friends and even some enemies, are in attendance. All the work has been done. All of the eyes are dotted and all of the tees have been crossed.

From her little window, in the top of the church, Ebony can see the multitude of people who have shown up to witness her and her only love, pledge their commitment to each other.
From his area, Ajay has peeked out of the door, at least 20 times, to see how many cars are outside. For as far as he can see, there is a car.
The parking lots are all full. So are the side streets and the neighboring parking areas and sidewalks. All 1000 announcements had responded. Those folks are seated. The overflow is another 300, easily. But the coordinators accommodate one and all. This is going to be a fabulous day. It's 4pm. It's time for Ebony Brown and Anthony Jackson's, Royal Wedding!

212

CHAPTER   31

THE ROYAL WEDDING

YOU ARE CORDIALLY INVITED

TO ATTEND THE WEDDING CEREMONY

OF

EBONY ELOISE *"BABY GIRL"* BROWN

TO

ANTHONY DEVANTE' *"AJAY"* JACKSON

ON THIS

THE THIRTY FIRST DAY

OF

DECEMBER

IN THE YEAR OF OUR LORD

NINETEEN HUNDRED AND NINETY SEVEN

AT

THE FIRST BAPTIST CHURCH OF CLEVELAND, OHIO

REVEREND LARRY EDWARD TUCKER, OFFICIATING

TIME 4:00 PM

WHAT GOD HAS BROUGHT TOGETHER, LET NO ONE PUT
ASUNDER!

TIME TO LOVE-RELOADED-TIME WILL REVEAL 3

Prelude..Soft Music

Lighting of the candles.......................By Ushers, Host and Hostesses

Entrance of Parents and Grandparents......................Soft Music

Mother of the Groom...................................Mrs. Joanna Williams Jackson
-Escorted by-
Father of the Groom.........................Mr. Allen Devante' Jackson, Jr.

Mother of the Bride......................................Mrs. Pearline Jones Brown
-Escorted by-
Uncle of the Bride...Mr. Gregory Brown, Sr.

Grandmother of the Bride...............Mrs. Eloise B*ig Mama* Wilkes Jones
-Escorted by-
Grandfather of the Bride..............................Mr. Percy *Poppa* Jones

Entrance of the Groom

.....................Mr. Anthony *Ajay* Devante' Jackson ....

-Best Men-
Honorary Best Man.............Cheston Wayne *Stoney* Coleman {deceased}
Best Man 3.......................Mr. Richard Trevon *Ritchie Rich* Williams, Jr.
Best Man 2...................................Mr. Brian *Big June* James, Jr.
Best Man 1.................................Mr. Jeremy Marcus *Tank* Brown

The Wedding Party-Wedding March Song

Senior Bridesmaids.........Escorted by..........Senior Groomsmen
Mrs. Renee Stewart Payne..........Mr. Kenneth *Big Chill* Ramon Payne, Sr.
Mrs. Latonya *Tonya* Walker Wilson..............Mr. Bradley *Jr* Lee Wilson, Jr.
Mrs. Janice *Jan* Logan Jenkins...................Mr. Robert *Lil Rob* Leon Jenkins
Miss Yolanda Marie Hall................................Mr. Jarvis Keith Rhodes
Mrs. Lynora *Lynn* Jackson Brown....................Mr. John *Jb* Brown, Jr.
Mrs. Breanna *Bre* Wilson Hamilton............Mr. Cedric *Ced* Leroy Hamilton
Miss Kimberly *Kim* Celine Logan............................Mr. Bruce Dalvin Wilson
Mrs. April Leshay Bradley......................................Mr. Terrell Allen Layton
214

TIME TO LOVE-RELOADED-TIME WILL REVEAL 3

-Matrons Of Honor-

Matron 3...............................Mrs. Latrisha *T-baby* Brown Williams
Matron 2...Mrs. Rebbie Wilson James
Matron 1...Mrs. Nina Jackson Brown

The Junior Wedding Party

Entrance Of The Junior Groom

........................Master Bradley Lee Wilson, III........................

Junior Best Man..............................Shannon Tyreek *Reaper* Wilson

Junior Bridesmaids..........Escorted by..........Junior Groomsmen

Erica Maureen Jackson......................................Gregory Brown, Jr
Ruthie *Roo* Nakia Williams...Jesse Lee Brown
Pamela Darius Jackson..Samuel Logan, Jr.
Alicia *Ally* Mallory Wilson................................Steven Davon Brown
Chaundra Denise Coleman...................................Kenneth Ramon Payne, Jr.
Brina Shawnice James..Archie Joseph Wilson, Jr.
Charlotte Ann Coleman...Brandon Shawn James

Junior Maid Of Honor........................Miss Brittany Neon James

...............................*Ring Bearers*................................
Honorary Ring Bearer ....Master John Brown, III
Ring Bearer..............................Master Richard Trevon Williams, III

...............................*Flower Girls*...........................

Honorary Flower Girl..........................Little Miss Orian Chanel James
Flower Girl 2.........................Little Miss Chastity *CJ* Jaquel Coleman
Flower Girl 1..............................Little Miss Jerica Eloise Brown

Entrance of the Junior Bride

Little Miss Destiny Jalene' Shante' Payne

EVERYONE PLEASE STAND FOR THE ENTRANCE OF THE BRIDE
215

TIME TO LOVE-RELOADED-TIME WILL REVEAL 3

Entrance of the Bride...*Bridal Song*

.....................Miss Ebony Eloise *Baby Girl* Brown...........................

Escorted by her Father...........................Mr. John *Big John* Brown, Sr.

PLEASE BE SEATED

Devotion...Pastor Larry E. Tucker
Prayer..............................Mr. Charles L. Wilson and Mr. Joshua Logan, Jr.

-Song to Anthony from Ebony-

I Feel Good.............................Mrs. Rena Baker Wilson-*Aunt of the groom*

Poem to the Couple ....Mrs. Eloise *Big Mama* Jones
Mr. Percy *Poppa* Jones
Mr. Jackson *Papa* Brown, Jr

}Moment of Silence for deceased loved ones{
Mr. and Mrs. Saul & Joanna Williams-*Grandparents of the Groom*
Mr. and Mrs. Allen & Bertha Jackson, Sr.-*Grandparents of the Groom*
Mrs. Pearline Anderson Granny Brown- *Grandmother of the Bride*
Mr. Cheston Wayne *Stoney* Coleman-*Crew Brother of the Couple*
Little Miss Angel Brown Jackson-*Daughter of the Couple*

-Song to the Couple from/by parents of the Groom-

If This World Were Mine...........Mr. and Mrs. Allen & Joanna Jackson, Jr

Scriptures....Mrs. Sally Greene Logan and Mrs. Annabelle Johnson Wilson

-Song to the Couple from the Grandparents-

Forever Mine...........................Performed by T*he Mighty, Mighty Ojay's*

-Song to the Couple from/by parents of the Bride-

Here And Now........................Mr. and Mrs. John & Pearline Brown, Sr.
216

TIME TO LOVE-RELOADED-TIME WILL REVEAL 3

}PLEDGING OF PERSONAL VOWS{

Bride-Ebony Eloise Brown

Groom-Anthony Devante' Jackson

Exchanging of Rings...Soft Music

Lighting of the Unity Candle...Soft Music

Pronouncement of Marriage...........................Pastor Larry E. Tucker

...............}SALUTE TO THE BRIDE AND GROOM{...................

-Song to Ebony from Anthony-

Vision of Love..*Miss Mariah Carey*
Accompanied by the Matrons of Honors
Mrs. Latrisha Brown Williams
Mrs. Rebbie Wilson James
Mrs. Nina Jackson Brown

..........Presenting the happy Couple..........

Mr. and Mrs. Anthony Devante' Jackson
Wednesday December 31, 1997

Blessing of the Couple.................................Pastor Larry E. Tucker

Recessional....................................Wedding March Exit Song

CONGRATULATIONS TO THE HAPPY COUPLE!

217

TIME TO LOVE-RELOADED-TIME WILL REVEAL 3

Coordinators
Mother of the Bride....................................Mrs. Pearline Jones Brown
Mother of the Groom..............................Mrs. Joanna Williams Jackson
Grandmother of the Bride.............................Mrs. Eloise Wilkes Jones
Aunt of the Bride...Mrs. Brenda Jones James

Seamstresses
Aunt of the Groom......................................Mrs. Rena Baker Wilson
Aunt of the Bride...Mrs. Sandy Logan Brown
Crew [Jan] Mother....................................Mrs. Belinda Carter Logan

Hostesses...
Aunt of the Groom...................................Mrs. Debbie Williams Wilson
Aunt of the Groom....................................Mrs. Anna Wilson Williams
Aunt of the Groom....................................Mrs. Jessica Jackson Layton
Crew [Stoney] mother................................Mrs. Jacquel Coleman Carr
Crew [Rob] mother....................................Mrs. Roberta Elise Jenkins
Crew [Ced] mother....................................Mrs. Sedina Faye Hamilton
Houston Crew...Mrs. Carolyn Davis Banks
Teammate of Bride.............................Miss Shantel Lanette Jacobson

Host...
Father of the Bride..Mr. John Brown, Sr.
Father of the Groom............................Mr. Allen Devante' Jackson, Jr.
Uncle of the Bride..Mr. Brian James, Sr.
Uncle of the Groom.....................................Mr. Bradley Lee Wilson, Sr.
Uncle of the Bride...Mr. Gregory Brown, Sr.
Uncle of the Groom.....................................Mr. Archie Joseph Wilson, Sr.
Uncle of the Groom............................Mr. Richard Trevon Williams, Sr.
Crew [Jan] Father..Mr. Samuel Logan, Sr.
Grandfather of the Bride..............................Mr. Jackson *Papa* Brown
Grandfather of the Bride...............................Mr. Percy *Poppa* Jones
Crew [Ced] Father............................Mr. George Leroy Hamilton, Sr.
Houston Crew..Mr. Ronald Lee Banks, Sr.
Houston Crew...............................Mr. Charles Edward Washington
Houston Crew..Mr. David Keith Jones
Uncle of the Groom......................................Dr. Jonathan T. Layton
Columbus Crew...Mr. Jason Michael Carr

218

TIME TO LOVE-RELOADED-TIME WILL REVEAL 3

Ushers.............Justine Carr & The Ladies of *Delta Sigma Theta, Inc* and The Gentlemen of *Omega Psi Phi, Inc.*

Decorations and floral arrangements:.............The mothers of the crew, coordinators and hostesses.

Catering and wedding cakes.....................*The Crews House of Soul Food*

Hair and nails...*Crew cuts & Styles*

Face and Makeup...................................*Crew Spa and Health Center*

Wedding Gown, Dresses and Female Attire:...... *Crew Gear & Alterations*

Photography and Video:.......Que Psi Phi Pictures- Arthur Lee Owens, CEO

Reception to follow at........................*The Chill Spot, CrewLand Mall*

Sounds for the Wedding and Reception.............*Jenkins Jams Co, Inc.* Robert Jenkins-CEO, Archie Wilson, Sr.-Manager, Bradley Wilson, Jr.-Ops Manager

Performing at the reception:
1. *Bone Thugs N Harmony W/ Mariah*
2. *Mo Thugs Family*
3. *The Ojay's f/ Levert*
4. Reaper f/ Miss Brittany J
5. Rebbie James Performing Arts Dance Group
6. Little Miss Jerica Eloise Brown

MR. AND MRS. ANTHONY DEVANTE' JACKSON
Will have their solo dance to *Voyage To Atlantis*. The Wedding party will join them for a couples dance to *Adore*.

Acknowledgements

MR. AND MRS. ANTHONY DEVANTE' JACKSON

We would like to thank God for showing us the way to each other. We have loved each other since birth and we will be together, even after death.

To Our Parents: We simply Adore you. No words can express what you are to us. Thanks for always protecting us and training us in a Godly way. We will not stray from your teachings and examples.

To Our Grandparents {Living and Deceased}: You are our foundation. The equalizers. You have shown us unconditional love for all our lives and we truly appreciate you all.

To Our Crew {Cleveland, Houston, Atlanta, Sacramento, Cincinnati, Miami, Baltimore, New York, Boston and Columbus}: You all know the good, the bad and the ugly but you love us anyway. {smile} We will always represent the crew in whatever paths we take from here. You are our family and we love all of you.

God bless our little Angel who was taken from us, Monday June 27, 1994. Mom and dad miss you, so much. We were *so* looking forward to your birth. But it wasn't in God's plan. We give God the glory for seeing us through to this day and the rest of our lives, together. We'll see you *One Sweet day*!

EBONY'S VOWS TO ANTHONY

Anthony, you are my love, my protector, my husband and my best friend. All my life, I've loved *only* you. My every waking moment and even my dreams, are filled with thoughts of you. Your loving touch, your thorough lovemaking, your sexy smooth demeanor. I am totally captured by your love for me. Thank you for showing me the love between a man and a woman. Today, I promise to love, honor, respect and obey you.
In sickness and in health
For richer or for poorer
For better or worse
In good times and bad
Even after death.
You are the only man for me and I truly love you, Anthony.

220

TIME TO LOVE-RELOADED-TIME WILL REVEAL 3

ANTHONY'S VOWS TO EBONY

Ebony, you are my love, the heart and soul of me, my wife and my best friend. You are the only woman that I've ever loved. You are the only woman I will *ever* love. Thank you for your dedication to me. Your unconditional Love, your loyalty and your optimism, when it comes to me. It is only my pleasure to love, honor, cherish, protect and caress you. You are my better half. My *reason* for living.

I adore you and you are forever mine.

From your beautiful face, your smile and heavenly body. To your warm heart, adoring personality, perfection on earth.

I promise to love, honor, respect and protect you, as long as we both shall live.

In sickness and in health

For richer, *richest* or poorer

For better or worse, in good times and bad.

If we are parted by death and that is the only way I would be without you. I only asked God that I go first.

For my life would be unbearable without you in it.

You are the only woman for me and

I truly love you, Ebony.

==

PRESENTING:

MR. AND MRS. ANTHONY [EBONY] JACKSON

WEDNESDAY DECEMBER 31, 1997

VISION OF LOVE

TIME TO LOVE-RELOADED-TIME WILL REVEAL 3

The soft music prelude continues as the final guest arrive and are seated. The church is huge and filled to capacity. The singing performances, scriptures and poems will take place up on the 2nd tier. Which overlooks the wedding party and the congregation on the floor of the church. It's time for a wedding.

"Alright! Places everybody," Brenda says, "Let's rock n roll."
She's in charge of lining up the guys, at the side entrance to the church.

"You got the girls ready, Sandy?" she asks, over her 2-way radio.

"It's all set, over here," Sandy answers back.

Sandy has all the females lined up and ready to march in. She alerts Anna to start the processional music. Her, Brenda, Anna, Belinda and Debbie, all have 2-way radios. So they can communicate with each other, at all times. The timing has to be perfect. Because of Ajay's celebrity status, this wedding is being covered by both national and local press. This includes; reporters from *ESPN*, Miami, Cincinnati, Houston and Cleveland. Arthur's company is in charge of the wedding video and photography. He has set up all the visiting media, in the appropriate places, so they won't interfere with his filming. Everything is a go. The ushers, host and hostesses march in, wearing tan dresses and tuxedo's, to light the candles.

The royal wedding is under way.

Mama Jo is the 1st to come down the aisle, escorted by big Al. She looks lovely in her Cream colored knee length, 2-piece skirt suit. Al is wearing a white tuxedo with a Cream tie, gloves and cummerbund.

Mama Pearl is next as she comes down the aisle, escorted by Greg Sr. She's wearing a form fitting Cream dress with a low neckline, similar to the top of Ebony's gown. Greg Sr is dressed identical to Al. Poppa Percy is too, as he escorts big mama. She's wearing her full length cream, 2-piece dress suit. All of the parents are wearing Cream or Tan.

Ajay strolls in from the side entrance, wearing an all White tuxedo. Complete with tails, top hat, cane and gloves. He looks dashingly debonair, handsome and surprisingly, calm. He's followed by Tank, June and Ritchie Rich, his best men. Who are all wearing white tuxedo's, purple gloves, ties and cummerbunds. After taking his place at the alter, Ajay smiles at Pearl and Jo. He blows a kiss to big mama. From her seat, Roc stretches her neck to get a full view of him. Darlene is in attendance. She's seated with her posse, minus Alana, who is still not allowed in Cleveland, legally. She didn't dare show up. Darlene has fantasies of speaking out when the pastor calls for *"anyone who can show just cause why these two should not be joined in holy matrimony, speak now or forever, hold your peace."*

222

Too bad the wedding isn't *by relevant invitation only.* But the fact is, she still has a fascination with Ajay, so when her posse joked about her causing a disruption, she just told them it was funny. Because even though she'd thought about it, in her wildest dreams, she knew if she so much as coughed aloud. Ajay would have her removed, then go right on with his wedding. And later, make arrangements to have her contract cancelled while he's on his honeymoon. She quietly clears her throat and takes in the ambience.

The wedding march song begins. Big Chill comes in from the side entrance and hugs Ajay, then he pauses to wait for Renee. She marches slowly down the aisle, wearing a gold full length bridesmaids gown with matching elbow length gloves. Her sparkling matching earrings, a gift from the bride, glows brightly as flashbulbs reflect off of them. Chill's accessories are gold, as well. All the groomsmen have on white tuxedo's with ties, gloves and cummerbunds to match *their* lady. The senior maids gowns are all full length. Chill escorts Renee to her place, then takes his spot behind Rich.

Jr waits for Tonya, who comes down the aisle in a beautiful blue gown. Next, Rob escorts Jan to her spot. They're 3rd in line and their color is green. Yolanda and Jarvis wear red and look wonderful in it. Lynn and Jb are the 2nd couple in gold, as they take the 5th mark behind Yolanda and Jarvis. Bre and Ced are in blue. Kim and Bruce, who wear green, attract much attention when they pretend to be heading to the alter. They go on to their marks, after a brief chuckle from Ajay and the rest of the crew. Many of the guest find them hilarious.

"Wait your turn," Ajay whispers, as they hit their marks.

April and Terrell, in red, go directly to their marks behind Kim and Bruce.

Now it's time for the Matrons of Honor. T-baby is first, as she strolls down the aisle in a purple 2-piece, full length skirt suit. Rich smiles broad as their eyes meet. He joins her at the end of the aisle, gives her a kiss, then escorts her to her mark in front of Renee. Rebbie and June do the same, just as they had rehearsed it. Rebbie is wearing a knee length form fitting purple dress. Nina has on a purple mini dress suit and she looks gorgeous. Tank tells her so, as he escorts her to her mark. The senior party are all inside and now it's time for the juniors.

"I'm sending Brad the third," Brenda radios to Sandy.

"Go for it," she replies back.

Brad III is dressed identical to Ajay but without the hat and cane. He's the junior groom. He's followed in by his junior best man, Reaper, who is also dressed in a white tux but with lavender accessories. They take their marks next to Ajay and Tank.

223

Erica is wearing a yellow dress. Greg Jr's accessories match hers, to a tee, as he takes her to her mark, next to Renee. The junior bridesmaids are all wearing knee length dresses. The styles and the colors are all blending perfectly, just as Ebony had visualized.

"This is so beautiful," Jo whispers to Al, who is all smiles.

Greg Jr stands next to Chill, as Jesse strolls in to wait for Ruthie. She comes down the aisle in light blue. Pam and Sam Jr wear mint green and take their marks next to Jan and Rob. Ally and Steven look splendid in Rose. Chaundra and Kenny Jr, in yellow, stand next to Lynn and Jb. Brina and Archie Jr's light blue, match their skin tones wonderfully as they slide in next to Bre and Ced. Charlotte is the final junior bridesmaid. She wears mint green, along with her escort Brandon.

Brittany coordinates with Reaper, in lavender. She's the junior maid of honor. Next, aunt Jessica comes in wearing cream as she carries John III. He's in an all white tuxedo, made by the ladies at Crew Gear, for his role as the honorary ring bearer. He sits in the pew with Jessica. Rich III is the *walking* ring bearer. His tuxedo and accessories are all white. Uncle Archie, in a tan tuxedo, carries in his granddaughter, Orian. She's the honorary flower girl, in an all white dress made at Crew Gear. She sits with her papa in their pew.

Then Belinda rolls out the white linen, full aisle length carpet for the flower girls, junior bride and the lady of honor, while she readies the last 3 females and Debbie goes to get Ebony.

"Are you little ladies ready to drop your flowers?" Sandy asks CJ and Jerica.

"*Yes!*" they sing.

They start down the aisle, dropping white rose petals as they go. CJ and Jerica are wearing all white, calf length gowns and gloves, with white laced baskets filled with white rose petals. They have giant ribbons in their hair, white tights and white paten leather shoes. Ajay starts to look anxious, for the 1st time since strolling in. He can't wait to see his bride.

Ebony has huge-sized butterflies in her stomach now, as she realizes it's almost time for her to walk down the aisle to see her man.

"Is my bride ready?" John asks.

"Yes, daddy. I'm ready," she says with a bright smile.

Destiny lines up behind the double doors. Matthew does a final check on Ebony's hair. Then he places her veil on. Sandy and Debbie open the doors for Destiny. She's the junior bride. She looks pretty in her little wedding gown and veil. Renee becomes misty eyed, watching her daughter stroll

224

perfectly, down the aisle. Chill smiles wide while he watches his little girl, not miss a beat and take her place next to Nina and Brittany.

"It's that time, man," Tank whispers to Ajay, as the audience is directed to stand.

The bridal song starts. Ajay holds his breath in anticipation. Ebony and John stand behind the double doors. When the doors open, Ajay squints his eyes trying to see his princess.

Ebony is striking. A very beautiful young bride and her gown is flawless. Her and John take the 1st step inside of the church. The audience gasp, at her radiance. Her wedding gown is all white, of course. It has short sleeves which coordinate perfectly, with her maids and matrons. She has a low neckline bodice, covered with shiny rhinestones and sequins. There are white roses around the edges of the sleeves. And around the bottom of the bodice, at the waistline. It's form fitting to the waist. From the waist down, it puffs out in *Princess Diana* like fashion with cascading ruffles which run from her waist, down to the hem. Her train is all fluffy ruffles, extending 10 feet behind her. A foot for every year, her and Ajay have dated. Her veil comes down to meet the white roses at her waist. She wears elbow length gloves with her ring finger exposed. She's a vision of elegance. Once she's close enough for Ajay to see her eyes, he smiles at her and she smiles back. Now they're captured in each other's stare. She can't wait to get to her mark and her man. But she's nearly blinded by the flashing of camera bulbs, as she squints. Her father John, can feel her trembling.

"Are you gonna make it, baby girl?" he whispers to her and smiles.

"Oh yes. I will," she manages.

Finally, they reach the alter. The audience sits down on cue as Ajay steps forward to meet Ebony.

"Hold on, Ajay. Not *quite* yet," pastor Tucker says and the audience laughs. "I have a line to say here. And dad here, has to *give* her away, first." Everybody laughs at Pastor Tucker. He's always humorous. Then he adds, *"Now,* who gives this beautiful young lady to be married today?" he asks with a smile.

"I do," John replies.

"Okay, Ajay. *Now* you may reach for her hand," pastor Tucker says with another smile.

Ajay obliges. John shakes hands with him. They make eye contact and then hug each other. Ajay thanks him quietly, once more. John joins Ebony's hand with Ajay's. Then he goes to his seat, next to Pearl. His job is done. Before pastor Tucker can start the devotion, Ajay reaches for Ebony's veil.
225

"Not yet, *Ant*," Jo whispers from her seat and everybody laughs again.

"You have to stay covered up, like *this*?" Ajay whispers to Ebony.

"Yes, baby. Until it's time for us to kiss," she whispers back.

"Ah man. What a tease," he says as they smile at each other.

They whisper frequently, as the devotion continues.

"You look so beautiful, baby girl," he says with a smile.

"You look handsome, yourself, baby," she whispers, "I knew you would."

This time, both Pearl and Jo *shush* them. Instantly, Ajay shows defiance.

"Ain't this *our* wedding?" he asks Ebony and they both snicker.

Ajay is heard over pastor Tucker's microphone and the audience laughs. Pearl and Jo look across the aisle at each other and shake their heads. Ajay and Ebony are going to do this their way. By now, their mothers know this.

"Now we'll have the prayer," Tucker says.

Grandpa's Charles and Joshua, go up on the 2nd tier, dressed in cream 3-piece suits. Everyone bows their head. Ebony and Ajay still manage to sneak peeks at each other, throughout the prayer.

"I'm in the mood," Ajay whispers and she blushes.

"*Amen*," the church says.

Everyone hears Ajay's comment, over pastor Tucker's microphone, again. Pastor Tucker smiles and says, "Perhaps we'll need to move this along, a little faster, for the groom." The entire church laughs.

Pastor Tucker continues, "This is a song to Anthony from Ebony."

Aunt Rena sings, *I feel good* by *Stephanie Mills*. Ebony's eyes start to mist. Ajay squeezes her hand.

"Are you scared?" he asks.

"I'm not," she answers.

"Why are you shaking, so bad?"

"I don't know. I can't stop," she says.

"I like the song, baby," he says and she smiles at him.

Rena receives a standing ovation.

Tucker reads from his program, "An original poem for Ebony and Ajay."

Big mama, poppa and papa, go up to the microphones. Their poem is beautiful, tear-jerking and humorous, all at the same time. Everyone applauds them.

"Now we'll have a moment of silence, in honor of the couples deceased family members, who are here in spirit," Tucker says.

The church is quiet. Except for John III and Orian's babbling and cooing.

226

"Next, we have a song for the couple, from the groom's parents." Al and Jo sing, *If this world were mine* by *Luther Vandross and Patti Austin,* from the 2nd tier. Once again, the audience stands and applauds.

"The scriptures will be done by sister Annabelle Wilson and sister Sally Logan," Tucker says.

These 2 grandmothers stop, just short of a sermon, on that elevated tier, as they move the entire church with their selection of scriptures fit for a wedding day.

"This next song is dedicated to the happy couple, from their loving grandparents. The song will be performed by, the *Mighty* O'Jays!" Tucker says with excitement.

The O'Jays sing *Forever Mine,* They receive a standing ovation, as well. A lot of the guest are misty eyed, from this point on.

"This is so beautiful," Ebony says to Ajay, "We have celebrities in our wedding."

"It's not over yet, baby," he says, then winks at her.

"A song to the couple, by the bride's parents. As you can all see, this is a very talented family," Tucker offers with a chuckle.

John and Pearl sing, *Here and Now* by *Luther Vandross.* The guest stand and applaud again.

"And now, we'll have the repeating of the vows. Ebony and Ajay have elected to recite original vows. Miss Ebony, you may go first," Tucker says as he holds the microphone for her.

She begins, as soft tears roll down her cheeks, just seconds into it.

"Anthony, you are my love, my protector, my husband and my best friend. All of my life, I've loved, *only* you. My every waking moment and even my dreams, are filled with thoughts of you. Your loving touch. Your thorough lovemaking and your sexy smooth demeanor. I'm totally captured by your love for me. Thank you for showing me the love between a man and a woman. Today, I stand here. Before God and all of these witnesses, and I promise to love, honor, respect and obey you. In sickness and in health. For richer and for poorer. For better or worse. In good times and bad times. Even after death. You are the only man, for me. And I truly love you, so much, Anthony," she says through teary eyes.

He can't resist lifting her veil to wipe away her tears. Nearly everyone in the church needed a tissue during her vows.

"Ajay, it's your turn," Tucker says, "I wonder if you can top that." Ajay clears his throat, as his groomsmen chuckle. Pastor Tucker holds the microphone for him.

227

TIME TO LOVE-RELOADED-TIME WILL REVEAL 3

"Ebony, you are my love, the heart and soul of me. My wife and my best friend. You are the only woman I've ever loved. You are the only woman, I will *ever* love. Thank you, so much, for your dedication to me and for your *unconditional love* for me. Your loyalty to me and for your optimism, when it comes to me." Everyone chuckles, as he continues. "It's only my pleasure to love, honor, cherish, protect, respect and caress you." She blushes. The audience sighs. The hopefuls, squirm in their seats. This is a side of Ajay, they've never seen.

He smiles and continues, "You are my better half. *My* reason for living and wanting to succeed. So I can give you the life, *I feel* you deserve," he says. He's choked up but he manages to go on, as she wipes a tear from his eye.

"I adore you and you are, forever mine. From your beautiful face, your bright smile and heavenly body. To your warm heart. Adoring personality. Perfection on earth. I promise to love, honor, respect and protect you, as long as we both shall live. Rather in sickness, thickness," he smiles as his groomsmen chuckle. He goes on, "And in health. For richer, *richest* or poorer." Everyone giggles.

"For better or worse. In good times and bad times. If we are ever parted by death, the only way I would be without you. I only pray that I go first, for life would be unbearable without you in it. I wouldn't know what to do with my days or nights. You are the only woman for me and I truly love you, Ebony."

There isn't a dry eye in the church. Not even the hopefuls, as the audience stands, cheers and applauds.

"Truly heart felt vows," Tucker says as he dries his own eyes.

"Let's continue with the rings, please. Ajay, please place the ring on Ebony's finger and repeat after me," Tucker says as he conducts Ajay and Ebony through the ring ceremony, then the marriage oath.

"Ebony, do you take Ajay to be your lawfully wedded husband?"
"I do!"
"Ajay, do you take Ebony to be your lawfully wedded wife?"
"Oh yes. Ajay does and Anthony does too. I do."

Everyone laughs again. Next, they go up to the 2nd tier to light their unity candle. Then they return to the alter, arm in arm and all smiles.

Pastor Tucker has 1 more hurdle to get over, before he can call them married.

"If there is anyone who sees just cause, why this couple should not be joined together, in holy matrimony," pastor Tucker starts, "Let them speak now. Or forever hold their peace."

228

No one says anything. But Ebony and Ajay can hear *some* mumbles throughout the audience.

"I thought I asked you to leave *that* part out," Ajay whispers to Pastor Tucker.

"I can't," Pastor says, "It's apart of the process."

They all chuckle and move on. The look on Chill, Jb and Jr's faces is 1 which says, *I wish a motherfuckah would say some dumb shit.* John, Al, papa and poppa have the same look. Al turns and looks directly at Darlene. As if he knows what she'd joked about. His look says, *it had best remain a joke.* Her invitation was a lure. Sort of a closure to her false, *Love Jones.* He hasn't liked her since she tried to latch onto his preteen son. Only after she couldn't get him. And because Ajay is an All-American and an heir to the crew throne. Al had told Ajay to fuck her, *once.* Only for sexual experience but she could never come to their home. Since that 1st night, in 1985, she was so sure her age meant she could trump his mentality. But she showed her true colors when he had no real interest in her, afterwards. She tried to slander his name. Saying he was black hearted, uncaring and a womanizer. A young thug, who didn't know how to give a damn about a female. She soon learned he was capable of love and *was*, in fact, interested in being in love. But what foiled her plan to lure him with money, oral sex and the freedom to treat her as disrespectful as he wanted too, so long as he came to see her? Was the fact that he was raised right and with something she wasn't familiar with. *Morals and pride.* He was looking for the best woman possible. Not some female willing to lower herself, as if that would hold his interest. He wanted a wholesome girl. One he could groom to be his partner for life. He had his eyes on Ebony, long before coming to know Darlene. Ebony gave him her hand, a year or so after and his search ended. He had his wife by age thirteen. Today, they complete that circle and invite her to witness it. From here on, there shouldn't be anymore doubt. He's capable of and wanted, just what he was raised on. *Unconditional Love.*

"By the power vested in me, in sight of God, the state of Ohio and these many witnesses. I now pronounce, Ebony Eloise and Anthony Devante' are husband and wife! Now Ajay!" Pastor says and chuckles because Ajay has taken the liberty upon himself to move this marriage on. "You may finally *kiss* your bride."

Ajay is way ahead of him. He has already lifted Ebony's veil and moved in for a long kiss. A kiss that is stretching into record time. The junior party are laughing. Al eventually clears his throat and Ajay releases Ebony's lips. Then follows the long kiss with a small peck. He's all smiles.

229

"Mmm," Ebony moans.

He gives her a look that assures her, he isn't done. Not by a long shot.

"The audience will now honor the couple with a short applause," Tucker says and the audience cheers, very loudly.

The wedding party and their teammates are the loudest of all.

"Hold on *now*," Tucker says, "We're not done yet. We have a song to Ebony from Ajay."

Nina, T-baby and Rebbie go up to the 2nd tier and stand behind 3 of the 4 microphones that have been set up for this song.

"Baby, they put out *too* many microphones," Ebony whispers.

"Oh *really*?" he asks in a slick tone, as he stares at his new bride.

He wants to see her reaction to his surprise. Suddenly, *Mariah* walks down the stairs, from the upstairs classrooms, smiling gorgeous and approaching the 4th microphone.

"*Oh my God! Oh God!*" Ebony screams, "*It's really her?!*"

She jumps straight into Ajay's arms and he hugs her tight.

"*Thank you, baby! Thank you!*" she screams, "*This is perfect! I love you!*"

He tries to calm her down, saying, "Wait, baby. She still has to sing for you," he says with a huge smile.

Mariah sings *Vision of Love* with T-baby, Nina and Rebbie accompanying her. Ebony cries the entire song, as she leans on her husband.

"You love me, so much," she says.

"You love me too, baby," he says.

They smile and kiss as the song comes to an end. The audience is already standing and cheering, loudly.

"Ladies and gentlemen! I present to you, mister and misses Anthony Devante' Jackson!" Pastor Tucker shouts.

The pianist and organist begin to play the wedding recessional song. Ajay escorts his wife up the aisle, as their wedding attendants follow. The whole congregation are already clapping, cheering and crying, behind this most beautiful and emotional display of true love. They stand, cheer, hiss and applaud until everyone of the attendants are outside with the happy couple.

"That was so beautiful, you guys," Brenda says as the newlyweds reach the double doors.

The doors have been propped open. The audience follows them outside, as many try to take pictures and congratulate them, immediately. But Sandy directs the whole wedding party back around to the side door, as they had rehearsed it. They have to go back inside for pictures.

"I got that look, after the kiss too, man," Arthur says to Ajay.

230

"Man, this is one big tease, right here," Ajay jokes.
He's happy to have their wedding done, as he carries his bride to the side door and back inside the church. He had told her, her feet wouldn't touch the ground until after she has given him some loving. They barely separate long enough for the male and female photo's.

"Y'all get your little time in, now," Ajay says to the females, as they take their photo's with his wife.

"I'm shutting everything down at ten o'clock."
Arthur takes a few pictures of Ajay carrying Ebony. The 1st 2 hours of their marriage has been all hands on. The church pictures are done. Now it's on to the reception, where the Houston Crew and their teams, past and present, are in charge.

}The Reception{

"To our distinguished guest! I present to you, mister and misses Anthony Devante' Jackson," Ron and Carolyn Banks announce.

The reception is filled to capacity, just as the church was. Ebony and Ajay go to their special table, which is set up in the middle of their wedding party and family tables.

"Oh baby, we finally get to sit down," Ebony say, as they make their way through their well wishers and take their seats.

"My feet are killing me."

"I'll handle *all* that for you, tonight," Ajay confirms.
Belinda and Debbie are in charge of the order at the reception. Arthur still has many more pictures to take.

Big Al and big John do a formal toast to their son and daughter. Then Ebony and Ajay salute each other with champagne. Shortly after, all of the single ladies gather for the bouquet toss. April catches it and Charles smiles, as all of the guys tease him.

"Come on over here and sit down, woman," Ajay demands with a smile.

"Oh, it's starting already, ha?" Ebony says and laughs.
She sits down in her Queen Anne chair, in the middle of the floor, so he can remove her garter. He puts his hand way past her garter, touching the rim of her Christian Dior panties. He cuts his eyes at her. She smiles. She likes.

"You know I didn't sleep with you, last night," he says, "I'm just trying to stay acquainted."

"It's *all* familiar to you, baby," she says and laughs as he smiles.

"Where is Charles at?" Ajay ask and tosses the garter, directly

231

at him. The other guys spread out, as the garter is tossed, leaving Charles standing alone to catch it.

After he does, he says, "Y'all not even right, man."

The newlyweds have their 1st slow dance, as husband and wife, to the song, *Voyage to Atlantis* by *the Isley Brothers.* Ajay can't stop kissing Ebony. He's real horny and she can *feel* him. All of their crew join them, for a dance to the *Prince* hit; *Adore*!

The newlyweds cut and serve each other wedding cake. After the wedding party and family are served, the guest form lines at the buffet tables. The performers are fed before and after they perform.

Jerica performs her version of *Funny Valentine.* Next, she joins Rebbie and the dance company. They performed an African dance routine. Brittany J and Reaper perform together. Next is *Levert* and *the OJay's.* *Bone Thugs N Harmony* performs a medley of their hits. They perform a song with *Mariah,* which will come out on her CD, *Butterfly,* next year. The song is titled, *Breakdown. Mariah* has to leave, immediately after their performance. Ajay and Ebony thank her for coming and performing for them. She gives them a trip to Hawaii, as a wedding gift. They can take the trip whenever they want. Before she is whisked away to her limo, Ebony tells her, "You have no idea how much this means to me. Your first CD got me through a lot of the hard times with him, back in the days. Thank you so much for being a part of our day."

Mo Thugs artist performed very well, also. All of the performances are great as the time winds down for the newlyweds.

"Time for you to change, baby girl," Debbie says as Ajay agrees.

"Okay. But before we leave, I have one more request from the DJ."

"Let me know and I'll get Rob on it," Ajay says.

"I'll do it, this one time, baby," she says, "You just go to the center of the dance floor, please."

He does. She goes and gets mama Jo and sends her to the dance floor. She gets all of the guys from the crew and tells them to go to the dance floor. She heads to the DJ booth. All of them look puzzled and so does Rob. That is until he hears her request. Once she asks him to play, *Dear Mama* by *Tupac, Parental Discretion is advized* by *N.W.A.* and *Pour Out A Little Liquor* by *Thug Life,* everybody understands why mama Jo and his crew brothers are on the floor. Ebony, the female crew and family gather around. Ajay dances with Jo and his boys. The whole crew family dances for Stoney.

"Baby, that was so fly," Ajay says, "But we need to leave now."

232

TIME TO LOVE-RELOADED-TIME WILL REVEAL 3

It's almost 10 o'clock and he wants his wife all to himself, when the New Year comes in. Ebony changes her clothes. Then they hurry to their Limo. Their guest throw rainbow confetti while Ajay carries her to the car.

}The Limousine{

Ajay had cradled Ebony, for nearly the entire reception. During the limousine ride, it's no different. He has her sitting on his lap as they hurry to the airport. There's a lot of heavy kissing, along the way. They have a 30 minute flight to Mount Pocono Pennsylvania's, Paradise Stream. He blindfolds her before they drive out to the jet. The UC alumni have provided this round trip flight, as 1 of the many wedding gifts they've given them. The G-4 crew congratulate them on their nuptials. Then, as Ebony waits in the limo, Ajay inspects the flight for all the riders he's ordered. They reconfirm the flight information with him, at this time. They have to be particularly careful not to divulge the destination to Ebony. It has to be a surprise to her. That's how he ordered it. He returns to the limo for his bride and carries her again, as they board the private jet. He puts her on her feet, only after she's inside. He removes the blind fold, allowing her to behold the ambiance. The jet is decorated in their wedding colors. There are bottles of *Dom Perignon* on ice, for them to share and a special CD with their wedding songs on it. The head flight attendant starts the CD player, then attends to her pre-departure duties. Ebony glares at the inside of this beautiful aircraft.

"They rented us our own *private* jet?" she asks.

"This belongs to Parkwood's company," Ajay answers, "He set it out for us, real nice. This thing is nicer than the condo."

They laugh and tour the jet. It has a complete living area, dining area and master bed and bath room. Plus a working office complete with copier, computer, email and faxing capabilities.

"This is gorgeous," she says.

"Our flight is only thirty minutes," he says, "But who *knows*. We may get to mess that bed up while we're up there."

She smiles at him and she's *more* than willing, if he so desires. But he tells her, he's saving that indulgence for their private honeymoon hideaway. They can join the mile high club, on the flight back.

"So where are we going? Can you tell me now?" she asks.

"No. You have to wait. It's all a surprise."

"Okay, husband," she giggles, "We have to be sure and thank the alumni, when we get back though. They set it out, big time."

233

"Mister Parkwood is on some *Donald Trump* type dough," he says, "He also told me to tell you he's got some starter clients and backing for you, from his firm, when you graduate. Your banking degree is gonna pull in some major figures with him."

"That's the bomb. I picked out my office at CrewLand, already. T-baby and me. We're sharing the split entrance suite, in building three."

"I married a real estate and investment banker. Our babies are gonna be set," he says and smiles.

"That's the truth," she says, "I married an NBA All-star, business mogul. Who is my *only* love."

"My only love is a *Tender Roni*," he says as they laugh at his *Bobby Brown* reference and he directs her to the loveseat.

She smiles at him and they kiss as the jet taxis the runway. He buckles them in for take off and they depart on time, listening to the songs which was just performed during their wedding and reception.

"It's so cool. The whole thing," she says, "When I saw *Mariah* come down those stairs, I felt weak."

"I thought you was gonna pass out. I saw how excited you was and I knew I had pick the right song," he says.

"Yes indeed. It was perfect. The wedding *and* the reception. Our day is perfect," she says.

"It's not over yet," he says, "It's gonna get better and better, from here on. That's my vow to you. I'm *on* mine," he says as she smiles and gives him another kiss.

‚The reception‚

As soon as the newlyweds left in the limousine, the crew changed out of their wedding dresses and tuxedo's. Then the party shifted gears. Rob took control of the deejay duties, for good. They're about to set the joint off, crew style. T-baby has changed into her dancing gear. She grabs Rich and takes to the dance floor to cut a rug.

"Come on, baby," she says, "Dance with me."

"Cool," Rich answers and leads the way, as the rest of the crew and many guest have the floor packed, within minutes.

"Party over here!" Jr and Tonya chant, along with Lynn and Jb. While Tank and Nina team with Bre and Ced and retort;
"Party over here! Ain't shit over there!"
Still, T-baby, Rich and Jan, with Rob on the deejay microphone screams,
"Where's the party at?"
234

Chill, Renee, the crew and the rest of the guest, scream back,
"Right here under my shoes!"
The reception is turning into another full blown party. The guest of honor have been gone less than half an hour and their crew are celebrating Bruce's 20th birthday. Which officially starts at midnight. But he's long gone too. He had flown out immediately after the wedding, to join his Ohio State team. They will be in a Bowl game on Monday, January 3rd. To which his family and some of the crew are going to attend.

On the dance floor, Rich tires out first and goes to get a seat. T-baby takes a break and gets him a cool drink. The rest of the crew continue to party.

CHAPTER   32

HONEYMOON OVER ALREADY?

}In Cleveland{

The news of the beautiful wedding travels fast. Darlene left the reception, moments after the happy couple. She phoned Alana in Pittsburgh with the details, before she was even 100 yards away from University heights. In Pittsburgh, Alana was expecting a call from her partner in crime. The incarcerated Angel. Though the psychotic actions of her fatal attraction had sent her to prison, she refuses to let go. She makes calls to Alana weekly, for her *"Ajay Information"* fix. Alana had only stopped her communication with Angel during their trials. But once she was in Pittsburgh, it started back. Alana had attended the bachelor party, last night. But her parole officer, through word from George Wheeler, had ordered her back to Pittsburgh, this morning. She has also stayed in touch with Samantha, Gloria, Nicole and Angie. Not only her aunt Darlene. Those 4 females still attend crew parties and are regulars at *The Chill Spot*. Darlene has fallen back from showing up at the weekly events. She only attends the *special occasions* which she feel Ajay may show up for. However, the other 4 girls party at the club every time the doors open. They keep Alana up on the latest crew news. The Ajay news, Alana passes on to Angel. The Tank news, she still loves to hear for herself. This late evening, after hanging up with her aunt Darlene, Alana is getting dressed to head out to a New Years Eve party when Angel calls.

"Hello."

"Hey, girl. What's good?" Angel asks.

"Happy New Year's. Well, almost," Alana says.

"Not in here, it's not," Angel says, "Everybody saying that shit. I'm in prison. It ain't shit happy about it."

"You're copping a little better, now though, right?" Alana asks.

"After two years. Kind of. But I can never get use to this, Alana," she says. Then switching gears to the real reason she called, she asks,

"So what have you heard about Ajay's wedding? I saw some highlights on sports center and the news."

"Darlene, Nicole and them, went to it. They said it was like royalty. Darlene said she wanted to scream out when the preacher said speak now," she says as she laughs, "Mariah Carey, Bone and Mo Thugs was there."

"I wish I could've been the bride," Angel says sadly.

TIME TO LOVE-RELOADED-TIME WILL REVEAL 3

"You are still in love with that man, ha girl?"

"I will always love Ajay. He fucks like nobody else I've ever been with," she says, "He made me cum. That shit was so good, wit his big dick ass. I be in here thinking about it and getting off."

Alana talks to her until the call expires. Then she has to go because her New Year's eve ride, *Farah Benson*, is tired of waiting.

}Paradise Stream{

Mr. and Mrs. Anthony Jackson arrives in Mount Pocono, ahead of schedule. It's only 11pm. They still have a full hour in which to get to their honeymoon cottage. The private cottage is another gift from Parkwood and the Cincinnati alumni. Parkwood owns a hotel, in Mt. Pocono. But the cottage is his personal getaway. He feels Ajay and Ebony are 2 of Cincinnati's most prized possessions and he wants them to feel like royalty. A limousine waits for them at Scranton airport. It pulls up to the aircraft steps. The flight crew assist them in embarking. The chauffeur loads in their bags and opens the door for Ajay, who carries Ebony from the aircraft to the car. He puts her down and she slides across the backseat. He slides in behind her. Before the chauffeur can close the door, he's already sliding closer to his wife. The driver starts up the limo and heads for Paradise Stream. Their drive will take 20 minutes. Mr. Jackson isn't wasting time.

"I missed you, last night," he says.

In the dark backseat of the limousine, he sits her on his lap, once again.

"I really like how you look in this dress," he says with a smile "So virgin like."

"I am to you. You got all of this, baby. You and you only."

"I'm proud of that stat," he says, "I want you to call me daddy, from now on," he says still smiling.

"Okay, baby, I mean, *daddy*," she says and smiles shyly, as she slips him her tongue.

He slips his handles under her crisp white cotton dress. It's made in a *Jacqueline Kennedy* style with wide shoulder straps, v-neck cut allowing for ample cleavage, with a matching crop cut jacket. The dress fits tight and contours to her body, with a sharp slit up the right side to her mid thigh. To accessorize it, Crew Gear had added white gloves, calf boots and a white petite handbag. She looks almost *British*. A very proper and prim, business and *hey I'm Marlo Thomas* from *That Girl,* type of style. She looks elegant and very sexy to him and he tells her so.

"You got your grown woman on today, baby girl."

237

"I feel like a business woman. All professional," she says between kisses.

He slips a couple of his fingers into her panties. Then checks to see that the privacy window is up. It is. He proceeds to play with her clitoris as she reaches for his bulge. They both moan in pleasure. Wet kisses aren't enough to contain these newlyweds. She pulls his shirt apart and exposes his abs. Then she unbuttons and unzips his pants releasing his *pleasure principle*. It seems to unfold as it's stiffness makes it stand straight up against his six pack.

"I get to try something new with this, *right*?" she asks.

He pulls back. He wants it but they're approaching their honeymoon spot. She's suppose to see it from the inside, first.

"Later on, you will," he says, "I have to put this back on, for right now, baby."

"Ah baby. Why? I wanna see," she whines.

"Not yet. It's a surprise," he says, "And I told you to call me daddy."

"Oh, I'm sorry, daddy. I wanna see. *Please*."

"In just a minute, baby," he says as he ties the blind fold back over her eyes and fix both of their clothes. "No peeking, either," he warns.

They arrive at the resort. The limo driver takes them directly to their private cottage, on the very top of the mountain. *The Garden of Eden, Apple cottage*. While the driver takes their bags in, Ajay helps Ebony to the edge of the seat and kisses her immediately. Then he picks her up, cradle style again and carries her in the night air.

"The air smells, *so* clean," she observes, "I wanna see, daddy."

"In a minute," he says as he carries her over the threshold.

"Mmm. It smells like apples in here," she says as he puts her down and removes the blind fold.

He tips the driver immediately, so he can leave.

"Wow! It's beautiful, Anthony! Daddy! It's so beautiful!" she says becoming misty.

"Do you like it?" he asks, "This is Parkwood's place. They remodeled and decorated it, just for us."

"It's perfect, daddy. I love it," she says, then she kisses him.

"Happy New Year, misses Jackson," he says.

"Happy New Year to you too, mister Jackson," she says with a bright smile as she watches him lock the door behind the driver and smile.

"Let's check it out," he offers and they take a tour.

238

TIME TO LOVE-RELOADED-TIME WILL REVEAL 3

The Garden of Eden Apple cottage is decorated in red. A red Heart-shaped Jacuzzi, a Heart-shaped king-sized bed and log burning fireplace. Their personal refrigerator contains many bottles of chilled champagne, water and sodas. There is a bottle of Champagne on ice and strawberries, setup for them, next to the Jacuzzi with 2 flutes. It's already filled with a warm bubble filled bath which is irresistible to Ebony.

"Can we get in?" she asks.

"We can do whatever you wanna do, Ebony," he answers, "Let me get you out of these clothes. I like 'em but the body underneath is banging."

"Then I must get you out of yours," she adds with a smile, "Because that's an award winning body under that suit too."

They undress each other and step into the Jacuzzi.

"It's so nice and warm," she says with a kiss, "Where are we?"

"The Pocono's mountains in Pennsylvania," he answers with another kiss. "I tried to think of somewhere we hadn't been, that was close enough to get to in less than an hour, with snow capped mountains."

He grabs and opens the champagne, then fills their glasses. He does a toast.

"To my beautiful wife and the love of my life," he says.

They toast, then take long sips.

"To my sexy husband and the love of my life," she says.

They toast and drink until they finish the 1st bottle. He exits the Jacuzzi and goes over to the fridge, grabs another bottle of Dom, then rejoins her. He fills their glasses again while she feeds him a strawberry.

"This is so nice, daddy," she says as she moves closer to him.

He looks into her eyes as she straddles him in the hot tub.

"I need to consummate this marriage," she says with a sexy smile.

"You've got control now, baby," he says throwing both of his arms behind his head.

"You're gonna have to participate *some*," she says.

"You've got my full attention," he says, "I've dreamed about this night, all of my life."

"Uh huh. I can feel that," she says as she takes him into her. "It's my job to fulfill your dreams, daddy."

"Come on," he says, "Get all you want. I want you to work this sweet little pussy for me, tonight. My dick's been hard since last night."

She takes as much as she can inside of her, as she gently grinds on his lap.

"Mmm," he moans, "I like it when you're in control."

"I love you, so much, daddy," she whispers in his ear as she grinds.

"I owe you something, right?" he whispers.

239

"Just a lifetime of loving me," she whispers back.

Suddenly, he lifts her up. She asks, "What are you doing, daddy?" He sits her on the 1st seat of the Jacuzzi and moves away. She asks, "Where are you going?" He doesn't answer. He stands and exits the Jacuzzi, leaving her in the hot tub alone. He retreats into the bathroom and grabs a large towel-for-2, then returns. He asks her to stand. She does as she's told and he quickly wraps the 2 of them in their towel.

"Are you cold?" he whispers, kissing on her neck.

"Uh huh. But it's warming up," she whispers back with a smile.

He dries her off, escorts her over to the large bed and tells her to lay down. She does. He climbs on top of her. Instead of reentering her, he kisses on her neck and breast, just as he's always done. After leaving her breast, he continues downward to her navel. In previous episodes, he would always return to her nipples and treat them again, before entering her. But this early morning, he has other options in mind. He continues southward to her outer, then her inner thighs.

"Oh my," she whispers as her whole body jolts.

This is a new sensation for her. Every inch of her inner thigh tingles with anticipation, as if they have a mind all their own. Her button throbs as if, somehow it knows that it is to be his tongue's final destination. She tries to lay still but her body won't allow her too. It's on automatic. Responding to his probing tongue as it draws circles on her inner thighs. First the right 1, then the left.

"Oh baby. Ssss," she moans.

He moans, as well. He's aroused, just from the reaction her body has to his present actions. His deep moan sends another shock through her. She grabs for something, anything to hold on too. Without warning, he touches the tip of his tongue to her clitoris.

"Oh! Ssss oh!" she gasp and her body jolts hard.

He takes her clit between his lips. She releases a long whining-like moan. She's experiencing yet another sensation which she has no idea of how to handle. She's unsure of what to expect, as he begins to draw circles around her clit with his tongue.

"No. Yes. No," she says aloud, "I can't take this."

She's afraid, almost. Not knowing how to react to this new feeling. Suddenly, she slides back and away from his lips.

"What's wrong, baby?" he whispers as he follows her further up onto the bed and pulls up, so he can look into her eyes.

240

TIME TO LOVE-RELOADED-TIME WILL REVEAL 3

"Just relax. Okay?" he whispers, "Let me do this."
He strokes her hair and tries to relax her. He can see that she's unsure. Afraid of the way she feels. He gets on his job of making her feel secure. He assures her this is something new to him too. He wants to experience it with her. His wife. But before he can. he has a question to help her relax.

"Did you tell somebody you was gonna get your pussy licked on our honeymoon?" he asks as he smiles.

"Yes I did. But not like that," she says as she smiles, shyly.

"You said you was gonna experience oral sex or something?"

"Yes. I said we was waiting until our honeymoon before we did it," she answers. Then she asks, "Why do you ask?"

"Because it's shaved," he says smiling big, "Except for this little fuzz on the top, there's no other hair around it."

She embarrassed as she smiles and says, "Aunt Anna said I needed a bikini wax, when I was at the spa. But not because I was gonna wear a bikini. I just said okay. Then they told me what they had to do and that my girls told them I needed one. I told my girls and they told them."

"I like it. It's smooth," he whispers as he rubs it. "It's like another set of lips. I'm looking forward to kissing it. I just need you to relax."

Her body jolts from that statement. All she can say is, "Okay."

"You told me you wanted to know what it feels like," he reminds her and smiles. "Since your girls getting it. Well, two of them. And they got you all trimmed up for it, so let me get to it. Okay?"

"Okay. I just don't know how I'm suppose to react to it," she says.

"Whatever comes natural," he says, then kisses her passionately.

She relaxes. He heads back downtown and begins again. But this time, he captures her body at the hips with both arms. Thus not allowing her to slide away from his lips again. He moans and dives in. He lets his tongue play little tricks with her throbbing clit. He seems to know this is a feeling that's so stimulating that she can't control her movements or her comments. She's talking to him but doesn't seem to be in control of what she's saying. His moans and whispers are so very erotic. She's spinning.
He knew I didn't really have control.

He arrogantly toys with her, asking, "Is this good to you?"
Are you kidding?

She wants to pull her hair out and maybe his too, as she says, "Yes."
He continues to lash her clit with his tongue. First licking it with the
241

consistency of a high speed mixer. At the same time, his soft tongue touching her is gentler than a feather. She rolls her hips and fucks his mouth, like she's been here before. It's what feels natural to her.

"Mmm, yes," he says, approving of her gyrations.

She's moving. She's moaning and panting. She's losing control of her inhibitions, her choice of words and sounds. With his hands guiding her, she grinds against his lips.

Whew! What the hell is this rumbling between my thighs? Is he gonna be okay with what's happening here?

All of sudden, her back arches and forms a perfect letter C. Her body lifts up off of the bed. She's in ecstasy.

"Uh huh," he moans, loving what his actions are doing to her.

This is what he's been waiting on. Hoping for. Working so hard toward, this morning. He knew he wasn't going to pass his own test, if he couldn't give his wife the same thing his guys brag about giving to theirs. But she's there and boy is she ever! He's conducting her body in a symphony of moves that she has absolutely no control over. He's arrogantly pleased at the outcome, it seems. She has been to ecstasy with him, many times before. But this time, it's pleasantly unfamiliar and strange. Good, nonetheless. But different. She doesn't have him to hold onto. Her body trembles like they're outside during that 40 below zero winter, 7 years ago, in Cleveland. She grabs but can't reach him. He's still busy with her south end and he isn't coming up until she stops gyrating. She pulls for him to come up. He doesn't. She screams in pleasure. He dives in, deeper and harder. Licking her with as much force as his tongue can put out. She grabs the head board and holds on. That sends him even deeper. He grabs her clit between his lips and kneads it, like it's having it's own little massage. Many pleasure waves fill her body as she raises her hips and ass, off of the bed. His lips follow her every twist, as he holds onto her. He's not about to let go. He moans loud but his mouth never releases her clitoris. It's held captive between his lips. She covers her face with a pillow. Partly from the insanity she's feeling. She also feels slight embarrassment for losing control, like she has. He licks her gentler now, as she spirals back to controllable jolts. But he doesn't let up until she's completely calm. Now she's forcefully pushing him away from her, *extremely* moist pussy. He finally moves his lips away. She closes her eyes. Tears are rolling down the side of her face, as he makes his way north and reaches her nipples again. She's out of breath. He suckles on them, looking up to make eye contact.

242

"How was it?" he asks arrogantly, as he slides up so he can look down into her eyes.

She can't speak because she feels suddenly shy.

He asks again, "Did you like it?"

"Yes. It was. It..., I feel so embarrassed," she finally confesses.

"Why?" he asks, still looking directly into her eyes.

"It's strange to get mine when I'm not holding you," she admits.

"Uh huh. So which is better?" he asks.

"Holding you is the best because you're always talking in my ear. But daddy, that's good too," she admits with a big smile, "It was like I was losing my mind. And like it was all about me and my pleasure."

He smiles and begins kissing her neck. Suddenly, she grabs his face with both hands and kisses him, aggressively. She can taste herself on his lips. He moans pleasantly. She releases his lips and looks into his eyes.

Then she asks, "Can I try it?"

"Later," he says, "One at a time. We have to save something."

"But you didn't," she tries.

"What did I say?" he whispers with a serious expression on his face. "I vowed to cherish you. You vowed to obey me. Let's not forget."

"Okay," she says as she wisely closes the subject.

"When I want you too. I'll be sure and let you know. Okay?"

"Okay."

They smile at each other. He adores her. She's willing to do whatever it takes to please him and he's sure of it. He'll give her the opportunity, while they enjoy this beautiful honeymoon. But at this moment, he wants to fuck her. He can see her eyes and they're begging for him, so he enters her with authority and grinds aggressively, from the onset.

"See baby. It's already wet," he whispers in her ear. "You're gonna have to give me some more of your juice, though. I wanna feel you come again. I wanna hear it. I love to hear that shit."

He begins kissing and sucking on her neck. From her neck, to her breast and back again. The trembles return. He raises his weight up off of her body, to see his work. He's drilling her thoroughly greased canal. She can see his sex faces, dripping sweat and they're turning her on. He looks from his work to her face and back again. He wants to see her fuck faces and how she reacts to each stroke. So he'll know if she still likes the strokes she use to like best. Or is her preference changing? He has always concerned himself with what fuck moves make her feel the best. So he can apply them and reapply them, over and over. Tonight, he wants there to be something new

243

in their sex life. It's always been good. He wants it to be better than the last time. *Each and every time.* He's the only man she's ever been intimate with. But she's sure she got the best-of-the-best on her 1st and only go round. No other man can be this thorough. Her husband takes the time to give her pleasure before getting his own. He takes pride in pleasing her. Plus he's *so* good at it. She wraps her legs around his waist and lays her head back. She's in this for a lifetime and she feels like the luckiest, most loved and sheltered woman in this world.

}The reception{
Arthur, Wayne, Kilo and Jr yell the Omega chant,
"I put my right hand in the air. I put my left hand in my underwear and just wiggle, wiggle, wiggle, wiggle, wiggle."
Everyone else chimes in, in the response,
"Just wiggle, wiggle, wiggle, wiggle, wiggle."
They yell this chant and cadence, over and over! It's 2am. The reception has gotten it's 2nd wind. The 1st and most of the 2nd generation and their friends are long gone. Chill, Reaper and Ron's crew's are still holding it down. The majority of the guest are still there. Many folks who showed up for *The Spot* club night, had been allowed in at no cover charge. With a 5 drink minimum. The party is definitely on.

"This ain't nothing but CrewLand party! That's all! That's all!"
The crew chant and yell, as all 3 floors are still packed and rocking. Nicole, Angie, Samantha and Gloria had shown back up, just before midnight, to ring in the New Year. Anita had come with them. Since being released from jail, she's cleaned up her act and hoped to see Ajay in the place. She looks descent. Or she looks like she can act decent. She's no longer on drugs. She didn't looked half bad, back in the day. Her whorish ways is what made her ugly. Tonight, she looks a little rough around the edges. Something drugs and jail can do to you. But in the words of Greg Jr, "She looks like she could be fuckable again. I wouldn't hit it. But one of these fools might."

"Back in the day, Ajay and the crew use to tear that shit up, man," Reaper tells him, "She went through all the crew. Renee's crew beat that ass, a few times. And those other tramps that's wit her too. Baby Girl and them, they beat the shit out of them, one night by Chill's house. Bruce told me about it."

"But they still keep hanging around cause they want that crew dick," Greg Jr says, "She want y'all to hit it. They all do." They laugh.
244

TIME TO LOVE-RELOADED-TIME WILL REVEAL 3

"Man, I wouldn't let my dick near that," Jesse offers, "That Anita chick. Tank told me she was a berry. She probably got the *HIV* by now." They talk on the females from they're older siblings past and know, messing around with them wouldn't be cool. They wouldn't have anyway. But just like the crew before them, they have their own groupies. And their girls in the crew, have constant beefs with them too. They're soon joined by Kim, Erica, Brittany and Ruthie. The girls pull them on the dance floor. They want to party. Kim is missing Bruce, already.

"Y'all got to hold me down until I get to the game with my baby," Kim says.

They all agree too. The girls want to dance. The guys oblige them. They join in the chanting, yelling and cadence. The New Year has definitely started off with a bang.

Rich has escape the dance floor again. This time he grabs the bag with his change of clothes and a bottle of Crown. He makes his way out of VIP and to his Benz. He leaves in a hurry. No one from his crew notice him leave and he hadn't bothered to tell anyone he was leaving. Rich has pulled this move, one other time. Him and T-baby had argued about it and he said he wouldn't do it, ever again. The party continues. No one notices Rich is absent. At least, not right away.

}Paradise Stream{

"Misses Jackson, you've got me sprung," Ajay says.

The newlyweds have a laugh as they cuddle on the loveseat, which sits on the enclosed patio of their cottage, overlooking Paradise Stream. They're watching snowflakes fall, with the New Year's Eve fireworks display. They have a postcard view of the ski slopes. The cottages sit on the mountain side. The one they're in, is at the very top. The Presidential Cottage, overlooking the entire village. It has 3 fireplaces. 1 in the bedroom, 1 in the living area and 1 outback, just off from the Jacuzzi, next to the patio where they're lounging. The crackling fire adds to the comfort and sexiness of this early morning. The newlyweds have taken a small break from sex, to cuddle, talk, have a meal and enjoy the view.

"Even this view is cozy and sexy," she says, "We can see this whole town, from up here."

"We're at the top of the mountain. Nothing but the very best, for my wife," he says and smiles. "On the way up here, I thought sure you could tell we was going up, the whole time we was driving. You couldn't tell we was in a constant inclined curve?"

245

"I thought so. Yes. But it was so gradual, I couldn't be sure," she says, "But then, I was on your lap and blindfolded. We was *kind* of busy, the whole way."

They smile and kiss. Then Ajay says, "That food smells good. This is as convenient as it gets."

They have assistants who will come in, at their beck and call, to stir up a meal or bring more refreshments. Whatever she wants or needs, they'll bring. A chef is in their kitchen, right now. Whipping up a stir fry meal of shrimp fried rice, broccoli beef, steamed dumplings and egg drop soup.

"You worked *all* of that reception food off me," he says with a smile.

"He's gonna be done in a second, daddy," she says and smiles.

"I'm gonna feed my husband. I can't have you loosing strength on me."

The chef lets them know their meal is ready and he asks, "*Where would you like me to serve you, sir?*"

"Baby, where do you wanna eat?"

"Here is fine, daddy," she says.

"Set it up out here, for us, please," Ajay says to the chef.

"*Yes sir*," chef says.

He sets a table on the patio, complete with candles and wine. Before leaving, he sets the music for them. They use only 1 chair at the table. Just as they had done on the loveseat, she sits on his lap and they feed each other. She takes the chopsticks and feeds him a mouthful.

"How does it taste?" she asks.

"Not as good as you," he says and smiles as she blushes.

"I can't say that," she says to him, "Because I don't know yet."

"Don't sweat it," he says, "We're gonna get to it."

They eat their meal. She can't help but wonder if he's afraid she can't please him, in the oral way.

Does he feel that I won't be good at oral sex? I would never fail this man. Ever!

"I know we will," she says, "If I have to take me some."

"You won't have to take it," he says.

They cuddle, kiss and finish their meal. The snow continues, as fireworks explode over the mountains. A beautiful sight to behold.

}The reception{

The reception winds down at an impressive 4am. The crew close up the club. That's when they notice Rich is absent.

246

"Have y'all seen Richard?" T-baby asks.

"Not for about an hour or so," Renee says, "I thought he wasn't feeling well and maybe he went home. He left without saying anything to you?"

"He didn't say anything," she answers, "I've been calling his cell. No answer. The house too. He hasn't been answering, if he's there."

"He was acting like he didn't feel good, all night," Roo offers.

"He probably went on to bed, knowing him," Jesse says.

"We'll go with y'all to check it out, T-baby," Chill says, "And make sure everything is alright."

They close up and head directly to *Jackson Heights*. Their upscale community was named Jackson Heights by Ajay, who owns the largest share of it. Tank, June and Rich had agreed *Jackson Heights* sounded much better than Brown, James or Williams Heights. Jackson Heights community is located only 10 miles east of the *Shaker Heights* community, where they had all grown up. It's less then 5 miles from *University Heights,* where their businesses are located. It doesn't take long for them to get home from *CrewLand Mall.* The crew arrives at T-baby's house to find it unoccupied and dark. There is no sign of Rich. The house is exactly as the guys had left it before going to the church. David and Charles verify that. T-baby continues calling his cell phone but still gets no answer.

"He wouldn't have gone back to New York without saying anything, I know," June says.

T-baby looks him over but doesn't offer a response. It was something about the way June's comment came out, that sounded phony to her. She holds her tongue, for now. But June and Rich are suppose to catch a flight, later this evening, going back to their respective teams.

"No. I don't believe he would," T-baby finally says.

She's feeling deserted, obviously. April, Charles, Yolanda and David offer to stay with her and she accepts their offer.

"I'll feel better knowing you're not here alone," Chill says.

"She was gonna stay with us, before we would've left her here alone," Nina says.

"True that," Rebbie agrees.

After knowing T-baby has plenty of company, for the rest of the morning, Chill and the rest of the crew prepare to leave.

"Tell his ass to call me when he gets in," Chill demands.

It's obvious he isn't pleased with Rich's actions. He knows the crew *are not* suppose to roll alone. Especially not after such a high profiled event.

247

"He'd better holla at me too," Tank adds.

Roo and Jesse are staying with Tank and Nina. They close the door behind them and yell back for T-baby to be sure and set the alarm. She does.

Her and her 4 house guest stay up and chat until sunlight. Rich finally arrives. He smells horrible and looks even worse.

"Baby, are you alright?" T-baby asks.

"Yea, baby. I'm just tired," he says.

"Where were you?" she asks.

"I had to go and clear my head. That's all."

"Is everything okay?" she asks.

"Yea Trisha! Damn!" he yells. But he calms down, instantly. He says, "I just had some stuff on my mind, about the team, That's all. Everything's alright with me. I just wanted to drive and clear my head. Let's get a shower and go to bed, baby. I'm cool."

"Okay," she says, "I was worried to death. I thought something happened to you."

"Nothing is gonna happen to me," he says.

He speaks to the Houston guest and thanks them for staying over with his wife. Then him and T-baby retire to their master suite to take a shower and turn in.

"You need to call your brothers, when you get up," she tells him.

"Okay, baby," he says, "I will."

After their shower, T-baby lays in bed and lets her mind wander. She can't help it. There is something wrong here. She thought all the way back to the nights when Rich use to try and convince her to sneak out and meet him at their new little private spot. It's a spot, all their own. No one else in the crew knows how to find them, when they go there. They wasn't even 18. Yet they could do whatever they wanted. Drugs, sex and liquor. With no type of guidance and no rules. Lots of folks hung out there too. She never knew how Rich knew those folks. She always thought maybe they were customers of his. Her and him had stayed there the night after Renee and Tonya's wedding. They had a large mansion filled with sport's memorabilia and antiques. They had a swimming pool, inside and out. Rich had told her the place belonged to 1 of the city's baseball players. Her not knowing baseball well, she wouldn't know where to start, if she was going to check into it. There use to be lots of women there. When he was in high school, they wanted him. She's sure they would have him, now that he's grown and playing professional football. Thing is, he's *married* to her now. Not just her

248

boyfriend, like he was then. He didn't fuck them then, as she knows of. Now, she isn't so sure what's going on. He's been doing something tonight that he wants to keep secret. Her gut tells her that much. Just the short temper he'd come home with, this morning, was enough to make her recall those days. Not to mention that distinctive smell. The same 1 he had when he came through the door today and that counts for everything. Plus he raised his voice to her. The last time he'd done that was the last time he was out at that mansion and wanted her to come see him. She wasn't able too, without getting caught by her uncle Sam. Rich use to have all those fancy cars to drive, at his leisure. Now he's a rich man, himself. The more she thinks, the more worried and uneasy she becomes. She wants to talk this over. She looks over at him but he has fallen fast asleep. She strains her memory but can't remember where that plush neighborhood was located. She remembers it was somewhere off of Shoreway drive. That's all she can recall, as she tries to recollect a name of someone from those days. She thinks of 1 guy. His name, "Clyde."
But Clyde who? Where is that sports guide for Cleveland teams?

She springs from the bed and runs down the hall to her library. She grabs the guide and tears it open. Frantically, she looks through it for someone named Clyde. Of all the sports teams in Cleveland; football, basketball, baseball, hockey and the WNBA. There is not 1 soul named Clyde. Not even an owner, manager or trainer. No one.
Who the hell is Clyde? I know there is a Clyde or is it Clive?

She does manage to find a Clive. Clive Reynolds. She rips through the pages for his photo and she sees it.
That's not him. This dude looks like he's about Eighty years old. This is not the guy I saw, out there. I'm going to drive out there, one day and see if I can find the house. As soon as he goes back to New York.

¦Paradise Stream¦
The chef is back this early morning, as scheduled, to make a fine breakfast for the newlyweds. Ajay takes his bride to the shower, where they shower together, dry off, brush their teeth, then sit down for breakfast. The chef sets the table, serves them and exits.
"This smells good," he says.
"It does. I'm hungry too," she says, "We just ate, like three hours ago and I'm hungry again."
249

"That's all this exercise," he says as he laughs and so does she. They have had 4 episodes since arriving here, 9 hours ago. They're only functioning on 3 hours of sleep and they're still raring to go.

"Are we gonna ski today?" she asks.

"Who?" he asks with a chuckle, "Baby, black folks don't ski."

"I wanna try it, though," she says, "I bet it's fun, Anthony."

"Who?" he smiles, "What did I ask you to call me?"

"Daddy. God," she says and laughs.

"Just daddy. Not God," he says, "I told you before. I don't want that kind of competition." He smiles at her and says, "We might try it tomorrow, baby. But I'm keeping you inside, for the first twenty four hours of our marriage. You remember?"

"Yes, daddy. I hear you," she says and she can't help but to blush. After an hour, they're done with breakfast. He gets up from the table and takes her hand. She stands. He wraps his arms around her, as they dance across the floor and stop in front of the patio window. He spins her around so that her back is to him. She looks out of the large patio windows. He stands close behind her, resting his chin on her left shoulder. His arms are around her waist and he's planting sweet kisses on the nape of her neck, as they take in the breathtaking view of the Pocono's mountains. The fresh Snowfall from over night, makes the village a winter wonderland. With the lights and decorations, left over from Christmas, plus all the wintered pine trees. It looks like frosty covered Christmas trees lining the mountains, from the top, to as far down as the eye can see. Standing and looking at this sexy view, combined with his kisses on her neck, is stimulating her. So much that she closes her eyes and lays her head back against him. He continues the kisses as he starts caressing her shoulders with his strong hands.

"Mmm, it's great," she moans and that's all it takes for him.

"We might ski tomorrow, baby," he says as he picks her up from the window.

They've had their fill of gazing at the scenery. He carries her back to bed.

"The first twenty four hours belong to your husband," he states.

"No problem with me," she concedes as he smothers her mouth with another sweet kiss.

"I love being with you, daddy," she says with a smile.

"I hope so," he says, "Because you're stuck with me, for life."

"It's *all good*," she says, "Daddy, I don't ever wanna be without you."

They pull the covers up over them and indulge in each other, once more.

250

TIME TO LOVE-RELOADED-TIME WILL REVEAL 3

"It's a new year. Filled with new possibilities," Jr whispers into Tonya's ear.

They're cuddled up in bed. After arriving home from the reception, a few hours ago, the 2 couldn't keep their hands off each other. Brad III had gone home, from the reception, with his grandparents, Deb and Brad Sr, last night. Jr and Tonya are *home alone*! They can make as much noise as they please and they're taking advantage of it. They have been making love since they came through the door. They finally stop to rest and talk.

"We haven't been to sleep yet, baby," she says and smiles.

"I'm not mad," he replies.

"We haven't had sex like that, since-"

"Since Lil Brad came," he finishes her sentence. "He needs someone to play with, though."

"He's got crew. And more coming," Tonya tries as she giggles.

"I mean, at *home*, baby," Jr says.

"What are you saying?" she asks.

"I've been thinking about it, for a minute. But ah," he clears his throat and asks, "Do you wanna have more kids?"

"Wow. I thought about it too," she admits.

"You have?" he asks.

"Yes I have."

"So do you want too?" he asks.

"You know Lil Bradley *is* six years old," she offers.

"It's pass time. Or we're gonna be like Chill and Renee, with our kids ages," he says.

"Lil Kenny and Destiny are nearly ten years apart," she says.

"If we start now, ours will still be seven years apart," he says, "Do you wanna start working on him or her?"

"I'd have to stop my pills," she says.

"Make an appointment to see Doc Weston," he suggests, "Lets get everything cosigned, first." They both giggle.

"I'm wit it," she says, "But you once said, we was gonna build in Jackson heights and move. We can get the appointment. Then we can have everything squared away. But let's move into the new house before I get pregnant, if we can wait that long."

"Cool. We can wait until then," he says. Then he changes the subject. "Ajay and baby girl had a great day, yesterday. Didn't they?"

"Oh yes. They did the damn thing. Finally," she says, "I always

251

thought she would be the first one, of the foursome, to get married. But at the same time, I knew Ajay would be the last one, of the foursome guys, to get married."

"I wasn't sure about cousin. For a long time, I didn't think dude would ever allow himself to fall in love with anybody," Jr says, "Ajay use to be a cold ass muafucka. He was emotionally dead, for years. No lie."

"I know when I first started going to Lincoln Middle school with y'all," she says, "Everybody was scared of him. He wasn't no joke."

"And he was younger than all of us," Jr says, "We was in eighth grade and he was in fifth grade," he says and laughs.
She laughs too, then says, "You're right. Ajay was hell."

"I bet he's fucking up a storm, on that honeymoon, too," Jr laughs.
"Poor Ebony," Tonya laughs.
"Shit, baby girl wit it. Y'all better recognize," he says, "She know who she married. She loves how my cousin be beating that shit up, just like you love it."
"Umm, I do love it, baby," she admits.
"Well come here," he says, "Come get some more of this dick, you love so much," and they return to their activities of the morning.
"This is gonna be a great year," Tonya giggles.

}Jackson Heights{

Tank and Nina are slow to rise today, as well. Their night hadn't officially ended when they got home, either. They've also been up since leaving the reception. They feel extra frisky, this morning, too.

"Let's bring the new year in the right way, woman," Tank says to Nina with a big smile. He has just received some serious oral sex.
"That's how you get the year off right!"
Nina grins proudly, as she says, "Anything for my man. You know that."
Noticing that Tank seemed to be distracted, all morning, she asks, "Or you okay, baby?"

"After that job? Hell yea," he replies, "Why, baby? Why would you even ask me that?"

"You seem distracted, that's all. It took forever for you to get off," she says and smiles. "That's how I can tell when your mind is *elsewhere*."

"In the back of mind, I can't quit wondering about where the hell Rich disappeared too," he says.

"Oh, I know, ha? He vamped out on us," she says, "Didn't even tell T-baby anything. But what are you thinking, baby?"
252

"I don't know yet," he says, "I know he's feeling real sad about the Jets, not making the playoffs."

"Jeremy, you know him and June are use to going all the way," she says, "Since junior high school, they've always won the championship," she offers, "I can understand him being side tracked, right now."

"I can too. But they'll bounce back," he says, "Richie Rich is not gonna settle for a losing season, for too long."

"As long as that's all it is," she says, as she scoots up under him and cuddles.

"I do get to suck on these tig ol' biddies, right?" he laughs as he fondles his wife, just as well as he intentionally fumbled his words.

"Please," she says and he obliges her right away.

}Shaker Heights{

It's moving past noon, on this, the 1st day of 1998. The entire crew family are slow to rise today. None of their businesses are opening except the clubs, the detail shop and the bar-n-grill. The clubs and bar-n-grill will open at 6pm. The detail shop will open at 2pm, so the crew take a little sleep in time. But Pearl and Jo are up early with their grandkids, Jerica and John III. Their husbands are preparing to go to CrewLand mall. Both sets of parents have received a call from the newlyweds to say they're, "Okay and having a great time."

John and Al walk over to Chill's house. The 3 of them are riding back to CrewLand Mall together, this afternoon. They're going to help with car detailing until time to open up the grill and the club, for the New Year's night party. Before they leave, they stack firewood on Chill's back porch. He had bought a load for all of the families and had it off loaded in his back yard, 2 days ago. Al and John help him load his portion onto his back porch. During the week, all the fathers will get together to distribute the rest of the load amongst the crew. This Thursday is especially chilly. This time of year, in Cleveland, is known to be cold. But today, it's almost frigid. Unlike just 24 hours ago, when the temperature hovered in the high 50's, all day, for the big wedding. Once all of the wood is stacked, the 3 men load up in Chill's blazer and head to the mall.

"This is going to be a cold winter," John says.

"I was just telling Renee that," Chill agrees, "This morning it feels like it use to feel, back in the seventies. Real bone chilling cold."

"When yesterday was mild," Al says, "I'll bet it's some real news around the corner too."

253

John and Chill inquire as to why he feels this way. He tells them it seems like every time the New Year starts off, extra cold, they get some shocking news during that year. For instance, 1990 started with sub zero temps and they buried Stoney. In 1991, Ebony was attacked that May, Chill and Jr got married in June and granny Pearline died in September.

"And Raymond was killed in November," Chill adds, "That was the other good news of that year, besides our double wedding."

"For real," John adds.

"It may not be a death. It may be new life," Al says, "But it's going to be something big and or unexpected."

"Ajay and baby girl off making a baby, right now, probably," Chill says as he laughs.

"He can make as many as he can take care of, now," John says and laughs too. "He kept his word to me. They're good to go now. I'm ready to see what kind of parents they're gonna be, anyway."

"Yes indeed, man. It's payback time for those two," Al says as they all laugh again.

"I knew they would make it, though," Chill adds, "I knew Ajay was in love with her, way back when everybody was riding him so hard. I knew he loved her."

"We knew it too," John says of he and Al. "But you're a married man. Try telling Renee something she thinks she already knows."
Chill laughs and says, "I see your point."

"We knew from birth," Al adds, "But Joanna and Pearl shut us down, for years." They all laugh again.

"I knew if any man's father, in this world, knew how important my only daughter was to me," John says, "I knew it was Al. I never worried about Ajay. Nor how he would treat my daughter. I was *on him* if he gave *her* too much slack." They laugh again.

"He sure was," Al says, "And the same go for him. Ant is my only blood son," he says to Chill, "John would call me from the road, asking me if Ebony and Ant broke up this week." He laughs and says, "If they was, he would call Ant himself. Or he would call big mama and put her on them."

"Chill, as a father, you know what you want for your daughter, right?" John asks.

"Right."

"My only daughter married a man who grew up in a house full of women," John says, "Raised by a strong father, who came from strong women and he married a strong woman, who was raised by a strong man
254

and woman. Like I said, I never worried about Ajay. I worried more about Ebony's spoiled ass." They laugh hard.

"She has always been spoiled," Al says, "And Ant spoils her too."

"Big time," John agrees, "But she listens to him."

"She sure does and yes, he does spoil her," Chill says, "And he enjoys it."

They arrive at CrewLand mall before 2pm. Jr is at Crew Details with Kilo, Ron and Rob. Rich Sr and Brian Sr had opened up early and have a line of cars, getting detailed. Chill, Al and John walk down to lend a hand.

"We're getting all the money," Brian Sr says and laughs.

"We opened up around noon, instead of waiting until two," Rich Sr adds, "It's been steady since. Folks wanna put that extra shine on, for the party tonight."

"And we don't mind" Brian Sr adds with more laughter.

Brad Sr, Sam Sr and Greg Sr are all there, helping out too. Archie Sr and Jason had gone to get lunch for all them and returned, just as John, Chill and Al grab a cloth and help dry vehicles.

"I guess this is father's day," Jason offers.

They all laugh. All the fathers take a break and grab a bite to eat, before getting back to work.

]Jackson Heights[

June rolls out of bed, after only a few hours of sleep. Without even a good morning kiss, he grabs his cell phone and retreats to the bathroom to shit, shower and shave. He places a phone call to Rich and T-baby's home.

"Hello."

"Yea, where's Rich at?" June asks T-baby.

"He's not up," T-baby answers.

"Wake his ass up for me," June demands.

"Hold on," she says as she goes into the bedroom to wake her husband.

He has been in a comma like sleep, for 6 hours straight. Not even turning over, once. T-baby shakes him to wake him up. He isn't in the best mood when he finally does come around.

"What girl?" he snaps.

"June is on the phone for you," she says, handing him the cordless.

Rich grabs the phone and retreats into the bathroom to wash his face. He says he has only 3 hours before his flight and he still has to pack, see his son, his family and the crew. Plus he has to spend some quality time with his

255

wife, before jetting out. T-baby is still anxious about his early morning activity. But she decides not to bother him with it, right now. She realizes he's stressed out about the outcome of their teams dismal season. After all, Rich is accustomed to being on winning teams. Teams that usually play and win their final game. His Jets team has struggled through a 6-10 season, with no post season play. She knows it's difficult for him to go back to New York, just to pack up for the off season.

But June's Ravens team isn't doing any better, so why isn't he acting like an asshole?

His team isn't playing anymore either. But he isn't disappearing on Rebbie in the middle of the night. She knows Rich and June had high hopes of competing against each other in the AFC Championship game. With the winner advancing to the grand finale, *The NFL Super Bowl game* in the *New Orleans Superdome*. She knows her husband has dreamed of an NFL Championship ring since junior high school. And even more so, since winning 2 college bowl games in that same Superdome. She's been right here with him and she knows. That ring has alluded him in this his 1st season as a professional football player. She certainly understands his killer instinct, his desire to win every game and play to the last possible game. She also knows that isn't going to happen this season. Undoubtedly, he's having a hard time accepting the disappointment of not making the playoffs. Let alone the Super Bowl, so she vows to support him and be understanding. Knowing full well the short comings, her and Ebony have faced on the collegiate level. They were use to winning the Ohio State Tournament, every year which was their final game.

"Honey, I got your stuff packed already and mama is on her way with the baby," she says through the bathroom door.

"Thanks, baby but I need to get out of here in an hour," he says.

"I thought your flight left at six?" she asks.

"Nah. We're leaving at four thirty," he says, "June needs to get back earlier, so we're leaving earlier."

She's disappointed. They haven't spent any quality time together, this trip home. Rich has been preoccupied, as of late. But with the season ending abruptly and not getting a wild card bid, she figures he just hasn't been in the mood for much else. Except drowning himself in *Crown Royal* and his sorrows.

"Baby, try to be in a better mood when you get back next week, alright?" she says as he emerges from the bathroom.

256

TIME TO LOVE-RELOADED-TIME WILL REVEAL 3

"I will, baby," he says with a warm smile.

He kisses her briefly, on the lips. Then grabs his bags and heads for the door, as if he his shuttle is already outside waiting.

"Aren't you gonna tell the baby goodbye?" she asks.

"Is he almost here?" he asks from the foyer. "Because the shuttle is on the way."

He opens the front door to see Sandy pulling up with Rich III in the car. Sandy jumps out and lets the toddler out of his car seat and out of the car.

"Daddy!" Rich III yells, running to his father.

"What's up, partner?" Rich says, dropping his bags and scooping up his son. "How you doing, man?"

"Fine," his son answers.

Rich greets his mother-in-law with a kiss on the cheek.

"Going back to get packed up this time, ha son?" Sandy offers with much sympathy in her voice.

"Yes ma'am. We couldn't pull it off this time. But we'll get back next season, though," he says with a smile.

T-baby is shocked by this jubilant reaction but says nothing. This morning when he strolled in, way passed dawn, in a shitty mood, he had blamed his depression on this season's outcome. Saying he just wasn't in the mood to be happy nor did he feel much like making love to her. Now all of a sudden, when he has less than 20 minutes to see her and their son, before he has to fly off to New York, just to pack up his clothes and return, he's acting chummy as a game mascot.

Why does it even matter when he packs his things? He owns the condo in Jersey. It's not like he lives in team housing or a dorm. He didn't even live in the dorms in college.

Something about this whole situation feels uneasy to her but she acts unaffected in the company of her son, her mother and her Houston guest. Rich all but runs out to the shuttle when it pulls up. June, who is more calm and less hurried, gets out and comes up to chat with T-baby, Sandy and the crew from H-town. He even tickles and plays with Rich III, for a few minutes. He doesn't seem to be rushed, at all. It's only when Rich reminds him that they need to leave, is when he gets hurried. They both load up in the van instantly and depart.

"That's a shame," April offers, "He had to leave, so fast. Y'all didn't even get to give each other a goodbye kiss."

"Good thing we took care of that inside," T-baby covers quickly.

257

TIME TO LOVE-RELOADED-TIME WILL REVEAL 3

Sandy says nothing as she grabs her grandsons hand and escorts him inside. T-baby, April and Yolanda follow. David and Charles left with Jr. He had come by to make sure Rich had made it home. They went to Crew Details with him to pitch in and help with detailing. Rich was too tired to go. All proceeds from the crews businesses today, are being donated to the *Boys and Girls Clubs of Ohio*. This is 1 of the main charities Ajay, June and Rich adopted, once they signed their multi-million dollar contracts. T-baby retreats to her bedroom and grabs the phone. She calls Nina and Rebbie, on 3-way, to chat about the events of the week.

"It's New Year's day," Rebbie says, "And I'm already pissed off."

"You are too?" T-baby asks.

"Hell yes. Brian left here soon as we left y'all, this morning," she says, "He said he was going to look for Rich. He didn't get back until eight thirty."

"That's what time Rich got here," T-baby offers, "So he must've found him."

"Found him or knew where he was and went to hang with him?" Rebbie offers.

"Y'all need to get a handle on these hours they're keeping," Nina suggest, "This is not the first time they've pulled this."

"I know that's right," T-baby says, "But let us try that. They'd be all in our grills about it."

"Even when we was at school and he calls," Rebbie says, "If I'm not there or he can't reach me, he was all agitated when we *did* talk."

"They're too jealous sometimes, that's for sure," T-baby adds.

"That's not jealousy, T-baby. That's insecurity," Nina offers.

"Yes, you're right," T-baby agrees, "But they don't have shit to be insecure about, though. They didn't help with the men's car wash benefit."

"And that's one of their main charity's," Rebbie continues.

"That's not a good look," Nina says and not wanting to make her girls feel more sad, she changes to a lighter subject, "I bet Ebony is having a good time."

"Heck yes! Mama said they called mama Pearl and Jo, this morning. She says they're in a cottage at the top of the mountain, over looking the whole village," Rebbie says, "That sounds so romantic."

"So where did they go?" T-baby asks.

"Pocono's mountains," Rebbie says.

"I'll bet you Ajay not even trying to leave that cottage to see shit else, either," Nina says and they all laugh.

258

"Ebony is gonna be sore as hell when she gets back," T-baby adds with more laughter.

"I'm not mad at her," Rebbie says, "At least she's getting hers."

"Kid, you didn't get any either?" T-baby asks Rebbie.

"Hell no. Ain't that a bitch?" she answers, "Why do you think I'm so tight, right now?"

"Damn, crew," Nina says, "I got more action than y'all did, this week and my fucking period on."

"What?" They exclaim simultaneously.

"I mean you know we couldn't do the penetration. Nor could I get any downtown action," Nina explains. "But he sucked the hell out of some titties and I gave him some serious lips, all week," she adds confidently.

"You *go*, Nina," T-baby says.

"Seriously, kids," Nina adds, "Y'all need to handle that shit, right now. Y'all have only been married eighteen months and the party is already *over*? Tell me it ain't so!"

T-baby and Rebbie both agree with her. They really have to talk with their men and see what the problem is, in the sex department.

"We're gonna do that, right away too," T-baby says.

"I'm gonna do it, this weekend. When I go meet him," Rebbie says, "Something has to give. Because your girl is tight, over here."

They all laugh. But each of them realize the seriousness of this situation. June and Rich are both failing to take care of their wives, sexually. *What's the problem?*

"We're gonna spice things up a bit and see if that works," T-baby says.

"It better work," Nina offers.

They discuss some of the options the girls can try. Tank comes into the kitchen, kisses Nina on the cheek and says, "Hey baby. I had to come back and get one more kiss," he says with a smile. "I'm going back over to Crew Details. You wanna go?"

"No. I'm gonna hang around here and get some work done," she says, "Will you pick up Jerica, on your way back?"

"Oh yea. That's automatic," he answers quickly. "I *have* to get my girl. I haven't seen her, all year."

They laugh. He kisses her again before leaving and adds, "Tell T-baby to let April and Yolanda know I'm ready to go," as he heads back out to the garage.

259

TIME TO LOVE-RELOADED-TIME WILL REVEAL 3

"Tell April and Yolanda, Jeremy is ready to take them to CrewLand to meet up with their crew," Nina relays.

T-baby alerts her guest. April and Yolanda have to meet Ron and the rest of their Houston crew at CrewLand mall. The fathers are getting them to the airport, from there. Nina gets back to their conversation.

"I'll bet you Ebony won't ever have this problem, T-baby and I are having," Rebbie says. "She'll get dicked down, twice a day, at least. Ajay will never, *not* want to have sex with her. So what is Brian's problem?"

"Hell no, kid," Nina agrees, "Ajay's *ever ready ass* is always gonna be in the mood. June best get his shit together and Rich too. I'm gonna put Jeremy on their asses, if they don't get right."

The 3 ladies finish their call but not before agreeing that each would help the other today, with housework, before time to go to work and play at the 2 clubs, this New Year's night.

Tank brings April and Yolanda to the mall. John and Al have opened Stoney's to cook for the entire Houston crew. They thank them for helping out at the detail shop and also for participating in the wedding. After closing the detail shop for the day, Rich Sr and Brian Sr take the Houston crew to catch their flight. They have their own New Year's night event to attend in Houston.

Around noon, Arthur had sent the wedding DVD to Ajay via *Express Mail* to Paradise stream. They have to view it before anyone else can have a copy. Ajay has plans of spending part of their 2nd day, viewing their wedding. Again, Ebony will be surprised. She doesn't know he's having it shipped to them. It should arrive before midnight.

T-baby, Rebbie and Nina help each other with housework until 6 pm. They spend an hour at each of their homes, then they spend an hour and a half cleaning Ebony and Ajay's home. All of their mothers plus Pearl and big mama, come over to help out with all of the chores. They tidy up the estate, from the things they had all left scattered about during the wedding morning's shuffle. They managed to get the place spic and span for when the newlyweds return home.

"They're gonna really appreciate us doing this," big mama says when they finish.

They finish cleaning and the kids go home with their grandmothers. T-baby, Rebbie and Nina return home to get dressed, then head to the mall to open up the clubs.

"I feel single again, damn near. That's the last time I wasn't having

260

sex on the regular," Rebbie says as T-baby drives them to their club in her Benz.

"Oh Rebbie. It's not that bad," Nina says.

"Look, I have needs, kid," she says and laughs. "Brian gave me more dick before we got married."

"Amen," T-baby chimes in, "Rich couldn't get enough, before we got hitched. I swear sometimes I feel like taking his ass back to Gordon Park, in Juniors cutlass." They burst out laughing.

"I'm still sorry for bursting into the car on y'all too, girl," Nina says as she continues to laugh.

"Me too," Rebbie offers, before they burst out laughing again.

"For real though, y'all," T-baby says, "That seemed like that's all our guys wanted to do then, remember?"

The other 2 ladies agree with her. Though they can't help but giggle when they reminisce about the night T-baby lost her virginity. When the 2 of them opened the car door and spoiled it.

"They made the earth move, if they had too, to find somewhere where we could be alone and get it on," Rebbie says.

"Amen. Fucking was the priority then, y'all," Nina tries, "But again, we didn't have any other responsibilities."

"Keeping your wife sexually satisfied is a responsibility too," T-baby says.

"A major one. I agree," Rebbie says, "We sound like the husbands, in the marriage, T-baby."

They all laugh again as they pull into VIP valet parking.

"We're gonna look back at this and laugh, in a month," Nina says, "Y'all will be calling me complaining that you can't get nothing else done because they pulling your panties down in every room."

"Not in a month," T-baby laughs.

"A year, maybe," Rebbie laughs too and adds, "Nee, you're getting dick regularly. You and Ebony will never know where we're coming from."

"Not ever. Especially not Ebony," T-baby laughs.

"I'll be complaining about Jeremy and Ebony still won't be missing any sex," Nina laughs, "My mama will tell you how the Jackson men are. They believe in having a healthy sexual relationship."

"And you *are* a Jackson woman," Rebbie points out.

"True that," Nina laughs, "I *gotta* get mine too!"

They laugh as they get out and head inside to help with the set up and opening of *The Chill Spot* and *The Spot II*.

261

CHAPTER 33

NEW HEIGHTS IN PARADISE

}Paradise Stream, Pa.{

Their 1st full day at Paradise Stream has been, *almost* perfect. Ebony cuddles with Ajay on what is known as, a chair and a half. It's a cross between an overstuffed chair and a loveseat. They have been closed up in their cottage for 22 hours and neither of them have a complaint about their private time. By now, they've given nicknames to every single body part, the other has. She's been to ecstasy, half as many time as hours they've been here. He'd made it his goal to give her an orgasm, every 2 hours of their honeymoon. Now that he has his oral sex skills as a weapon too, he's twice the threat. He still hasn't allowed her to pleasure him, orally. She still has no idea if she can take him to the point of no return orally. Because he still insist on treating her like a virgin, around the mouth. She doesn't even know what to make of it, at this point. He has eaten her pussy 9 times to her serving him, zero. He'd said he wanted to save something so they would have a new move to try later, on in *this* trip. The trip only last through Sunday. It's Thursday night! Something has to give. She's thinking as she cuddles with her slumbering husband. She doesn't know why *he's* sleeping. She's the 1 being drained of bodily fluids. She should be limp, like a cooked cabbage leaf, by now. But her devotion to being able to satisfy his every need, won't allow her to sleep.

"Daddy," she whispers.

"Yes."

He's holding her, next to him. He'd drifted into a light sleep after taking her to sexual heights, for the 11th time since they'd taken possession of the cottage. He adjusts himself, on the big chair, pulls her mouth to his and plants a sweet little kiss on her pouting lips.

He whispers, "What's the problem, baby. Huh? Why are you looking sad?"

"Daddy," she starts, "I don't understand something."

"What is it?"

"When, daddy?"

"When?"

"Yes."

"When, *what*?" he asks.

"When do I get to try it?" she asks.

"Try what, baby?" he asks.

"When do I get to try oral sex on-"

"When I ask you for it," he answers, cutting her off.

"You don't think I can, do you?" she asks.

"Yes, I do."

"I don't believe you do," she tries.

"I believe you can try, just like I did," he says, "And I know you wanna please me. So I know you won't stop until you do. I know this, already."

"Then why don't you let me try?" she asks.

"I *will* let you try, " he says, "And when I want you too, I'll let you know."

"You don't believe in me, daddy?" she asks.

"I just told you, I do," he says, "I really don't wanna discuss it further."

She folds her arms and sticks her lips out. Then rolls her eyes and sighs heavy.

"Getting angry is not an option, baby," he says with a smile and his father's calmness. "Not for the rest of your life. We have to talk things out."

"We don't talk it out, though," she says with her mothers impatience. "You just tell me what we're gonna do."

He lays in silence, for a few seconds. He's thinking of what he should say next.

First, he chuckles. Then he says, "I never thought we would have this type of disagreement about me *not* letting you suck my dick."

Those words startle her.

He adds, "I always thought it would be the other way around."

Hearing him say; *"suck my dick"* catches her off guard. She doesn't know how to even take the phrase into context. She questions herself.

Am I upset about not being able to do something that he doesn't even like? I thought all men liked it?

"Do you like it?" she asks suddenly.

"Hell yea, I like it," he says, "I love it when it's done right. And you'll do it right. I have no doubts about that. Because I'll talk you through it, if I have too. But your willingness to please me, leaves no doubt in my mind that you'll be good at it."

"When you messed around with other girls," she says, "You let them do it. I'm your wife. Why can't I?"

263

He looks into her eyes, then kisses her with fervor. As if he hadn't been having sex with her the majority of the time they've been in this cottage. Then he smiles at her and says, "Baby girl, it's not you. There's nothing wrong with you. It's me. I just always saw the girls who gave head as.., whores." He finds it hard to finish his sentence but he continues saying, "I see you as a good girl. I always have. Because I know you're the *wifey* type. I knew I wanted to marry you, a long time ago. In the very beginning. Before you even said you would be my girlfriend. That's why I got myself right. To be, in my opinion, deserving of an honest woman like you. I use to just tell myself we'll get to all of that after we're married."

"Well, we're married now," she says, "And I *was* a good girl. Now, I'm a good woman. Your woman and your wife. You told me you like how it feels. It's my job to please you."

"I do like how it feels," he chuckles, "All men like head. If they say they don't, they're lying or that girl is just not doing it right. It's just that females, the good girl types, don't usually like to do it."

"You always said you wouldn't want to kiss a girl who did that," she says, "I know you like to kiss me. I always thought that's why you never wanted me to do it. But you said when we got married, we both would."

"I never wanted to kiss no other girl, once you let me kiss you, the first time," he admits, "I really didn't. I can say with all honesty, that I've never kissed another female, in any way. Not since kissing you."
She smiles and says, "Not tongue, ha?"

"Not *anything*. I use to kiss on their necks and breasts too," he clarifies without a smile. "My lips haven't been on another female since kissing you."

"Neither have mine," she says, "And no male either."
They both laugh. She has never been with another guy, in any sort of way. He is the extent of her intimacy. He knows this. He's *quite* proud of it and so is she.

"Do you think you're the problem or me?" he asks.

"I think, *you think,* that I won't be good like the whores was," she says and laughs, "You think you have to see me as a whore, for me to do it." He sits in silence and stares at her. She stares back. Neither of them say anything. They just stare at each other.
The door buzzer sounds!

"I got it," he says as he gets up and covers her with the throw, from the back of the large chair, then he goes to answer the door.
264

"Is the chef back, already?" she asks, "He's really early."

Ajay opens the door. It's the concierge, with an Express envelope for him.

"You have a package up here?" she asks with a smile as she starts to get up.

"Wait there, baby," he says.

He doesn't want the concierge to see her in her sexy attire. And even though she's wrapped in a throw, while he's away from her side, he doesn't even want anyone to see her with her legs or shoulders exposed. He's stingy with his woman. She remains on the chair and a half and waits for her King to return. He signs for the *Express mail*, closes the door and locks it back. Then he rejoins her.

"What is it?" she asks.

"It's a surprise."

She smiles and says, "You surprise me a lot but you don't like surprises."

"No. But you love them," he says, "That's why I do it for you. You love to be surprised."

"I love to be surprised *by you*."

He smiles and looks at her. She watches as he pulls a DVD case from the envelope with a photo of them, posing at the alter, on the front.

"It's *us*!" she shrieks and giggles. "What is this?"

He removes the DVD, which has the same picture from the case. He hands it too her. She takes it from him and looks at it. Then she looks at him and smiles big.

"It's our wedding," he answers, "I arranged for Money shot to rush it up here to us. So we can check it out, as a honeymoon surprise. I thought you'd like that."

He smiles. She grabs his face with both hands and plants a huge kiss on him, with tongue. Then she looks into his eyes as her eyes well up with tears and says, "I do love it. You're the man. I really wanted to see how it looked to everyone else. I didn't get to see anything before I came out because I wanted to be surprised. You are so good to me. I should've known you would have this done, early."

"Keep kissing me like that and I'll give you anything you want."

"Even the pleasure of giving you some lip service?" she asks.

"Baby. Lynn and Nina got you talking like a stripper," he says as he looks at her and laughs. "You would never had said something like that when we use to play basketball together, on the driveway."

She laughs too and asks, "Well will you? If I keep kissing you like this?"

She kisses him again as he looks into her eyes. They're silent. She can see it in his eyes. He's conflicted with the thought of his goody-2-shoes, baby girl,

265

actually giving him some serious head. She already has a clue that he's more concerned with how he feels it will make her look, then he is with being satisfied.

"You wanna be freaky for me, don't you baby?" he ask kissing her again.

"Yes, daddy," she says, "I really do. I don't want there to be any, *one thing*, that we haven't experienced with each other," she says, "Except that anal stuff. That's not for me."

He laughs and says, "Me either."

"I know you don't."

They laugh again, then kiss again. He gets up, puts in the DVD and starts the player. He rejoins her on the chair and a half and they watch their wedding.

"Your vision was on point," he says, after seeing a shot of the entire wedding party at the front of the church.

"Well thank you, daddy," she says, "It looks *so* grand. We did good."

Arthur had put it together, well. This DVD is only a fraction of what the final will be. Their wedding will be a box set. Of everything from the days leading up to the engagement, right through to them leaving in the limo. They'll have more footage as their lives and marriage progresses. Ajay thought of this video diary, while spending so much time apart from her, at college. And now with them living in Cincinnati and Miami, it's something they can both watch when they're missing each other. Arthur has footage on film and/or video, of them dating. Back to the start of their relationship. But on this honeymoon DVD, he tries to keep it simple. He has scenes from the engagement party, then the wedding morning before they leave from Jackson Heights. Their spa, salon and grooming stages. The entire party getting dressed at the church and clowning around. Then the grand finale. Their wedding was lavish. It's followed up with their scenes from the reception and a bit of the party, after they had left in the Limousine.

}Cleveland{

"Hey auntie. Happy new year," Alana says to Darlene as she arrives back from Pittsburgh.

She has come back to Cleveland to attend the New Year's night party with Angie, Nicole and the other girls in their clique.

"Happy New Year to you too," Darlene says, "I didn't get to ask you at the bachelor party or on the phone. But how's my niece?"

266

TIME TO LOVE-RELOADED-TIME WILL REVEAL 3

"She's good and getting big," Alana says of her soon-to-be 8 year old daughter, Olivia Denise Casey. "She really likes second grade too." Alana had named her daughter after 2 of her favorite TV character's, from her then favorite TV sitcom, *The Cosby show*. *Raven Symone*, who played Olivia and *Lisa Bonet*, who played Denise.

"She's already in second *grade*? Time flies," Darlene says.

"It sure does. My probation ends in a few more weeks," Alana says, "On Jeremy's birthday, actually."

"He looked good in that wedding, yesterday," Darlene says, "But not better than the groom. Too bad you couldn't go with me."

"I didn't wanna risk messing up my probation," she says, "We still almost came back. But Farah had to be there for her old man's party, last night," Alana says, "He wasn't about to let her go back out of town in the car."

"Isn't it *her* car?" Darlene asks.

"Her name's on the title," Alana says, "She just needs to find her another black dick and she'll let his ass go, *again*." They laugh.

Farah Benson is a Caucasian friend, Alana met while attending Allegheny community college, in the Steel City. Farah isn't a student. She was student teaching. That's when her and Alana met and became fast friends. Farah helps Alana get through her classes with a much better understanding of the curriculum. Alana's doing better in college, then she'd done in high school. She's 2 classes shy of being a sophomore. She credits Farah with being the one who cared for her and Olivia enough, to set her on the right path to knowledge. Farah will complete her student teaching at the end of this semester. She has been offered a teaching job in Cleveland. At none other then, MLK high school. She has an interview in 3 weeks. She had Alana to drive down with her today and show her directions to the school, for when she has to come back. Further, Alana has convinced her to attend the party at The Chill Spot, tonight. The sweetener is, her being able to meet some professional athletes. Alana had bragged to Farah about the bachelor party having pro athletes, wall to wall. Farah found her offer to be one, she couldn't refuse. She takes this opportunity to join in on the conversation, as she lets Darlene in on another surprise.

"Alana is moving back when I move here," Farah says, "She'll enroll at Cleveland State and finish up. She'll have me to help her out."

"We're gonna get a house together," Alana adds, "She has already started the paperwork."

"A *house*?" Darlene asks.

267

"Yes," they answer in unison, "A house."

"Where is this house?" Darlene questions.

"The Point," Alana answers with a smile.

The ladies go wash up and get dressed for the party. They convince Darlene to go with them. Samantha, Nicole, Angie and Gloria show up, just after 11pm. The 7 ladies head out to *The Chill Spot*.

It's nearly midnight and the place is jumping already. Alana and company arrive and try to sneak through VIP valet and up to the door of the VIP lobby. They ring the buzzer and are attempting to go in. The regulars, in this pack, know full well that cards are required for this door. VIP's have card keys which activate both the VIP door and the elevator. Once you get off the elevator, there's the lobby, then the velvet rope and the entrance which Renee usually monitors. Those who don't have a card can either phone in to Renee or ring the buzzer. Then the crew checks the video monitors to see who it is. If it's a legitimate VIP guest, they send someone down to escort them up. During the course of the night, they offer them VIP membership to The Chill Spot. That's not the case with these females. Renee waste very little time having them escorted to the regular entrance. She can see the smirks on their faces as they stand there awaiting their fate.

"I'm not even in the mood," Renee says as security heads down and directs them around to the front, immediately.

"I guess Jeremy isn't on the door," Alana says, trying to save face. Farah laughs and says, "I guess I'll have to apply for a card." They all laugh as they jump on line for the front door.

Meanwhile, Renee calls Nina, who's at *The Spot II*. She wants her to know that her past nemesis is on the property.

"Guess who showed up over here with the regulars?" she says.

"*Who*?" Nina asks.

"Darlene. And she brought her niece, this time," Renee says.

"*Alana!?!*"

"Uh huh. I knew when I saw Darlene at the wedding, yesterday," she says, "She was gonna start back coming around. But I didn't expect to see Alana. Not ever."

"What the *hell*? She must be visiting," Nina says, "I know that bitch haven't moved back here."

"I don't know but get this," she says, "Her dumb ass was down there ringing the buzzer for the VIP lobby." They laugh.

268

TIME TO LOVE-RELOADED-TIME WILL REVEAL 3

"She's stupid," Nina says, "Trying to front, I guess."

"There's a white girl with them," Renee says, "I haven't seen her, before. But looks like she's got some bread. She's *D&G,* to the hilt."

"*Dolce?* She must've came in from Pittsburgh, with Alana," Nina says, "I hear Alana's in college."

"When did she finish high school?" Renee asks and they laugh again.

Renee and Nina are actually more up on Alana's recent activity, than they discuss. They knew, through frequent visits from Nicole and Angie, that she had gotten her G.E.D. They've kept them up on everything that's gone on with the 2 females. Which is why Chill had gone investigative, following the Angel phone calls. Renee and Nina hang up.

Nina calls T-baby and Rebbie, who are inside VIP, at The Spot. She tells them Alana is about to be in the building. T-baby puts her speaker on.

"So ah, what? You wanna kick her ass?" T-baby ask and laughs.

"Don't rule it out," Nina says to them.

"We're sexually frustrated," Rebbie says, "It ain't no *thang.*"

They laugh again. Then Rebbie and T-baby go to their private window, overlooking the club below. They're watching the patrons as they enter. They're going to call Nina back and let her know when they see Alana enter the club.

Meanwhile Nina seeks Tank out, immediately. She finds him at the concessions bar on the 1st floor, talking to the 99 crew, which is Jesse, Brittany, Erica, Greg Jr and Sam Jr. They are the 5 crew members who will graduate from MLK in 1999. They'll be the largest number of crew to graduate together, in the history of the families. The foursome are the largest, thus far. After seeing the 6 of them laughing and giggling, Nina knows her husband has been telling them jokes about how their crew had done things at their age. And they're telling him that his crew is not as fly as theirs. They go back and forth, like this, all the time. While the 99 crew works concession at their under 18 club.

"What's good, Nina boo?" Erica asks as she grins.

"It's all good, lil sis," she says and smiles. "I just need to steal my husband away from you guys, for a minute or two."

"Tank, you bout to go get busy, man?" Greg Jr asks as he laughs.

"Hey crew," Tank smiles but doesn't say another word as he walks off toward the elevators with Nina.

He gives the 99 crew the thumbs up and she does too. The 99's whoop and holler their approval. Nina and Tank hop on the elevator and head upstairs.

269

The Spot II is designed very similar to the adult club. It's become famous for being the plushest spot for teens. Nina and Tank have their offices on the 3rd floor, just as Chill and Renee do, at The Spot. The Spot II has VIP and a dance floor on 2 levels, just as the adult club. Instead of a Strip Club and poker room on the 2nd floor, it has a state of art Arcade arena which includes interactive games, a computer and study lab and the latest in video games and technology. The Spot II is also endorsed by *EA Sports,* as is the *Kids Arena* in Atlanta. They receive immediate upgrades each time a new game gets released. June, Rich, Lynn and Ajay secured that link for Tank and Jb. Tank hosts tournaments, weekly. They're highly attended by all demographics of Cleveland and surrounding areas. The prerequisite to enter, is all participants have to be enrolled and in good standings in school.

Tank and Nina reach the 3rd floor and dip into her office. She closes the door as he moves in for a sweet kiss. She reciprocates. Then she asks him to have a seat.

"This sounds serious, baby," he says.

"Alana is at the spot," she says.

"So," he says, "She paid to get in, *right*?"

"I'm sure she did but," Nina answers, "It doesn't bother you *any*?"

"Of course it does," he says, "When I think about her part in hurting my sister and my partner."

"I think she should be banned from our properties," Nina suggests.

"I don't agree," he says.

"And why not?"

"Because, baby," he says, "we're in business to make money. If we ban her, we're banning dollars. Not only from her but do you realize the money sluts and tramps bring into our businesses? The men show up for easy ass. She can dance in the strip club, if she wants too. I don't have a problem with making money. I don't care who's money it is."

He laughs. She doesn't. She asks, "Is that the only reason?"

"*Baby*?" he asks in shock.

"Is it?" she asks again.

"Yes it is," he says as he stands up and steps close to her, pulling her close to him and holding her there. "There's nothing or no one who can come between what we have. Do you *hear* me? Not one *muthafucking* thing. My home is happy. My baby girl is happy, *in it*. I'll kill a motherfuckah for even dreaming about trying to fuck wit it. You understand?"

270

He kisses her with passion before she can answer him. He holds her tongue hostage as he grabs a fist full of her hair, tilting her head back. He kisses her on her neck, taking it further down into her bosom. Then he asks, "It's still not a go yet, is it?" referring to her *time of the month.*

"Not quite. *Damn!*" she giggles.

"Well you'd better stop looking so damn good," he warns, "Or you're gonna get me in trouble with God, this week. Because I'll fuck you, right here." They laugh and kiss again. "I love you Nina Shalon Jackson Brown. You do know that, right?"

"Yes Jeremy Marcus Brown. I do. And I love you too. But-"

"This is the only butt," he says, grabbing a hardy handful of hers, "This is all I see. All I want and all I need. Understand me? I married the woman I wanna fuck, *every* night. Do you feel me?"

"Yes, dear," she says and smiles.

"We had the only argument and break up that we're gonna have, behind that tramp," he says, "That was before I had to move to Houston," he reminds her. "That shit tore me up. I told you back then, I was gonna prove to you that I hadn't started a future with that bitch. I did that, did I not?"

"You did," she admits.

"Then if I did," he says, "The uneasiness about Alana should be dead, after tonight," he says, "Just like T-baby did with Tameka. She works for us now. Is T-baby and Rich thing stronger than *ours*, baby?"

"Of course not," she smiles, "Nobody's is, if you ask me."

"I just asked you," he says and smiles.

"No. Theirs is *not*," she says with a smile and emphasis.

"Listen, Nina boo," he says, "The only way Alana will be a factor in us being apart, is if she get in my motherfuckin way or fuck with my Jerica or you. Because I'll set her ass up and bury her alive. Get caught and go to prison, for life."

"We can't have that," she says, "I trust you, Jeremy."

They smile at each other. There's no need to speak on it, anymore. She had been on edge momentarily, about the resurgence of her husband's ex-lover, long before he was her husband. It brought back a few memories. A few hurtful ones. He reminds her of how those memories was put to rest. How they had helped to close that chapter and also showed her what kind of team they are. What kind of trust they have in each other. That night at the University Apartments, when the crew brought in Alana and Angel, was monumental to him. It showed him how much she trusted him. How much

271

his word meant to her. And even though he had to be around Alana to get it accomplished, she never doubted him and had even helped to arrange it.

"I will never lose your trust again," he says "You have my word on that, Nee Nee."

She smiles. He hasn't called her by that pet name in a long time. They kiss. Then head back to get ready for closing. They're asking themselves what kind of names have Ajay and Ebony come up with for each other.

"Oh man," Nina laughs, "*Lord and master.*"

"*Cleopatra and Delilah!*" he says as they laugh loud.

They start the closing, so they can join the others at The Spot. Alana's name is dismissed as a past fling. Which will stay in the past, whether she accepts it or not. The best thing would be for her to accept it. Because Nina is fresh out of patience for her type. The crew are on their grown up shit, these days and they aren't in the mood to waste time with a nothing ass bitch like her. She's the type of enemy that encountered the mild side of the crew. She was allowed to live, where others were killed for less. She can learn and live on. Or fuck up and feel the wrath. Ain't shit changed when the matter of a crew's happy home gets threatened. And that goes for all 3 generations.

}Paradise stream @ 130am{

The DVD was 2 and a half hours long. They watched it, in it's entirety. It's past midnight and into Friday morning. Ajay is ready for some more loving. He still hasn't answered her question about her performing oral sex on him. But he has certainly served her again. He takes her to the bed, for this latest episode. He licks her honey and moans like it's the sweetest thing he's ever tasted, as he takes her to new heights. Now she's feeling vulnerable and deeply loved, all at the same time. She just wants to give him the same pleasure but he still hasn't allowed it. Laying there, her mind takes her back to motel room 111. The real beginning of ecstasy for her. She remembers feeling as though she would never be able to handle him. *That hasn't changed.* He still has way too much dick for her. For awhile now, she has looked forward to giving him oral sex. She wants to get up close and personal with this tool which has kept her subservient, for all of these years. She wants to coax it, caress it, kiss it and assure it that she will always be good to it and it's owner. So then maybe, it will have a little mercy on her sweet box during their pleasure sessions. But he won't allow her to meet his member, up close. That she feels is the way to his ultimate vulnerability and pleasure.

It must make him lose control.

272

TIME TO LOVE-RELOADED-TIME WILL REVEAL 3

It has to be the key to evening up their sex sessions. She feels it's about him being dominate. He has to master oral sex before allowing her to try it, just like it was with sex. He knew it all, then she learned through him. But that's not what they agreed on for their wedding night. He said and she agreed, they would start on their honeymoon. *He has.* But he's still denying her the opportunity. And if she can't give him the ultimate, will he stray to get it? She remembers what she thought that night when she couldn't handle the thrust of his dick.

How will I ever be able to be his lady, if I can't please him in bed?

Her mind comes back to the present. She's trembling. He's finishing up her honey. She's making sounds that she can't even recognize. He comes up to look at her face. He knows what her question is, even before she can ask it.

"Not yet," he whispers as he enters her vigorously, taking the air from her lungs and her hair in both hands.

He drills her. He rides her while kissing her wildly, all over her breast, neck and face. He grunts every time he pushes his nearly 14 inch slab into her. He's talking to her but she can't hear him over her own screams. His hopes are to tire her out and maybe she won't pressure him about allowing her to perform.

He's got something to prove? But why? I know this look. What is he afraid of? Is it his vulnerability too?

She can't figure this out. His mind drifts as he fucks her, very well. His thoughts are totally different from hers. He's still her protector, the guardian of her virtue plus she has been through enough. How is he going to marry her and then turn her into some slut? Have her doing things his whores did for him? She has been through things in her life that even his own father doubted he could handle. But he has. He can't fuck that up now. He promised he would make her an honest woman. He promised his father-in-law he would.

Can I really stick to that part? Is that ruining her virtue, if we're already married? Can I make that part make sense to her? Why do I think it'll make me look at her differently? She's my baby. I love her. I know she's not gonna accept me not giving her the chance to please me, the same way. I know she's not gonna be denied.

He's considering not even going there with her, at all. He's afraid to risk it and doesn't know how to tell her.

273

If I say I don't want her to do it, what will she think of me?

"Baby, you feel so good," he moans as he's out in the zone somewhere and still fucking her vigorously.

She's digging the covers off the bed as his thrust are so powerful that she reminisces back to the night when he'd helped to kill Stoney's murderers.

"What's wrong, daddy?" she screams and he finally hears her.

He stops instantly and finds her eyes. She's crying, as she asks, "What is it? Are you mad with me? What did I do?"

"No, baby," he says, "Of course not."

He finds her lips and kisses her over and over, while wiping away her tears. He realize he was fucking her like an angry man, only because he's at war with himself. He pulls out and tries to get a grip on the situation but she has questions for him.

"Or you okay?" she asks.

He sees tear tracks down her face. He wipes them away again and apologizes, over and over. This wasn't suppose to happen, like this. He cuddles her close to him, continuously apologizing. Now she's confused. Maybe she shouldn't bother him with her longing. If he doesn't desire oral sex from her, then maybe she shouldn't offer it. This wife thing is already complicated. She thought he would love for her to try something new. But it seems apparent he doesn't want it, after all.

"I'm sorry too, daddy," she says, "I didn't mean too. I want say it, anymore."

"Say what?" he asks.

"I want ask you to let me do oral sex on you," she says, "I didn't mean to make you mad."

"I'm not mad," he says with a kiss, "Just leave that to me. We'll get there. I didn't mean to hurt you, baby girl. I'm sorry for that, okay?"

"Okay."

They cuddle together. Within minutes, she falls fast asleep. It's nearly 5am. The chef will be there at 9am to make breakfast. He's still awake, watching her sleep. He kisses her forehead over and over, as he looks at her.

"I love you, baby girl," he says as she sleeps.

He's more or less trying to convince himself that he won't stop seeing her as a good girl, if she gives him head. He's taking her skiing and hiking, this morning, around 10a.m. That's the plan. She wants to go. He's willing to give her whatever she wants, if it's possible. He adores this woman. He really does. She's sleeping peacefully and no longer crying because he had

274

bugged out on her during sex. No, none of that's going on now. The tiring her out plan has worked to perfection. But now he's curious about her oral sex abilities. He has convinced himself that it's going down today. All she has to do is stop asking him. He's kissing her lips. She sighs and moves closer to him. He had tired himself out too. He dozes off.

}*Late Friday morning at Jackson Heights*{
T-baby visited Rich III at Daycare, early this morning. Rebbie, her and Nina had let their children go home with the grandmothers, after house cleaning was done yesterday. They had let them stay the night and go to daycare from there, this morning. They knew they wouldn't leave the spot until they closed up. The kids club had closed at 1a.m. Nina and Tank had joined their crew at the adult club. They didn't have a confrontation with Alana during the evening. She had wisely kept her distance and behaved herself. Still, Rebbie and T-baby told Nina they felt like she was up to some dirt and left it at that. The ladies have their priorities in order, these days. They have to get up and see their children early, because they'll be heading back to Cincinnati tonight. The beginning of the 2nd semester starts Monday. But all 3 of them have practice, early tomorrow morning. Ebony will return to school for Monday practice. They'll play *Southern Mississippi* on Tuesday night. T-baby visits her son, then leaves before Rebbie and Nina show up. She has something else to attend too before she can leave Cleveland. Something which has been on her mind since early yesterday. She rushes back home to map out her strategy. She has to get some lead way into where her husband had spent yesterday morning. Her intuition tells her that he's cheating.
Who the hell is Clive?

Clive Reynolds. She had ripped through the photo's and found a picture of him, only to determine that he wasn't the guy who had hung out with them at the mansion, back in the day. That wasn't him. The dude in the photo looked like he was 80 years old. That wasn't the guy, so it's time to take a ride.
I remember how to get there. I can find it. When he gets back from New York, I have to have something to confront him with. Who is the bitch? That's all I wanna know!

She has her hand written directions as she grabs the Benz keys and heads out to the garage. She lets up the garage door and starts the car. She backs
275

out and heads toward the entry gate. She drives through it, speaks to Jacobson and moves on outside of their community. She follows her directions. Before long, she's in the well kept neighborhood, out in Lake County, known as *Madison-on-the-lake*. She maneuvers through this well manicured subdivision. She has visions of her own, Jackson Heights community. She realizes they're just a pond away from this same elegance. She turns up Rhodes drive.

"There it is," she says to herself, as she drives up the hill towards the huge mansion.

She pulls in front of it, pauses but doesn't stop. She drives on, passing the mansion slowly and on to the cul-de-sac. She loops around and heads back. On her way back towards the house, she sees a female. She has run out to the end of the drive in anticipation of the Benz pulling back up to the house. *Oh fuck! Who is this bitch?*

She puts her window down and drives slower. The female walks up to the car. But when she leans down and sees T-baby, she excuses herself.

"Sorry, No. I think you some one," the female says, in broken English.

The woman is foreign. Asian. She hasn't quite gotten a hold of the English language yet.

"Who was you looking for, *bitch*? My husband?!" T-baby screams at her.

The woman doesn't answer. She turns and runs back up the drive. T-baby turns into the driveway, pulls up and parks. She gets out and runs up to the door. She can't see or hear anyone. She knows that Asian woman just went inside. She rings the bell frantically. But no one answers. She waits at the door, for nearly 10 minutes, ringing the bell and knocking. She's puzzled but she's convinced she's found something. Finally, she heads back to the Benz.

"That bitch is fucking my husband," she asserts. "That's why she ran in there and hid. He was probably fucking someone out here, yesterday. Probably years ago too. When he use to bring me with his *scandalous* ass!" She talks to herself as she stomps back to the car.

Ring! Ring! Ring!

Her cell phone is ringing. She jumps into the car and looks at the caller I.D. It's Rich. She doesn't answer. She lets it ring as she starts up the car, backs
276

out and pulls away. She cursing, a whole lot, as she drives back home. *Did your bitch call you and tell you I was out here? You dirty muthafucker! What the fuck is going on?*

She drives out of Madison-by-the-lake and back onto Memorial Shoreway drive. She takes highway 44 to 87 and back into Jackson Heights.

Ring! Ring! Ring!

Rich is blowing her cell phone up. She decides to answer it as she pulls up their driveway, into the garage and closes it down again.

"Hello," she says, her voice dry.

"Hey, what's up, baby?" he says very jubilantly.

"Not much. What's up with you?" she asks, still dry.

She's playing it off since her suspicions are telling her that he's satisfied with doing the same.

"I'm done packing and I'm about to head out of here," he says. "I was trying to see you before you leave for Natty."

He's sounding as if he's in a great mood.

Maybe he's just checking to see what time I'll be gone, so he don't have to waste time coming by the house. He can go straight to hell. Him and his bitch.

"What time is your flight?" she asks, as she seethes.

"Two forty. One forty, your time," he says, "I'm at the airport now. I get in at five fifteen. Can you pick me up?"

"Sure," she says.

"Cool. We can pick up the baby, on the way in and grab some soul food too."

"Sounds like a plan," she says.

"Okay, baby. I'll see you at the airport," he says.

He hangs up and so does she.

"Sounds like a plan," she repeats her last sentence.

Now her mind has switched to total detective mode. She's not going to tell him she's been to Mentor. She's not going to tell him shit. She's going to let him tell her.

}Late morning at Paradise Stream{

The newlyweds have a late breakfast this morning. They shower, dress and prepare to hit the slopes. They take the short ride to a nearby ski
277

lodge. Before they even board the trolley, they watch a video tutorial about skiing. Then they stand and observe as 1 by 1, skiers reach the bottom of the mountain. Ebony still wants to try skiing. Ajay has a promise to keep. They head over to the sky lift and climb on. He has hired 1 of the resort photographers to snap pictures of them. He climbs into the lift with them.

"Are you ready to do this?" Ajay asks Ebony.

"Yes I am," she answers, "I'm excited. I'm kind of nervous too."
They're riding the ski lift to the top.
"What a view," she says as she asks the photographer, "Please get this?"

"It *would* be interesting, if he wasn't here," Ajay says and smiles, as he looks at the photographer.

"Daddy, we're gonna get something else out of this honeymoon."

"Why?" he asks as they laugh and so does the photographer.
They're going to ski the beginner slopes. Still, it takes a great deal of encouragement and flat out begging, for her to get Ajay to even come to the ski resort.

"My legs are my career," he says as they laugh.
But she knows he's being truthful.

"I know. You have some nice looking legs too," she says, "I promise not to let anything happen to them."

"Coach made me promise I wouldn't go near these ski slopes," he says, "Now look at me."

"Coach didn't look at your wife," Ebony says and smiles. "But it's the baby slopes, daddy. We're gonna be on flat land, the entire way."

"Flat *land*? Then how do we get back down there?" he asks with a chuckle as he points back toward the bottom.

"Well, it's a very gradual decline," she adds and laughs.

"Yea, okay," he says and they laugh again.

"It's a beautiful view, daddy," she says, "Thank you for bringing me here."

"Thank you for marrying me," he says.

"You're welcome. Thank you too," she says as they kiss.
A perfect snapshot with the slopes in the background. They finally arrive at the top. The resort team member opens the lift door. They disembark from the lift and take in the view from the top. It's gorgeous.

"There are slopes for racing, slopes for fast skiers, slopes for intermediate, slopes for learning and performing jumps and procedures. And slopes for beginners."

"That's us," Ajay says with a laugh.

278

TIME TO LOVE-RELOADED-TIME WILL REVEAL 3

There's no shame in his game. He sloshes over to the beginner slopes with pride and his bride in tow.

}Cleveland{

Alana and Farah are just waking up. Darlene had gone in to work, hours ago. Farah phones her boyfriend Marvin, back in Pittsburgh. She tells him they'll be home Sunday. He isn't pleased and she doesn't care. She will deal with his attitude when she returns to the Steel City. Her and Alana had a good time, last night with the girls from Cleveland. Alana had made certain Farah knew which guy was Tank. She had also pointed out all of the crew members, she saw and recognized.

"So is he Olivia's father or not?" Farah asks.

"Could be. Could be not. Depends on if he wants the job," Alana says and laughs.

Farah was only joking. She knows about the blood test Tank *insisted* Alana have done, when Olivia was born. It proved he wasn't the father. She also knows about the accident Angel caused to Ebony and Alana's part in it. She knows pretty much the entire history and scene, where her girl Alana is concerned. She knows about her multiple group orgy's too. So it doesn't surprise her that the welcome mat wasn't rolled out for her, last night at *The Chill Spot nightclub.* Or anytime since being here. But she's being a bitch about the whole thing. Much like Alana, who doesn't seem to have learned much from her last encounter with the crew.

"He seemed secure with his wife, last night," Farah says, "I don't think he noticed you was there."

"He knew I was there," she says, "I guarantee you that. His crew saw me. They told him I was in the club. I bet you she dared him to look my way. Now *that's* what the deal was."

"From what you told me about your final meeting," Farah says, "I'd be afraid to even go around them."

"I lived through last night," she says boastfully, "That says to me that they have grown past it. Besides, Ebony just married Ajay, two days ago. All of them was in a good mood. My probation ends in twenty three days and that's also Tank's twenty third birthday. You come back for your interview with the high school, on Monday the twenty sixth," she lays it out, "I know they'll have a party for him. Either Saturday or Sunday, before your interview. They're famous for their parties. I told you that."

"We're coming back that Friday, before the interview," Farah says, "So I can meet with the realtor, about the house."

279

TIME TO LOVE-RELOADED-TIME WILL REVEAL 3

"Marvin still don't know you're going to move here, does he?"

"Why *should* he? He's not moving with me," Farah says and laughs. "I'm so sick of him trying to be my owner. Besides, the dude who owns the chill spot. He's fine! I know I'm going to go through a few of these cards," she says as she holds up her Chill Spot card which she received, last night. "If that's what it takes to get to him because he made me feel extra special and welcomed, last night. I want to know him better."

Chill makes it a point to welcome each new guest, who comes into the nightclub. All new patrons receive what is known as, a frequent Chill Spot partygoer card on their 1st visit. It's a card which contains 24 punch out slots. On each visit, when the card is presented, a slot is stamped and recorded. On the 25th visit, there is no cover charge and drinks are half price before midnight.

"You're talking about Chill. He's a kingpin," Alana says, "He's a boss, *for real* girlfriend. He's the one who keeps all of the crew's shit together and in order." Alana eggs her on. "If you can get with him, you'll be the a *fucking* boss bitch."

"Give me time to get my feet wet," Farah says, "I'm a white bitch with money. I'll be looking to invest in his business and not just with cash."

"Farah, how is Marvin gonna react when you tell him it's over?"

"He's gonna think I'm leaving him for you." They laugh.

It's amusing to them that Farah's boyfriend since her freshman year in college, thinks she's having a lesbian affair. It isn't like he doesn't have good reason for thinking it. She experimented with her roommate while in college and he had walked in on them, several times. Her and Alana have also dabbled in it a bit too. Theirs wasn't seen by Marvin but he had automatically assumed it because of Farah's past actions. These 2 are both so promiscuous with men, that they only keep each other as a back up. Just in case they aren't able to pick up a masculine human, who's packing *God given* hardware.

"If Marvin gives me trouble, I'll have the crew to deal with him," Farah says and they laugh wildly.

"Oh he'd better not go there," Alana says, "When Chill is your man, he'll eighty six his corny ass, quicker than you can dump him."

"I needs to see him, girl," Farah says, "I'm Jonesing for him."

"Well I'm hungry girl," Alana says, "Let's check out their new restaurant. I heard a couple of my ex-home girls are working for them now too. I wanna see if they gonna keep it real with me or act fake, like before."

"Let's do it," Farah says.

280

TIME TO LOVE-RELOADED-TIME WILL REVEAL 3

They get dressed and head out to University heights CrewLand mall, for an early dinner.

}Mount Pocono's, early evening{

Mr. and Mrs. Jackson spent 2 hours on the slopes. From there, they went ice fishing but it got too cold, sitting on the ice. So Ajay suggested they go snowmobiling instead and she accepted.

"You've got me all out of my comfort zone, baby girl," he says as he laughs. "That's another exclusive for you. Only you can get me to do things that I wouldn't normally do."

She smiles big. They finish up, just before dusk. They had a light lunch at the ski resort. But they're both hungry now and ready for dinner. She wants to dress for dinner but she isn't sure how he'll feel about it. Not until she brings it up.

"Should we go back to the cottage and have the chef come in and cook?" she asks.

"It's up to you," he says, "What do you wanna do?"

"I saw a steak and rib restaurant, right outside of the village," she says, "I know you love prime rib, daddy."

"Are you trying to stay out of the cottage as long as possible?" he ask and chuckles.

"Of course not," she laughs too. "I just wanna see some of this gorgeous place, before we leave."

"We'll hike tomorrow," he says, "It's almost dark. They got wolves up here."

The horrified look on her face, makes him laugh. He laughs hard. She laughs too.

"I'd rather get inside before dark," she suggest with laughter. "We'll go to the restaurant."

"Oh yes. That sounds like a winner," he says, "Let's go back and wash up."

They go back to their cottage and took a bath together. They change into elegant dinner attire, then they catch their limo to *Bailey's Rib and Steakhouse restaurant.* They're seated at a very secluded and private table. Immediately, they're server takes their full order and turns it in to the kitchen. She returns with a glass of *Lindemans Bin 65 Chardonnay* for Ebony and a Heineken for Ajay. No glass.

"I love how private this table is," she says.

The look on his face tells her he likes the private spot, as well and he's
281

TIME TO LOVE-RELOADED-TIME WILL REVEAL 3

planning to take advantage of it. They can't see the other patrons in the restaurant from where they're seated and vice versa. They're also seated side by side and close enough to smooch during dinner.

"Admit it. You had fun skiing today," she says giving him a kiss.

"It was fun. Cold but fun," he smiles.

"You did good, daddy," she says, "Better than me."

"I don't think so," he says, "But you was too cold, most of the time, though."

"It wasn't as cold as ice fishing though, right?" she asks smiling.

"Not even," he says, "But the snowmobiles was the most fun."

"Mmm yes. Because we could cuddle," she says and smiles.

"Do you still want to go hiking?"

"Not with wolves out there," she says.

"I'm the only wolf you've got to worry about, baby," he says.

He kisses her. Their server arrives with their appetizers. 2 dozen fresh steamed jumbo shrimp and a dozen oysters, on the half shell.

"These right here will get you right," he says as he smiles.

He puts an oyster on a cracker, sprinkles it with salt and pepper, adds a dash of Tabasco, then offers it to her.

"You first," she says and laughs, as he devours it and winks at her.

"These will have you horny, all over again," he says with a smile.

"As if we need an aphrodisiac," she says as she lets him serve her the next oyster.

The server refills their drinks and leaves them a basket of bread. They sit and enjoy their appetizers and drinks. He feeds her oysters and sexy looks. She feeds him shrimp cocktail and inviting smiles. She can tell he's already in the mood. But when *isn't* he? She knows he doesn't need any help getting up for sex.

"You're not giving me any more oysters?" he asks as he laughs.

She serves him 2 back to back.

"You don't really need any help, daddy," she says again.

He smiles and says, "Neither do you." Their server alerts him that their entrees are ready. "We're ready for them," he tells her.

She retreats to the kitchen and returns with their main courses. They dine on Prime rib with Maryland Crab cake. They added lobster tails and sautéed mushrooms with sweet potato fries, salad and sweet tea to drink. They eat as much as they can hold, between kisses and fooling around. After dinner, he has a *Courvoisier* chaser. She sips from his.

"This is *strong*," she says after her 1st sip.

282

"Cognac is for Don's," he says and smiles. "Godfather types."

"But you're daddy. Not Godfather," she giggles.

"One in the same," he says.

"Then what does that make me?" she asks.

"Mama or Godmother," he says and they both laugh.

"It just doesn't have the same kick to it, for a girl," she says.

They laugh some more and enjoy each others company and conversation. It isn't long before the topic turns to sex. She still wants to do oral sex on him. She's hoping he wants it and as always with him, she gets her wish.

"I was shocked when you ask me, *do I like oral sex?*" he says, "You think I don't like it or that I don't think I will like you doing it."

"It don't seem like you do," she says, "You act like you don't want me to *ever* do it. I guess I just don't understand that part and why?"

"It's like I said before," he says, "I see you as my baby. My good girl. From a good family. *Respectable.* I can't asked big *John's* daughter to give head." They laugh.

"I know you do," she says, "I see you the same way. I have mad respect for you daddy but you've been-"

"-eating the hell out of your pussy since we've been married," he says, seizing her lips as if that was something she had just demanded.

He kisses her with fervor, heated passion and heavy breathing, at the same time. The Cognac taste better on his tongue, then it did from the glass. He finally pulls up. She feels drunk, at this point.

"Yes," she answers, clearing her throat, "Yes, you have been."

She giggles. She's noticeably turned on and a little buzzed. The oysters are working. There are little beads of sweat forming on her nose and on her smooth forehead, as she plays with her earlobes. He has learned, too well, the sexual signs that she puts off. She learned his too. His eyes become very narrow, like he's in deep thought. He stares at her with glazed over eyes while biting down on his bottom lip. His chest rising and falling, rapidly under his dress shirt. He's doing that, right now.

"Are you horny, baby?" she asks, "Because you got that sexy look in your eyes and you're biting your lip. It looks so good to me."

"I could fuck. Yes," he says, "But I want some lips, tonight. I want you to taste me," he says suddenly.

"I wanna know what you taste like, daddy," she says as she lets the oysters talk for her. "Oh *God*! I wanna taste your dick so bad, my mouth is watering."

"*Check please!*"

283

}The CrewLand Mall{

Alana and Farah arrive at *The Crews House of Soul Food*. They request and are given seats, in Tameka's section. She comes over to greet them.

"Hi Alana," Tameka says, "I never expected to see you here."

"Likewise," Alana says, "So you're working for your man now?"

"*Sshh.* Lower your voice," Tameka says, "I am not interested in Rich, anymore. Please don't come in here with that nonsense."

"You're really serious too, aren't you?" Alana asks.

"As a heart attack. That's over and done with," she says, "I work with some of the nicest people, I know. Their grandparents and fathers run this restaurant. They treat me like family, Alana. I'm not gonna let you come back here and mess up my situation."

"*Whatever*," Alana says, "This is my girl, Farah Benson. Farah this is Tameka. The two of us, Angel and another partner Michelle, was aces when I lived here."

"Nice to meet you," Tameka says to Farah, before turning back to Alana and saying, "I'm serious, Alana. Don't start any mess here. I'm doing good for myself now. Plus I'm still on probation, for four more years."

"Alright girl, *damn*. I'm cool," she says, "So where's Michelle? What's up with her?"

"She's still with Arthur and they moved from the U," she answers, "I heard they're suppose to be getting one of the crew houses, in Shaker Heights."

"Are they getting *married*?"

"I haven't heard," Tameka says, "But they're doing well and I'm happy for her. He has his own business, out here. He's still doing his thing with the lens."

She points, just down the side walk, to *Que Psi Phi Photography and video Studio*.

"Okay, cool," Alana says, "I'm gonna go ask him to call her for me. Before we head back to Darlene's."

"We're gonna be moving here," Farah says suddenly, "We'll Alana is moving back here to live with me."

"*Really*?" Tameka asks, looking at both women as if she knows they're up to no good. Then she asks, "When?"

"I have an interview to teach at MLK, in three weeks," Farah tells her. "I know I'll get it," she says confidently. "I have an offer on a house out in an area called, the *point*."

284

TIME TO LOVE-RELOADED-TIME WILL REVEAL 3

"Oh that's out there where my bosses live," Tameka says. *The Point* is where the 1st generation of the crew reside. Papa Brown and his crew. Tameka can't help but suspect the 2 women of being up to no good. It's in the tone of voice Farah used when she spoke of *"moving back here to live with me."*

As for Alana, Tameka is very familiar with her catty ways. She's almost certain her reason for moving back, is ultimately to cause trouble. Trouble for Tank and Nina which is going to cause trouble with the crew and then ultimately, trouble for her, as a former friend.

She warns Alana, "If you're coming back to bother the crew, then don't contact me. I love my job here. They make sure I have benefits and can go to college. They are *all* good to me and I won't be apart of any trouble being brought to them. I don't think Michelle would want to be bothered either. She's in more than I am and she loves Arthur. They're doing good. So just leave that part alone and start over, if you want too. Just don't be a bother to the crew."

"I'll bet they *are* good to you," Alana says with a sly grin. She acts like she thinks it's a game. A joke even, as she tells Tameka, "Okay girl. I'm not gonna get you in no trouble. I can't mess with nobody who don't wanna mess with me. Now can I? If Jeremy is happily married, we'll all see and I'm leaving that, right *there*."

Her and Farah giggle as Tameka goes and turns in their food order. Then tends to her next table. She had only told Alana about Michelle's success to make her jealous and hopefully, for her to back off. It doesn't seem to matter to Alana that Michelle had helped to turn her and Angel in. Or maybe it does. Farah's words; *"moving back here,"* echoes in her head. *Is Alana coming back here to get with Tank or does she want revenge?*

She's thinking both and she has to warn Michelle. She keeps her eyes on the 2 of them while she tends to her other tables and waits for their food to come up. It's obvious to her, they're plotting on something, every second she's away from their table and she's absolutely right.

"The crew must be the shit, around here?" Farah asks.

"I told you," Alana says, "The crew will fuck you up, if you fuck with them wrong."

"Alana, are you sure you should even approach this Jeremy guy?" Farah asks.

"I'm not approaching him," she answers, "At least, not right away. But every chance I get, I'll be down here at the mall until he talks to me.
285

He's gonna say something to me before long. I know it."

"It could be, *Alana get the fuck out of town before I kill your ass*," Farah offers.

"I would have to have meant something to him, for him to be that fucking angry, right?" she asks.

Farah agrees with her friend. Not so much because she thinks the same way. But she knows if she's ever going to get close enough to Chill to get his attention, then she's going to need Alana around doing whatever it is that she does.

Several minutes later, Tameka returns with their orders.

"Oh this looks good," Farah says.

"And it smells good too," Alana says.

They both have today's special of Catfish, mac-n-cheese, cabbage and sweet cornbread. Tameka slides their platters in front of them and says, "And don't forget my tip." She smiles as she refills their ice tea's.

"No problem, girl," Alana says, "She's loaded."

Farah nods her head, affirmative. Tameka leaves the check on the edge of the table, then she takes a break to make a quick phone call while Alana and Farah dig in and continue plotting.

"Do you think Tameka still considers you a friend?" Farah asks.

"It don't seem like it, does it?" Alana asks, "Fuck her. Her shit can be ruined, in a heartbeat, if she pisses me off."

Farah tells her, she doesn't think Tameka wants to be aligned with her anymore. Again, she tries to advise Alana against pushing the crew buttons. Alana promises her, that isn't what she's doing and that she really loves Tank and wants to make things right between them. So he want hold a grudge against her for what Angel did.

"Just be absolutely sure of what you're doing," Farah says, "Before you make a move."

"I am absolutely sure that I hate that bitch he's married too," she says, "She thinks she's better than me. I'm just gonna show her and him, that she's not."

Meanwhile, just down the walk at Que Psi Phi Studios, Michelle is still reacting to the call she's received from Tameka. She's happy she had taken that short break to call her. Tameka was afraid that seeing Alana means trouble for both of them. She had to warn her that Alana was in the restaurant asking about her. Tameka may be afraid but Michelle isn't. Tameka admitted that she had told Alana about her still being with Arthur

286

and him having business with the crew. That was in hopes of making her jealous and cautious enough to back off. But it hadn't worked. Tameka also alerted her of Alana's plan to return to the Cleveland area and where Farah plans to move and teach. Michelle already knew Alana was in town and she was at the club, last night. Because Michelle was there, in VIP, with Arthur, the entire time. She didn't want to see Alana, last night. Just her presence in the club made Michelle feel antsy about how the crew would view *her*. The very same way Tameka is feeling, right now. Still, she isn't afraid. For the most part, the crew as a whole treats her no different. But Rebbie and T-baby had said to her,

"Did you hear? Your old home girl is in the club." And how they hoped, *"She start some shit, so we can finish it."*

It gave Michelle psychological hives, last night. Just to reminisce about all of the pain those ex-friends had caused the crew. For the most part, the crew had cast aside or ignored many doubts they'd once had about Michelle. They have accepted her as a part of their business family, just as they've done with Tameka. That alone gives her hope that this too shall pass. But she knows, without a doubt, Alana being back in Cleveland spells trouble. *Period*! She didn't care to see her last night and today is no different. She immediately tells Arthur, Pam and Ruthie the reason Tameka had called her.

"Moving back to Cleveland?" Arthur asks, "Her probation must be up?"

"In three weeks or so," Michelle answers, "I've got a bad feeling about it."

"I do too and it's not good for her," Arthur says.

"Baby, I'm gonna step in the back and do some developing until they've come and gone," she says to him.

"No problem," he says, "You know I'll get rid of their asses, quick like," Arthur assures her and she can tell he's looking forward to it.

He's pissed off that Alana even had the nerve to show back up in Cleveland. Let alone, move back. And on top of all of that, come by the crew's places of business.

"I'm looking forward to reminding that silly bitch of just how crucial it can get," he says, "When you fuck with the crew wrong, they'll get your ass gone." He loves to rhyme his words. "If they're not buying shit. They'll get excused up out of here, real quick."

Arthur has always been the comedian of the crew. Always saying something witty to make everybody laugh. Although this time, he's quite serious about
287

getting rid of Alana, for good. Michelle, Ruthie and Pam laugh at his wit, as they do, daily. This is Ruthie and Pam's, after school and summer job. They run the front end and keep the store front window with fresh designs that are eye-catching. This frees up Arthur and Michelle to go in the back and develop film and edit videos. Michelle escapes to the back of the store, in the nick of time.

Alana and Farah slither into the quiet shop. Arthur stays up front. He wants to deal with these 2, himself. First, they pretend to be looking at digital camera's. Farah shows interest in 1 camera, in particular. She asks Arthur if he can help her with it. He comes over to assist her. Alana walks around, checking out the merchandise. The store offers some of the latest digital equipment available and some of the most popular cellular phones too. Pam and Ruthie watch Alana, like a hawk while Arthur is with Farah. Finally, Farah decides to purchase a digital camera and a hand held video camera, as well. Arthur sends her to the counter where Pam and Ruthie wait to bag her purchases and ring her out. Then he sets his sights on Alana. Wisely, she joins Farah at the counter and even suggest Farah get herself the newest cell phone. She does. Arthur figures she did that to show that she has power over Farah. Since it's obvious Farah has money. He feels that's the saddest part of all.

"Will this be all for you?" Ruthie asks.

"I want the bags for the camera's, the batteries and all of the accessories for the three items, please," Farah says with a smile.
Arthur grabs the necessary items and the accessories. The girls ring everything up and give Farah her total.

"That will be two thousand, five hundred, seventy dollars and forty seven cents," Pam says.

"How would you like to pay for this?" Ruthie asks.

"Platinum American Express," Farah gloats.
Ruthie takes her credit card, swipes it and it goes through, instantly. Pam gives her the printout and a pen for her signature. She signs and receives her copy.

"Thank you," Pam and Ruthie say to Farah.
Alana has a conniving look about her face, as she asks, "Is Michelle here?"

"No, she's already gone for today," Pam says.

"You look familiar to me," Alana goes on.

"I don't know you," Pam says.

"You look like Nina Jackson," she says, "Do you know her?"

"I do," Arthur interrupts, "I know you too and you know me."

288

"Right," she says, "I remember you. That's why I ask if Michelle-"

"-Michelle is none of your fucking business," he says, "Y'all are done purchasing. Alana you can get the fuck out and stay out," He says directly to her, then turns to Farah. "Ma'am, if you need anymore photo equipment or help with your warranties, please let us know and bring your receipt. Have a nice day."

With that, the ladies leave immediately. Alana may be an idiot but Farah isn't willing to be. She saw a look in Arthur's eyes that frightened her enough to move on off the crews property. She convinces Alana to get in the drop top BMW with her and leave the premises. Farah peels out of the lot, as if something was behind her. Then Michelle reemerges, after the coast is clear of Alana. Ruthie and Pam are giving Arthur props on how he had gotten rid of her.

"I heard you, baby," Michelle says and smiles, "Thank you."

"So that's the girl who helped Angel?" Pam asks.

Michelle explains the entire story to them, of how her and Tameka use to be friends with Alana and Angel. But how the whole thing turned sour for those 2, when they couldn't have Tank and Ajay.

"Tameka showed remorse for causing T-baby and Rich to lose their first baby," Arthur says, "And she paid her debt to society, then moved on. Rich was telling her lies about how serious him and T-baby was. She found out the truth, after all of that happened."

"He admitted that to me too," Ruthie says, "He was trying to be a player."

"But Tank never wanted Alana and Ajay never wanted Angel. And they both knew it and I knew it," Michelle says, "When Tameka found out that Rich didn't want her either, she got over him. But she had to do time, for her mistake. She really is a good person, who learned from her mistakes. Just like me."

"Who was you with?" Pam asks.

"Me," Arthur says with a smile. "She was always with me, as far as the crew go. But she came around us looking to holla at Ced and Jr. She wanted a dog. An Omega Psi Phi man, in her life," he says with a smile. "She made a mistake or two, back then. But still, she was smarter than them. She knew she didn't want to cross that line with the crew."

"The point of no return," Michelle adds, "As soon as I saw how close all of y'all was. And how loyal y'all are to your girl or guy, as in having their backs. Cause most men mess around. That's when I stepped off. I'm not that type. I was looking for love, from day one. Not just to be

289

somebody's jump off. I never wanted to be the other woman. But those two, they didn't care how they had them, as long as they had them."

Ruthie says, "That miscarriage made my mama so mad, she wanted to kill Tameka. But now look. She works for us and nobody holds a grudge against her, anymore. Mama and the foursome said they was all just young and stupid, at one point."

"My mama said that too. But Angel," Pam says as she shakes her head, "No one will ever forgive her. Because she *intended* to kill my niece and she tried to kill Ebony too. Tameka and T-baby was fighting each other. Tameka didn't come out of the blue at her. Ebony wasn't given a fair shot and T-baby was."

"Yes. That's different than sneaking up in a car," Ruthie says.

"Like the coward, Angel is," Michelle says, "She threatened Ebony for awhile, before she did that. I was so scared Ajay was gonna kill that girl," she says.

"I'll bet you *she'd* better not be dumb enough to come back around here, like Alana has," Arthur says, "Because she *will* die. I'd do her myself, to keep Ajay from doing it."

"Or Jesse," Ruthie says, "Because I remember how mad he was too. All of her brothers wanted to kill that girl."

"My sisters too," Pam adds, "Lynn still do."

"We all was," Arthur says, "Ebony actually saved her life, that night. She said turn them in to the police. Nobody else wanted too."

"Even me. I wanted them dead because I know Alana. See how she came back here with a white girl," Michelle says, "Like she can't die too. Alana don't care about nobody. Not even her *own* baby. That's why I cut off all ties. That was the end of my friendly contact with them." She says, "Everything I said to them, after I found out they was apart of that accident, was to help the crew."

"Michelle was the one who helped the crew bring them in to the police," Arthur offers.

"For real?" Ruthie says.

"I heard about that," Pam says, "My big sister Lynn told us that, Roo. You don't *remember*?"

"Wasn't that at your coming out party?" Ruthie asks.

"Yes. That same year of her trial," Pam says, "Alana got sentenced and had to move. Angel was in jail, awaiting her trial."

"And she went to trial in November of that year," Arthur says.

"She got life and has been locked up, since that night we brought

290

her back from Pittsburgh," Michelle adds, "And that bitch that just left, was the one hiding her in Pittsburgh. I learned a whole new respect for the crew, that night."

"And she has been down with me, the right way, every since," Arthur says as they all laugh.

"Why would she ever wanna come back around here?" Pam asks.

"Let alone move back," Ruthie adds.

"She's up to no good," Michelle says, "I'll bet anything, she is."

"The Point. M-L-K?," Arthur says, "Let's see what Chill thinks." He's up to his usual. Alerting Chill and the crew of potential hazards. Arthur's nickname had become *money shot* because he's a wealth of information, all the time. And sometimes, he'll even have information and a photo to go with it. Chill always reminds him of how valuable he is and always has been to the crew. He calls Chill on his cell phone. Chill is at *The Spot*. He tells Arthur to walk over when he gets down time and fill him in. Arthur tells Chill he's going to grab a bite to eat, drop his night deposit and change his clothes for the club. Then he'll be on over. He leaves the 3 ladies to tend to the closing of the photo studio, in another hour or so. Him and Michelle will meet at the adult club, later to do snapshots of club goers. While Ruthie and Pam will go to work at the kids club, when the store closes at 7pm.

Alana and Farah are back at Darlene's apartment. After they left the CrewLand Mall, they had stopped at a boutique and bought an outfit for Darlene, before returning. Darlene is home from work when they arrive. The ladies waste no time telling her about their visit to the mall.

"I met Tameka at the restaurant," Farah says, "But Michelle wasn't at the photo store."

"Alana, I told you don't come back here with that same shit," Darlene warns, "You will go to jail, this time. Those folks are successful assets to Cleveland, nowadays. These courts won't be as kind to you, as they was before."

"Auntie Darlene, I'm not doing anything but visiting," she says, "I haven't said one word to Jeremy. Nor have I been to his *particular* business. I haven't mentioned him."

Farah smiles. Alana is lying about not even mentioning Jeremy. She had made a remark to Tameka about him. Farah can see the signs but still she has no idea of what she's really dealing with, when it comes to the crew.

"Alana, don't start no shit you can't shake yourself out of. I mean

291

that," Darlene says, "And don't get me into no shit because of you, either."

"I won't auntie and who knows? I might get you another meeting with Ajay," Alana laughs.

Darlene smiles. She still wants Ajay, after all of these years. She just knows she can never have him. But if she can fuck him, from time to time, she would still be more than willing.

"I don't want a death meeting," she says and laughs. "He'll show up here to kill me because of your mess."

"Nah. He's coming to ease your woes and kill that cat, like you use to tell me he did," Alana smiles.

"I'd take that meeting," Darlene admits.

}Ohio State Penitentiary{

Angel has tried to reach Alana, today. She's heard that she's in Cleveland and wants to know why she hadn't told her she was going.

"Her bitch ass auntie likes your nigga, Ay," a tier buddy named Willie Mae offers. "She done cliqued up with her aunt, I'll bet you. They scheming on how she can get with your nigga and they ain't *thankin* bout you, home girl."

She calls Angel, Ay, as in the letter of the alphabet, for short.

"First of all, don't call him a nigga, okay?" Angel says, "He don't get down like that. He told me that shit, personally. He's on some come up off the dumb shit, type of vibe. I'm telling you, Ajay was so next level, back then. That's why I can't get over him. I always told guys I was a virgin. But I really didn't care to be for them. I just thought guys wanted you to be. But with Ajay, I wanted to be because I know that's the only reason why he put that bitch Ebony before me. He wanted a virgin because of his morals and his family. And he wasn't about being called no nigga. I ain't never had a man like him."

"Now he done married the bitch," Willie Mae says, "So what you gone do bout that? I mean you still trying to take her out or what?"

"Hell yea," she says, "She has to go or he will never get back with me. She has to be gone, for *good*. Then he can focus on us."

"Yo girl Alana ain't working for you, right now," Willie Mae says, "She on her auntie's team. See, she ain't leave you no way to contact her. She could be setting shit in motion to get rid of his wife, if she was down."

"Yea, I know," Angel says, "Ebony and Alana's fuckin auntie too. Both of them bitches need to go. *Fuck* it."

"Set that shit off, then Ay," Willie Mae encourages.

292

CHAPTER 34

SOMETHING TO BUILD ON

{Jackson Heights, after dusk{

T-baby and Rich pick up their son from daycare and arrive home, just before 7pm. Rich heads directly for the shower. T-baby sets the table for the *to-go* dinner, they had just grabbed from their restaurant. She isn't even wanting to start the conversation tonight because she has to leave for Natty, at 10pm. If they get into talking about the mansion in Mentor and he admits to an affair, someone is going to lose their life, tonight. Rebbie is suppose to drive them back in her Camry but T-baby is feeling spiteful. She has considered taking the Benz back to school. Still, she wants her son to enjoy it and he'll be here with his father. Rich emerges from the shower, still in a great mood. T-baby's mood is somber.

"Why do you seem so down today?" Rich asks.

"I've got to go back to school tonight," she says, "I'm gonna miss my baby."

She lies and gives her son a kiss, as she helps him get seated at the table.

"What about me?" Rich asks, "You're not gonna miss me?"

"It seems like I do that, all the time," she answers.

He won't dare touch that comment and wisely changes the subject.

"I hear Alana is back in town?" he says.

"How'd you hear that?"

"Tank called me before my flight," he says, "He *ain't* feeling it."

"She was in the club, last night," she says, "Rebbie and I saw her, as soon as she got there. But she stayed her distance, wisely."

It's obvious to Rich that she's disconnected about something. She continues, "Mama said she was at the restaurant, earlier today. I was hoping they would be there when I picked up our food. But grandma Sally said they had come and gone. I wanna catch that ho outta pocket."

"They who?"

"Some white girl from Pittsburgh, who came wit her," she says, "Do you know her?"

"No. I don't know her," he says, "How could I know her? I'm just hearing about all of it."

"It's weird that they show up at the restaurant and ask for Tameka to serve them," she says.

"Is she down with her again?" he asks, treading lightly.

"You tell me!"

"I wouldn't know, Trisha," he says offensively, "I haven't talked to *any* of them."

T-baby looks at him briefly, then she says, "Seems like everybody is up on shit before I am, these days."

He won't touch that either. He surfs this conversation, very carefully.

"I guess her probation must be almost up," he says, "since she's resurfacing."

"This month is the last of her, third year," T-baby says, "But she won't need probation if she fucks up again. Because she's going to hell."

He can see his wife isn't in the mood for idle chatter. There's something heavy on her mind.

"What time do you leave for Natty?" he asks.

"In a few minutes," she lies.

They aren't suppose to leave until 10pm. But she's going to ask Rebbie to leave, as soon as possible. She can't stand the sight of her husband, right now. She has convinced herself that he's cheating on her. She doesn't even want to be in the same room with him, at the moment. But he's thinking differently.

"I can take you, later," he says, "And maybe we can hang out, awhile longer."

He's interested in sex with his wife. She isn't interested in helping him to hide the lie that is the affair, she's now convinced that he's having.

After they finish dinner, she calls Rebbie and says no to her husband, without even saying it. She wants to know if they're ready to leave early.

"I'm packed. Nina's packed. We can leave when y'all get ready," Rebbie says, "I'm here by myself, anyway. Orian is at mama Brenda's. Brian is meeting me in Cincinnati before coming here. He'd better be ready to get on his job too."

June's team hadn't made the playoffs either. He'd said, from day 1, that he was coming right back. Rich was the 1 who said it would take him a whole week to pack and then get back to Cleveland. But suddenly, he's back early. *Is the Asian whore expecting him, earlier? Is that why he came back, so soon? Is it because he knows I'm going back to school today? Is that why he's in such a great mood because he can frolic with his whore, at his leisure. Since I won't be around to inquire about his errands? Are is it because his homeboy June's team didn't do any better than his did?*

294

She doubts the latter is the reason for his bubbly demeanor. She would rather believe that he's up to no good. Even though he could be happy, just to be home with his son. Anyway, that's what she'll tell herself for now.

Rebbie pulls up to their garage and honks. Her and Nina jump out and come in to speak to Rich III and his father. They make light conversation while T-baby puts her bags in the trunk. She kisses her son goodbye. She barely pecks Rich on the lips, then says, "goodbye."

He doesn't protest, at all. His demeanor is still jolly as he stands in the garage with Rich III and watch as the Camry passes the marble entry sign, then passes through the gate. They honk at Jacobson's crew and disappear outside the wrought iron gates.

}Paradise Stream, Friday night, January 2{

At the Garden of Eden Apple cottage, the newlyweds had made it back from dinner, peeled out of their attire and made passionate love. Not once but twice, before Ajay held up on his word. They are about to go for penetration number 3, as they have now feasted on each other. It took Ajay awhile but he did stick to the words he'd said over dinner. He let his wife taste him, a little while ago. It was awkward, at first. But they gelled right into the act, as if there had been a script to follow. If it had been a movie role, then his baby girl had given an Oscar winning performance. He's at a lost for words, right now.

"Was it good, daddy? Was I good?" she asks.

He can't speak, at the moment. He feels a little embarrassed, this time. A feeling he isn't use to having and definitely not with her.

"Are you okay?" she asks.

"Uh huh."

He's laying on his back with his eyes closed. He's unable to look at her.

"So are you still gonna kiss me?" she asks.

"I think so," he says, keeping his answers short.

On night 3, after a day out on the slopes, then ice fishing, snowmobiling and an elegant romantic and filling dinner at Bailey's, they had come back to their cottage to bathe in the Jacuzzi and relax. His curiosity about her ability to perform oral sex, had finally gotten the better of him. About 15 minutes ago, after taking her to the highest heights with his oral ability, he had asked that she show him what she could do with his southern exposure. She didn't disappoint him, at all. He probably thought she would fumble around with his member, like a virgin school girl on her prom night. But she hadn't. What she had done was given him the shock of the honeymoon, 295 when she'd brought him to undeniable ecstasy, in just under 10 minutes. She was and seemed to be determined to please him. She wasn't willing to stop performing until he had been thoroughly satisfied. He came. Did he ever! He pulled her away in the nick of time, just before he sprayed. Now his breathing is normal again. He can talk without gasping for air. He wipes himself clean, after first wiping his deposits from her neck and chest. Then he has to get some answers, before his mind drives him nuts.

"Where in the *fuck* did you learn how to do that?" he asks as he looks into her eyes, almost in desperation.

"Porno movies, cucumbers, pickles and my girls. All of them," she says with a smile. "I've been practicing to do that to you, for five years."

"*How?*" he asks.

"Just by watching what the girls in the movies do. Plus Renee, Tonya, Lynn and Carolyn. All of them telling me what to do and what not to do."

"You must've *really* paid attention, ha?"

"Of course, I did," she says, still smiling, "Because I wanna be good at it."

"You didn't know if I was gonna like it," he says, "Why did you want to learn it?"

"Daddy, the word was out on the crew guys, all the time. Plus big mama use to tell me," she starts, "Men love when you do oral sex on them. I told her that neither one of us was doing it to the other one. But she said when we got older, we would probably both start doing it. When I was living with them, I was crying and worried about you being with Darlene and she told me that."

"What did she say?" he asks.

"She said oral sex was the main thing that an older woman can do to a young man, to hold his interest in her," she says, "Besides giving him money and material things. And she told me that she would bet her last dollar, she was doing it to you. More than you was penetrating her. She said that was the only thing she could attract you with, sexually."

"She told you that?" he asks.

"Yes and she said the freedom to do what you wanted, was why you went and lived with her," she says, "Because she would let you do whatever *you thought* was important, just to keep you with her. And on that same day, she told me we was going to Cleveland for Christmas, so I could get my man back." she smiles.

"So you was suppose to do it, then?" he asks.

296

"She said I should try it," she says, "But you wasn't gonna let me. So I didn't and when you got mad about Shuntay telling the lie about me and Raymond. Plus my dumb letter. I knew not to go there, then. Because it would've just confused you."

"Oh no," he says, "That would've made me think you had got turned out. That, along with the letter you wrote."

"That's what big mama and my girls said too," she says, "We called big mama and we was talking about that, at your mama's house, that same night. Then we came back and you was gone with Shuntay."

"So I could've got some head from you, *that* night?" he asks with a smile.

"Yes if you wanted me to do it," she says, "I would have. But I never got a chance to even talk about it because you got mad. Madder than I've ever seen you, in my life."

"I *was* mad as hell, that night," he says, "But I knew you wasn't fuckin wit nobody. But you going down on me *then*, I know I would've freaked out. Because I have always been use to introducing new things to you, when it comes to sex."

"That's how it's been the whole honeymoon but that's why big mama told me to talk with you about it and see if you were open to it" she says, "She said that was all Darlene did to you that I wasn't doing and it had nothing to do with her age or her having an apartment or a car."

"Big mama is the bomb," he says and laughs, "She was dead on, with that one. Darlene did suck a mean dick, baby." He still laughs. She doesn't like hearing him give Darlene positive credit, for anything. She brushes it off with a shoulder shrug.

"So daddy, was it right? Was I good at it?" she asks again.

"Hell yea, Ebony," he says, "Any time a man get a nut, it's right. It's off the chain, baby. *Damn!*"

"So are you gonna-"

Before she can even ask him again, he kisses her, taking her tongue into his mouth and sucking on it, for almost a full minute.

"How could I ever think I would ever, *not* wanna kiss you?" he asks with a smile.

"You must've been crazy then," she says, quoting *Rick James* from *Fire and Desire,* one of her parents favorite love songs and they laugh.

"Daddy, that's a lot of pressure off me," she admits.

"Is it really?"

"Yes," she says, "I was so worried about being good to you. You

297

have no idea how much that act has stressed me out. For *years*."

"Why baby?" he asks.

"Because I knew that had to be the only thing that the Darlene's, the Angel's and *Nicole's*," she says shocking him. He didn't realize she was aware of his rendezvous with Nicole and Angie, back in the day. But she tells him she found out about them during college. She continues, "So yes, I know about Nicole and Angie but they had that one weapon that I didn't have because you wouldn't teach me. But now that you have allowed me too, it's *on*, daddy." She smiles.

"Is that right?" he asks, smiling too.

"Yes it is," she says, "And I know you got head at your bachelor party too."

He's totally shocked with that one. But he has never lied to her about any of his indiscretions.

"I told you about Miami," he stalls.

"Your bachelor party wasn't in Miami," she smiles and says, "Stop playing with me, daddy."

"I'll tell you about my bachelor party, if you tell me about your shower," he says.

"Deal!" she says.

He didn't expect her to give in that quick but she has. He's a man of his word, so he tells her the truth.

"Okay, yes. I got head from Roc," he admits.

She lays there on top of him, looking down into his eyes. He doesn't know what her next reaction will be but he's poised for it. Whatever it may be.

"Was she better than me?" she asks, totally shocking the hell out of him again.

"No way," he says quickly, "None of them was better than you," he says, "I *mean* that shit. Your sex was always better. That's all they had on you was giving head. Only because, like you said, I didn't teach you to do it. But now, *hell* no. They have no wind and no win. I love you and to get head from you, knowing that you love me too. That makes it *ten* times nicer because we kiss and rub and hold each other too. I didn't give them none of that type of affection, Ebony."

"It's because you have *always* loved me," she says, "And I always knew that."

"True that," he agrees, "Now about that shower."

She laughs and stalls. He looks impatient. She doesn't want him to get angry, unnecessarily. She clears her throat and spills the beans.

298

"I didn't get any head," she says and laughs.

But he doesn't. He gives her a serious look, as he waits.

"I got lap dances," she admits.

"Lap *dances*?" he asks, "*Damn*. How many?"

"Ah. About eight?"

"How many *naked* men was in my house?" he asks, as he sits up.

"Four."

"So you got two from each of them?" he asks.

"No."

"Spill it, woman." he says impatiently.

"I got one, from all four," she says, "Then the first guy went again. The second guy went again. Then the first guy kept coming back to me."

"So the first one was in love with you and he couldn't get enough?" his expression is serious, as he asks, "What's his name?"

She's slow to answer. As she thinks it over, he's watching her expression and her eyes. She couldn't get away with a lie, if she wanted too. But she doesn't want to lie. She wants to tell him everything. *And live, afterwards.*

"I don't know his name," she finally says, "But he was just doing his job. And he wasn't rude or pushy. I wouldn't have allowed that."

"Uh huh. What else did he do?"

"Not much."

"What else?" he persists.

"Shaking it, in my face."

"*Naked*?!"

She doesn't say anything. He puts it all together and doesn't like the visual. He says, "I don't wanna hear no more of it. I can figure the rest out. I'm kicking Nina and Lynn's ass, when I see them. And his naked ass too."

She freezes and lays quiet. Then he burst out laughing. She's afraid to laugh with him, until he says, "I'm just kidding, baby. I know what they do at those things. I know you wasn't rubbing on them until they put your hands there."

"Not even then. I wouldn't go that far," she says.

"You'd better not."

They smile at each other. He kisses her again.

"You can come on and give me some of my sweet pussy," he adds.

He has fully recovered from his lack of breathe, after the draining orgasm she'd given him. He pulls her on top of him.

"Come on with some rodeo style. Since you're shocking the hell out me, this week," he says as she straddles him.

299

She knows Rodeo-style isn't her best event and so does he. But just like anything else, she's willing to risk it, if this is the position her man desires. He enters her eager and quick. He's ready to prove who really has control, as his throttle invades every inch of her tight shaft. Before she can complain or ask for gentleness, he pauses, pulls out, flips her over and goes back to work. He has to recapture his dominance, in a hurry.

"You're working with something, baby girl," he whispers, "You've got the complete package. I knew you did. I can't let you turn me out, like that. I gotta save face, up in here. Baby, looking down at your face, always did turn me on. You're always licking your lips," he gives her a heated kiss and says, "That good head, just adds one more thing to think about. Baby girl, I don't even know how I'm suppose to go to work."

He's fucking her, like his life depends on it and working her over with sheer excellence. Even though on their wedding night, 2 nights ago, he'd declared she was in control. She knows for certain, right now, he is *still the man*. No matter what she did or will do to him, sexually. He will always trump her. He will always overshadow it with an outstanding performance that will top anything she can do. 1 thing is for sure. When it comes to intercourse, he is, has always been and will always be, the dominant 1 in their relationship and marriage. She is *definitely* alright with that too.

}The Chill Spot{

Arthur arrives at the club, to talk with Chill, around 10pm. Just after the doors open. They dip into his office to vibe.

"So what's up, money shot?" Chill asks.

"That bitch Alana is back, as you might know," he says.

"I know," Chill tells him.

"She's planning to move back here before next school year."

"Talk to me."

"First off, the white chick she's with. She's got some money," he says, "She spent over two grand in my store today."

"She dropped nine hundred in here, last night," Chill offers, "But we're not mad at that."

They laugh, as Arthur continues, "Oh no! We're not. The chick's name is Farah Benson, from Pittsburgh. Her folks got Steel Plant money. Anyway, she has an interview at MLK, the last Monday of this month. And she's already bidding on a house in The Point."

"And we want to stop her from moving here, why?" he asks.

"Well, I don't know if we do," he says, "That's why I'm bringing it

300

to you. Alana is moving back with her and she's already coming around Tameka and Michelle. Neither of them wanna upset the crew."

"I don't blame them," Chill says, "I wouldn't want too either. Farah is hot for your man too. She's one of those bold type women. She'll run her ass up in here and try to make a boss move."

"And make these crew ladies, knock the top out of her head," Arthur laughs, "A white woman go missing, will fuck up a lot o' shit."

"Do you think Michelle would whoop Alana's ass, for what she's trying to do now?" Chill asks.

"She'd whoop her ass for less than that. I'd put my worth on it." Chill smiles. He thinks it over, for a few minutes while rubbing his goatee. Then he says, "She might get her chance."

He grabs his desk phone and calls *The Spot II.*

"The Spot II. This is Erica. How may I help you?" Erica answers. She takes over as receptionist while Nina is in Cincinnati.

"Hey P-Y-T! You holding it down for your big sister, over there?" Chill asks.

Erica laughs and says, "Hey, big Chill. Of course I am. How are you doing, tonight?"

"Great and getting better," he laughs, "Let me holla at Tank, a minute. Tell him it's urgent or I wouldn't even call on a Saturday night." She says okay, then she tells him, "Hang on while I check his radio." He holds while she hits the talk button on the 2-way radio and says, *"Tank, you got your ears on?"*

"Yea, lil sis. What you need?" he asks.

"Chill's on the phone, for you," she says, *"I'll patch him through to your office."*

"I'm thirty seconds away," he says, *"Thanks."*

She reaches back at Chill, "He's picking up, any second."

"Alright. I'll see ya," he says.

"In a minute," she says as she releases the call to Tank's line and goes back to her station, next to VIP.

Tank takes the call in his office. "What's up, player?" he asks with a laugh.

"Getting money, homeboy and you?"

"The same and loving it. What's so crucial?" Tank asks.

"Alana is moving back. Do you give a fuck?" Chill asks.

"Hell no. But since you're asking me," he says, "I figure it's more to the game, than just her popping up over there, last night."

"She ate at Crews house today, then she shopped at the photo

301

studio," Chill says. "She's trying to hook back up with Tameka and Michelle. They want no parts of her."

"I don't blame them, at all," he says, "But how is that moving back here?"

"She told Tameka she's moving back with that chick Farah, from last night," he says, "She's shopping for a house out in The Point and she has an interview at MLK, in a few weeks."

"The point?" Tank asks.

"Yes."

"Somebody got some money," Tank says, "You can't just move into that retirement community without some money," he asserts. "There's no renting out there. Papa is on the board."

"Arthur says Farah dropped, over two grand, in his store today. Platinum American Express."

"I see," Tank says.

"He says her folks got Steel Plant money."

"Sounds like Steelers *owner,* money to me," Tank laughs, "She done dropped over four grand with us. She got rich family and Alana probably sucking her dry."

"She didn't seem to mind it, last night," he says, "I think they're fucking each other, anyway."

"Some shit don't change," Tank says, "*Good.* As long as she leave me the fuck alone. I'll get June, Ajay and Rich to give principal Myers a call. Maybe block the hiring? But for me, it don't matter."

"I know Arthur don't want that bitch around Michelle," Chill says, "She's doing good. Her nor Tameka don't want us to feel like they can't be trusted."

"Again, I don't blame them," Tank says and they both laugh. Then he asks, "What do you want me to do?"

"Let her get the job and the crew can keep an eye on her, at school," he says, "And she'll still be close enough to spend that cash, wit us," Chill suggests. "But have Ajay talk to Parkwood and we'll talk to papa Brown. Block the real estate and send her further west. Like the other side of seventy seven. Parma or pass the airport, maybe."

"Cool," Tank says, "Oh yea. They're breaking ground for you and Junior, next week bro."

"That's what's up."

Chill and Jr are next to have homes built in Jackson Heights. They break ground, in a few days. Their streets have already been cut in and named in
302

their honor. They're still the leaders of this crew and crew are never too far from each other.

"Oh yes," Chill says, "We're coming to Jackson Heights. Y'all can't get away *that* easy." They laugh.

"We've been hounding you, long enough," Tank says, "Money's good. May as well bring the whole damn family out there."

"It will be, soon enough," Chill says as he laughs, "It's like three miles of land and Ajay is trying to get us to get every foot of it."

"We're all gonna be investing in it, once twin gets her office opened up," Tank says, "That's gonna be her thing. She said Parkwood has already acquisitioned all of the property that Ajay wants to get."

"Real Estate banking and Investments," Chill says as he smiles, "Go ahead, baby girl. And T-baby will do Accounting, for us. We're doing this shit, man."

"Yes sir," Tank responds as they laugh arrogantly.

"Oh, I wanted to tell you one more thing about that Pittsburgh business," Chill says.

"What's up wit it?"

"That Farah chick is playing a dangerous game," Chill says, "I've already peeped it."

"She trying to get at you, is what it looked like to me," Tank says.

"Hell yea. But she don't have the game to play big Chill," he says, "I'm going real deep in her steel plant pockets. *Trust*." They laugh.

"She's fucking with the ace and don't even know it," Tank adds.

"But now, you know white girls have never been *my* thing," he says, "My mama would come back from the grave, on my black ass. She was insistent that I get *and stick with,* some *black* pussy."

"True that and at the same time, she taught you that all money was green," Tank says as he laughs.

"Hell yea," Chill says as he laughs too. "It takes big John to talk about the hustler my mama was, man."

"She was about her business," Tank says. "That's what he always said, when he talked about her. She was about big Paul too. She would whoop a muthafuckaz ass, about *her* Paul. Male or female."

Chill says, "Big Al said that's why they never got around to having other kids."

"She had enough raising to do," Tank says as they laugh hard.

"And it's a many humbug women, my old man was fucking with too," he says, "When I was little, she *stayed* fighting *some* woman."

303

"And you married a sister, just like mama Willa," Tank says.

"And you know it," Chill agrees, "Renee will beat her ass and then, make it a political situation."

They both laugh before getting back to the reason for the call.

"I don't want no bullshit for my family, like that. Because I already know Alana is on that old humbug shit," Tank says, "Same shit she was doing before. Renee will bust a cap in both they're asses, these days," he says, "She's got a lot of Willamena Payne, in her."

"Arthur said similar bullshit, about Alana," Chill laughs, "I didn't get to know her until after the accident with baby girl. But really, she needs to recognize that the game has gotten grown like a muthafucka, nowadays. We about our money and we're not taking *no shorts, no loses*."

"No shit. And I agree, one hundred percent," Tank says, "Well man, speaking of money. Let's get more!" They laugh again.

"See ya," Chill says.

"In a minute," Tank says and they hang up.

Then Chill assures Arthur that everything will be handled with Alana and Farah.

"That's cool. I'm gonna get started," he says, "See ya, man."

"In a minute, money shot!" Chill yells behind Arthur, as he's leaving.

Arthur does pictures within both clubs, during club hours. Michelle, Kilo and Justine assists him. Kilo and Justine work the camera's at *The Spot II* while Arthur and Michelle do the honors at *The Chill Spot*.

The Chill Spot is just starting to buzz! The Spot II has an hour to go before closing. Justine and Kilo are finishing up last minute photo's, for guest. As Kilo sets up the last couple for their shots, Justine bags her camera and the other equipment and loads it onto the cart. Kilo will bag his camera when he's done. Then take all of the equipment to their storage room, on the 3rd floor, until the next evening.

"Okay, I've got everything bagged except your camera," she says.

"Alright, you can go to Stoney's and put our orders in," Kilo says, "I'll be there by the time it comes up."

Justine says okay and heads out. She says goodnight to Tank, the 99 crew, Reaper and the rest of the staff.

On her way out the Spot II doors, she glances over at the long line of patrons, waiting to get into The Chill Spot.

"Gotta get that money man, it's still the same, now!"

304

TIME TO LOVE-RELOADED-TIME WILL REVEAL 3

She sings the lyrics to *Bone Thugs and Harmony's,* 1994 hit, *Foe da Luv of money,* as she heads into *Stoney's Bar n Grill.* John and Al have a packed house and they greet her as she comes in.

"Good Evening to our surrogate daughter," Al says.

Him, John and Justine laugh, as she says, "Good evening, almost morning. I'm ordering the usual, my play daddies."

"The usual is *usually,* two shrimp baskets," John says, "I don't see the usual fellow."

"Oh, he's coming, in a minute," she says, "He has one last group to shoot."

They make small talk as Al drops the food for their late night snacks. Kilo shows up, just as John slides the baskets onto the counter. Him and Justine pay. Then take a seat at a booth to eat. Later, they'll join the crew at *The Chill Spot.*

Alana and her posse make their entrance, just before midnight. Darlene decided to come, since she had a new outfit, thanks to Farah. With Nicole, Angie and Samantha, they show up looking like regulars in new clothes. The ladies don't even try the VIP route. They go through the regular entrance. After nearly an hour wait, they get in and go straight to a booth, on the back wall. Courtney Freeman, who's Wayne's girlfriend, is their server.

"Welcome back, ladies. What can I get for you?" Courtney asks.

Farah orders for the table. It figures since she's doing the paying, as well.

"We're gonna have a fifth of *Courvoisier,* a liter of *coke*, a bucket of ice and four glasses. For these two ladies," she points to Darlene and Samantha, "They can't handle the brown liquor," she laughs as the others giggle, "They'll have a *sex on the beach* and a *slow screw.*"

"*Literally,*" Darlene adds as they all laugh.

Courtney leaves with their order and heads to the bar.

"I'm ready to party," Angie says.

Her and Nicole begin to circle the club, looking for dance partners. Samantha is more reserved and doesn't talk much. Darlene feels out of place, only because she hasn't done the club scene, *quite* as much, lately. She's nearly 35 years old and her sons, who are 18 and 19 now, go to *The Spot II,* all the time. She'd been self conscience about running into them, while out clubbing. They aren't very respectful of her, as their mother and many say it's because she wasn't a stable mother to them, over the years. When Ajay was seeing her, 10 years ago, she didn't even bother to make

305

them go to school. Ajay would tell them to go and they would. Sometimes, he made sure they got there before going, himself. Each 1 had juvenile records. 1 was very extensive, for everything from shoplifting to possession.

}Cincinnati{

Nina, T-baby and Rebbie arrive in Natty, just after midnight. June is already there. His former football teammates had picked him up from the airport and brought him to the Cincinnati house. They're still hanging out, in the driveway, when the ladies pull up, park and go inside. June has a warm bath drawn for all 3 of them and he's turned down their beds. This is the same thing they use to do for the guys, when they was still students here. Rebbie was thinking he was meeting her here to make up for time lost. Now with his team hanging around outside, she's not so sure.

"Oh June, you're such a sweetheart," Nina says with a smile.

"Thank you, June," T-baby says giving him a kiss on the cheek.

"Baby, thank you," Rebbie says, "Are you joining me in my bath?" He's slow to answer, so she gives him her assumption. "Oh never mind," she says, "Your teammates are still outside, anyway. They're not gonna be able to do anything without you. I already know the drill." She grabs her gown and heads for the bathroom. She says, "Goodnight!" and slams the door. As it turns out, she was right. He had plans to go to a bar with his former teammates from UC. She takes her bath and turns in for the night.

T-baby gets a call from Rich while she's in the tub. She only answers out of concern for her son. She soon learns that Rich III is fine, so she cuts her talk short with Rich and tells him, "Come to Natty if you really wanna talk to me. You know the way."

"I wanted to take you back but you never said anything," he tries.

"I'm saying it now."

"It's late now, Trisha. I-"

"Yea, I figured that. Goodnight, Richard," she says and hangs up.

Tank calls Nina, just as she's about to lay down. He asks her if she wants him to skip the main club tonight and just go on home.

"No baby, you always help out at The Chill Spot," she says, "We're not gonna up root or change anything because of that tramp."
Suddenly, Tank hears gunfire outside.

"I have to go," he says, "I hear shots outside. I'll call you back as soon as I know what's going on."

"Be careful and I love you," she says quickly.

306

TIME TO LOVE-RELOADED-TIME WILL REVEAL 3

"I love you too, Nina boo," he says and they hang up.

The disturbance outside of The Spot II, happened just after Tank had locked up. He comes outside to investigate. 2 teens had decided to show off by shooting their guns into the air, while in the parking lot preparing to leave. McDaniel and officer Teddy Joiner of Jacobson security have already apprehended them. They're waiting for crew. The 2 teens they have are Darlene's sons, 18 year old Jamal Warren and 19 year old Rodney Casey.

"Hey you can go get my mama, man," Jamal says, "She's in the club, right now."

"She not gonna do nothing for you, nigga," Rodney says, "I'll get Swag boy to come get us, bro. You know mama don't give a fuck what happens to us."

Tank tells McDaniel and Joiner, he can get her out there by 2-way radio. He wants to do the guys a solid, in hopes that they won't bring their disturbance back on crew property. He does an all-call on his radio and gets Jr and Tonya to locate Darlene and bring her outside.

"We're not no Juveniles, no more, man," Rodney screams at officer Joiner, "You ain't gotta call our mama, homie."

"Hey, chill out Rodney," Tank says, "Show some respect, man. These guys work for us. If you chill out, you might not even have to deal with Cleveland PD. But if you wanna stay rowdy, then we won't have no other choice but to call them folks out here."

They calm down and wait for their mother. They appreciate the lick from Tank too.

Tonya goes to the booth where Darlene is seated and informs her of the situation. She asks her to step outside. She gets up to follow Tonya as Jr comes over to escort them.

"Hey, where is Chill?" Farah asks as they're walking off.

"He's in the club, somewhere," Tonya says, "Is there a problem?"

"I just wanted to speak to him about an investment," she says with a sly grin.

"We can deal with that, a bit later," Tonya tells her, "You're not leaving without your companion, are you?" she asks, not liking the slimy way Farah inquires about her best girlfriends husband.

"Oh no," Farah says, "I'll be here till I get that business handled."

Tonya, Jr and Darlene go outside.

Security confiscates the weapons, then allow the young men to go home. Darlene volunteers to leave with them, to make sure they go. Nicole
307

drives them, then her and Darlene return to the club at 230am.

Tank calls Nina back and tells her what the disturbance was about. She was worried and hadn't gone to sleep.

"They get in trouble, a lot, don't they?" Nina asks.

"Rodney does," he says, "Do you remember when Darlene came to that fourth celebration with them?"

"Yes and granny whooped both of them for cursing," she says with a giggle.

"They doing way more than cursing now," he says, "But Jamal not as bad as Rodney yet. Rodney had beef wit somebody. Jamal was trying to hold up for him."

They talk for 45 minutes until she gets sleepy. Then they hang up. She goes to bed and he goes back to help in the adult club.

In the meantime, Chill has met with Renee in her office to tell her the latest news. After some kissing and fooling around, he gets down to the real point of the meeting.

"Baby, look here. That white girl who showed up with Alana is on some shit."

"That's not a shock, baby. Considering the company she keeps."

"She wants to meet with me, supposedly about investing," he says.

"*Wow*. Last night, she was trying to suck your dick. And already, she's turned it to *business*," Renee says sarcastically, "So she's a multi-faceted whore?" They laugh.

"Apparently she thinks I'm a rookie," he says, "Or maybe she believes the hype."

"What hype?"

"That all black men secretly desire white women," he says as they laugh.

"Oh boy. She really don't know who she's going after, does she?"

"That proves to me that she don't do her homework," he says, "She's about trying to fuck me and getting some type of rank. More than investing. She don't know nothing about Willamena Payne's only child. I'm pledged to some sweet black pussy, for life."

"Then it's time to make it clear to her that you've got that, *who fuck's you area,* covered too," Renee says with a smile.

"I agree with you and it has nothing to do with, will she be able to invest," he says, "That's not *gonna* happen. But if she just wants to fuck up some money, we can help her with that. *Right* baby?"

308

TIME TO LOVE-RELOADED-TIME WILL REVEAL 3

"That's for damn sure," Renee says, "We can buy another parking lot and name it after her."

"Wow. You think she got that much traffic?" he asks.

Renee laughs, then says, "Maybe. Maybe not. But she's been run over and through, a few times. Can't you tell?"

He tells her to dial his office when Farah is being escorted up. He'll pick up the phone. Then she is to record the entire conversation, he'll have with Farah Benson.

"Have Tonya to tell her, I can meet with her when the club closes." The meeting is set and the matter is closed. He'll meet with Farah in his office, at 430am, once the club is closed for business. Tonya passes the word on to Courtney, then goes on about her duties.

In the meantime, Alana and her clique drink and party with all the willing participants until the patrons start to thin out. Angie and Nicole find leeches to take home with them. Samantha's on again off again baby's father, wants to take her with him. While Darlene, Alana and Farah, now have their eyes on a much bigger prize. Farah wants to make her 2nd move on Chill. Alana plans to make new contact with Tank, this morning. While Darlene tries to look as spoken for as possible. She isn't going to take anyone home from this club which Ajay is part owner of. Unless it's Ajay, himself. Anyone else, in her opinion, would be stepping down. As the time to close nears, Courtney tells Farah her meeting with Chill has been set.

"You can come to the second floor lounge and someone will come get you," Courtney says.

"Alright," Farah says as her, Darlene and Alana follow Courtney to the 2nd floor.

]Around Cleveland{

For Rich, being in trouble with T-baby isn't enough to make him stay home. This morning, he's out riding and looking for Tameka, of all people. He had gotten her address through her background check info. It's 4am and he's pounding on her door. She looks through the peep hole, sees him and refuses to answer. She doesn't make a sound. Partially out of fear and the other, out of respect for the family she works for. She wonders how they would feel, knowing he has come to her apartment, demanding she open the door and let him in. This is the 2nd time, in as many weeks. He had followed her home, last week and didn't get in. He certainly isn't going to get in this morning, unless he breaks down the door. She wanted to tell Michelle when she talked to her, yesterday. But she knew she would tell

309

Arthur. Then the crew would find out and fire her. That is her worst fear and she doesn't need that to happen. So she hid it from Michelle and now, she's stuck with hiding in her own apartment.

}The Chill Spot{

"Chill is ready to see you," Tonya says to Farah, "Are all three of you meeting?"

"No. They rode with me," Farah says.

"They can wait here, then," Tonya says as she signals to the staff. Then she takes Farah up the elevator and into Chill's office, where he sits behind his huge granite top desk with a freshly lit *Cuban* and a *Chivas,* on the rocks.

"Good morning, misses-"

"Miss," Farah corrects him.

"Miss Benson."

"Farah. Call me, Farah."

"Okay. Farah Benson, I'm a business man," he says, "So we're going to deal with first and last names, okay?"

"Okay. What should I call you?" she asks.

"Mister Payne is fine."

"That would be correct," she says as she giggles flirtatiously.

Chill lets that 1 slide as he glances at his speakerphone and half smiles. He knows Renee is in the adjoining office. Listening, recording and probably plotting to kick Farah Benson's ass, soon.

"So what can I do for you, Farah Benson?" he asks.

"A lot. A whole lot. But first, I wanted to know how would a person interested in investing, get in on this great business thing you've got here?"

He answers, "Birth, love or luck."

"Excuse me?" she asks.

"The businesses you see, aren't *all* mine," he says, "This is a family thing. Three generations of family."

"So if I wanted to say, invest in a piece of property, to run a business under the Crew Enterprise umbrella, would that be *doable*?"

"Only by a vote," he says.

"Who votes?" she asks.

"Shareholders. All of the shareholders," he says.

"Would it be possible to get a vote started?" she asks.

"On what? You haven't pitch anything," he says with a lack of patience to his tone.

310

"I have a few ideas," she says as she stands and starts to pace the floor. "I was thinking of a boutique. An accessories shop, you know?"

"I don't know if there's a fit for that at CrewLand," he says.

"I saw the Alterations shop," she says, "They have some original pieces in there. But I didn't see any accessories for them."

"They make those, custom," he says, "They're in the window."

"I didn't notice them," she tries.

"Do you have anything drawn up and a figure sheet? What's your top line?" he asks.

"Not quite *drawn up*, so to say. But I would pay whatever I had to, to get in *your* business," she says assertively.

He tells her, she can leave her contact information with his Co-CEO, "Misses Payne. She'll be in, momentarily."

That's Renee's cue to come in and end the meeting. Which she is just *too happy* to do. They wrap up, then close up the club and leave.

ʲCincinnatiʲ

T-baby has tossed and turned, all night. She finally sits up and decides she has to know where Rich was, during Ebony and Ajay's reception. She grabs her cell phone and hits the speed dial number for their house phone. The phone rings 10 times, on 4 separate occasions.

No answer in forty rings?

She tries his cell phone. He picks up but says nothing.

"Richard. Richard?" she says into the phone, then there's the dial tone.

She dials the phone back but his time no one picks up. By the 4th try, the voice mail picks up immediately and she knows he's turned the phone off. It's 5am. She calls her mother's house. Sandy answers in her usual good spirits.

"Hey, Trisha. How are you all doing, down there at school?"

"We're good," she says, "I'm just bored and can't sleep. I thought I'd call you."

"Are y'all still acting like newlyweds?" she says with a giggle.

T-baby doesn't have an answer. Her mother giggles more and continues to talk. "I figure since I got my grandson at midnight, so my son-in-law could hit the road for Cincinnati, that you two was back on that riding the highway thing, again," Sandy says, "Like y'all did, last year."

Coming to see me? My mama has the baby?

311

TIME TO LOVE-RELOADED-TIME WILL REVEAL 3

"I wouldn't say newlyweds, ma. It has been a year and a half," she say as she tries to sound jubilant.

Her mother continues with the chat and never even knows that Rich hadn't come to Natty. T-baby never tells her. Which is something she may live to regret. Keeping her husbands inconsistencies a secret, instead of putting him on blast. At least then, she would have the entire family aware and watching. But she's more concerned with how it would make *her* look, so she talks to her mother for another 20 minutes until Sandy is getting Rich III ready for daycare. She even talks to her son, then she tells her mother that Rich had too much to drink and can't get up. Instead of telling her, he didn't come. They hang up. Suddenly, she feels alone and abandoned. Used and mislead. She's sure she's being cheated on. She has an idea of where Rich is but she's all the way in Cincinnati. There's no way she can drive to Mentor and get back in time for practice. And she has practice twice, today. One in the morning and one in the evening. She decides to stay at school and try to focus on something else. She isn't going to let Rich worry her to the point of exhaustion. If her crew doesn't call her, then things must be okay. She doesn't take into account that she hasn't given her crew the heads up.

Why does my relationship have to be the one that's fucked up, in the crew?

She turns on the TV and watches insomniac video's until it's time to get up and eat breakfast. Still, she hasn't decided to tell anyone about her situation because she doesn't want to be the 1st crew marriage to fail.

}Paradise Stream, PA Saturday January 3{

Ajay wakes up, stretching at first. Then trembling. Next, he's panting and moaning like he's having sex. Because he *is*. Sort of. Ebony had awakened 5 minutes earlier then him and went *downtown*. She's licking him like a *lollipop* and sucking the tip, like a shaved ice cup. He loves it. She takes him to the back of her throat and he gasps. Then he clutches a huge handful of the bed sheet. It feels good, as she moans to his reactions. Which brings more reaction from him.

"Does it feel good, daddy?" she whispers.

"Ssss yes."

She continues taking him deep to her throat, then sucking the head. Licking it. Keeping it moist. Then back to the base of her throat, over and over. He grabs the back of her head, tangles his fingers into her hair and fucks her mouth.

312

TIME TO LOVE-RELOADED-TIME WILL REVEAL 3

Finally! I was wondering was he ever going to get all the way into it.

"Oh, baby," he moans.
She gets faster with her actions. Moaning while churning his dick in her mouth. She wants him to love it, need it and he had damn well better request it, from now on. He needs to feel confident that his wife can suck his dick, better than any groupie can. And that he'll cum too. She's trying to make him skeet in her mouth but he's pushing her away from his dick. *My dick!*
> "Uh Ugh, daddy. You have to cum first," she demands.
> "It's cumin, baby," he manages.
He sprays and she accepts. It's a medium load but more than enough for her 1st experience with, as *lil Kim* would say it; *drinking babies*. This isn't her favorite part of the drill but he's in ecstasy and there's nothing to clean up. He's loving it, so she stays on it until it's only semi-hard. Then she goes to brush her teeth and he follows her. They brush their teeth with him staring at her, through the mirror, the entire time. She feels proud of herself. He starts the shower for 2, then her kisses her. Taking her tongue into his mouth and sucking on it for 30 seconds.
> "I couldn't start my day without that," she says.
> "I love how I started my day," he says and smiles.
> "You have a lifetime of *those* starts, to look forward too, daddy. I'm yours, completely."
He smiles. He's speechless. She has finally found his sexual weak spot, if he has one. He *is* vulnerable. Now she understands why he was hesitant about letting her serve him, initially. Having his dick sucked and getting a nut, makes him lose control too. It shows his vulnerability. He didn't want to show that to her until he knew she would love and serve, only him, forever. Because he always loved her and didn't want her to get the upper hand on him. Then misuse it. Anyway, that's her best guess. She knows he has none of that to worry about. It's him, she'll be fucking and sucking until eternity. *God willing.* They take a shower, then go back to bed at 7am. They can go hiking, in the late morning. He has to get his rank back and she's willing. *Yes Lord, I'm willing.*

}Late morning, in Cincinnati{
June is making breakfast for the girls, to get out of the dog house with Rebbie. He has 3 dozen roses delivered from the campus flower and gift shop, for each of them. He has to make things right with his wife, so he
313

doesn't need her girls upset with him, to start with. The girls really appreciate him cooking for them.

"Now you need to take Rebbie in that room and handle your business," Nina says.

"I'll vote for that," he says as he picks Rebbie up and they retire to the room they'd shared before he graduated.

}Paradise Stream, PA{

The newlyweds go out on a short hike, just before 11a.m. They hike to *Overlook Ridge*. Their photographer and chef takes the outing with them. Ajay wants to have a picnic, out there. Overlook has enclosures where you can sit, eat, view the surroundings and still remain warm. The enclosures are similar to ski lifts, as they're made of mostly glass. The chef sets up their lunch there, while the photographer takes snapshots.

"What time would you like me to return sir?" the chef asks Ajay. Ajay looks at Ebony and she says, "It's our last day. We can go back to the cottage, after we eat."

"Give us thirty minutes," Ajay tells him, then he excuses them both as they sit down to their lunch and conversation.

"I'm sad to see our honeymoon come to an end," he says.

"Me too. But it's not gonna end," she says, "I do feel like it's gonna be impossible to just go back to our regular lives. After the time we've spent up *here*, though."

"Baby, my life will never be regular again, after spending this time with you," he says, "I feel closer to you, then I have ever felt to anyone. Even Tank."

"Well, *that's* good to know," she says and they laugh.
She cuts up his beef tips and serves them to him, as he keeps 1 arm around her, the entire lunch.
"When do you wanna start on our family?" she asks.

"As soon as you stop taking the pills," he says.

"I can stop when we go back," she says, "I finished a pack today. I should get my period, next week. Then I can just not start another pack."

"I timed this wedding and honeymoon, perfectly," he says as he smiles, then they laugh.

"So did I," she says, "I counted it up since ninety three, when it came on, *on* my birthday."

"So don't start a new pack," he says, "Because it'll take a few months for them to flush your system. But don't get impatient, baby girl."

314

"I'll try not too," she says, as her eyes start to well up. "I just can't believe we're finally talking about trying. You know how long I've wanted to get pregnant again."

"I don't wanna get it in there to soon, before your season ends," he says, "Y'all might go to the big dance."

"I know we're playing well enough too," she says, "Our record is solid. We can stay unbeaten in the conference. We should go to the tourney. But I want to have a baby, more than I want to go to the NCAA."

"Wow. I've just taken your love for the game, completely."

"No daddy, that's not it," she says, "I've loved you, way longer than I've loved the game."

He smiles. He really loves that answer. They finish their lunch. The chef and photographer are back to meet them and they head back to the cottage. She has to pack up their things. Their limousine to Scranton Airport will be there at noon tomorrow, to take them to their private jet. She'll return to Cincinnati. He has to go back to Miami. They're regular lives await them.

****

The construction on Chill and Jr's new homes has started. They're expected to be complete in less than 3 months. Arthur and Michelle have lived with Chill and Renee since moving from the U. Kilo moved into the house with Jr and Tonya and brought Justine. Chill and Jr plan to allow them to remain in the homes, when they take possession of their new ones.

With Rob's label taking off in Atlanta, Reaper is guaranteed a chance to release a CD, this year. He's looking forward to his high school graduation, this May. He plans to attend college at *Clark-Atlanta*. From there, he can work on his album and promotions with Rob. Atlanta has become a Mecca for Hip-Hop, in recent years. They're happy to be there.

Jacobson security is in full effect now. David Jacobson mans the entry gate, personally. Ajay had requested Jacobson be the main officer on the gate because as he had said to Jacobson, "You saved my baby girl, one time. I know you'll keep her safe while I'm away."

Jacobson feels privileged to be asked to guard what is to Ajay, such a pure and precious commodity. He knows he loves Ebony, very much and wants her to feel secure. Jacobson has 2 relief officers for Jackson Heights, in Carl Bronson and Larry Davidson. Jacobson made Lieutenant before he retired, based on his rescue efforts out at cliff ridge road in 1994. Parkwood played a key role in the promotion. Jacobson will man the booth while Davidson or

315

TIME TO LOVE-RELOADED-TIME WILL REVEAL 3

Bronson, do random drives around and past the homes, to insure they are secure.

****

Today, Tank contacts Ajay down in Miami and asks him to give Principal Myers a call. He tells him he wants a tight lid on Farah Benson. But she can get the job. He also tells Ajay, they don't want Farah to get the property in The Point. They prefer The Grove area or farther away.

"So we get married, leave and all hell breaks lose, ha?" Ajay asks.

"Darlene told that bitch about your wedding," Tank says, "I know that's why she showed back up here, at the bachelor party. Wheeler did what I ask him to do and she couldn't stay for the wedding. But then, she was back by New Years night. Ajay, I could kill that bitch. I play it off for Nina. But on the real, I don't' wanna fuck her. I wanna fuck her *up*."

Ajay tells him he'd love to fuck Angel up, as well. But he ask Tank not to do anything rash and he'll have Parkwood to block the property deal.

"I'll call baby girl and have her to get him on the line," Ajay says, "That'll be blocked today and Jason can call Farah's agent and suggest another spot."

"Chill says put her out in Parma or farther west," Tank says.

He says he'll get Ebony on it right away and by the end of business today, he'll have something solid to report back to him.

"So the honeymoon was cool, ha?" Tank asks.

"Bro, I'm in love with your sister, man," he says, "I hate being away from her. We grew a lot closer, up there. It was cool as fuck."

"I'm in love with yours too, bro," he says, "We're *grown*, man."

They talk for a few more minutes, then hang up. Ajay has to call his wife and his high school principal, then attend a team meeting.

Ebony talks with Parkwood, who guarantees the property in The Point will not go through for Farah Benson. He gives her a number for Jason Carr to call and set up something in Parma Heights. Parkwood *acquires* the property in The Point and deeds it to Ebony's company, which isn't even open yet. She'll be in charge of any future sell of that property. Then he sends Jason Carr, Farah's agent's info and instructs him to send them the options in Parma Heights. It's listed now, as the only thing in her range opening before May. That will take care of Farah, momentarily. The crew don't want them out near their grandparents because of Alana and her mess. They know she'll seize the 1st opportunity she gets, to seek them
316

out and meddle. Keeping her out of that gated community is insurance for the crew. Farah's agent will deliver her the bad news by the close of today's business.

}January 6, in Natty{
Ebony doesn't start her birth control pills after she returns from her honeymoon, as they had discussed. They plan to start their family, immediately. Her and T-baby have a game at UC, tonight. Nina and Rebbie have to cheer. Jerica is the mini-cheerleader for their squad. Rebbie and Nina have worked hard, with her, teaching her all of the routines. Jerica is quite the little professional. At the game tonight, they discover she has a wealthy fan named Mrs. Judith Briar. Mrs. Briar is a UC dance team alumni and lead contributor to the cheering and dance programs. After the game, she approaches Jo and offers to sponsor Jerica for dance school.

"I have several programs throughout the state," Mrs. Briar says, "I would love to enroll little Jerica in one of my schools, if there's no objection to it."
Jo is thrilled but she tells her, she'll have to clear it with Jerica's parents.

"I don't think they'll have a problem with it," Jo says, "But they *are* her parents."

The next day, Mrs. Briar speaks with Nina and Tank. They include Rebbie in the meeting. She speaks with Rebbie about a future venture. Mrs. Briar offers to fund a new school at CrewLand and the 1st scholarships.

"I know you want to open a dance school, in the future," she says, "I can help you get up and running, if you'd like."
Rebbie is ecstatic. She accepts the proposal, graciously. Nina and Tank accept her offer to give Jerica the 1st scholarship.

Later that night, Rebbie and Nina discuss Mrs. Briar's offer.
Rebbie says, "That's just the break I was looking for. Misses Briar is gonna sponsor Jerica and me, to go to dance tryouts in New York, after the local classes are complete. Oh, it's *on* now."
They begin looking into how and where, at CrewLand mall, they will build the structure for her school. It's still a few years off but Rebbie can get the plans for it and pick out a site. She calls Renee to tell her about the offer. Renee thinks it's a great idea and the crew are definitely going to invest too. They hang up and Renee and Tonya go over the books for the last quarter.

"You know junior wanna have another baby," Tonya says, this late morning in January, while they plan the January-February celebration.
317

It will include birthday parties for Tank, Jesse, Bruce, Erica and Sam.

"You said you wanted another baby, right?" Renee asks.

"Yes, I do," Tonya says.

"Well there you go," Renee says, "Kenny has been talking about it too. But he can forget it. I think I'm done, girl."

"You're just saying that, right now," Tonya says, "But you'll give him another one, one day."

"Tonya, I am twenty eight years old," she says, "If we have another baby now. I'll be damn near fifty before that kid is grown." They laugh.

The celebration is tonight. Tank had managed to avoid a run in with Alana when her and Farah was here visiting for New Year's. Now, Farah is back for her interview tomorrow and to look at home sites in Parma Heights. She had found out by phone that she couldn't get a spot in The Point. Her agent told her they will tour spots in Parma, *"because you need something before May. That's the only availability, right now."* She accepts his word and they set up an appointment to tour homes.

T-baby has allowed the lack of communication and lack of sex to go on in her marriage, for long enough. Before the celebration tonight, she feels like something has to shake out between her and Rich. Or she's going to lose her mind. She decides to go for broke.

"We really need to talk about what's been bothering you lately, baby," she starts.

"What's to talk about?" he asks, "The season's over. We didn't make the Super Bowl."

"Yea but how long are you gonna let it bring you down, honey?"

"I don't know, Trisha," he says, "It's just hard to adjust to being on a losing team."

He acted like he wanted to fuck me so bad, when he called me at school. I'm home now.

"I know what you mean," she says, "We can't seem to get to the big game either. But I'm not gonna let that interfere with my home life."

"I just can't seem to handle it, as well as you are," he says.

"Can I help?" she asks.

"How?"

"Well, I was thinking maybe I can help to get your mind on other things," she says.

318

"What other things?" he asks.

"Richard, haven't you noticed we haven't had sex, this *year*?"

He sits quietly on the couch, thinking of what his next words should be.

"Baby, it's been almost two months since we've had sex," she adds.

"So is that the problem?" he asks, "Because we haven't had sex?"

"It's a problem for me," she says.

"How about tonight, after the celebration," he asks.

"Do we have to schedule it now?" she asks, "Why not before the celebration?"

"Look, I'm just trying to work with you here," he says.

"*Work* with me?" she blurts out, then tries to calm her tone as she continues. "Is that how you see it? *Working* with me?"

"That's not how I meant it, Trisha," he says, "Look, I know I haven't been in the mood, lately. Maybe I have a problem or something. I don't know. What can I say?"

"Say you wanna fuck your wife, Richard!" she yells before she grabs her keys and heads to the garage. "You can start with saying that!"

He locks the doors and gets into the car with her. They drive to the celebration, in silence.

No one is shocked to see Farah, Alana and their clique show up. The crew know they're in town for the interview. Alana approaches Michelle, as her and Arthur do photo's on the 1st floor in the picture room. Michelle is cordial but she lets Alana know, in so many words, that she isn't intending to rehash their friendship or lack there of.

"It seems like you guys are doing good," Alana says, "Got a business with the crew and all that."

She's trying to sound genuine but it isn't working. Michelle's patience is short tonight. She wastes no time speaking her mind.

"Alana, *I know* your coming back here is to be on some bullshit," she says, "But if you start some shit for this family, me or Arthur. Then I'm gonna kick your fucking ass, myself. Now bitch, I want you to *try me*."

"Get the fuck from back here, anyway," Arthur says, "You know nobody around here is interested in you or your conversation."

Tank comes in to see that they have everything they need before he goes up to VIP. Jr and Tonya are running The Spot II and Jesse's party, so Tank and Nina can celebrate his birthday at the adult club.

"Well, Jeremy. Hello," Alana says and he ignores her.

"Arthur, y'all straight down here?" he asks, "You got your radio?"

319

"Yea partner. We're good," Arthur says.

"I'm out," Tank says as he heads to the VIP elevator.

Alana gives chase and Michelle follows Alana.

"Jeremy," she says, "I don't wanna be trouble."

"Then don't," he says as he pushes the button to call the elevator. She continues, "I just wanted to say hi and happy birthday."

"I don't give a fuck what you want," he says, "Just stay the fuck away from me."

Before she can respond, the elevator door opens and Nina is on it.

"Oh, here we go," Nina says, "You're back to chasing my man again? He's my husband now. Which means I'll push a blade through your windpipe slow." She quotes *Puff Daddy* on that *biggie* joint, as she continues, "Do you hear me, bitch?" she asks as she starts to advance and Tank gets on the elevator and holds her there.

"Nina, I'll do the honors for you," Michelle says, "Just let me know when. I'll save you the headache. Because this bitch is on my last nerve, now too."

"Michelle can get it done, for you, miss Nina," Arthur says, "And bring in some other chicks who use to stomp her ass for sport, back before she transferred to MLK."

"I just hate the game she plays," Michelle says, "Trying to fuck up my relationship and my connection with the crew family. And ain't no bitch gonna salt up my name, then come back here *all chummy,* like we're gonna be alright. Bitch, I'll beat the brakes off you. Nina just holla when you want this bitch done."

"We'll get together on it. Trust me," Nina tells her with a wink, "Go on ahead back to Arthur. Don't get your nice outfit wrinkled, for this dumb *bitch.*"

Michelle goes back to her station. Alana doesn't say anything. Tank puts Nina's finger on the elevator button, the doors closes and they leave Alana where she stands, looking dumbfounded.

Later, Farah catches Chill as he's making his rounds. She tells him about her displeasure of having to live so far away from CrewLand mall and him. She tells him she wanted to move into the point but the property was unavailable. She also tells him, she wants to be closer because of him.

"I don't need that kind of action in my life, Farah Benson," he says, "I'm good in the woman department. I'm *damn* good."

CHAPTER   35

CARRYING THE TORCH

}Jackson Heights{

Ajay makes a call to his bride, this morning. She's already up and sounding very cranky. He loves to hear her make the pinch for getting her way. He gets a kick out of it.

"Hello," she says.

"Good morning, baby," he says, "Did you sleep good?"

"No," she whines.

"Why not?"

"It's too lonely in this house," she says, "I don't like being here when you're not home. This house is too big and lonely, when you're gone."

"So you want a smaller house?" he jokes.

"No. I want my husband to come home," she says.

He says, "I miss you too. I can't wait to see you."

They parted after their honeymoon and haven't seen each other since.

"You know if I had a baby, I wouldn't be so lonely," she says as she smiles.

"We're working on that, though," he offers.

"We can't work on it without seeing each other," she says.

"I know, baby. But daddy's gonna handle all that, as soon as I can," he says in a sexy tone. "I'm so full, I'm bout to explode."

"Anthony-"

"What did I tell you to call me?" he asks in that same sexy tone.

"You were serious about that, wasn't you?"

"As a heart attack," he says.

"I thought that was just for the honeymoon," she says.

"That's for life," he says.

"Then what am I suppose to call *my daddy*?" she asks.

"You can still call him daddy."

"Our families are gonna think we're *crazy*," she tries.

"I ask you to do that," he says, "You promised to obey me, right?"

"Yes I did," she says as she giggles.

"Then do it, baby girl," he says, this time in a more serious tone.

"Okay, daddy," she says, "When can we work on this baby situation?"

"When I get home," he says, "Unless you get a break in your

schedule and come see me."

"We only got last night off," she says, "We have to go back for practice today."

"I knew that," he says, "That's why I wasn't insisting on you trying to come down here."

"I miss you though, daddy," she says, "I wish this season was already over."

"Don't say that," he says, "How are you gonna get your mind right to make it to *March Madness*?"

"I don't know, daddy, shoot," she says, "I'm trying to deal with February madness, right about now."

"That pussy hot, girl?" he ask as he's back to the sexy tone.

"Uh huh," she says in her baby voice.

"Damn, baby girl," he says, "You got me hard as a muthafuckah."

"I guess that thang hot too, ha?" she says with a smile.

"For you, it stays hot on this side," he says, "Don't forget that."

It's a week before Valentines Day. Their schedules are hectic during this time of the year. They won't have a break for another 2 weeks.

"We have to spend our first Valentines Day, as husband and wife, apart," she says, "That really sucks."

"I'll come up with something, baby," he says, "Daddy can't have his girl being lonely and sad, up there. You know that, right?"

"Yes, daddy. I know you'll make it alright," she says.

"Believe that."

As soon as they hang up, he calls Chill and lets him know about Ebony's reluctance to stay, *home alone*. He asks him to find a way to keep her content until he can get there. Chill tells him he'll get on it and they hang up. He'll suggest to the younger crew that they go over and stay with her, the next time she's *home*. They'll be more than willing to stay. Since it means they'll get to hang out in the big house, which is what they want to do.

{Afternoon, in Miami{

"I need to send something to Cincinnati, for my wife," Ajay says.

He's picking out Valentine gifts to send, before his team hits the road tonight.

"I want seven pairs of those edible panties, with the days of the week on them and that big teddy bear, over there," he says, "I need jewelry too. What do you recommend? It's our six week anniversary," he says.

322

The associate shows him the in-store collection, he can pick from and more choices online.

"I need it sent today. Can you assure me everything will ship today?"

"Yes sir, Ajay," he says, "We'll get it out, as soon as we get your shipping label done. Even if you order from our online store, it'll process as soon as I press send."

"Okay, cool," he says, "I want that diamond necklace. Oh yea, give me two dozen of those roses. One white and one red and the biggest and best box of milk chocolates you got. That's her favorite. Not the mixed up kind. Just milk chocolate and chocolate covered pecans, alright? You got me, man?"

"You know I'm going to make sure you take care of that beautiful bride of yours," he says, "She's very exquisite and you always spare no expense, when you send her gifts. She's a lucky lady."

"I'm the lucky one," he says as he looks at their wedding photo in his wallet and smiles.

The clerk fills out his invoice and makes small talk. They had sent a crystal wine set as a wedding gift, to the bride and groom. In exchange, they have a wedding photo on display in their Jewelry and novelty store. In the meantime, Ajay spots something else he likes.

"Can you put one of those daddy's girl bibs on the teddy bear?" he asks with a smile.

"Yes sir, Ajay," the clerk answers, "We'll do anything our platinum clients request."

"It's got to be there by eleven a-m, Saturday," he says, "Will that work out?"

"Oh *yes*," the clerk assures him. "All we need is the delivery info and we'll get in there, on time. And we have that already. It's charged to your account and I'm going to package it personally. Right now."

Ajay knows Ebony has to play a game on Valentines night. Her teams pre-game meeting will be at 9am. She'll be back at the Cincinnati house by 10:30, where she'll chill out all day, listening to music until she has to report back to the arena for pre-game. He knows her game day ritual, as well as he knows his own.

}Early evening, in Natty{

T-baby and Ebony leave practice, in Ebony's Camry, heading off campus to the flower and gift shop owned by their teammate Katrina Dobbs, whom T-baby nor Ajay care for. Ebony isn't to fond of her disposition either but
323

she tolerates her, for the sake of the team. Still, she has to get gifts for her man and this store is closest. This is their first Valentine's as husband and wife. No way is she going to miss sending him gifts. Not for some uppity snotty acting, overstuffed bitch in a sweatshirt, who seems to have anxiety attacks in her presence. They pull up and park at the store. Ebony makes T-baby swear to be cordial, just until they can get their husbands gifts, ship them and get out of there. T-baby says she will be. They see Shantel Jacobson heading in and catch up to her and they enter together. Once inside, they see Katrina, 1st thing. T-baby snorts like a bull. She's been itching to kick her ass since before they signed their scholarships. She had moved her out of her spot, the 1st week of freshman year. Moving her ass down to the concrete and stomping her into it, would not be a problem either. So far, Ebony has kept the peace between all of the above.

"Valentines day is next week," T-baby says.

"And I've got to send daddy something sexy, for it," Ebony says to T-baby and Shantel, as all 3 of them giggle.

They approach the counter. Everything T-baby see that she needs to have assistance with and Katrina has to be asked, she gets Shantel to asked for it. Ebony isn't so fickle. She asks Katrina for whatever she needs.

"I want a bottle of that chocolate flavored body oil," Ebony says to Katrina.

"Ebony, your ass has gotten freaky as hell since that honeymoon, kid," T-baby says as Shantel and Katrina laugh.

"Don't hate, cousin," Ebony says with a smile. "I got turned out though. I must admit."

"What else do you want. Ebony?" Katrina asks.

"Oh your ass don't see me shopping?" T-baby asks.

"Yes cousin. she see us both," Ebony says, "Just chill. okay?"

She calms down but rolls her eyes at Katrina. Soon. another associate comes over to assist T-baby while Katrina's older sister comes to assist Ebony. They send Katrina to the back.

"I want that big tiger and I want one of those bibs. I want it to read, *Baby Girl's Daddy*. Send it back to Katrina. so she can do it now."

"What I tell you. Shanny," T-baby says, "Freak-o-the-week, right here." They all laugh.

"So you call him daddy?" Shantel asks.

"Yes. He likes that. It turns him on," Ebony says with a grin.

"Like I said," T-baby starts, "Freaky deaky," and they laugh loud.

Then she asks, "What is this body paint about?"

324

"Oh and *I'm* the freak?" Ebony says with a smile.

"That's body paint for two," the clerk explains, "You and your partner get to paint each others favorite body parts. Then imprint them on the two big cards that come with it and save the cards. You know, the gift that keeps on giving. The paint is safe for eating too. It's food coloring."

"*Edible*? Oh let me get that too. *Chocolate*," Ebony says, "And that big tub of Turtles. That's daddy's favorite sticky chocolate. Besides me."

"Cousin, you're out of control," T-baby says with a giggle.

Shantel loves it. The 2 clerks find it cute and say as much.

"No, she's way out of control though," T-baby emphasizes.

"When it comes to my man. When have I ever *really* been *in* control?"

"You've got a point there," T-baby agrees as they all laugh again.

Ebony spots a special action poster of Ajay, made from a photo she's never seen. She inquires instantly, asking, "Where did y'all get this?"

"It's a game shot we had blown up to poster size," the clerk says.

Katrina's sister is quiet and doesn't offer any information.

"My husband doesn't know about it," Ebony says, "Does my big brother, John Brown junior know about it?"

"I'm not sure," the clerk says.

"I'm checking now," Ebony say as she dials Jb. "Box them all up. All your stock and the negative. I'm buying them all. We'll settle up later."

She adds a diamond laced money clip and the new UC school pin that came out this season. JB answers. T-baby finishes her shopping. Jb tells Ebony it's not authorized, confiscate the merchandise and to order a cease, which she already has. She tells them, he'll be in touch. Then they check out.

"I need this delivered by Friday morning, to Miami," Ebony says, "Can you do that?"

Katrina's sister tells her they can accommodate her. Ebony fills out her invoice and the delivery information.

"Keep this information on the low," Ebony tells her, "I don't want no groupies getting my husband's address and stalking him."

"It's all confidential, Ebony," Katrina's sister says.

T-baby picks out some candy for Rich and some crouch-less underwear.

"Freak of the month!" Ebony says and the laughter continues.

They pay for their items, then leaves the store.

}Cleveland{

John, Pearl, Jo and Al fly to the Bahamas for Valentine's. This is a

325

gift from their children. Jesse, Erica and Pam stay in Jackson heights while their parents are away. Ebony drives to Cleveland after her 4 o'clock game ends. Jesse, Roo, Steven and Ally, along with Erica and Greg Jr, come over to keep her company. She goes to her room to shower and change clothes before Ajay calls.

Trisha and Rich exchange gifts at their home tonight.
"What is this paint stuff for?" he asks.
T-baby explains it to him.
"Well, I guess we need to get started then, ha?" he suggests.
"I'm wit it," she says with a smile, as they tear open their Valentines paint and proceed with their arts and crafts assignments.
It's a beautiful evening for them. The best 1 in months and she's happy. And for a change, sexually fulfilled. They talk a lot tonight and really get some things out in the open. Still, she doesn't mention Mentor or the night that he was suppose to be in Cincinnati. She's satisfied with his answer to her question, as he answers, "Of course, you still turn me on."
His actions in their bedroom later, solidifies his answer.
"Tonight was wonderful, Richard," she says.
"Tonight isn't over until the morning, baby," he corrects her.
"Oh hell yea," she says as they indulge in session 3.
They have made so many different patterns on their cards by now, that the art looks like 1 big circular swirl. They're having a wonderful Valentines night.

Meanwhile, down the boulevard and around the curve, Ebony has finished her shower. She's in her bedroom waiting on the phone to ring. Ajay calls, just as she lays across the bed. She picks up on the 2nd ring.
"Hello, daddy. Happy Valentines day!" she says with a smile.
"Same to you, baby girl," he says from his 1st class seat on *Southwest Airlines.*
His team is in the middle of a 2 week road trip which will land them in Cleveland by Friday night.
"I'll see you in six days, right?" she asks.
"Yes you will," he says, "And I wanna see you in those *Friday* panties."
"Okay."
"That's henny and penny on that card you sent to me," he says.
She laughs loud. They had come up with several pet names for their body
326

parts while in the Pocono's. Henny and Penny are the names he had given her breast. The left one is Henny and the right one is Penny.

"I know those nipples anywhere, baby. And you know I was tripping," he says as he smiles. "You are freaky as *hell*, baby girl. I'm learning more and more about my baby. You got everything, just like I need and want it." His teammate Jim, looks at him and grins.

"You said you wanted me to be your little freak, didn't you?" she asks, "I promised to do whatever you tell me to do."

"I'm not complaining," he assures her, "I love it, baby. I got a surprise for you, when I get home."

"What is it?" she asks.

"A surprise."

She leaves it alone. He isn't going to tell her. She knows too well that even though he hates surprises, he loves to surprise her.

"Henny and Penny are missing daddy," she says.

"Daddy is missing them too," he says, "Is that edible paint? It smells like chocolate." Jim looks at him and grins again.

"Yes it is," she says.

"Uh huh. Are you ready for me, baby girl," he asks, "I mean *really* ready?"

"I think so," she says.

"You better be sure about it. Because I got something that won't quit." She tells him she's ready. "You'd better be," he says as he can hear chatter in the background. "Who is all that in my house, baby?" he asks.

"Jesse, Roo, Steven, Ally, lil Greg and Erica," she says, "Chill sent them to keep me company. They're in the game room on the playstation. You can hear them, all the way in our room?"

"Yes, I hear them," he says, "Tell them to hold it down."

She does. Then she returns to the bedroom.

"Can you sleep better with them there?" he asks.

"I don't know. I'll see, tonight. I'll pretend you're *here with me*."

"How do you do that?"

"I pretend you're here," she says.

"How?" he persist.

"You know," she says, "I try to do the things you do-"

"Are you touching on my pussy?" he asks.

Jim can't help but laugh, out loud. The whole team knows Ajay is a cut up. He keeps them laughing, all the time. But he's serious, right now.

"I don't want you touching my pussy."

327

TIME TO LOVE-RELOADED-TIME WILL REVEAL 3

Jim burst out laughing and she can hear him.

"Daddy, can somebody hear what you're saying?" she asks.

"I don't know and I don't care. Have you been?" he asks.

"Daddy," she whines.

"Answer me," he demands.

"Yes."

"Don't do it, no more," he says.

"But you told me too," she tries.

"That's for when you're on the phone with me," he says, "But not when I'm not telling you too. I have to know every time my pussy gets service." Jim explodes.

"Okay, daddy. I don't wanna talk about it, on the phone," she says.

"Then you understand me, right?" he asks for clarity.

"Yes, I understand," she says and he lets her go with that.

"I'll see you Friday night," he says, sounding as sexy as ever.

"I can't wait," she says.

"You'd better wait," he says and they share a laugh.

They exchange *I love you* before they hang up.

****

Friday, when Ajay arrives, he has not 1 but twin surprises. He had purchased 2 Pekingese to keep her company.

"They're so *cute*," she says, "I haven't had a dog in fifteen years."

She has a boy and a girl Pekinese. She had a Scottish terrier when she was 7 years old. It had been run over by a car when it got out of the house. She was very attached to that dog. When she was killed, Ebony never wanted another dog around the house again. Her parents never got one which prevented the boys from having one, as well. And it further fueled the, *she is spoiled* talk. Many say she's even more spoiled now. Ajay counters the talk by saying, *"She's suppose to be,"* and that settles it.

"I figure since you're in a new house," he says, "Then we can get you a dog. Are you okay?"

"Yes, daddy," she says, "I am. I've got two babies for this big house. What are their names?" she asks.

"I've been calling them *Ike* and *Tina*," he says with a chuckle.

"But daddy, they don't stay together," she says, "And Ike was abusive."

"That's how he acts," he says, "Whenever she don't wanna play

328

with him, he tries to fight her. He chases her all around until she gives in."

"Well we're gonna have to get him some anger management," she say, as they laugh. "We won't have domestic violence going on up in here." She plays with her new pets. They take to her immediately and are already following her and learning the house. He goes to the master suite and starts a Jacuzzi for 2. He's arranged with big mama to have dinner delivered from their restaurant. He has some time to make up for.

"We want be leaving here tonight, baby," he says, "We need to work on some more company for you."

He's kissing her on the back of her neck while undressing her for their bath. Once she's naked, he leads her to the bathroom. Ike and Tina follow them into the master suite. He instructs her to *"get in"* and she does. He whips into the bedroom and grabs Champagne from the portable fridge, then joins her in the tub. After a few sips, he begins to kiss her. As the room becomes steamy, Ike and Tina exit as if they sense this is a private moment.

"They left when we started kissing," she says, "Did you see that?"

"Good. They're learning early," he says, "Maybe they need some privacy too."

"They'd better not have been seeing any kissing going on, down there."

He says, "Well, they may have."

"What do you mean?" she asks as she giggles.

"The couple I bought them from, kept them while I was on the road," he says, "So maybe they trained them, like that. They was a loving couple too."

"Have you thought anymore, on what we talked about?"

"We talked about a lot of things," he says.

"The clinic," she says, "The fertility clinic?"

He asks, "Do you really think we need to take drugs, to have a baby?"

"I don't know," she says, "But we haven't been successful."

"You just stopped the pills, last month," he says, "You was taking them for years and we haven't been together since the honeymoon."

"I was taking them longer than that, before the *first baby* and it didn't take long-"

"Baby," he says, cutting her off in mid sentence. "Take your time and don't think about it, so much."

"I try but I want a baby, so bad," she says and her eyes well up.

"I know and so do I. But it won't happen until the time is right. I want you to try to be a little more patient. Just let it happen, when it

329

happens. We fuck, a lot. We'll have plenty of chances for me to send one."
She sits in silence. He can tell she's conflicted over his optimistic answer.
"I tell you what," he says, "Set up an appointment with doctor Weston. Let's get everything checked out. We can talk to her about it and see what she thinks. Okay?"
"Okay," she says as she's satisfied with his suggestion.
After their bath and getting reacquainted session, they emerge from the bathroom, towel dry each other as poppa and big mama arrive with dinner.
"Hello Ajay," big mama says, "How are you, baby?"
"I'm good, big mama," he says, "Come on in. How y'all doing?"
"We're feeling young and spunky, all of a sudden," poppa says, "It must be the atmosphere in this house," he adds with a chuckle.
"I know that's right," Ajay says, returning the chuckle.
They have brought dinner for 4, as Ajay had requested. He wants them to join them so he can run a few things by them. The offer of them moving into the guest house and the fertility drugs. He starts with offering them the guest house, as Ebony helps him make the case.
"We want y'all to be closer to us," Ebony says, "And papa too."
"I don't want baby girl to be lonely, when I'm not here," Ajay says.
Big mama and poppa say they'll think it over, once more. Big mama does however agree to come and stay with Ebony whenever she needs her.
"Now baby, you know big mama is here for you, whenever you need me," she says.
They accept that answer for now and move on.
"Big mama, I wanna ask you something else too," Ajay says.
"What is it?" big mama asks.
"You know we're trying to have a baby, right?"
"Yes I heard something about that," big mama says batting her eyes at Ebony, as they both smile.
"Your impatient granddaughter thinks we need to try fertility drugs," he says, "What do you think about that?"
"Y'all don't need no drugs to have a baby," she says, "Everything y'all need, you already got."
"How long do I need to wait for the pills to wear off?" Ebony asks.
"It's different for each person, baby," big mama says, "And each pregnancy and cycle is different too."
"So the best thing to do, is to continue to count the days and keep trying, right?" Ajay asks, knowing big mama will agree.
Big mama is always stressing they do *things* the natural way and leave it in
330

TIME TO LOVE-RELOADED-TIME WILL REVEAL 3

God's hands. Naturally, she agrees with Ajay and tells Ebony to be patient.

"But when we lost the baby, doctor Weston said I might have trouble conceiving the next time," Ebony tries.

"I know she did but she didn't say you *wouldn't* be able to get pregnant, *naturally*," big mama says, "You gotta have faith."

"I do but…-"

"There ain't no butts to it," poppa adds, "Twins run in this family, baby girl. You start messing with fertility and y'all gonna have a litter, like these dogs do."

Ajay cracks up laughing as Ebony laughs too. Then smiling, he says, "Baby, let's just keep trying. We'll talk to doctor Weston too. But we're not taking anything, right away. Okay?"

"Alright," she says sadly, "I don't wanna go *too* long though."

"At least wait until after you graduate," poppa suggests, "You only have a few months of college left. And baby, God has blessed y'all, *so* much. He has a whole lot more blessings in the works. Look at this place. You have fifteen foot ceilings in the bedrooms and I know these are at least twenty."

"Twenty five," Ajay says and smiles, "And paid for."

"Shit yea!" poppa says with a chuckle, "We can fit a lot of houses inside this one. And all those rooms God blessed y'all to build. He's gonna bless you to fill. Do you believe I know what I'm talking about?"

"Yes sir, poppa," she says as she agrees to be patient.

Though Ajay knows she won't let go of the fertility drugs idea, he's happy to have big mama and poppa on board, against it. They'll bring it up to Pearl and John too. He knows they won't want them to use drugs either. That will go a long way in convincing his wife that she shouldn't do it.

"Set up an appointment for Friday the twentieth," he says, "That's our bye weekend. I can fly back and go to the doctor with you. That's if you're not in the tournament, somewhere."

Ebony has been so focused on trying to get pregnant that she hasn't even considered the fact that her team will get an NCAA bid.

"Oh yea, that's right," she says, "I know we're going because we're winning the conference. We've got the best conference record. The bid is automatic."

"I don't want you to be pregnant, trying to finish the season," he says as he kisses her on the cheek.

"I know you're right, daddy," she says.

Big mama and poppa smile. They think the pet names are cute. They adore the fact that he's so patient and understanding with her. And also, they like
331

that the 2 of them communicate with each other, on all matters.
Golden.

Farah receives mail saying she got the Computer Technologies teaching job at MLK. She'll start teaching in the fall of 1999. She still has a year of student teaching to do. And she still hasn't made her boyfriend Marvin Huntley, aware of her plans. After she reads the letter of confirmation, she calls her real estate agent and tells him to go ahead with the house in Parma Heights. She's definitely moving. She has chosen a home with 6 bedrooms and 4 bathrooms. Alana is moving with her and bringing her daughter, Olivia. There's been some discussion about Darlene moving too. But she isn't going to bring her sons. Or actually, that part hasn't been finalized yet. After Farah heard Rodney and Jamal's explanation for why they were firing guns at CrewLand mall, she started to see them as leverage. The 2 young black males had clowned outside of *The Spot II,* hoping to gain the crew's attention because they want to be initiated. They want to be down with Ajay, Chill and the crew. Farah is going to try to work their fascination to her advantage. After all, *she's* fascinated too.

"Hey, Sandy. How are you feeling, girl?" Rena asks.
She has decided to call Sandy tonight, to discuss their kid's behavior, lately.
"I'm living. *Barely,*" Sandy jokes, "What's up with you?"
"I'm about sick and tired of these hardhead ass kids of mine," Rena says, "Have you seen Alicia?"
"Not today but Steven isn't here either," Sandy says, "His ass acts like he lives out there at Trisha's."
"Well Ally acts like she can't do anything without him being there, Sandy," Rena tells her, "They claim they're in love."
"I know, honey," Sandy says, "He'd better get his ass to this house and at a decent time."
"I'm getting ready to go out there to get Ally," Rena says, "I didn't tell her she could stay, when Rebbie is in Cincinnati."
"Well bring Steven and Greg junior when you go, please," she says, "And Pearl told me that Jesse has a key to Ebony and Ajay's house."
"*What*? Do they know it?" Rena asks.
"I doubt it," she says, "Ajay isn't about to let them run all over his mansion, when they're not there."
332

TIME TO LOVE-RELOADED-TIME WILL REVEAL 3

Rena tells Sandy, she'll bring her sons home with her. They hang up and Sandy finishes feeding Rich III, bathes him and puts him to bed. Then she calls the Cincinnati house to speak to T-baby.

"Hey Mama," T-baby says, "How's my little man doing?"
Rich is down in Natty with her and their mothers are keeping their son until the weekend.

"He's fine. I just put him to bed," Sandy says, "Is Ebony around?"

"She has to tutor tonight," T-baby says, "What's up?"

"I wanted to ask if you gave Jesse and Greg junior, keys to your houses."

"No. *I* didn't," T-baby says, "And I know she didn't either."

"Well they're out there, right now. Rena is bringing them home."

"Rich is down here until we come home, Friday," T-baby says, "But Tank is home with Jerica. I'm calling him to handle this, right now."

"Well tell Ebony, she needs to find out where Jesse got a key from too," Sandy says, "He sure has one. But he doesn't know the security code, I guess. Jacobson called Pearl and Jo, four times, about the silent alarm."
T-baby tells her mother she's passing the word on to Ebony, when she gets home. They hang up. T-baby tells Nina, who calls Tank and tells him to get the keys.

"*What*? They at *Ajay's* house?" Tank asks, "I'll go get them out of there. Ajay is gonna go off, if they fuck up something."
After hanging up with Nina, Tank drives around to Ajay's house. Sure enough, Jesse, Roo, Ally and Steven are there with Erica, Greg Jr, Sam Jr and Pam. He gets them back up to his house and Rena meets them there. Tank gets the keys to Ajay and Rich's homes, from Jesse and Greg Jr.

"I'm telling Ajay and T-baby, what y'all did man," Tank says.
Jesse had taken the spare key from the house, 1 day when he was there keeping Ebony company. She didn't know he had taken it. Greg Jr had taken T-baby's spare key from their parents house, for him and Erica to use at their leisure.

"I'm telling on you," Tank says and laughs, "Yes, I'm snitchin. You should know better than that. We *never* stole Chill or Stoney's keys."
Him and Rena make sure all of them get home.

Later that night, Ajay calls and talks to Jesse about taking advantage of Ebony.

"That's your only sister, man," he says, "And that's *our* home. What if y'all had burned it down or something? Y'all didn't have neither one of our permission to be up in there. Y'all shouldn't have been there."
333

TIME TO LOVE-RELOADED-TIME WILL REVEAL 3

He adds, "Each one of y'all are welcome to come over, *when* we're home. But don't ever do that again. And y'all *will* apologize to my wife."

"My bad, Ajay," Jesse says, "I was just trying to chill with my girl. Like y'all use to do at big Chill's. I'm tell baby girl, I'm sorry. For sho."

"Okay. Just know, you need permission to do that, bro," Ajay says, "I don't have a problem with y'all staying there, when baby girl is there. But don't steal the damn key and let yourself in, like that. Jacobson says my silent alarm has been going crazy. And he knew who was there, so *he called* y'all parents and not me. They called Tank. Tank called me."

Jesse apologizes repeatedly and says he understands and won't do it again.

"You know Reaper still got the apartment," Ajay says, "Why can't y'all chill out there, when we're gone? Nobody is there but him and Brit."

"We can but it ain't that much room," Jesse tries.

"Room for what?" Ajay asks and chuckles, "*Bedrooms*, man?"

"Yea man. You know," Jesse says and laughs too.

"Bro, are y'all using any protection?" Ajay asks with a smile.

"I got some rubbers but I don't like using them with Ruthie."

"Then you'd better make sure she got some pills. Before y'all end up with a baby," Ajay suggests, "You're seventeen. She's sixteen. Neither one of y'all are out of high school yet. Be careful, bro. Still, there's three bedrooms at the U."

"But Reaper don't want nobody to come there unless Bruce come home. And him and Kim go over there," Jesse says, "He'll let Kenny and Chaundra use the other room. But when the rest of us go, he trips out. He's trying to let little Archie and Brina hook up over there and they're not even thirteen yet."

"I'll put Tank and Chill on it," he says, "They'll get it straight for y'all. You make sure y'all tell my woman, you're sorry. Done deal."

Jesse is satisfied that Ajay is going to help him out. He hangs up, smiling.

UC makes it to the sweet 16, this year, before loosing to Georgia. The following weekend, Ajay and Ebony talk to Dr. Weston about fertility drugs. She suggest they don't try anything, right away.

"I feel like you can conceive on your own," Dr. Weston says, "You've got to give yourself some time." Ajay hugs his wife as her eyes are welling up with tears. "Let's see you all back in 2 months. If nothing has happened, by then. I'll run some more test. But right now, you're ovulating fine, honey," she says as she suggests the same thing Ajay, big mama, poppa and their parents have been saying for 3 months.

334

TIME TO LOVE-RELOADED-TIME WILL REVEAL 3

"Give your system time to cleanse from the birth control pills. Don't think about it so much and you'll get pregnant."

"Okay," Ebony says but she's disappointed that Dr. Weston hasn't supported her on fertility.

After leaving the clinic, they have lunch at Crew's House, then go home.

Rebbie has been talking to her younger sister Ally, about calls she keeps getting from their mother. Rena has been calling Rebbie, at school, complaining about Ally's attitude. She's not wanting to go to school. And she only wants to stay out at the U or in Jackson Heights, way too much. The foursome come home today for Spring Break, which starts Monday. April and Yolanda are coming for the week. Rebbie has plans of getting her housework done before they come. Before she starts studying, Ally calls.

"Hey Ree, what are you doing?" Ally asks, sounding as if she's been crying, on this last Friday in March.

"Nothing much," Rebbie answers, "I'm gonna clean this house thoroughly, while I'm home for spring Break. You sound upset. You wanna come over and help me, so we can talk?"

"I will," Ally says, "I need to talk to you about something."

"What's up?"

"I missed my period," Ally confides in her, "I think I'm pregnant."

"I'm on my way, kid," she says, "I'll get a pregnancy test and we'll find out."

****

Ajay's team is finishing up the regular season on a high. Their record gets them into the playoffs. He's happy about the playoff birth. But he knows it'll keep him away from Ebony, even longer. He talks to her about it and sure enough, she's happy about the teams success. But she knows she'll miss him too. However, she's looking forward to the visit from her best friends from Houston. April and Yolanda are coming to visit for spring break. The ladies plan to do some shopping and partying while their friends are in town.

The ladies arrive and get right into flow with the foursome. Ebony, Nina and T-baby pick them up from the airport while Rebbie takes care of Ally. Then they all meet up at Rebbie's house, where she's doing the pregnancy test. It doesn't take long to see that the test is positive. Ally and Steven have conceived a child. Ally calls Steven, right away to tell him.

335

Rebbie and T-baby vow to be there for both of their younger siblings.

"We've got your back, Ally," T-baby tells her, while smiling, "I'm gonna be an *auntie*."

Alicia is only 14 years old. Steven just turned 15. They're afraid to tell their parents, so Rebbie and T-baby agree to go with them.

"My sister just found out she's pregnant," Yolanda says, "She's thirteen."

"And my cousin has a baby on the way," April says, "He's fourteen and the girl is fifteen."

The 6 ladies, along with Ally, go pick up Steven and go to Crew Gear to talk with their mothers. Neither of them want to tell big Greg or Archie Sr.

Rena and Sandy are upset but they don't try to make Ally and Steven feel bad. They leave the foursome, April and Yolanda to help at the store, while they take Ally and Steven to Dr. Weston for prenatal care. Their child is due, 12 days into October.

They return and the foursome are ready to shop. They're keeping Ally close to them. She shops and hangs out with them, all week.

The next week, for MLK's spring break, Ally goes with them to Cincinnati too. April and Yolanda had spent a week in Cleveland and are now returning to Houston, only to pack all of their things and move to Atlanta. The 2 of them, Charles, David and Terrell are making the move to help Jb and the crew, manage the new southern businesses. It's already known that Jb, Lynn and Terrell will manage *the Dirty South Chill Spot*. Jb, Yolanda and David will manage the new restaurant, *Southern Exposure*. Rob and Jan already manage the studio and record shop, *Jenkins Jams Company Inc.* April, Charles and Chrissy, who is Terrell's girlfriend, will manage *the Southern Complex*, a sports arena for all athletic activities. The arena will offer concessions, like The Spot II. Bre and Ced will have *The Hideaway bar and grill,* to open and manage next year, when Bre finishes OTC. The other businesses are on tap to open in June of this year.

April calls Ebony after getting settled in Atlanta. She has things she wants to reveal to her. Personal things, they'd touched on while Ebony lived in Houston. Those things which helped to shape their friendship. Things about April's family that Ebony found very disturbing and rather sad.

"I was so glad to have this opportunity in Atlanta," April says, "Just to get away from it all."

"I'm glad for you," Ebony says, "But did you speak your peace about the lies and the issues you have, before you moved?"

336

"No Ebony. I didn't bother," she says, "They're in denial. Plus most of their actions are so deeply rooted and have been going on, for generations. I just pray for them, cling to my bible and spare peoples feelings."

"You really should've told your mother, both grandmothers and your aunt, *the hypocrites* as you call them, how you felt, before you moved," Ebony suggests, "That's the part that I feel you was the most upset about."

"They just talk about each other and my daddy, like they hate each other. I feel like they want me to hate too. They don't even think about how it makes me feel about all of them."

"And still you didn't tell them?" Ebony asks.

"Well, one of my grandmothers live in Mississippi," she says, "And my aunt moves around a lot, staying with people. But Ebony, they won't pay it any attention. Even if I do tell them. Both sides of my family is screwed up. My mama and her mom, talk about them too. They all, *always* talk bad about my daddy. But to me, my daddy is okay. But he don't come around much anymore because of his *problem.*"

"Do you still feel like the pressure in his life led to the problem?" Ebony asks.

"Of course, I do," she says, "I know it did and they don't think I even know about the problems that led to it. His mother gave his sister everything. Trying to live some lifestyle they couldn't afford. Fancy car and designer clothes, she's still paying for twenty years later. If she didn't buy it, then my aunt would shoplift. She use to run away, sleep around with older men, use drugs, dress like lil Kim. You name it," she giggles. "She's very insecure. But my daddy, he worked for almost everything he's got. I just want to marry Charles and make a clean break from all of them."

"Do you still confide in your cousin Black?" Ebony asks.

"Yes indeed. I talked to her, last night. She listens to me and I don't have to worry about her saying anything to anybody about what I've told her."

April had confided in Ebony about the fact, she feels she lives in the crossfire of a war, between fake ass people. Her mother's side doesn't like her father's side. Her father's side doesn't like her mother's side. But they all pretend when in each others presence. Neither side supports her father. They all tend to love her but she sees things for what they are and prays to God everyday, to take her away from all of it.

"That's why I am so strong in my faith, Ebony," she says, "Only God can help them and keep me sane, while I deal with all of them."
337

TIME TO LOVE-RELOADED-TIME WILL REVEAL 3

"Well, you know we're here whenever you need us," Ebony says.

"I had a blast up there," April says, "Every time I visit you and see how your family behaves. I really know what's missing in my life. My dad has one aunt that he's close too. And she's close to Black. I talk to her too. But we keep that a secret. She doesn't let any of their insecurities hold her back. I know that's really what they hate about her. I talk to her every week, about my life. She tells me don't let what they say hold me back. She says, *'If I love Charles, then I should be able to make my own decisions. Since I'm over eighteen.'* Her mother, *she's a granny too.* Always tells them that they're just jealous of her and I say that's what it is too."

"Like I said," Ebony says, "Anytime you wanna get away, the crew are here for you."

"Are you and Ajay still gonna let me and Yolanda, Christian your first baby?" she asks.

"No doubt. If we ever make one," she says and they both laugh.

"Y'all will, sis," she says, "The love is too strong not too."

They make plans for the next time they'll call and visit. Then they hang up. April has to get to *The Southern Complex* for their 1st staff meeting.

It's late April and the heat are back in the playoffs against New York, in the 1st round this time. Last year, they had gone to the finals of the Eastern conference. This year, they meet New York in the 1st round. Renee and Tonya are planning the May celebration which will include college graduates, the foursome, from UC and Reaper is finishing MLK. Celebrating a birthday is Kim, who'll be 19 and Pam will turn 16. John III and Orian will make 1.

Jb and Lynn are coming home for the foursome's graduation, on the 16th of May. Lynn and Rebbie plan a party at Granny's *House* for their 1 year olds. The crew will celebrate anniversary 43 for grandpa Joshua and grandma Sally Logan. Also, anniversary 26, for Al and Jo. The crew will attend the foursome's graduation in Cincinnati, then travel back to Cleveland for the birthday parties and a celebration, at both clubs.

Early morning, in early May. Ebony has been up all night, on the phone with Ajay. In his game last night, there was a fight. Worse than that, New York tied the series. He wasn't in the best of spirits and she had to be there for him. She has had her fill of studying for finals too. Her and her girls need a break, so they drive to Cleveland for the weekend. If it wasn't for finals next week, she'd be flying to New York for game 5, tonight.

338

TIME TO LOVE-RELOADED-TIME WILL REVEAL 3

Instead, she goes to Tank's house to get Ike and Tina and take them for a walk. She's still longing to get pregnant and Weston told them to come back in 8 weeks. She doesn't want to wait, so she calls the clinic from her cell and ask if she can come in to talk. Weston says, "Of course you can."

T-baby has convinced herself to lay off Rich because his moods have changed. He has been more attentive to her needs, for the past 2 months. They have spent quiet time together, both in Natty and at home. He's playing the role and she still hasn't hinted to anyone that she feels like he's been unfaithful. Not even to him. He spends quality time with his son. Taking him to daycare, picking him up, playing with him at the park and taking him shopping. The things a father does. Every since Valentine's day, he's stepped his game up. There are still a few hours per night when she can't contact him. As far as that night when she called him and he picked up, then hung up, he'd told her he was sleeping it off and didn't even remember answering. For why he didn't come to Natty, like he'd told her mother, he said he had too much alcohol before he knew it and didn't feel safe driving that far. And he was at home passed out. When he was actually at Tameka's apartment door, hounding her.

Ebony shows up for her appointment. When she's called back, Dr. Weston is surprised to see her there without Ajay.

"So where's that husband of yours?" Dr. Weston asks "He let you come in here *alone*?"

"I didn't tell him I was coming," she says, "And he's in New York."

"Oh no," Dr. Weston says, "What are you trying to get me into?"

"Do you really think fertility is a bad idea?" she asks.

"I think fertility is fine for my patients who need it," she says, "But I don't think you all need any assistance."

"But we're still not *pregnant*," Ebony tries.

"Have you all been able to see each other?" Weston asks.

"Yes but not much."

"During your ovulation period?" Weston asks, for clarity.

"No," she says, "We missed it by three days."

"Keep trying. And there's still a chance, the pills aren't completely gone," Weston says, "You took them for a lot of years."

"So there's really nothing wrong with my reproductive system?" She wants to hear her doctor say it.

"There's absolutely nothing wrong with your reproductive organs, sweetheart," Dr. Weston says, "You're as healthy as a horse."

339

Dr Weston tells her, her *and Anthony* can come in anytime with any questions and she'll be at their disposal. She also suggests that Ebony think long and hard about fertility because they can have negative repercussions.

"You're going to be a high risk pregnancy because of the anemia," Weston says, "So I don't want to have to factor in anymore risk."
Ebony accepts her doctor's advice.

"Please don't tell Anthony about this visit," Ebony says.

"And why not?" Weston says, "He'll see your charts when you come back. He always looks at it."

"I'll tell him I came in. But I'm gonna have to figure out how to tell him without him thinking I'm being sneaky."

"Well you *are*," Weston says with a smile.
Ebony smiles and thanks her doctor for seeing her on such short notice.

In the lobby, the receptionist makes her an appointment for the first day of July. Which is 8 weeks later.

"That's two weeks before we go on our extended honeymoon," she says aloud, "Hopefully we'll be pregnant by then."
She takes her appointment card and leaves. Disappointed that she still wasn't able to convince Weston to say they need help getting pregnant, she hangs her head and walks out to her car. She drags herself across the parking lot, feeling dejected and wondering will they ever conceive. She makes it to her Camry, unlocks it and gets in. She sits there a few minutes, thinking of how she'll explain this visit to her husband. Just before starting her car up, she looks across the parking area and notices June's car. She's about to get out and go over to speak. But she remembers Ajay doesn't know she's there and he has to know, *first*. There are 4 people in June's car. *My girls didn't say they had to come down here. But I didn't tell them either. There are females in... That's not Rebbie or T-baby. Who is that in the car?*

She sees Rich in the back seat. He's kissing on a woman, who isn't T-baby.

"Oh my God," she says, "Rich is messing around on my cousin. What is going on?!"
June is in the drivers seat with his arm around a woman, in his passenger seat, who isn't Rebbie.

"Oh no. *No. No!*" she screams, "What the *hell* is going on!?"
Her 1st impulse is to run up to the car and demand they stop what they're doing. She jumps out. She thinks she'll run over and confront them. But as she's getting out of her car, she notices Rich and the woman getting out. She freezes in her tracks and crouches down, next to her car. She gets a better
340

look at the woman. It's not Tameka or Selina, from his past. She's never seen *this* woman. Rich is smiling and hugging her, like they're life long lovers. June's friend has gotten out. She's standing near June's driver's door, waiting for the woman Rich is kissing, *again*. He's leaning her up against the car like they're some hot teenagers, stealing any opportunity they can, to be affectionate. Like he use to be with T-baby, after the games in grade school. June is still seated in the drivers seat with his door open. The other woman is leaning into him, using his door rest as her foot prop. He's playing with the calf of her leg. Ebony is *pissed*. Rich is married to her cousin. This bastard owns a home just behind her and Ajay's, with his wife of less than 2 years. This is her husbands, 1st cousin. The 1 who tried to advise Ajay on what to do and not do, when he got married. She was happy when Ajay told him to, *"mind your business. I got mine."*

The longer she crouches there and thinks of the reasons why she should confront them, the less she thinks about her being there, unannounced. She has hyped herself up to tell both of them a piece of her mind. But then, she talks herself down and gets back in her car. She watches her 1st cousin's husband, trade spit with this unknown woman. She becomes visibly upset, as tears well up in her eyes. She gets out of her car again and this time she starts towards them. June gets out of the car. Still, he doesn't see her and neither does Rich. She freezes again. She thinks she should stay at a safe distance, to witness what they'll undoubtedly try to lie to their wives about, later. She waits. She doesn't want them to see her now. She doesn't want to give them the opportunity to come up with a lie, in advance. She turns, goes back and gets into her car. This scenario has already upset her to tears. She doesn't want to be the 1 seeing this infidelity. Nor does she want to be the 1 to break her girls hearts. At this point, she knows what she wants to do. She wants to just leave. She opens her car and gets in. She glances back toward her cheating cousin and her cousin's cheating husband. They're looking directly at her. Rich is walking toward her car.

"Oh hell no, you don't!" she screams as she starts her car.

She backs out and rips through the parking lot, like she's seen a ghost. She shoots out into traffic, out of control of her steering and nearly smashes into oncoming traffic. She manages to get control, then she accelerates to speeding, within seconds. A police officer witnessed the whole thing and gets behind her with sirens blaring and lights flashing. Ebony has control of her car but not herself. She realizes she has a cop on her tail and slows down, then pulls over to the side of the road. She's still not in control of her emotions. She's crying frantically as the police woman approaches her car.
341

"Ma'am, put your window down," the police woman instructs. Ebony is crying, so hard, she doesn't even hear her. The officer taps the window with her night stick.

"Ma'am, turn your engine off and unlock your door."
Ebony shuts off the car and releases the locks. The officer opens the door.

"Ma'am, are you okay?" The female officer asks.

"I saw them! They was cheating!" Ebony cries.

"Ma'am, I need you to take a deep breath and calm down. Or I'll be forced to get you off of the roadway. Are you okay?"
Ebony tells her she's not okay. Then she tells the officer what she saw, at the Medical center. The officer talks to her, for several minutes. Until she calms down. The officer recognizes her, before getting her license. She asks her where she's headed. Ebony tells her to Jackson Heights.

"That's where I live," Ebony says.
The officers name is Deloris Miles. She tells Ebony she knows her from playing basketball and she has a relative who played on her team, in Natty. She also tells Ebony, she knows Jacobson and all of his staff. Officer Miles calls ahead and tells Jacobson to be on the look out for her and that she's upset. Miles doesn't give her a ticket. Nor does she say whom her relative is. She warns her to slow down. Ebony says she will. From there, she proceeds with caution to the restaurant. She wants to see big mama. She doesn't want to go home. She doesn't want to run into T-baby nor Rebbie. Not now. *What will I say to them? How will I act, knowing what I know?*

She doesn't want to tell them *this* news. They're her best friends, in this world. She just can't hurt them, with this. She stops at *Crews House of Soul Food* to pick up big mama. She tells her what she witnessed. Big mama orders lunch for the 2 of them and tells poppa, she'll be leaving to go to Ebony's house. While they wait for their food, she can see that Ebony is trembling and still visibly upset. Big mama rubs her hands and tells her repeatedly, to calm down. Eventually, she gets their lunch plates and they head to Jackson heights.

As they pass the entry gate, Jacobson is curious about Ebony's well being. She looks a mess as she drives past. She parks in the garage, leaving the door up. Her and big mama get out and enter the estate, through the kitchen. Big mama suggests Ebony go get a cold towel to avoid puffiness under her eyes. Then join her for lunch while she sets up their lunch on the kitchen terrace. Ebony joins her and they eat. They talk after they finish.

"Baby, there's really nothing you can do about them being

342

unfaithful," big mama says, "But you're gonna make problems in your *own* marriage, if you let this upset you, like you're doing."

"How am I suppose to be around Rebbie and T-baby, when I know their husbands are cheating on them?"

"Maybe you don't have to tell them, just yet," big mama says, "But you do need to tell *your* husband."

"I know. But he don't-"she starts, "He didn't know I was going to see doctor Weston today. He's gonna wanna know *why I was there*."

"Then you need to start with that," big mama suggests, "You don't wanna keep secrets from your husband. At least, not this kind of stuff."

"I know. But he's in the playoffs, right now. I don't wanna distract him with my problems. It's a crucial game, tonight."

"Trying to get pregnant is a concern for both of you," big mama says, "And anything that upsets you, *this much*, is something he should know. If you try to harbor Rich and June's secret, it will tear at the fabric of your own marriage. I won't have that, *lil* Eloise."

"I know you're right, big mama," she says, "But-"

"There is no but, sweetheart," she says, "Tell your husband about everything that happened today. Let him help you figure out what to do."

Just then, the phone rings. It's Lieutenant Jacobson.

He says, "I'm calling to check on you. You looked troubled when you came through. And officer Deloris Miles called after she stopped you earlier. She told me you was upset. I need to know if you're okay?"

"Yes sir, I am," she says, "I needed to talk to my big mama about some things. She's always been able to make things, make *sense*."

Jacobson doesn't pry but he does tell her, "Ajay hired me to keep an eye on you and keep things cool, around here. So I wanted to check in with you. Just to see if there is anything I need to do. That's all."

She tells him thanks and she's fine. They hang up.

"Big Mama, I am gonna tell Anthony but not on the phone," she says, "I have to tell him, face to face. That's how it's done in this family. But not until after his series deciding game, tonight."

"That's fine," big mama says, "Just be sure and tell him, as soon as you see him. Okay?"

"Okay."

They smile and pinky swear. The doorbell, at the kitchen entrance, rings.

"I hope this isn't T-baby or Ree Ree. Because I don't think I can play this off," she says as she heads to the door, leaving big mama on the terrace.

343

She rounds the large island counter and answers the door to find Rich standing there. *Seething.*

"What do you want?" she asks, "I don't wanna hear about the complex."

"Good. Then you can just *listen!*" he spits, "If you tell Trisha about this, you're gonna crush her!"

"That's a given."

"I don't think it's any of your fucking business, anyway!" he yells, "Stay the fuck out of it!"

"I wasn't trying to be in it. Do you think I wanted to see that?"

"What the fuck was you doing down there, anyway?!"

"Watch your language in my home. I don't answer to you."

"Whatever, Ebony," he says, "You're going behind my cousin's back and being sneaky. So how can you judge me?!"

"I'm not judging you," she says, "And I'm not going behind Anthony's back. I don't check in with you. Anthony and I talk about every doctor's visit. Now when are you gonna tell *Tee* about her wife-in-law?"

"Yea, you'll tell him because we *saw* yo ass there!" he screams, deliberately trying to push her buttons. "You're a slick bitch!"

"You can leave with that language, Rich. See, I wasn't cheating," she says, "You're bothered about getting *caught*? Stop cheating!"

"I was seeing a friend of mine!"

"Y'all was doing more than *seeing,* each other," she says.

He starts to raise his voice more. He's getting up in her face, so she takes a step backward. Big mama can hear the commotion getting fevered, so she starts inside. She gets inside of the door where she can hear them better.

"Ajay treats your ass, like some spoiled ass kid! Like you're living in a fantasy world!" he yells, "*Bitch* please! All niggas cheat! He needs to shock your ass again, one good time! Do something to keep your ass in line! Stop you from turning into the sneaky little bitch that you're becoming!"

"Get out of our house!" Ebony screams, shocked at the words he's using to her, "Y'all got caught! Don't try to make this about Anthony!"

"He needs to get your ass in line, before you-"

"She asked you to leave her home," big mama says, "You need to leave and leave now. Any of those suggestions you have for *Ajay*? Sugar, how about you tell those directly to him, the same way you've just expressed them to his wife and best friend. I'd love to get his opinion on these colorful words and names you've labeled her. I happen to know for a fact, *his names for her* are quite the contrary."

344

TIME TO LOVE-RELOADED-TIME WILL REVEAL 3

Rich is shocked and surprised to see big mama there. He knows not to take his verbal assault any further. He gives Ebony an evil look, then he leaves without another word. Big mama sizes him up as she calms Ebony down.

"The nerve of some people," big mama says, "Instead of him going home and apologizing to his wife. He's over here stirring it up thicker." Ebony is totally disgusted as she says, "I know I'm telling Anthony now. I really felt like he wanted to hit me or something. Did you see his face?"

"Yes indeed. I did," big mama answers, "That man has got *way* more problems than just being unfaithful."

"Tell me about it," Ebony says thinking of what Ajay will do.

Big mama is a very wise woman. She watches all of her crew children closely. She's felt like Rich has more problems than just infidelity, for a while. And she's right. It'll be only be a matter of time before he falls apart.

}Pittsburgh{

Farah and Alana are at Farah's condo. They're on her computer taking the virtual tour of the home in Parma which Farah closes on, in just a few weeks. After learning she had gotten the job in Cleveland, she'd started shopping for her new house. She'd decided, a long time ago, that Marvin wouldn't be invited along on the move. She's hired a decorator to furnish it, once the closing is complete.

"So when are you gonna tell Marvin about the move?" Alana asks.

"I don't know. Why? Can you think of when and how? Because I don't have a clue."

"Fare, you have to tell him it's over, at *least*," Alana says, "You can't just change zip codes on a man, that's been your roommate and not even tell him you're moving."

"Suddenly you have a conscience?" Farah ask as they laugh. Then she says, "Okay. Maybe you're right but how do I tell him?"

"Marvin's a rational guy," she says, "He has to know something's different. Think of a way and just tell him and tell him soon. Like today."

"Okay, I'll tell Marvin," Farah says, "Maybe I'll take him to dinner and tell him there."

"Tell me what?" Marvin asks.

}Cleveland{

T-baby calls Ebony and ask what she's going to do, today. Ebony plays her off, saying she's going to study for her finals. Then arrange some things in their home until Anthony makes it in.

345

"We was suppose to be studying together," T-baby says, "You wanna study at your house or what?"

"Nah. I'm gonna study alone," she says, "I need to clear my head."

"What's wrong. Are you okay?"

"Yea, I'm cool. I just need to be by myself today."

Rebbie and Nina are on the line also. They ask if she needs them to come over, so they can talk. She says no. Which makes them even more suspicious. Before they left Cincinnati, they had agreed they were going to study for finals together, at 1 of their homes.

"Why are you changing your mind now?" Nina ask as T-baby and Rebbie wonder the same thing.

Ebony doesn't have an answer. They figure maybe she's just feeling lonely right now and she'll snap out of it in an hour and come to the study session. She all but hangs up on them, as she tries to get off the phone before she lets loose of anything. Her girls still get together at T-baby's house. Ebony never shows up.

}Pittsburgh{

Farah and Alana was caught off guard when Marvin, who has taken off work early, walked in on their conversation. He had taken off at the start of the lunch hour, to take his girlfriend to lunch and to discuss why there's such a distance between them, lately.

"Tell me what? What do you need to tell me, Farah?" he asks.

"I got a new job, *Marv*. That's good news, right?" she asks dryly.

"And you couldn't tell me?"

"I'm telling you now," she says.

"Well that's great, honey," he says, "What job is it? Where is the job at, sweetheart?"

"It's a high school teaching job, for Computer Technologies," she says, "It starts in the Fall. We was sitting here looking up the curriculum, to see if I'll even be able to handle it," she lies.

"Sure you can. You can do anything, baby," he says, "Are you taking it?"

"Yes I am."

"So which school did you get? Carrier. Brashear. Langley or where?" he asks.

"It's not in the Pittsburgh district," she says.

"Oh okay. But that's even better. Test scores wise, that is," he says, "So where did you get? East Allegheny, Fox Chapel, Hampton?"

346

"Neither."

"Where is the job?" he asks.

"Cleveland."

He's already familiar with Alana's background. He know she has relatives in Cleveland, as well as a past lover whom she's hell bent on getting back there too. He's curious about how their 2 trips to Cleveland had gone, now that he knows Farah has been going over there because she had a job offer. A fact she had failed to make him aware of. What else is she not telling him?

"You was going to Cleveland for a job offer?" he asks.

"Yes."

"When were you going to inform me?"

"I guess *now*," she says.

"Farah dear, you took a job in Cleveland?" he says, "When do you start it? What about housing?"

"This fall," she lies again, "I have that covered. I've seen a place."

"Were you going to tell me about it or not?"

"Of course I was," she says, "I had to be sure I got the job first."

"You've established housing?" Marvin probes.

"Yes."

"Where? A good area?"

"It depends," she says.

"On?"

"What you mean by a good area," she says.

"Well, you know. Low to no crime. Good neighbors, adequate lighting and county attention-"

"Oh you mean a non *urban* area?" she snaps.

Marvin doesn't say anything. He ponders her question. Alana is still present. Farah seizes the moment to push him into bad light by elaborating on her question.

"Do you mean a non-ethnic area? No Blacks, no Hispanics, no Asians. Is that what you mean by a good area? Ha? White only?" she asks.

"No. I meant upscale, Farah. A nice area where I want have to worry about you, if you walk out of the house," he says, "Or if I wanna go for a run."

"Oh you want have to worry," she says.

"So you picked a good neighborhood, then?" he asks.

"Yes I did."

"Where is it, may I ask?"

"No you may not," she says, "I have some affluent business

347

owners and professional athletes there, who have guaranteed me the spot. Only because they met me *unattached*."

"What does that mean, Farah?" he asks, "You're not, *unattached*. We've been a couple since freshman year. We've lived together since our sophomore year. That's not unattached."

"It's the only way I could get the house, so I went for it," she says.

"Are you trying to tell me something?" he asks.

"Am I? Telling you something, that is. Am I?"

Marvin doesn't say anymore. He's not only hurt but he's disappointed and angry, as he darts out of the front door. Farah doesn't chase him. He feels as if he's been used. Farah had clung to him and his money when they 1st met. Marvin's family had become rich through insurance, on his fathers side and Textile manufacturing, on his mothers side. Marvin is a 4th generation, spoiled ass rich kid, on both sides. Though Farah comes from a rich family too, her parents had cut her off from her trust fund because they hadn't approved of the men she had been seeing since high school. Simply put, Farah dated Black. Her parents prefer she date and marry a white man or she won't inherit their fortune. She met Marvin Huntley during their freshman year at Pittsburgh University. She paraded him in front of her parents, less than a week after knowing him. Initially, he thought she was just that taken by him. But a month later, he caught her and her roommate Marla, in the act. They had invited him to join them that night, only because Farah still hadn't convinced her slightly prejudiced parents that she was off of the mixed races express, enough for them to give her her credit cards back. Marla was white, as well. But Farah's parents would never have approved of a lesbian relationship either. They want a pure bred, white boy for their daughter. Marvin Huntley was picture perfect, in their eyes.

"You think he'll call your dad?" Alana asks.

"If he does, he'll find out he's not in, anymore. My parents don't want me with an abusive person. White or other," she says as they giggle.

Alana isn't even aware of what Farah had done to insure that her parents wouldn't flip on her about breaking up with Marvin. She had told them he'd beat her up, New Year's Eve. And she had gone away to heal her wounds because she didn't want them to see her like that. Plus she didn't want him to find her, in the city. Her parents had agreed with her that she needed to get away from him, immediately. However, she didn't tell them that she was getting all the way away, in Cleveland.

348

{Cleveland{

After closing the restaurant and going home, big mama tells poppa and papa what Ebony had told her earlier. Poppa calls June and demands he come over to their house. He agrees to do so and comes right away.

They had called papa Charles about Rich, by the time June arrived. Then they talked to June about this mornings event. He denies any wrongdoing.

"I was just driving them," he tries.

"Then you're just as guilty as they are," poppa says, "Son, don't y'all mistreat those ladies, like that. This family is too close and if y'all do them wrong, it'll ripple through this *entire* family."

June agrees with his grandparents and says he won't do it again. He wants to get out of the hot seat, quickly. So basically, he denies any involvement with the woman who had sat in his front seat. They warn him, "Anything done in the dark, will come to light."

June says he understands. They leave the conversation, at that. June leaves and heads back to Jackson Heights. He picks up a light snack for him, Rebbie and Orian, on the way. He isn't planning to tell Rebbie about the complex. His plans are to plan better and to be more careful.

Miami lost game 5 to New York. The season's over. Ajay is heading home. He calls Ebony, just as they're getting ready to board their flight.

"Hi daddy," she says, "I'm sorry about the game."

"Yea, I know," he says, "We're out again. We didn't even get out of the first round, this time."

"Are you okay?" she asks.

"No. I'm getting a flight home. I should be in, just after midnight."

"I'll be there to pick you up," she says.

"I'm feeling better already," he says smiling, "But what's wrong, baby girl?"

"Nothing," she says, "I've just been studying, all evening. I'm ready to *throw* something."

"Make sure it's those hips then, alright," he says, "Throw 'em at me when I get there." She smiles and says she will.

"We've got until preseason to work on that baby," he says, "Are you looking forward to graduation?"

"Yes."

"I'm so proud of you," he says.

"I know. Thank you, daddy," she says.

349

"I don't like your tone, right now, baby girl," he says, "You can talk to me when I get home, about whatever's really bothering you since you prefer to wait. Okay?"

She can never hide anything from him, for long. He knows her, too well.

"My flight lands at one fifteen," he says, "Tell Tank I'll get with him when we get up tomorrow."

She agrees to call her brother and relay the message. They hang up.

She calls Tank, who has found out from Nina that she's not talking to them.

"What's wrong with you today, twin?" Tank asks immediately.

"Nothing."

"Why you not talking to Nina and your girls?" he asks.

"I am talking to them," she says, "I just wanted to chill by myself today. That's all."

She can hear Nina asking Tank to let her have the phone.

"Not right now, Tank," Ebony says, "I just need to think some things out. Then I'll have to talk it over with Anthony," she says and hangs up immediately.

Nina calls her back and asks her if she's going to come to the clubs to help out tonight. She declines to hang out again. Nina doesn't pressure her but she knows something's going on.

So does Ajay and he calls Jacobson from the aircraft and ask him if everything is alright in Jackson Heights. Jacobson tells him everything has been quiet, as of late. Then he tells him about the call from officer Deloris Miles, earlier.

"She said Ebony was *pretty* upset that someone was cheating and she almost wrecked her car," Jacobson says, "When she came through the gate, she looked worried. But when I called her, she said she just needed to talk with her big mama. She had big mama with her. I assumed she was working it out. Whatever it was."

Ajay tells him he'll handle it in a little while.

At the kids club, Nina, T-baby and Rebbie discuss Ebony's reluctance to be around them.

"This is just weird to me," T-baby says, "I don't get it."

"She's stressed out about getting pregnant, y'all," Rebbie says, "It's bothering her more now that Ally's pregnant."

350

"Didn't Ally and Steven ask her and Ajay to Christian their baby?" Nina asks.

"They did," T-baby answers, "Y'all think she's upset about that?"

"No. She wasn't last week," Rebbie says, "It's something else. Something that went down since we got home. Why won't she tell us what it *is*?"

"Where did she go today?" T-baby asks.

"I don't know but that's the key to it," Rebbie says, "I'm telling you, if we find out where she spent today. We'll be on to it."

"It's not like Ebony, not to talk to us," T-baby says.

"Unless it's something about Ajay," Nina says, "Y'all know they started being more independent when we got to Natty."

"She ain't gonna tell us shit about Ajay," T-baby says, "Especially not if he's fucking up."

"No, it's not that," Rebbie says, "She has something to tell. But that ain't it. But how come she don't wanna tell us what's bothering her?"

"Oh she's gonna have to tell me something," Nina says, "I'm calling Ajay and see if he knows anything."

Immediately, she calls her brother's cell phone. He can't talk long because his flight is ready to land. Nina tells him to find out why Ebony doesn't want to hang with them and he says he'll get to the bottom of it. They hang up.

"Ajay's on the case," Nina says, "He'll find out what's going on."

"I hope it's not *his* ass," T-baby says, "He'd better not be fucking up on my cousin, already."

"I doubt that," Rebbie says, "I already told you, he's not."

"I doubt that too," Nina adds, "But there's something fucked up, that's for sure. She either heard or saw something today, since we've been home."

"I wonder what it is?" Rebbie asks.

"So do I," T-baby agrees, "So do I."

THE END OF PART 3!

351

Also by Black Coffee:

Be sure to pick up the sequels to this Time Will Reveal Series
Time To Learn-RELOADED-Time Will Reveal part 1
Time To Grow-RELOADED-Time Will Reveal part 2

(Time Will Reveal, short stories)
#1 MORE THE 4 ADMIRERS-RELOADED
#2 MR. WRONG AND THE RATS-RELOADED
#3 THE CREW'S PRIORITY [TBA]

And more of the Time Will Reveal series!
Time To Know-RELOADED-Time Will Reveal part 4
Time To Feel-RELOADED-Time Will Reveal part 5
The Making of Ajay-Every Man-RELOADED, A Time Will Reveal novel
Time To Show-RELOADED-Time Will Reveal part 6 [TBA]
Ajay and Ebony 1-Time Will Reveal 7-Time To Give [TBA]
Ajay and Ebony 2-Time Will Reveal 8-Time To Live [TBA]

If you were charged more the $25 [US dollars] and shipping wasn't included in that price, contact us at the following websites, immediately.
www.blackdollone.com
www.truesrelatepublishing.com

[future releases]
The Foe, The Friend-Poetry [print & audio] [Late Fall 2014]
All By My Lonely-The Organization-part one [Released 1/1/2014]
Still By My Lonely-The Organization-part two [TBA]

"Join our group on Facebook: **Black Coffee's Crew Nation & True's Relate publishing and Black Coffee's Books, NOW** and let me know what you think of this book. You can make the READERS PAGE on my website."-Black Coffee aka #ABC

www.ingramcontent.com/pod-product-compliance
Lightning Source LLC
Chambersburg PA
CBHW061318170626
46817CB00001B/229